Let #1 *New York Times* bestselling author Nora Roberts fly you into Lunacy, Alaska, and into a colorful, compelling new novel about two lonely souls who find love—and redemption . . .

Lunacy was Nate Burke's last chance. As a Baltimore cop, he'd watched his partner die on the street—and the guilt still haunts him. With nowhere else to go, he accepts the job as chief of police in this tiny, remote Alaskan town, where the peace provides a balm for his shattered soul—and an unexpected affair with pilot Meg Galloway warms his nights . . .

But other things in Lunacy are heating up. Nate suspects the killer in an unsolved murder still walks the snowy streets. His investigation will unearth the secrets and suspicions that lurk beneath the placid surface, as well as bring out the big-city survival instincts that made him a cop in the first place. And his discovery will threaten the new life—and the new love—that he has finally found for himself.

NORTHERN LIGHTS

"While Alaska is an unfamiliar setting for a Roberts novel, the song she sings here remains—happily for fans of the romantic suspense genre—the same."

—*The New York Times*

"[An] engaging mix of suspense and romance."

—*Seattle Post-Intelligencer*

"The characters in *Northern Lights* . . . come alive on the pages . . . If you have time for only one good read this fall, make it this book. It's well written, has intriguing characters, a tantalizing plot, wit, and romance."

—*Times Union* (Albany, NY)

continued . . .

"The setting is economically but beautifully evoked, the spare style balancing the breathtaking grandeur of Alaska. Pace, dialogue, and scenes are cunningly shaped, and the police procedural skillfully dovetails with romance. Wit abounds . . . [A] shapely hybrid of the mystery and romance." —*The Washington Post Book World*

"I was hooked . . . This is a good book . . . [Roberts] makes wonderful, descriptive use of her setting in wilderness-edge, small-town Alaska . . . memorable characters . . . a challenging mystery and mounting suspense . . . *Northern Lights* has enlightened me in more ways than one." —*Winston-Salem Journal*

"Roberts shines again with a nuanced tale of the Alaskan wilderness and the appealing eccentrics who cluster there . . . A richly textured novel that captures the intimacy of small-town police work, the prickliness of the pioneer spirit, and the paradox of a setting at once intimate and expansive, welcoming and hostile, indisputably American and yet profoundly exotic to those in the Lower 48." —*Publishers Weekly* (starred)

Turn the page for a complete list of titles
by Nora Roberts and J. D. Robb
from The Berkley Publishing Group . . .

Anthologies

FROM THE HEART
A LITTLE MAGIC
A LITTLE FATE

MOON SHADOWS
(with Jill Gregory, Ruth Ryan Langan, and Marianne Willman)

The Once Upon Series
(with Jill Gregory, Ruth Ryan Langan, and Marianne Willman)
ONCE UPON A CASTLE
ONCE UPON A STAR
ONCE UPON A DREAM
ONCE UPON A ROSE
ONCE UPON A KISS
ONCE UPON A MIDNIGHT

* * *

SILENT NIGHT
(with Susan Plunkett, Dee Holmes, and Claire Cross)

OUT OF THIS WORLD
(with Laurell K. Hamilton, Susan Krinard, and Maggie Shayne)

BUMP IN THE NIGHT
(with Mary Blayney, Ruth Ryan Langan, and Mary Kay McComas)

DEAD OF NIGHT
(with Mary Blayney, Ruth Ryan Langan, and Mary Kay McComas)

THREE IN DEATH

SUITE 606
(with Mary Blayney, Ruth Ryan Langan, and Mary Kay McComas)

Also available . . .

THE OFFICIAL NORA ROBERTS COMPANION
(edited by Denise Little and Laura Hayden)

NORTHERN
LIGHTS

Nora Roberts

JOVE BOOKS, NEW YORK

THE BERKLEY PUBLISHING GROUP
Published by the Penguin Group
Penguin Group (USA) Inc.
375 Hudson Street, New York, New York 10014, USA
Penguin Group (Canada), 90 Eglinton Avenue East, Suite 700, Toronto, Ontario M4P 2Y3, Canada
(a division of Pearson Penguin Canada Inc.)
Penguin Books Ltd., 80 Strand, London WC2R 0RL, England
Penguin Group Ireland, 25 St. Stephen's Green, Dublin 2, Ireland (a division of Penguin Books Ltd.)
Penguin Group (Australia), 250 Camberwell Road, Camberwell, Victoria 3124, Australia
(a division of Pearson Australia Group Pty. Ltd.)
Penguin Books India Pvt. Ltd., 11 Community Centre, Panchsheel Park, New Delhi—110 017, India
Penguin Group (NZ), 67 Apollo Drive, Rosedale, North Shore 0632, New Zealand
(a division of Pearson New Zealand Ltd.)
Penguin Books (South Africa) (Pty.) Ltd., 24 Sturdee Avenue, Rosebank, Johannesburg 2196, South
Africa

Penguin Books Ltd., Registered Offices: 80 Strand, London WC2R 0RL, England

This is a work of fiction. Names, characters, places, and incidents either are the product of the author's imagination or are used fictitiously, and any resemblance to actual persons, living or dead, business establishments, events, or locales is entirely coincidental. The publisher does not have any control over and does not assume any responsibility for author or third-party websites or their content.

NORTHERN LIGHTS

A Jove Book / published by arrangement with the author

PRINTING HISTORY
G. P. Putnam's Son hardcover edition / October 2004
Jove premium edition / October 2005

Copyright © 2004 by Nora Roberts.
Excerpt from *Naked in Death* by J. D. Robb copyright © 1995 by Nora Roberts.

ISBN: 978-0-515-13974-7

JOVE®
Jove Books are published by The Berkley Publishing Group,
a division of Penguin Group (USA) Inc.,
375 Hudson Street, New York, New York 10014.
JOVE® is a registered trademark of Penguin Group (USA) Inc.
The "J" design is a trademark belonging to Penguin Group (USA) Inc.

PRINTED IN THE UNITED STATES OF AMERICA

15   14   13   12

To my precious Logan, son of my son.
Life will be your treasure box, filled
with the sparkle of laughter, the
gleam of adventure, the shine of
discovery, the flash of magic. And
through all these jewels streams
the steady glow of love.

NORTHERN LIGHTS

DARK

Finish, good lady; the bright day is done,
And we are for the dark.

WILLIAM SHAKESPEARE

O dark, dark, dark, amid the blaze of noon,
Irrecoverably dark, total eclipse
Without all hope of day!

JOHN MILTON

PROLOGUE

Landed on Sun Glacier about noon. The flight in rattled the hangover right out of me, and severed those strangling roots of reality that is the world below. The sky's clear, like blue crystal. The kind of sky they slap on postcards to lure the tourists in, complete with a shimmering sun dog around the cold, white sun. I'm taking it as a sign that this climb was meant to be. The wind's about ten knots. Temp's a balmy ten below. Glacier's broad as Whoring Kate's ass, and icy as her heart.

Even so, Kate gave us a proper send-off last night. Even gave us what you could call a group rate.

Don't know what the hell we're doing here, except you gotta be somewhere doing something. A winter climb on No Name's as good a something as any, and better than most.

A man needs a week's adventuring now and then, adventuring that excludes bad liquor and loose women. How else are you going to appreciate the liquor and the women if you don't get away from them for a while?

And bumping into a couple of fellow Lunatics turned not only my luck at the table but my mood in general. There's little that bums me more than working a job for a daily wage like the rest of the mice on the wheel, but the woman sure will push the buttons.

My windfall should satisfy my girls, so now I'm taking a few days with pals just for me.

Going up against the elements, risking life and limb in the company of other men just as foolish is something I've got to have, just to remind me I'm alive. To do it not for pay, not for duty, not because a woman's nagging your balls blue, but just for pure idiocy is what keeps the spirit sparked.

It's getting too crowded below. Roads going where they never used to go, people living where they never used to live. When I first came, there weren't so many, and the damn Feds weren't regulating everything.

A permit to climb? To walk on a mountain? Screw that, and screw the tight-assed Feds with their rules and their paperwork. The mountains were here long before some government bureaucrat figured out a way to make a buck off them. And they'll be here long after he's winding red tape in hell.

And I'm here now, on this land that belongs to no one. Holy ground never can.

If there was a way to live on the mountain, I'd plant my tent and never leave. But holy or not, she'll kill you, quicker than a nagging wife, and with less mercy.

So I'll take my week, with like-minded men, climbing this peak that has no name and rises above the town and the river and the lakes, that skirts the boundaries the Feds throw up on land that mocks their puny attempts to tame and preserve.

Alaska belongs to none but itself, no matter how

many roads or signs or rules are erected on her. She is the last of the wild women, and God love her for it. I do.

We've established our base camp, and already the sun's dropped below the great peaks and plunged us into the dark of winter. Huddled in our tent, we eat well, pass a joint around, and talk of tomorrow.

Tomorrow we climb.

ONE

Strapped into the quivering soup can laughingly called a plane, bouncing his way on the pummeling air through the stingy window of light that was winter, through the gaps and breaks in snow-sheathed mountains toward a town called Lunacy, Ignatious Burke had an epiphany.

He wasn't nearly as prepared to die as he'd believed.

It was a hell of a thing to realize when his fate hung precariously in the hands of a stranger who was buried in a canary yellow parka and whose face was nearly concealed by a battered leather bush hat perched on top of a purple watch cap.

The stranger had seemed competent enough in Anchorage, and had given Nate's hand a hearty slap before wagging a thumb at the soup can with propellers.

Then he'd told Nate to "just call me Jerk." That's when the initial unease had set in.

What kind of an idiot got into a flying tin can piloted by a guy named Jerk?

But flying was the only sure way to reach Lunacy this late in the year. Or so Mayor Hopp had informed him when he'd conferred with her over his travel arrangements.

The plane dipped hard to the right, and as Nate's stomach followed, he wondered just how Mayor Hopp defined *sure*.

He'd thought he hadn't given a good damn one way or the other. Live or die, what did it matter in the big scheme? When he'd boarded the big jet at Baltimore-Washington, he'd resigned himself that he was heading to the end of his life in any case.

The department shrink had warned him about making major decisions when he was suffering from depression, but he'd applied for the position as chief of police in Lunacy for no reason other than that the name seemed apt.

And he'd accepted the position with a who-gives-a-shit shrug.

Even now, reeling with nausea, shivering with his epiphany, Nate realized it wasn't so much death that worried him, but the method. He just didn't want to end the whole deal by smashing into a mountain in the fucking gloom.

At least if he'd stayed in Baltimore, had danced more affably with the shrink and his captain, he could've gone down in the line of duty. That wouldn't have been so bad.

But no, he'd tossed in his badge, hadn't just burned his bridges but had incinerated them. And now he was going to end up a bloody smear somewhere in the Alaska Range.

"Gonna get a little rough through here," Jerk said with a drawn-out Texas drawl.

Nate swallowed bile. "And it's been so smooth up to now."

Jerk grinned, winked. "This ain't nothing. Ought to try it fighting a headwind."

"No, thanks. How much longer?"

"Not much."

The plane bucked and shuddered. Nate gave up and closed his eyes. He prayed he wouldn't add to the indignity of his death by puking on his boots first.

He was never going up in a plane again. If he lived, he'd drive out of Alaska. Or walk. Or crawl. But he was never going into the air again.

The plane gave a kind of jerking leap that had Nate's eyes popping open. And he saw through the windscreen the triumphant victory of the sun, a wondrous sort of lessening of gloom that turned the sky pearly so that the world below was defined in long ripples of white and blue, sudden rises, shimmering swarms of icy lakes and what had to be miles of snow-draped trees.

Just east, the sky was all but blotted out by the mass the locals called Denali, or just The Mountain. Even his sketchy research had told him only Outsiders referred to it as McKinley.

His only coherent thought as they shuddered along was that nothing real should be that massive. As the sun beamed God fingers through the heavy sky around it, the shadows began to drip and spread, blue over white, and its icy face glinted.

Something shifted inside him so that, for a moment, he forgot the roiling of his belly, the constant buzzing roar of the engine, even the chill that had hung in the plane like fog.

"Big bastard, ain't he?"

"Yeah." Nate let out a breath. "Big bastard."

They eased west, but he never lost sight of the mountain. He could see now that what he'd taken as an icy road was a winding, frozen river. And near its bank, the spread of man with its houses and buildings and cars and trucks.

It looked to him like the inside of a snow globe that had yet to be shaken, with everything still and white and waiting.

Something clunked under the floor. "What was that?"

"Landing gear. That's Lunacy."

The plane roared into a descent that had Nate gripping his seat, bracing his feet. "What? We're landing? Where? Where?"

"On the river. Frozen solid this time of year. No worries."

"But—"

"Going in on the skis."

"Skis?" Nate abruptly remembered he hated winter sports. "Wouldn't skates make more sense?"

Jerk let out a wild laugh as the plane zeroed in on the ribbon of ice. "Wouldn't that be some shit? Skate plane. Hot damn."

The plane bumped, skidded, slid along with Nate's belly. Then glided gracefully to a stop. Jerk cut the engines, and in the sudden silence Nate could hear his own heart tattooing in his ears.

"They can't pay you enough," Nate managed. "They can't possibly pay you enough."

"Hell." He slapped Nate on the arm. "Ain't about the pay. Welcome to Lunacy, Chief."

"You're damn right."

He decided against kissing the ground. Not only would he look ridiculous, but he'd probably freeze to it. Instead, he swung his weak legs out into the unspeakable cold and prayed they'd hold him up until he could get somewhere warm, still and sane.

His main problem was crossing the ice without breaking his leg, or his neck.

"Don't worry about your stuff, Chief," Jerk called out. "I'll haul it for you."

"Thanks."

Steadying himself, Nate spotted a figure standing in the snow. It was wrapped in a brown, hooded parka with black fur trim. And smoking in short, impatient puffs. Using it as a guide, Nate picked his way over the ripply ice with as much dignity as he could muster.

"Ignatious Burke."

The voice was raspy and female, and came to him on a puff of vapor. He slipped, managed to right himself, and with his heart banging against his ribs, made the snowy bank.

"Anastasia Hopp." She stuck out a mittened hand, somehow gripped his with it and pumped righteously. "Little green around the gills yet. Jerk, you play with our new chief on the way from the city?"

"No, ma'am. Had a little weather though."

"Always do. Good-looking, aren't you? Even sickly. Here, have a pull."

She yanked a silver flask out of her pocket, pushed it at him.

"Ah—"

"Go ahead. You're not on duty yet. Little brandy'll settle you down."

Deciding it couldn't make things worse, he uncapped the flask, took a slow sip and felt it punch straight to his quivering belly. "Thanks."

"We'll get you settled in The Lodge, give you a chance to catch your breath." She led the way along a tromped-down path. "Show you around town later, when your head's clear. Long way from Baltimore."

"Yeah, it is."

It looked like a movie set to him. The green and white trees, the river, the snow, buildings made of split logs, smoke pumping out of chimneys and pipes. It was all in a dreamy blur that made him realize he was as exhausted as he was sick. He hadn't been able to sleep on any of the flights and calculated it had been nearly twenty-four hours since he'd last been horizontal.

"Good, clear day," she said. "Mountains put on a show. Kind of picture brings the tourists in."

It was postcard perfect, and just a little overwhelming. He felt like he'd walked into that movie—or someone else's dream.

"Glad to see you geared up good." She measured him as she spoke. "Lot of Lower 48ers show up in fancy overcoats and showroom boots, and freeze their asses off."

He'd ordered everything he was wearing, right down to the thermal underwear, along with most of the contents of his suitcase from Eddie Bauer online—after receiving an e-mail list of suggestions from Mayor Hopp. "You were pretty specific about what I'd need."

She nodded. "Specific, too, about what we need. Don't disappoint me, Ignatious."

"Nate. I don't intend to, Mayor Hopp."

"Just Hopp. That's what they call me."

She stepped up on a long wooden porch. "This is The Lodge. Hotel, bar, diner, social club. You got a room here, part of your salary. You decide you want to live elsewhere, that's on you. Place belongs to Charlene Hidel. She serves a good meal, keeps the place clean. She'll take care of you. She'll also try to get into your pants."

"Excuse me?"

"You're a good-looking man, and Charlene's got a weakness. She's too old for you, but she won't think so. You decide you don't either, that's up to you."

Then she smiled, and he saw that under her hood she had a face ruddy as an apple and shaped the same way. Her eyes were nut brown and lively, her mouth long and thin and quirked at the corners.

"We got us a surplus of men, like most of Alaska. That doesn't mean the local female population won't come sniffing. You're fresh meat and a lot of them are going to want a taste. You do what you please on your free time, Ignatious. Just don't go banging the girls on town time."

"I'll write that down."

Her laugh was like a foghorn—two quick blasts. To punctuate it, she slapped him on the arm. "You might do."

She yanked open the door and led him into blessed warmth.

He smelled wood smoke and coffee, something frying with onions, and a woman's come-get-me perfume.

It was a wide room informally sectioned into a diner

with two- and four-tops, five booths, and a bar with stools lined up with their red seats worn in the center from years of asses settling down.

There was a wide opening to the right, and through it he could see a pool table and what looked like foosball, and the starry lights of a jukebox.

On the right, another opening showed what looked like a lobby. He saw a section of counter, and cubbyholes filled with keys, a few envelopes or message sheets.

A log fire burned briskly, and the front windows were angled to catch the spectacular mountain view.

There was one enormously pregnant waitress with her hair done in a long, glossy black braid. Her face was so arresting, so serenely beautiful, he actually blinked. She looked to him like the Native Alaskan version of the Madonna with her soft, dark eyes and golden skin.

She was topping off coffee for two men in a booth. A boy of about four sat at a table coloring in a book. A man in a tweed jacket sat at the bar, smoking, and reading a tattered copy of *Ulysses*.

At a far table a man with a brown beard that spilled onto the chest of his faded buffalo-check flannel shirt appeared to be holding an angry conversation with himself.

Heads turned in their direction, and greetings were called out to Hopp as she tossed her hood back to reveal a springy mop of silver hair. Gazes locked on to Nate that ranged from curiosity and speculation to open hostility from the beard.

"This here's Ignatious Burke, our new chief of police." Hopp announced this as she yanked down the zipper of her parka. "We got Dex Trilby and Hans Finkle

there in the booth, and that's Bing Karlovski over there
with the scowl on what you can see of his face. Rose Itu
is waiting tables. How's that baby today, Rose?"

"Restless. Welcome, Chief Burke."

"Thanks."

"This is The Professor." Hopp tapped Tweed Jacket
on the shoulder as she crossed to the bar. "Anything different in that book since the last time you read it?"

"Always something." He tipped down a pair of metal-
framed reading glasses to get a better view of Nate.
"Long trip."

"It was," Nate agreed.

"Not over yet." Shoving his glasses back into place,
The Professor went back to his book.

"And this handsome devil is Jesse, Rose's boy."

The boy kept his head bent over his coloring book,
but lifted his gaze so his big, dark eyes peered out under
a thick fringe of black bangs. He reached out, tugged
Hopp's parka so that she bent down to hear his whisper.

"Don't you worry. We'll get him one."

The door behind the bar swung open and a big, black
truck in a big, white apron came out. "Big Mike," Hopp
announced. "He's the cook. Was a Navy man until one
of our local girls caught his eye when she was down in
Kodiak."

"Snared me like a trout," Big Mike said with a grin.
"Welcome to Lunacy."

"Thanks."

"We're going to want something good and hot for
our new chief of police."

"Fish chowder's good today," Big Mike told her.

"Ought to do the trick. Unless you'd rather bite into some red meat, Chief."

It took Nate a moment to identify himself as *chief*. A moment when he felt every eye in the room focused on him. "Chowder's fine. Sounds good."

"We'll have it right up for you then." He swung back into the kitchen, and Nate could hear his bone-deep baritone croon out on "Baby, It's Cold Outside."

Stage set, postcard, he thought. Or a play. Anyway you sliced it, he felt like some sort of dusty prop.

Hopp held up a finger to hold Nate in place before marching into the lobby. He watched her scoot around the counter and snag a key from one of the cubbies.

As she did, the door behind the counter swung open. And the bombshell walked out.

She was blonde—as Nate thought suited bombshells best—with the wavy mass of sunlight hair spilling down to brush very impressive breasts that were showcased by the low scoop of her snug, blue sweater. It took him a minute to get to the face as the sweater was tucked into jeans so tight they must have bruised several internal organs.

Not that he was complaining.

The face boasted bright blue eyes with an innocence in direct contrast with the plump, red lips. She was a little generous on the paint, and put him in mind of a Barbie doll.

Man-killer Barbie.

Despite the restriction of the outfit, everything that could jiggle did so as she strolled around the counter on skinny, backless heels, wiggled her way into the diner. And posed languidly against the bar.

"Well, hello, handsome."

Her voice was a throaty purr—she must've practiced it—designed to drain the blood out of a man's head and send his IQ plummeting to that of a green turnip.

"Charlene, you behave." Hopp rattled the key. "This boy's tired and half sick. He doesn't have the reserves to deal with you right now. Chief Burke, Charlene Hidel. This is her place. Town budget's paying your room and board here as part of your pay, so don't feel obliged to offer anything out in trade."

"Hopp, you're so *bad*." But Charlene smiled like a stroked kitten as she said it. "Why don't I just take you up, Chief Burke, get you all settled in? Then we'll bring you something hot to eat."

"I'll take him up." Deliberately Hopp closed her fist around the key, letting the big black room number tag dangle. "Jerk's bringing in his gear. Wouldn't hurt to have Rose bring him the chowder Mike's dishing up for him though. Come on, Ignatious. You can socialize when you're not so ready to drop."

He could've spoken for himself, but he didn't see the point. He followed Hopp through a doorway and up a flight of steps as obediently as a puppy follows its master.

He heard someone mutter, "Cheechako," in the tone a man uses to spit out bad meat. He assumed it was an insult, but let it go.

"Charlene doesn't mean any harm," Hopp was saying. "But she does like to tease a man to death given half a chance."

"Don't worry about me, Mom."

She gave that foghorn laugh again, and slid the key into the lock on room 203.

"Man took off on her about fifteen years back, left her with a girl to raise on her own. Did a decent enough job with Meg, though they're at each other like she-cats half the time. Had plenty of men since, and they get younger every year. I said she was too old for you before." Hopp looked over her shoulder. "Fact is, the way she's been going, you're too old for her. Thirty-two, aren't you?"

"I was when I left Baltimore. How many years ago was that?"

Hopp shook her head, pushed open the door. "Charlene's got better than a dozen years on you. Got a grown daughter nearly your age. Might want to keep that in mind."

"I thought you women got off when one of your kind bags a younger man."

"Shows what you know about females. Pisses us off is what it does, because we didn't bag him first. Well, this is it."

He stepped into a wood-paneled room with an iron bed, a dresser and mirror on one side, and a small round table, two chairs and a little desk on the other.

It was clean, it was spare and about as interesting as a bag of white rice.

"Little kitchen through here." Hopp walked over, yanked back a blue curtain to reveal a pint-sized refrigerator, a two-burner stove and a sink the size of Nate's cupped palm. "Unless cooking's your passion or hobby, I'd take my meals downstairs. Food's good here.

"It's not the Ritz, and she's got fancier rooms, but we're on a budget." She crossed to the other side, pushed open a door. "Bathroom. This one has indoor plumbing."

"Woo-hoo." He poked his head in.

The sink was bigger than the kitchen's but not by much. It didn't rate a tub, but the shower stall would do him well enough.

"Got your gear, Chief." Jerk hauled in two suitcases and a duffel as if they were empty. He dumped them on the bed where their weight sagged the mattress. "Need me for anything, I'll be downstairs grabbing a meal. I'll bunk here tonight, fly back to Talkeetna in the morning."

He tapped a finger on his forehead in salute and clomped out again.

"Shit. Hold on." Nate started to dig into his pocket.

"I'll take care of tipping him," Hopp said. "Till you're on the clock, you're a guest of the Lunacy town council."

"Appreciate it."

"I plan to see you work for it, so we'll see how it goes."

"Room service!" Charlene sang out when she carried a tray into the room. Her hips swayed like a metronome as she walked over to set it on the table. "Brought you up some nice fish chowder, Chief, and a good man-sized sandwich. Coffee's hot."

"Smells great. I appreciate it, Ms. Hidel."

"Oh now, that's Charlene to you." She batted the baby blues, and yeah, Nate thought, she practiced. "We're just one big happy family around here."

"That were the case, we wouldn't need a chief of police."

"Oh, don't go scaring him off, Hopp. Is the room all right for you, Ignatious?"

"Nate. Yes, thanks. It's fine."

"Put some food in your belly and get some rest," Hopp advised. "You get your second wind, just give me a call. I'll show you around. Your first official duty will be attending the meeting tomorrow afternoon at Town Hall, where we'll introduce you to everybody who cares to attend. You'll want to see the station house before that, meet your two deputies and Peach. And we'll get you that star."

"Star?"

"Jesse wanted to make sure you were getting a star. Come on, Charlene. Let's leave the man alone."

"You call downstairs you need any little thing." Charlene sent him an invitational smile. "*Any* little thing."

Behind Charlene's back, Hopp rolled her eyes toward heaven. To settle the matter, she clamped a hand on Charlene's arm, yanked her toward the door. There was a clatter of heels on wood, a feminine squeak, then the slam of the door behind them.

Through it, Nate could hear Charlene's hushed and insulted: "What's the *matter* with you, Hopp. I was only being friendly."

"There's innkeeper friendly, then there's bordello friendly. One of these days, you're going to figure out the difference."

He waited until he was sure they were gone before he crossed over to flip the locks. Then he pulled off his parka, let it fall to the floor, dragged off his watch cap, dropped it. Unwound his scarf, dropped that. Unzipped his insulated vest and added it to the heap.

Down to shirt, pants, thermal underwear and boots, he went to the table, picked up the soup, a spoon, and carried both to the dark windows.

Three-thirty in the afternoon, according to the bedside clock—and dark as midnight. There were streetlights glowing, he noted as he spooned up soup, and he could make out the shapes of buildings. Christmas decorations in colored lights, in rooftop Santas and cartoon reindeers.

But no people, no life, no movement.

He ate mechanically, too tired, too hungry to notice the taste.

There was nothing out that window but the movie set, he thought. The buildings might have been false fronts, the handful of people he'd met downstairs just characters in the illusion.

Maybe this was all some elaborate hallucination, born out of depression, grief, anger—whatever ugly mix had sent him pinwheeling into the void.

He'd wake up back in his own place in Baltimore and try to drum up the energy to go through the motions for another day.

He got the sandwich, ate that standing at the window as well, looking out at the empty black-and-white world with its oddly celebrational lights.

Maybe he'd walk out there, into that empty world. He'd become a character in the odd illusion. Then he'd fade to black, like the last reel of an old movie. And it would be over.

As he stood, half thinking it could be over, half wishing it would be, a figure stepped into frame. It wore red—bright and bold—that seemed to leap out of that colorless scene and thrum movement into it.

Those movements were definite and brisk. Life with a mission, movement with purpose. Quick, competent strides over the white that left the shadow of footprints in the snow.

I was here. I'm alive and I was here.

He couldn't tell if it was a man or woman, or a child, but there was something about the slash of color, the confidence of the gait, that caught his eye and interest.

As if sensing observation, the figure stopped, looked up.

Nate had the impression of white and black again. White face, black hair. But even that was blurred with the dark and the distance.

There was a long moment of stillness, of silence. Then the figure began to walk again, striding toward The Lodge, and disappearing from view.

Nate yanked the drapes over the glass, stepped away from the window.

After a moment's debate, he dragged his cases off the bed, left them dumped, unpacked, on the floor. He stripped down, ignored the chill of the room against his naked skin, and crawled under the mountain of blankets the way a bear crawls into his winter cave.

He lay there, a man of thirty-two with a thick, disordered mass of chestnut hair that waved around a long, thin face gone lax with exhaustion and a despair that blurred eyes of smoky gray. Under a day's worth of stubble, his skin was pale with the drag of fatigue. Though the food had eased the rawness in his belly, his system remained sluggish, like that of a man who couldn't quite shake off a debilitating flu.

He wished Barbie—Charlene—had brought up a bottle instead of the coffee. He wasn't much of a drinker, which he figured is what had saved him from spiraling into alcoholism along with everything else. Still, a couple of good belts would help turn off his brain and let him sleep.

He could hear the wind now. It hadn't been there before, but it was moaning at the windows. With it, he heard the building creak and the sound of his own breathing.

Three lonely sounds only more lonely as a trio.

Tune them out, he told himself. Tune them all out.

He'd get a couple hours' sleep, he thought. Then he'd shower off the travel grime, pump himself full of coffee.

After that, he'd decide what the hell he was going to do.

He turned off the light so the room plunged into the dark. Within seconds, so did he.

TWO

THE DARK SURROUNDED HIM, sucked at him like mud when the dream shoved him out of sleep. His breath whooshed out as he broke the surface, floundered his way to the air. His skin was clammy with sweat as he fought his way clear of blankets.

The scent in the air was unfamiliar—cedar, stale coffee, some underlying tone of lemon. Then he remembered he wasn't in his Baltimore apartment.

He'd gone crazy, and he was in Alaska.

The luminous dial of the bedside clock read five forty-eight.

So he'd gotten some sleep before the dream had chased him back to reality.

It was always dark in the dream, too. Black night, pale, dirty rain. The smell of cordite and blood.

Jesus, Nate, Jesus. I'm hit.

Cold rain streaming down his face, warm blood oozing through his fingers. His blood, and Jack's blood.

He hadn't been able to stop the blood from oozing any more than he'd been able to stop the rain from streaming. They were both beyond him and, in that Baltimore alley, had washed away what had been left of him.

Should've been me, he thought. Not Jack. He should've

been home with his wife, with his kids, and it should've been me dying in a filthy alley in the filthy rain.

But he'd gotten off with a bullet in the leg, and a second, in-and-out punch in the side just above the waist, just enough to take him down, slow him down, so Jack had gone in first.

Seconds, small mistakes, and a good man was dead.

He had to live with it. He'd considered ending his own life, but it was a selfish solution and did nothing to honor his friend, his partner. Living with it was harder than dying.

Living was more punishment.

He got up, walked into the bathroom. He found himself pathetically grateful for the thin spurt of hot water out of the showerhead. It was going to take a while for the spurt to carve away what felt like layers of grime and sweat, but that was okay. Time wasn't a problem.

He'd get himself dressed, go downstairs, have some coffee. Maybe he'd give Mayor Hopp a call and go down to take a look at the station house. See if he could be a little more coherent and brush off some of that first impression of a bleary-eyed moron.

He felt more like himself once he'd showered and shaved. Digging out fresh clothes, he layered himself into them.

Picking up his outdoor gear, he glanced at himself in the mirror. "Chief of Police Ignatious Burke, Lunacy, Alaska." He shook his head, nearly smiled. "Well, Chief, let's go get you a star."

He headed downstairs, surprised at the relative quiet.

From what he'd read, places like The Lodge were the gathering spots for locals. Winter nights were long and dark and lonely, and he'd expected to hear some bar noise, maybe the clatter of pool balls, some ancient country-western tune from the juke.

But when he stepped in, the beautiful Alaskan Rose was topping off coffee, much as she'd been before. It might've been for the same two men, Nate wasn't sure. Her boy was sitting at a table, coloring industriously.

Nate checked the watch he'd set to local time. Seven ten.

Rose turned from the table, smiled at him. "Chief."

"Quiet tonight."

Her whole face lit with a smile. "It's morning."

"I'm sorry?"

"It's seven o'clock, in the morning. Bet you could use some breakfast."

"I . . ."

"Takes a while to get used to it." She nodded toward the dark windows. "It'll lighten up for a while, in a few hours. Why don't you have a seat. I'll bring you coffee to start you off."

He'd slept around the clock, and didn't know whether to be embarrassed or delighted. He couldn't remember the last time he'd gotten more than four or five patchy hours of sleep.

He dumped his outer gear on the bench of a booth, then decided to make an effort at community relations. Walking over to Jesse's table, he tapped the back of a chair. "This seat taken?"

The boy took a slow, under-the-bangs peek, and shook

his head. With his tongue caught between his teeth, he continued to color as Nate sat down.

"Pretty cool purple cow," Nate commented, studying the current work-in-progress.

"Cows don't come in purple 'less you color them that way."

"I heard that. You take art in high school?"

Jesse's eyes rounded. "I don't go to school yet 'cause I'm only four."

"You're kidding. Four? I figured you for about sixteen." Nate eased back, winked at Rose as she brought him a thick, white mug and poured coffee into it.

"I had a birthday and we had cake, and a million balloons. Right, Mom?"

"That's right, Jesse." She laid a menu beside Nate's elbow.

"And we're having a baby really soon. And I've got two dogs, and—"

"Jesse, let Chief Burke look at his menu."

"Actually, I was going to ask Jesse to give me a recommendation. What's good for breakfast, Jesse?"

"Short stack!"

"Short stack it is." He handed the menu back to Rose. "We're fine."

"If that changes, you let me know." But she was pink in the cheeks with pleasure.

"What kind of dogs?" Nate asked, and was entertained with the exploits of Jesse's pets throughout breakfast.

A plate of pancakes and a charming young boy were a much better way to start the day than a recurring nightmare. His mood improved, Nate was on the point of calling Hopp when she came through the door.

"Heard you were up and around," she said, and tossed back her hood. Snow showered from her parka. "You look some sturdier than you did yesterday."

"Sorry I faded on you."

"No problem. Got yourself a good night's sleep, decent breakfast, good company," she added with a grin for Jesse. "You up for a tour?"

"Sure." He got up to pile on his outdoor gear.

"Skinnier than I expected."

He looked over at Hopp. He knew he looked gaunt. A man dropped more than ten pounds from a tuned-up one-sixty on a five-ten frame, gaunt was the usual result. "Won't be, I keep eating short stacks."

"Lot of hair."

He pulled on his watch cap. "It just keeps growing out of my head."

"I like hair on a man." She yanked open the door. "Red hair, too."

"It's brown," he corrected automatically, and pulled the cap lower.

"All right. Get off your feet awhile, Rose," she called back, then trudged out into the wind and snow.

The cold struck him like a runaway train. "Jesus Christ. It freezes your eyeballs."

He jumped into the Ford Explorer she'd parked at the curb. "Your blood's thin yet."

"It could be thick as paste, and it'd still be fucking cold. Sorry."

"I don't blush at frank language. Of course it's fucking cold; it's December." With her blasting laugh, she started the engine. "We'll start the tour on wheels. No point stumbling around in the dark."

"How many do you lose to exposure and hypothermia in a year?"

"Lost more than one to the mountains, but those mostly tourists or crazies. Man called Teek got himself stupid drunk one night, three years ago this January, and froze to death in his own outhouse, reading *Playboy* magazine. But he was an idiot. People who live here know how to take care of themselves, and cheechakos who make it through a winter learn—or leave."

"Cheechakos?"

"Newcomers. You don't want to take nature casually, but you learn to live with it, and if you're smart, you make it work for you. Get out in it—ski, snowshoe, skate the river, ice fish." She shrugged. "Take precautions and enjoy it, because it's not going anywhere."

She drove with steady competence on the snow-packed street. "There's our clinic. We got a doctor and a practical nurse."

Nate studied the small, squat building. "And if they can't handle it?"

"Fly to Anchorage. We've got a bush pilot lives outside of town. Meg Galloway."

"A woman?"

"You sexist, Ignatious?"

"No." Maybe. "Just asking."

"Meg's Charlene's daughter. Damn good pilot. A little crazy, but a good bush pilot's got to be, in my opinion. She'd've brought you in from Anchorage, but you were a day later than we'd hoped, and she had another booking, so we called Jerk in from Talkeetna. You'll probably see Meg at the town meeting later."

And won't that be fun, Nate thought.

"The Corner Store—got everything you need, or they'll find a way to get it. Oldest building in Lunacy. Trappers built it back in the early 1800s, and Harry and Deb have added to it since they bought the place in '83."

It was twice as big as the clinic, and two stories. Lights were already gleaming in the windows.

"Post office runs out of the bank there for now, but we're going to break ground for one this summer. And the skinny place next to it's The Italian Place. Good pizza. No deliveries outside of town."

"Pizza parlor."

"New York Italian, came up here three years back on a hunting trip. Fell in love. Never left. Johnny Trivani. Named it Trivani's at the start, but everybody called it The Italian Place, so he went with it. Talks about adding on a bakery. Says he's going to get himself one of those Russian mail-order brides you hear about on the Internet. Maybe he will."

"Will there be fresh blinis?"

"We can hope. Town newspaper runs out of that storefront," she said, pointing. "The couple who run it are out of town. Took the kids to San Diego for the school break right after Christmas. KLUN—local radio—broadcasts from that one there. Mitch Dauber runs it almost singlehanded. He's an entertaining son of a bitch most of the time."

"I'll tune in."

She circled around, headed back the way they'd come. "About a half mile west of town is the school—kindergarten through twelfth. We've got seventy-eight students right now. We hold adult classes there, too. Exercise classes, art classes, that sort of thing. Breakup to freeze-up we hold them in the evenings. Otherwise, it's daytime."

"Breakup? Freeze-up?"

"Ice breaks up on the river, spring's coming. River freezes up, get out the long johns."

"Gotcha."

"What we got is five hundred and six souls within what we'd call town limits, and another hundred and ten—give or take—living outside and still in our district. Your district now."

It still looked like that stage set to Nate, and far from real. Even farther from being his.

"Fire department—all volunteer—runs out of there. And here's the town hall." She eased the car to a stop in front of a wide log building. "My husband helped build this hall thirteen years ago. He was the first mayor of Lunacy, and held that post until he died, four years ago next February."

"How'd he die?"

"Heart attack. Playing hockey out on the lake. Slapped in a goal, keeled over and died. Just like him."

Nate waited a beat. "Who won?"

Hopp hooted with laughter. "His goal tied it up. They never did finish that game." She eased the car forward. "Here's your place."

Nate peered out through the dark and the spitting

snow. It was a trim building, wood frame, and obviously newer than its companions. It was bungalow style, with a small, enclosed porch and two windows on either side of the door, both of them framed with dark green shutters.

A path had been shoveled out or tromped down from the street to the door, and a short driveway, recently plowed from the looks of it, was already buried under a couple inches of fresh snow. A blue pickup truck was parked on it, and another narrow walking path snaked its way to the door.

Lights burned against both windows, and smoke puffed out, a gray cloud, from the black chimney pipe in the roof.

"We open for business?"

"That you are. They know you're coming in today." She swung in behind the pickup. "Ready to meet your team?"

"As I'll ever be."

He got out, found he was just as shocked by the cold this time around. Breathing through his teeth, he walked behind Hopp down the single-lane path to the outer door.

"This is what we call an Arctic entry up here." She stepped inside the enclosure, out of the wind and weather. "Helps keep down the heat loss from the main building. Good place to stow your parka."

She pulled hers off, hung it on a hook beside another. Nate followed suit, then dragged off his gloves, stuck them in one of the parka's pockets. Then came the watch cap, the scarf. He wondered if he'd ever get used to outfitting himself like an explorer on the North Pole every time he had to go out a door.

Hopp pushed through the other door, and into the scent of wood smoke and coffee.

The walls were painted industrial beige, the floors were speckled linoleum. A squat woodstove stood in the back right corner. On it a big cast-iron kettle chugged steam from its spout.

There were two metal desks, kissing each other on the right side of the room, and a line of plastic chairs, a low table with magazines arranged on the other. Along the back wall ranged a counter topped with a two-way, a computer and ceramic tabletop Christmas tree in a green that nature never intended.

He noted the doors on either side of it, the bulletin board where notes and notices were pinned.

And the three people who were pretending not to stare at him.

He assumed the two men were his deputies. One looked barely old enough to vote, and the other looked old enough to have voted for Kennedy. Both wore heavy wool pants, sturdy boots, and flannel shirts with badges pinned to them.

The younger one was native Alaskan, with black, ruler-straight hair falling nearly to his shoulders, deep-set almond-shaped eyes dark as midnight, and a painfully young, innocent look to his fine-boned face.

The older was wind-burned, crew cut, sagging in the jowls, and was squinting out of faded, blue eyes fanned by deep grooves. His thick build contrasted with the delicacy of his counterpart. Nate thought he might be ex-military.

The woman was round as a berry, with plump pink cheeks and a generous bosom under a pink sweater embroidered with white snowflakes. Her salt-and-pepper hair was braided into a top-of-the-head bun. She had a pencil sticking out of it and a plate of sticky buns in her hands.

"Well, the gang's all here. Chief Ignatious Burke, this is your staff. Deputy Otto Gruber."

Crew cut stepped forward, held out a hand. "Chief."

"Deputy Gruber."

"Deputy Peter Notti."

"Chief Burke."

Something in the hesitant smile rang a bell. "Deputy, are you and Rose related?"

"Yes, sir. She's my sister."

"And last but not least, your dispatcher, secretary and bearer of cinnamon buns, Marietta Peach."

"Happy you're here, Chief Burke." Her voice was as southern as a mint julep sipped on a veranda. "Hope you're feeling better."

"Fine. Thank you, Ms. Peach."

"I'm going to show the chief the rest of the station, then I'll leave you all to get acquainted. Ignatious, why don't we take a look at your . . . guest quarters."

She led the way through the door on the right. There were two cells, both with bunk-style cots. The walls looked freshly painted, the floor recently scrubbed. He smelled Lysol.

There were no tenants.

"These get much use?" Nate asked her.

"Drunks and disorderlies, primarily. You have to be pretty drunk and disorderly to warrant a night in jail in Lunacy. You're going to see some assaults, occasional vandalism, but that one's mostly from bored kids. I'll let your staff give you the lowdown on crime in Lunacy. We don't have a lawyer, so if somebody wants one bad enough, they have to call down to Anchorage or over to Fairbanks, unless they know one somewhere else. We do have a retired judge, but he's more likely to be off ice fishing than answering legal questions."

"Okay."

"Boy, you going to keep talking my ear off?"

"I never could learn to keep my mouth shut."

With a half-chuckle, she shook her head. "Let's take a look at your office."

They cut back through the main area where everyone was pretending to work. On the other side of Ms. Peach's counter, just through the doorway, stood the weapons cabinet. He counted six shotguns, five rifles, eight handguns and four wicked-looking knives.

He tucked his hands in his pockets, pursed his lips. "What? No broadsword?"

"Pays to be prepared."

"Yeah. For the coming invasion."

She only smiled and walked through the door next to the cabinet. "Here's your office."

It was about ten feet square with a window behind a gray metal desk. The desk held a computer, a phone and a black gooseneck lamp. Two file cabinets were shoved against the side wall with a short counter running beside them. It held a coffeemaker—already full—and two brown stoneware mugs, a basket with packaged creamer and sugar. There was a corkboard—empty—two folding chairs for visitors and pegs for hanging coats.

The lights mirroring against the black window glass made it seem all the more impersonal and foreign.

"Peach loaded up your desk, but if you need anything else, supply cabinet's down the hall. John's across from it."

"Okay."

"Got any questions?"

"I've got a lot of questions."

"Why don't you ask them?"

"All right. I'll ask this one, since the rest fall down from it anyway. Why'd you hire me?"

"Fair enough. Mind?" she said as she gestured to the coffeepot.

"Help yourself."

She poured mugs for both of them, handed him one, then sat in one of the folding chairs. "We needed a chief of police."

"Maybe."

"We're small, we're remote and we pretty much handle our own, but that doesn't mean we don't need structure, Ignatious. That we don't need a line between the right and the wrong and somebody to stand on that line. My man worked for that a lot of years before he sank his last puck."

"And now you do."

"That's right. Now I do. Added to that, having our own police force here means we keep on handling our own. Keep the Feds and the State out of it. Town like this can get ignored because of what it is and where it is. But we got a police force here now, a fire department. We've got a good school, good lodge, a weekly newspaper, a radio station. Weather comes in and cuts us off, we know how to be self-sufficient. But we need order, and this building and the people in it are symbols of that order."

"You hired a symbol."

"On one hand, that's just what I did." Her nut-brown eyes held his. "People feel more secure with symbols. On the other, I expect you to do your job, and a big part of the job, besides keeping order, is community relations—which is why I took the time to show you some of the town's businesses, give you names of who runs what. There's more. Bing's got a garage, fix any engine you bring in, and he runs heavy equipment. Snowplow, backhoe. Lunatic Air runs cargo and people, and brings supplies into town, takes them into the bush."

"Lunatic Air."

"That's Meg for you," Hopp said with a half-smile. "We're on the edge of the Interior here, and we've built ourselves up from a settlement of boomers and hippies and badasses to a solid town. You'll get to know the people of that town, the relationships, the grudges and the connections. Then you'll know how to handle them."

"Which brings me back. Why did you hire me? Why not somebody who knows all that already?"

"Seems to me somebody who knew all that already might come into this job with an agenda of his or her own. Grudges, connections of his or her own. Bring somebody from Outside, they come in fresh. You're young; that weighed in your favor. You don't have a wife and children who might not take to the life here and pressure you to go back to the Lower 48. You've got over ten years experience with the police. You had the qualifications I was looking for—and you didn't haggle over the salary."

"I see your point, but there's the other side. I don't know what the hell I'm doing."

"Mmm." She finished off her coffee. "You strike me as a bright young man. You'll figure it out. Now." She pushed to her feet. "I'm going to let you get started. Meeting's at two, Town Hall. You're going to want to say a few words."

"Oh boy."

"One more thing." She dug in her pocket, pulled out a box. "You'll need this." Opening it, she took out the silver star, then pinned it to his shirt. "See you at two, Chief."

He stood where he was, in the center of the room, contemplating his coffee as he heard the muted voices outside. He didn't know what he was doing—that was God's truth—so the best he could think of was to mark some sort of beginning and go from there.

Hopp was right. He had no wife, no children. He had no one and nothing pulling him back to the Lower 48. To the world. If he was going to stay here, then he had to make good. If he blew this, this strange chance at the end of the universe, there was nowhere left to go. Nothing left to do.

His stomach jittered with the same sort of queasy nerves he'd experienced on the plane as he carried his coffee out to the communal area.

"Ah, if I could have a couple minutes."

He wasn't sure where to stand, then realized he shouldn't be standing at all. He set down his coffee, then walked over to grab two of the plastic chairs. After carrying them over to the desks, he retrieved his coffee, worked up a smile for Peach.

"Ms. Peach? Would you come on over and sit down?" And though the short stack was heavy in his belly, he boosted up the smile. "Maybe you could bring those cinnamon buns with you. They sure smell tempting."

Obviously pleased, she brought over the plate and a stack of napkins. "You boys just help yourselves."

"I gotta figure this is at least as awkward for all of you as it is for me," Nate began as he plopped a bun on a napkin. "You don't know me. Don't know what kind of cop I am, what kind of man I am. I'm not from around here, and I don't know a damn thing about this part of the world. And you're supposed to take orders from me. You're going to take orders from me," he corrected, and bit into the bun.

"This is pure sin, Ms. Peach."

"It's the lard that does it."

"I bet." He envisioned every one of his arteries slamming shut. "It's hard to take orders from somebody you don't know, don't trust. You've got no reason to trust me. Yet. I'm going to make mistakes. I don't mind you pointing them out to me, as long as you point them out in private. I'm also going to rely on you, all of you, to bring me up to speed. Things I should know, people I should know. But for right now, I'm going to ask if any of you have a problem with me. Let's get it out in the open now, deal with it."

Otto took a slurp of his coffee. "I don't know if I've got a problem until I see what you're made of."

"Fair enough. You find you've got one, you tell me. Maybe I'll see it your way, maybe I'll tell you to go to hell. But we'll know where we stand."

"Chief Burke?"

Nate looked over at Peter. "It's Nate. I hope to God you people aren't going to take a page from Mayor Hopp and call me Ignatious all the damn time."

"Well, I was thinking that maybe at first me or Otto should go with you on calls, and on patrol. Until you get to know your way around."

"That's a good idea. Ms. Peach and I'll start working out a shift schedule, week by week."

"You can start calling me Peach now. I'd just like to say I expect this place to stay clean, and that chores— which includes scrubbing the bathroom, Otto—get put on the schedule like everything else. Mops and buckets and brooms aren't tools just for women."

"I signed on as deputy, not as a maid."

She had a soft, motherly face. And, like any mother worth her salt, could sear a hole through steel with one firm look. "And I'm being paid to work as dispatcher and secretary, not to scrub toilets. But what has to be done, has to be done."

"Why don't we rotate those chores for the time being?" Nate interrupted as he could see combat fire light both faces. "And I'll talk to Mayor Hopp about our budget. Maybe we can squeeze out enough to hire somebody to come in and swab us out once a week. Who has the keys to the weapon cabinet?"

"They're locked in my drawer," Peach told him.

"I'd like to have them. And I'd like to know what weapons each of you deputies is qualified for."

"If it's a gun, I can shoot it," Otto retorted.

"That may be true, but we're wearing badges." He tipped his chair back so he could see the gun Otto wore in a belt holster. "You want to stick with the .38 for your service revolver?"

"It's my own, and it suits me."

"That's fine. I'm going to take the 9mm SIG from the cabinet. Peter, you comfortable with the nine you're carrying?"

"Yes, sir."

"Peach, can you handle a firearm?"

"I've got my father's Colt .45 revolver locked in my desk, too. He taught me how to shoot when I was five. And I can handle anything in that cabinet, the same as GI Joe here."

"I served in the Corps," Otto retorted, with some heat. "I'm a Marine."

"Okay then." Nate cleared his throat. "How many residents, would you say, own weapons?"

The three of them stared at him until, finally, Otto's lips quirked up. "That'd be about all of them."

"Great. Do we have a list of those residents who're licensed to carry concealed?"

"I can get that for you," Peach offered.

"That'll be good. And would there be a copy of town ordinances?"

"I'll get it."

"One last," Nate said as Peach got up. "If we have occasion to arrest anyone, who sets bail, decides on the term, the payment of fine, and so on?"

There was a long silence before Peter spoke. "I guess you do, Chief."

Nate blew out a breath. "Won't that be fun?"

He went back into his office, taking the paperwork Peach gave him. It didn't take long to read through it, but it gave him something to pin up on his corkboard.

He was lining up pages, tacking them on when Peach came in. "Got those keys for you, Nate. These here are for the gun cabinet. These are for the station doors, front and back, the cells and your car. Everything's labeled."

"My car? What've I got?"

"Grand Cherokee. It's parked out on the street." She dumped keys into his hand. "Hopp said one of us should show you how you work the heat block for the engine."

He'd read about those, too. Heaters designed to keep an engine warm when at rest in subzero temperatures. "We'll get to it."

"Sun's coming up."

"What?" He turned, looked out the window.

Then he just stood, his arms at his sides, the keys weighing down his hand, as the sun bloomed orange and rose in the sky. The mountains came alive under it, massive and white with the gold streaks sliding over them.

They filled his window. Left him speechless.

"Nothing like your first winter sunrise in Alaska."

"I guess not." Mesmerized, he stepped closer to the window.

He could see the river where he'd landed—a long, saggy dock he hadn't noticed before, and the sheen of ice under the lightening sky. There were hills of snow, a huddle of houses, stands of trees—and he noted, people. There were people, bundled up so thickly they looked like globs of color gliding over the white.

There was smoke rising, and Jesus, was that an eagle soaring overhead? And as he watched, a group of kids went running toward the iced ribbon of river, hockey sticks and skates over their shoulders.

And the mountains stood over it all, like gods.

Watching them, he forgot about the cold, the wind, the isolation and his own quiet misery.

Watching them, he felt alive.

"That
the c

THREE

MAYBE IT WAS too damn cold, maybe people were on their best behavior, or it might have been that the holiday spirit was entrenched in that week between Christmas and New Year's, but it was nearly noon before the first call came in.

"Nate?" Peach came to his door holding a couple of knitting needles and a hank of purple wool. "Charlene called from The Lodge. Seems a couple of the boys got into a ruckus over a game of pool. Some pushy-shovey going on."

"All right." He got to his feet, fishing a quarter out of his pocket as he walked out. "Call it," he said to Otto and Peter.

"Heads." Otto set down his *Field & Stream* while Nate flipped the coin in the air.

He slapped it on the back of his hand. "Tails. Okay, Peter, you'll come with me. Little altercation over at The Lodge." He snagged a two-way, hooked it to his belt.

He stepped into the entry, began dragging on gear. "If it hasn't broken up by the time we get there," he said to Peter, "I want you to tell me the players straight off, give me the picture. Is it something that's going to turn nasty or can we resolve it with a few strong words?"

He shoved out the door, into the blast of cold air.

"That mine?" he asked, nodding toward the black Jeep at the curb.

"Yes, sir."

"And that cord plugged into that pole there would be attached to the heater on the engine."

"You'll need it if it's going to sit for any time. There's a Mylar blanket in the back, and that'll cover up the engine and keep the heat in for up to twenty-four hours, maybe. But sometimes people forget to take them off, and then you're going to overheat. Jumper cables in the back, too," he continued as he pulled the plug. "Emergency flares and first-aid kit and—"

"We'll go over all that," Nate interrupted, and wondered if navigating down a road called Lunatic Street would entail the need of emergency flares and first aid. "Let's see if I can get us to The Lodge in one piece."

He climbed behind the wheel, stuck the key in the ignition. "Heated seats," he noted. "There is a God."

The town looked different in the daylight, no doubt about it. Smaller somehow, Nate thought as he maneuvered on the hard-packed snow. Exhaust had blacked the white at the curbs, and the storefront windows weren't exactly sparkling, and most of the Christmas decorations looked the worse for wear in the sunlight.

It wasn't a postcard, unless you looked beyond to the mountains, but it was a few solid steps up from dreary.

Rugged was a better term, he decided. It was a settlement carved out of ice and snow and rock, snugged tight to a winding river, flanked by forests where he could easily imagine wolves roaming.

He wondered if forest meant bear, too, but decided it

wasn't worth worrying about until spring. Unless all that
hibernation talk was bullshit.

It took less than two minutes to drive from station
house to lodge. He saw a total of ten people on the street
and passed a brawny pickup, a clunky SUV, and counted
three parked snowmobiles and one set of skis propped
against the side of The Italian Place.

It seemed people didn't exactly hibernate in Lunacy,
whatever the bears did.

He went to the main door of The Lodge and walked
through it just ahead of Peter.

It hadn't broken up. He could hear that plainly
enough through the shouts of encouragement—*kick his
fat ass, Mackie!*—and the thud of bodies and grunts.
What Nate calculated was that a Lunacy-style crowd had
gathered, consisting of five men in flannel, one of which
turned out to be a woman on closer inspection.

Encircled by them, two men with shaggy, brown hair
were rolling around on the floor, trying to land short-
arm punches on each other. The only weapon he saw was
a broken pool cue.

"Mackie brothers," Peter told him.

"Brothers?"

"Yeah. Twins. They've been beating the hell out of
each other since they were in the womb. Hardly ever take
a swing at anyone else."

"Okay."

Nate nudged his way through the press of bodies. The
sight of him had the shouts toning down to murmurs as
he waded in and hauled the top Mackie off the bottom
Mackie.

"All right, break it up. Stay down," he ordered, but Mackie number two was already springing up, rearing back. He landed a solid roundhouse to his brother's jaw.

"*Red River,* numbnuts!" He shouted, then did a victory dance, fists lifted high, as his brother slumped in Nate's arms.

"Peter, for Christ's sake," Nate said as his deputy remained immobile.

"Oh, sorry, Chief. Jim, settle down."

Instead, Jim Mackie continued to bounce in his Wolverines to the cheers of the crowd.

Nate saw money being exchanged, but decided to ignore it.

"Take this one." Nate shoved the unconscious man into Peter, then stepped up to the self-proclaimed champ. "The deputy gave you an order."

"Yeah?" He grinned, showing blood on his teeth and an unholy gleam in a pair of brown eyes. "So what? I don't have to take orders from that shithead."

"Yeah, you do. I'll show you why." Nate spun the man around, shoved him against the wall, had his hands behind his back and cuffed in under ten seconds.

"Hey!" was the best the reigning champ could manage.

"Give me grief, and you'll sit in a cell for resisting arrest, among other things. Peter, bring that one over to the station when he wakes up."

With no apparent loyalty, the crowd shifted its support to Nate with catcalls and whistles as he muscled Jim Mackie toward the door.

Nate paused when he saw Charlene ease out of the kitchen. "You looking to press charges?" he asked her.

She stared, finally blinked. "I . . . well, hell, I don't know. Nobody's ever asked me that before. What kind of charges?"

"They broke some stuff back there."

"Oh. Well, they always pay for it after. But they did run off a couple of tourists who were going to order lunch."

"Bill started it."

"Oh now, Jim, you both start it. Every time. I've told you I don't want you coming in here fighting and causing a ruckus that runs people off. I don't want to press charges exactly. I just want this nonsense to stop. And payment for damages."

"Got it. Let's go sort this out, Jim."

"I don't see why I have to—"

Nate solved the matter by pushing him out into the cold.

"Hey, Christ's sake, I need my gear."

"Deputy Notti will bring it. Get in the car, or stand here and get frostbite. Up to you." He yanked the door open, gave Jim a heave inside.

Once Nate was behind the wheel, Jim had recovered some dignity, despite the bleeding mouth and puffy eye. "I don't think this is the way to treat people. It ain't right."

"I don't think it's right to coldcock your brother when somebody's holding his arms."

Jim had the grace to look chagrined, and dipped his chin onto his chest. "I was caught up. Heat of the moment. And the son of a bitch *pissed* me off. You're that Outsider's come to be chief of police, aren't you?"

"You're a quick study, Jim."

Jim sulked during the short drive to the station house. Then he trudged along as Nate took him inside.

"Lower 48 here," he said the minute he spotted Otto and Peach, "he doesn't understand how things are done in Lunacy."

"Why don't you explain it all to him?" There was a light in Otto's eyes. It might've been glee.

"Need the first-aid kit. Step into my office, Jim."

Nate led him in, pushed him into a chair, then, after unhooking one of the cuffs, snapped it onto the arm of the chair.

"Aw, come on. If I was going anywhere, I could just take this little dink of a chair with me."

"Sure you could. Then I'd add stealing police property to the mix."

Jim sulked some more. He was a bony man of about thirty, with a shaggy mop of brown hair, a narrow face sunken at the cheeks. His eyes were brown, with the left puffing up nicely from one of those short-armed punches. His lip was split and continued to dribble blood.

"I don't like you," he decided.

"That's not against the law. Disturbing the peace, destroying property, assault. Those are."

"'Round here, a man wants to pound on his fool of a brother, it's his business."

"Not anymore. 'Round here, these days, a man's going to show respect for private property, and public property. He's going to show respect for duly designated officers of the law."

"Peter? That little shithead."

"That's Deputy Shithead now."

Jim blew a sighing breath that had blood spitting out along with the air. "Christ's sake, I've known him since before he was born."

"When he's wearing a badge, and he tells you to settle down, you settle, whether or not you've known him in vitro."

Jim managed to look both interested and baffled. "I don't know what the hell you're talking about."

"I get that." He glanced over as Peach came in.

"Got the first-aid kit and an ice pack." She flipped the ice pack to Jim, set the kit on the desk in front of Nate. Then she fisted her hands on her hips. "Jim Mackie, you just don't grow any smarter, do you?"

"It was Bill started it." Flushing, he pressed the ice pack to his bleeding lip.

"So you say. Where is Bill?"

"Peter's bringing him along," Nate said. "When he wakes up."

Peach sniffed. "Your mother's likely to blacken your other eye when she has to bail you out." With that pre-diction, she walked out, snapped the door closed.

"*Jeez!* You're not going to put me in jail for punching my own brother."

"I could. Maybe I'll cut you some slack, seeing as this is my first day on the job." Nate leaned back. "What were you fighting about?"

"Okay, listen to this." Gearing up for his own defense, Jim slapped his hands on his knees. "That brainless jack-ass said how *Stagecoach* was the best Western ever made when everybody knows it's *Red River*."

Nate said nothing for a long moment. "That's it?"

"Well, *Christ's sake!*"

"Just want to be clear. You and your brother whaled on each other because you disagreed about the relative merits of *Stagecoach* versus *Red River* in the John Wayne oeuvre."

"In his what?"

"You were fighting over John Wayne movies."

Jim shifted on his seat. "Guess. We'll settle up with Charlene. Can I go now?"

"You'll settle up with Charlene, and you'll pay a fine of a hundred dollars *each* for creating a public nuisance."

"Oh hell now. You can't—"

"I can." Nate leaned forward, and Jim got a good look at cool, quiet gray eyes that made him want to squirm in his seat. "Jim, listen to what I'm saying to you. I don't want you or Bill fighting in The Lodge. Anywhere else for that matter, but for just this minute, we'll pinpoint The Lodge. There's a young boy who spends most of his day there."

"Well, hell, Rose always takes Jesse back in the kitchen if there's a ruckus. Me and Bill, we wouldn't do nothing to hurt that kid. We're just, you know, high-spirited."

"You'll have to lower those spirits when you're in town."

"A hundred dollars?"

"You can pay Peach, within the next twenty-four hours. You don't, I'm going to double the fine for every day you're late meeting the terms. If you don't want to pay the fine, you can spend the next three days in our fine accommodations here."

"We'll pay it." He muttered, shifted, sighed. "But Christ's sake. *Stagecoach*."

"Personally, I like *Rio Bravo*."

Jim opened his mouth, shut it again. Obviously he took a moment to consider the consequences. "It's a damn good movie," he said after a moment, "but it ain't no *Red River*."

IF NUISANCE CALLS were to be the norm, Nate considered he might have made the right decision in coming to Lunacy. Sibling brawls were probably his top speed these days.

He wasn't looking for challenges.

The Mackie brothers hadn't posed one. His round with Bill had gone along the same lines as his round with Jim, though Bill had argued passionately, and with considerable articulation, regarding *Stagecoach*. He hadn't seemed nearly as upset at being punched in the face as he was about having his favorite movie dissed.

Peter stuck his head in the door. "Chief? Charlene says you should come over and have lunch on the house."

"I appreciate that, but I've got to get ready for this meeting." And he hadn't missed the gleam in Charlene's eyes when he'd hauled off Jim Mackie. "I'd like you to follow this one through, Peter. Go on over there, get a list of damages and replacement costs from Charlene. See that the Mackie boys get it, and pay the freight within forty-eight hours."

"Sure thing. You handled that real slick, Chief."

"Wasn't much to handle. I'm going to write the report. I'm going to want you to look it over, add anything you feel necessary."

He looked around when he heard a window-rattling roar. "Earthquake? Volcano? Nuclear war?"

"Beaver," Peter told him.

"I don't care if it is Alaska, you don't have beavers big enough to sound like that."

With an appreciative laugh, Peter gestured to the window. "Meg Galloway's plane. It's a Beaver. She's bringing in supplies."

Swiveling around, Nate caught sight of the red plane, one that looked the size of a toy to him. Recalling he'd actually flown on one of about the same size, he felt the little pitch in the belly and turned away again.

Grateful for the distraction, he pressed his intercom button when it buzzed. "Yes, Peach."

"A couple of kids pitching ice balls at the school windows. Broke one before they ran off."

"We got ID?"

"Yes indeed. All three of them."

He considered a moment, worked down the order of things. "See if Otto can take it."

He looked back at Pete. "Question?"

"No. No, sir." Then he grinned. "Just nice to be doing, that's all."

"Yeah. Doing's good."

He kept himself busy doing until it was time to leave for the meeting. They were primarily housekeeping and organizational chores, but it helped Nate feel as if he was making his place.

For however long the place was his.

He'd signed on for a year, but both he and the town council had a sixty-day grace period when either side could opt out.

It steadied him to know he could leave tomorrow if he chose. Or next week. If he *was* here at the end of two months, he should know if he'd stick for the term of contract.

He opted to walk to Town Hall. It seemed wimpy somehow to drive so short a distance.

The sky was a clear, hard blue that had the white mass of mountains standing against it as if etched with a thin, sharp knife. The temperatures hovered at inhuman, but he saw a couple of kids burst out of The Corner Store with candy bars in their fists just as kids everywhere burst out of doors with candy. Full of greed and anticipation.

The minute they raced down the sidewalk, hands appeared at the door to turn the Open sign around to Closed.

More cars and trucks were parked on the street now, and others easing along the snow-packed road.

It looked like they'd have a full house at the town meeting.

He felt a quick twist in his gut, one he recognized from his public speaking course in college. A hideous mistake as an elective. Live and learn.

He enjoyed a reasonable amount of conversation. Give him a suspect to interrogate, a witness to interview, no problem—or it hadn't been once upon a time. But ask him to stand up in front of an audience of some sort and speak in coherent sentences? Flop sweat was already snaking a line down his back.

Just get through it, he ordered himself. Get through the next hour, and you'll never have to do this again. Probably.

He stepped inside, into heat and a hubbub of voices. A number of people stood around a lobby area dominated by the biggest fish Nate had ever seen. He was baffled enough to focus on it, wonder if it was, perhaps, some sort of small, mutant whale—and how in God's name someone had caught it much less managed to mount it to the wall.

The distraction saved him from worrying overmuch about the number of people looking in his direction, and the number already inside the meeting area, sitting on folding chairs and facing a stage and lectern.

"King salmon," Hopp said from behind him.

He kept staring at the enormous silver fish that showed its black gums in a kind of sneer. "*That's* a salmon? I've eaten salmon. I've had salmon in restaurants. They're like this big." He held out his hands to measure.

"You haven't eaten Alaskan king salmon, then. But truth to tell, this one's a big son of a bitch. My husband caught it. Came in at ninety-two pounds, two ounces. Short of the state record, but a hell of a prize."

"What did he use? A forklift?"

She let out her foghorn laugh, slapped him merrily on the shoulder. "You fish?"

"No."

"At all?"

"Got nothing against it, just never have." He turned then, and his brows shot up. She'd decked herself out in a sharp-looking business suit with tiny black and white checks. There were pearls at her ears, and a slick coat of red lipstick on her mouth.

"You look . . . impressive, mayor."

"A two-hundred-year-old redwood looks impressive."

"Well, I was going to say you look hot, but I thought it would be inappropriate."

She smiled broadly. "You're a clever boy, Ignatious."

"Not really. Not so much."

"If I can look hot, you can be clever. It's all presentation. Now why don't we get this show on the road by me introducing you to the town council members. Then we'll do our little speeches." She took his arm the way a woman might as she led a man through a cocktail party crowd. "Heard you dealt with the Mackie brothers already."

"Just a little disagreement over Westerns."

"I like those Clint Eastwood movies, myself. The early ones. Ed Woolcott, come over here and meet our new chief of police."

He met Woolcott, a tough-looking man in his fifties who gave Nate's hand a politician's shake. His hair was gray and full, brushed back from a craggy face. A tiny, white scar cut through his left eyebrow.

"I run the bank," he told Nate—which explained the navy blue suit and pinstriped tie. "I expect you'll be opening an account with us shortly."

"I'll have to take care of that."

"We're not here to drum up business, Ed. Let me finish showing Ignatious off."

He met Deb and Harry Miner, who ran The Corner Store, Alan B. Royce, the retired judge, Walter Notti, Peter's father, musher and sled-dog breeder—all of whom were on the town council.

"Ken Darby, our doctor, will be along when he can."

"That's okay. It's going to take a while to keep this all straight anyway."

Then there was Bess Mackie—a beanpole with a shock of henna-colored hair who planted herself in front of him, crossed her arms over her thin chest and sniffed.

"You roust my boys today?"

"Yes, ma'am, you could say that."

She drew another sharp breath through her thin nostrils, nodded twice. "Good. Next time, you knock their heads together, save me the trouble."

It was, Nate decided as she strode off to find a seat, a warm enough welcome, considering.

Hopp worked him toward the stage where chairs were set up for her and Nate, and for Woolcott, who served as deputy mayor.

"Deb's going to start things off with some town business, announcements and such," Hopp explained. "Then Ed'll have his say, introduce me. I'll have mine, introduce you. After you say your piece, we'll close it down. Might be some questions here and there."

Nate felt his stomach sink. "Okay."

She motioned him to a chair, took her own, then nodded at Deb Miner.

Deb, a stocky woman with a pretty face framed by

wispy blond hair, stepped onto the stage, took her place behind the lectern.

The mike buzzed and squeaked while she adjusted it, and her throat clearing could be heard echoing through the hall. "Afternoon, everybody. Before we get to our main business, I have some announcements. The New Year's Eve celebration at The Lodge is going to get rolling about nine o'clock. Live music's provided by The Caribous. We'll be passing the hat for the entertainment, so don't be stingy. The school's holding a spaghetti supper a week from Friday, proceeds going to the uniform fund for the hockey team. We got a good chance at making regional champs, so let's put the team in uniforms we can be proud of. They start serving at five. Dinner includes the entree, a salad, a roll and a soft drink. Adults six dollars, children six to twelve, four dollars. Under six eat free."

She went from there to details about an upcoming movie night being held at Town Hall. Nate listened with half an ear, tried not to obsess about his turn at the mike.

Then he saw her walk in.

The red parka, and something about the way she moved told him he was looking at the same woman he'd seen out his window the night before. Her hood was back, and she wore a black watch cap over her hair.

A lot of black, straight hair.

Her face seemed very pale against the two strong colors, her cheekbones very high in that black frame. Even across the hall he could see her eyes were blue. A bright, glacial blue.

She carried a canvas satchel over her shoulder and wore baggy, mannish trousers with scarred black boots.

Those icy blue eyes zeroed straight to his, held as she strode down the center aisle formed by the folding chairs, then scooted into one beside a whippily built man who looked to be Native.

They didn't speak, but something told Nate they were—not intimate, not physically—but in tune. She shrugged out of the parka while Deb moved from movie night to announcements about the upcoming hockey game.

Under the parka was an olive green sweater. Under the sweater, if Nate was any judge, was a tough, athletic little body.

He was trying to decide if she was pretty. She shouldn't have been—her eyebrows were too straight, her nose a little crooked, her mouth was top-heavy.

But even as he mentally listed the flaws, something stirred in his belly. Interesting, was all he could think. He'd stayed away from women the last several months, which, given his state of mind, hadn't been a real hardship. But this chilly-looking woman had his juices flowing again.

She opened the knapsack, took out a brown bag. And to Nate's baffled amusement dipped a hand in and came out with a fistful of popcorn. She munched away, offering some to her seat companion while Deb finished up the announcements.

While Ed took the lectern, made his comments about the town council and the progress they'd made, the newcomer pulled a silver thermos out of her sack, and poured what looked to be black coffee into its cup.

Who the hell was she? The daughter of the Native guy? The ages were about right, but there was no family resemblance he could see.

She didn't flush or flutter when he stared at her, but nibbled her snack, sipped her coffee and stared right back.

There was applause as Hopp was introduced. With an effort, Nate forced himself to put his head back in the game.

"I'm not going to waste time politicking up here. We decided to incorporate our town because we want to take care of our own in the tradition of our great state. We voted to build the police station, to form a police department. Now we went through a lot of debating, a lot of hot words on all sides and a lot of good, hard sense, too, on all sides. The upshot was, we voted to bring in a man from Outside, a man with experience and no connection to Lunacy. So he'd be fair, so he'd be smart, so he'd enforce the law without prejudice and with equality. Proved that much today when he slapped cuffs on Jim Mackie for wrestling around with his brother at The Lodge."

There were some chuckles over that, and the Mackie brothers, faces battered, grinned from their chairs.

"Fined us, too," Jim called out.

"And that's two hundred in the town coffers. Way you two carry on, you'll pay for the new fire truck we're wanting by yourselves. Ignatious Burke comes to us from Baltimore, Maryland, where he served on the Baltimore Police Department for eleven years, eight of those years as detective. We're lucky to have somebody with Chief Burke's qualifications looking after us Lunatics. So put your hands together and welcome our new chief of police."

As they did, Nate thought: Oh, shit, and pushed himself to his feet. He stepped toward the lectern, his mind as blank as a fresh blackboard. And from the crowd, someone called out, "Cheechako."

There were murmurs, mutters and a rise of voices poised on argument. The irritation that spiked through him carved away the nerves.

"That's right, I am. Cheechako. An Outsider. Fresh from the Lower 48."

The murmurs quieted as he scanned the crowd.

"Most of what I know about Alaska I got out of a guidebook or off the Internet or from movies. I don't know much more about this town except it's damn cold, the Mackie brothers like to pound each other and you've got a view that'll stop a man's heart in his chest. But I know how to be a cop, and that's why I'm here."

Used to know, he thought. Used to know how. And his palms went damp.

He was going to fumble—he could feel it—then his gaze met those glacier blue eyes of the woman in red. Her lips curved, just a little, and her eyes stayed on his as she lifted the silver cup to sip.

He heard himself speak. Maybe it was just to her. "It's my job to protect and serve this town, and that's what I'll do. Maybe you'll resent me, coming from Outside and telling you what you can't do, but we'll all have to get used to it. I'll do my best. You're the ones who'll decide if that's good enough. That's it."

There was a sprinkling of applause, then it grew. Nate found his gaze locked with the blue-eyed woman's again. His stomach knotted, unknotted, knotted up again as that top-heavy mouth tipped up at one corner in an odd little smile.

He heard Hopp adjourn the meeting. Several people surged forward to speak to him, and he lost the woman in the crowd. When he caught sight of her again, it was to see the red parka heading out the back doors.

"Who was that?" He eased back until he could touch Hopp's arm. "The woman who came in late—red parka, black hair, blue eyes."

"That would be Meg. Meg Galloway. Charlene's girl."

SHE'D WANTED A GOOD LOOK at him, a better look than the one she'd caught the day before when he'd stood in the window looking like the brooding and bitter hero of some Gothic novel.

He was good-looking enough for the part, she decided, but up close he seemed more sad than bitter.

Too bad really. Bitter was more her style.

He'd handled himself, she'd give him that. Rolled with the insult—that asshole Bing—said his piece and after a little hitch, moved on.

She supposed if they had to have a police force poking around Lunacy, they could've done worse. Didn't matter to her, as long as he didn't stick his nose in her business.

Since she was in town, she decided to run a few errands, load up on supplies.

She saw the CLOSED sign on The Corner Store, sighed

heavily. Then fished her ring of keys out of her bag. She found the one marked CS, then let herself in.

Grabbing a couple of boxes, she began to work her way through the aisle. Dry cereal, pasta, eggs, canned goods, toilet paper, flour, sugar. She dumped one box on the counter, filled the second.

She was hauling over a fifty-pound bag of Dog Chow when the door opened, and Nate walked in.

"They're closed," Meg huffed out as she set the bag on the floor by the counter.

"So I see."

"If you see they're closed, what're you doing in here?"

"Funny. That was my question."

"Need stuff." She walked behind the counter, picked out a couple of boxes of ammo to add to her box.

"Figured that, but generally when people who need stuff take it from a closed store it's called stealing."

"I've heard that." From under the counter she took a large record book, flipped through. "I bet they arrest people for that down the Lower 48."

"They do. Regularly."

"You intend to implement that policy here in Lunacy?"

"I do. Regularly."

She gave a quick laugh—the fog to Hopp's foghorn—found a pen and began writing in the book. "Well, just let me finish up here, then you can take me in. That'll be three arrests for you today. Gotta be a record."

He leaned on the counter, noted that she was neatly listing all the items in her two boxes. "Be wasting my time."

"Yeah, but we got plenty of that around here. Damn, forgot the Murphy's. You mind? Murphy's Oil Soap, right over there."

"Sure." He walked over, scanned the contents on the shelves and picked up a bottle. "I saw you last night, out my window."

She wrote down the Murphy's. "I saw you back."

"You're a bush pilot."

"I'm a lot of things." Her gaze lifted to his. "That's one of them."

"What else are you?"

"Big city cop like you should be able to find that out quick enough."

"Got some of it. You cook. Got a dog. Probably a couple good-sized dogs. You like your own space. You're honest, at least when it suits you. You like your coffee black and plenty of butter on your popcorn."

"Not much of a scratch on the surface." She tapped the pen against the book. "You looking to scratch some more, Chief Burke?"

Direct, he thought. He'd left out direct. So he'd be direct back. "Thinking about it."

She smiled the way she had in the hall, with the right corner of her mouth lifting before the left. "Charlene jumped you yet?"

"Excuse me?"

"I'm wondering if you got Charlene's special welcome to Lunacy last night."

He wasn't sure which irritated him more, the question or the cool way she watched him as she asked. "No."

"Not your type?"

"Not so much, no. And I'm not real comfortable discussing your mother this way."

"Got sensitivity, do you? Don't worry about it. Everybody knows Charlene likes to rattle the headboard with every good-looking man comes through here. Thing is, I tend to steer clear of her leftovers. But seeing the way it is, for now, maybe I'll give you a chance to scratch."

She closed the book, replaced it. "Want to give me a hand loading this stuff into the truck?"

"Sure. But I thought you flew in."

"Did. A friend and I switched modes of transportation."

"Okay." He hauled the dog food bag over his shoulder.

She had a brawny red pickup outside, with a tarp, camping gear, snowshoes and a couple of cans of gas already in the bed. There was a gun rack in the cab, loaded with a shotgun and a rifle.

"You hunt?" he asked her.

"Depends on the game." She slapped the gate of the truck bed into place, then just grinned at him. "What the hell are you doing here, Chief Burke?"

"Nate. And I'll let you know when I figure it out."

"Fair enough. Maybe I'll see you New Year's Eve. We'll see how we socialize."

She climbed into the truck, turned the key. Aerosmith blasted out about the same old song and dance, and she pulled into the street. She headed west, where the sun was already sliding behind the peaks, turning them flaming gold while the light went soft with twilight.

It was three-fifteen in the afternoon.

FOUR

Fucking cold. We're not talking about it, or we'll go crazy, but I'll write about it here. Then I can look back one day—maybe in July, when I'm sitting out with a beer, covered in bug dope and slapping at the sparrow-sized mosquitoes—and staring out at this white bitch.

I'll know I was here, that I did it. And that beer will taste all the sweeter.

But right now it's February, and July's a century away. The bitch rules.

Wind's taking us down to thirty or forty below. Once you're down that far, it doesn't seem like a few degrees one way or another matters. Cold broke one of the lanterns and snapped the zipper on my parka.

With night lasting sixteen hours, we make and break camp in the dark. Taking a piss becomes an exercise in exhaustion and misery. Still our spirits are holding, for the most part.

You can't buy this kind of experience. When the cold is like broken glass lacerating your throat, you know you're alive in a way you can only be alive on a mountain. When you risk a moment outside shelter and see the northern lights, so brilliant, so electric that you think you could reach up and grab some of that shimmering green and pull it inside yourself for a charge, you know you don't want to be alive anywhere else.

Our progress is slow, but we're not giving up on the goal of reaching the summit. We were slowed by avalanche debris. I wondered how many had camped there, under what is now buried and barren, and how soon the mountain will shift or shimmy and bury the snow cave we fought to hack into her.

We had a short, screaming argument over how to circumvent the debris. I took the lead. We spent what seemed like two lifetimes getting through and around it, but it couldn't have been done any faster, no matter what anyone else thinks. It's a hazardous area, known as Quicksand Pass because the glacier's moving under you. You can't see it, can't feel it, but she's slipping and sliding her way under you. And she can suck you down, because beneath that world of white are crevices just waiting to make themselves your coffin.

We picked our way up Lonely Ridge, ice axes ringing, frost clinging to our eyelashes, and after battling our way around Satan's Chimney, had lunch on a picnic blanket of untouched snow.

The sun was a ball of gold ice.

I risked a few pictures, but was afraid the cold would break the camera.

There was little grace but plenty of passion in the post-lunch climb. Maybe it was the speed we'd popped for dessert, but we kicked and cursed the mountain and each other. We beat steps into the snow for what seemed like hours, while that golden ball began to sink and turn a vicious, violent orange, that set fire to the snow. Then left us in the killing dark.

We used our headlamps to give us enough light to chop a tent ledge into the ice. We're camped here, listening to the wind blow like a storm surf through the night, easing our exhaustion with some prime weed and the success of the day.

We've taken to calling one another by code names from *Star Wars*. We're now Han, Luke and Darth. I'm Luke. We entertained ourselves pretending we were on the ice planet Hoth, on a mission to destroy an Empire stronghold. Of course, that means Darth's working against us, but that adds to the fun.

Hey, whatever floats your boat.

We made good progress today, but we're getting jumpy. It felt good to carve my ice ax into No Name's belly, inching my way up her. There was a lot of shouting, insults—motivational at first, then turning on an edge as ice chunks rained down. Darth took some in the face, and cursed me for the next hour.

For a minute today I thought he was going to lose it and try to bloody my face as I had his. Even now I can feel him stewing about it, boring the occasional dirty look at the back of my head while Han's snoring starts to compete with the wind.

He'll get over it. We're a team, and each one of us has the others' lives in his hands. So he'll get over it when we start climbing again.

Maybe we should ease off the speed, but a couple of

pops gives you a nice rush and helps beat off the cold and fatigue.

There's nothing like this in the world. The blinding sparkle of snow, the sound of axes slapping ice, or squeaking through snow, the scrape of crampon on rock, the free-falling wonder of the rope, and watching the ice fire with sunset.

Even now, huddled in the tent as I write this, my belly roiling from our dinner of freeze-dried stew, my body aching from the abuse, and fear of frostbite and death gnawing like a rat at the back of my brain, I wouldn't be anywhere else.

BY SEVEN, NATE FIGURED he'd put in a long enough day. He carried a radio phone with him. If anyone called the station after hours, the call would be bounced to his phone.

He'd have preferred eating in his room, alone, in the quiet, so his brain could unclog from all the details jammed into it throughout the day. And because he'd prefer alone.

But he wasn't going to get anywhere in this town by secluding himself, so he slid into an empty booth in The Lodge.

He could hear the crack of pool balls, and the whining country on the juke from the next room. Several men were hoisted on bar stools, downing beers while they watched a hockey game on television. The eating area was more than half full, with a waitress he'd yet to meet serving and clearing.

The man Hopp had introduced as The Professor wound his way through tables to Nate's booth.

He wore his tweed jacket with *Ulysses* tucked in the pocket, and carried a mug of beer. "Mind if I join you?"

"Go ahead."

"John Malmont. You're after a drink, you'd get it faster going to the bar. You're after food, Cissy'll work her way around here in a minute."

"Food's what I want, no hurry. Place is busy tonight. Is that usual?"

"Only two places you can get hot food you don't have to cook yourself. Only one you can get hard liquor."

"Well, that answers that."

"Lunatics are a fairly social lot—with each other, in any case. Add the holidays, you get full tables. Halibut's good tonight."

"Yeah?" Nate picked up the menu. "You lived here long?"

"Sixteen years now. Pittsburgh, originally," he said, anticipating the question. "Taught at Carnegie Mellon."

"What did you teach?"

"English literature to ambitious young minds. Many of whom enjoyed the smug position of dissecting and critiquing the long-dead white men they'd come to study."

"And now?"

"Now I teach literature and composition to bored teenagers, many of whom would prefer to be groping one another rather than exploring the wonders of the written word."

"Hey, Professor."

"Cissy. Chief Burke, meet Cecilia Fisher."

"Nice to meet you, Cissy." She was skinny as a broomstick with short, spiky hair in several shades of red, and a silver ring pierced into her left eyebrow.

She offered him a sunny smile. "You, too. What can I get for you?"

"I'll have the halibut. I hear it's good."

"Sure is." She started scribbling on her pad. "How do you want it cooked?"

"Grilled?"

"Fine. You get a house salad with that, choice of dressing. House dressing's real special. Big Mike makes it himself."

"That'd be fine."

"Got your choice of baked potato, mashed potato, fries, wild rice."

"I'll take the rice."

"Get you a drink?"

"Coffee, thanks."

"I'll be right back with that."

"Nice girl," John commented, giving his glasses a quick polish with a snowy white handkerchief. "Came into town a couple years ago, hanging out with a bunch here to do some climbing. Boy she was with slapped her around, dumped her out with nothing but her knapsack. She didn't have the money to get home—said she wasn't going back anyhow. Charlene gave her a room and a job."

He sipped his beer. "Boy came back for her a week later. Charlene ran him off."

"Charlene?"

"Keeps an over-and-under back in the kitchen. The boy decided to leave town without Cissy after looking down those barrels for a minute." John turned his head, and the amusement in his eyes turned to longing—just for an instant.

Nate saw the object of it gliding across the room with a coffeepot.

"Look at this. The two handsomest men in Lunacy at the same table." Charlene poured Nate's coffee, then slid cozily into the booth beside him. "And what would you two be talking about?"

"A beautiful woman, naturally." John picked up his beer. "Enjoy your dinner, Chief."

"So . . ." Charlene angled her body so her breast brushed Nate's arm. "What woman would that be?"

"John was telling me how Cissy came to be working for you."

"Oh?" She traced her tongue over her freshly slicked bottom lip. "You got your eye on my waitress, Nate?"

"Only with the hope she brings my dinner out soon." He couldn't scoot away without looking, and feeling, like an idiot. He couldn't move without bumping up against some part of her body. "The Mackie brothers pay you damages yet?"

"They came in about an hour ago, made it good. I want to thank you for taking care of me, Nate. Makes me feel secure knowing you're just a phone call away."

"Having an over-and-under in your kitchen ought to make you feel pretty secure."

"Well." She dipped her head, smiled. "That's really just for show." She angled her body closer, so that the come-get-me perfume seemed to rise out of her cleavage.

"It's hard being a woman alone in a place like this. Long winter nights. They get cold. And they get lonely. I like knowing a man like you's sleeping under the same roof. Maybe you and I could keep each other company later."

"Charlene. That's . . . That's an offer, all right." Her hand slid up his thigh. He grabbed her hand, pressed it on top of the table, even as he went hard and hot. "Let's just take a minute here."

"I'm hoping it'll take longer than a minute."

"Ha ha." If she kept rubbing that body against him, reminding him how long he'd been celibate, he might not make the full sixty seconds. "Charlene, I like you, and you're a pleasure to look at, but I don't think it'd be a good idea for us to . . . keep each other company. I'm just feeling my way around here."

"Me, too." She twined a lock of his hair around her finger. "You get restless tonight, you just give me a call. I'll show you what I mean about this being a full-service establishment."

She kept her baby blues on him as she wiggled out of the booth—and managed to slide her hand suggestively along his thigh again. Nate waited until she'd crossed the room in that hip-rolling gait before he let out a hoarse whistle of breath.

HE DIDN'T SLEEP WELL. The mother-daughter tag team kept him churned up and edgy. And the dark was endless and complete. A primitive dark that urged a man to burrow in a warm cave—with a warm woman.

He kept a light burning late—read through town ordinances by it, brooded by it, and ultimately slept by it until the alarm shrilled.

He started off the day as he had the one before, breakfasting with little Jesse.

It was routine he wanted. More than routine, he craved a rut where he wouldn't have to think, one that got deeper and deeper so he didn't have to see what was beyond it. He could go through the motions here, handling minor disputes, easing through the day with the same faces, the same voices, the same tasks repeating like a loop.

He could be the mouse on the wheel. And maybe the ridiculous cold would keep him from decomposing. That way no one would know he was already dead.

He liked sitting in his office, hours on end, juggling among Otto, Peter and himself the scatter of calls that came in. When he went out on one, he took one of the deputies with him to let him fill in background and set the rhythm.

He was getting a handle on his staff, in any case. Peter was twenty-three, had lived in the area all of his life, and appeared to know everyone. He also appeared to be liked by everyone who knew him.

Otto—staff sergeant, USMC, retired—had come to Alaska for the hunting and fishing. Eighteen years before, after his first divorce, he'd decided to make it his permanent home. He had three grown children in the Lower 48, and four grandchildren.

He'd married again—some blonde with a bustline bigger than her IQ, according to Peach—and had divorced again in under two years.

Both he and Bing had considered themselves qualified for the position Nate now held. But while Bing had gotten pissy about the town council's decision to bring in an Outsider, Otto—perhaps more accustomed to taking orders—had accepted the job as deputy.

As for Peach herself, the source of most of his information, she'd lived more than thirty years in Alaska, ever since she'd eloped with a boy from Macon and hightailed it with him to Sitka. He'd died on her, poor lamb, lost at sea on a fishing trawler less than six months after the elopement.

She'd married again and had lived with husband number two—a strapping, handsome grizzly bear of a man who'd taken her into the bush where they'd lived off the land, with occasional forays into the fledgling town of Lunacy.

When he'd died on her, too—went through the overflow on the lake and froze to death before he could get back to their cabin—she'd packed up and moved to Lunacy.

She'd married again, but that was a mistake, and she kicked his drunk, cheating ass all the way back to North Dakota, where he'd come from.

She'd consider husband number four, should the right candidate come along.

Peach gave him tidbits on others. Ed Woolcott would've liked the job of mayor, but he'd have to cool his heels until Hopp decided she'd had enough. His wife, Arlene, was snooty, but then she came from money, so it wasn't surprising.

Like Peter, Bing had lived here all of his life, the son of a Russian father and a Norwegian mother. His mother had run off with a piano player in '74, when Bing had been about thirteen. His father—and that man could down a pint of vodka at one sitting—had gone back to Russia about twelve years later and taken Bing's younger sister, Nadia, with him.

Rumor was she was pregnant, and there'd been whispers the father had been married.

Rose's husband, David, worked as a guide, a damn good one, and did odd jobs when he had time on his hands.

Harry and Deb had two kids—the boy was giving them some trouble—and Deb ruled the roost.

There was more. Peach always had more. Nate figured in a week, maybe two, he'd know whatever he needed to know about Lunacy and its population. Then the work would be another routine digging itself into a comfortable rut.

But whenever he stood at his window, watched the sun rise over the mountains, sheening them with gold, he felt that spark simmer inside him. The little flare of heat that told him there was still life in him.

Afraid it would spread, he'd turn away to face the blank wall.

On his third day, Nate dealt with a vehicular accident involving a pickup, an SUV and a moose. The moose got the best of the bargain and stood about fifty yards from the tangle of metal as if watching the show.

Since it was the first time Nate had seen an actual moose—bigger and uglier than he'd imagined—he was more interested in it than the two men currently bitching at each other and passing blame.

It was eight-twenty A.M. and black as pitch out on the road the locals called Lake Drive.

He had the deputy mayor and a mountain guide named Hawley going nose to nose, a Ford Explorer tipped into a ditch with its wheelbase buried in the snow, its hood crinkled like an accordion, and a Chevy pickup lying on its side as if it had decided to take a nap.

Both men had blood on their faces and mayhem in their eyes.

"Settle down." Deliberately, Nate shined his flashlight into the eyes of each man in turn. Both, he noted, were going to need stitches. "I said settle down! We'll sort this out in a minute. Otto? Anybody got a tow truck?"

"Bing's got one. He's the one handles this sort of thing."

"Well, give him a call. Get him out here to haul these vehicles into town. I want them off the road ASAP. They're a hazard. Now . . ."

He turned back to the men. "Which one of you can tell me what happened in a calm, coherent manner?"

They both started to rant at once, but since he smelled the whiskey fumes on Hawley, he held up a hand, then pointed at Ed Woolcott. "You start."

"I was driving into work, in a reasonable and safe manner—"

"Load of bullshit," Hawley commented.

"You'll get your turn. Mr. Woolcott?"

"I saw the headlights coming toward me, entirely too fast for safety."

Even as Hawley opened his mouth, Nate stabbed a finger at him.

"Then the moose came out of nowhere. I slowed and swerved to avoid collision, and the next thing I know, this, this *heap* is barreling down on me. I tried to cut over to the side of the road, but he, he *aimed* at me. Next thing I know, he ran me off the road, crashed my car. That car's only six months old! He was driving recklessly, *and* he's been drinking."

With a sharp nod, Ed folded his arms and glowered.

"Okay."

"Bing's heading out," Otto announced.

"Good. Mr. Woolcott, why don't you step over there, give your statement to Otto. Hawley?" Nate jerked his head, wandered over to the pickup. And stood there a moment exchanging baleful glances with the moose. "You been drinking?"

Hawley stood about five-eight and sported a golden brown beard. The blood that had trickled down from the gash on his jaw had frozen.

"Well, sure, I had a couple of belts."

"It's shy of nine A.M."

"Shit. Been ice fishing. I don't pay attention to what the hell the time of day is. I got some good fish in the cooler in my truck. I was heading home to store them, get something to eat and turn in. Then bankerman sees a damn moose in the road and goes into a tailspin. He's all over the damn road, doing doughnuts, and the moose is standing there—they're brainless animals, you ask me— and I have to swerve. Went into a little skid, and Woolcott spun right into me. We smashed, and this is where we ended up."

It had been a long time since he'd been on Traffic, and he'd never had to do an accident reconstruction in the dark, in the snow, at somewhere under zero degrees. But when he played his light over the road, studied the tracks, Hawley's version hit closer to home.

"Fact is, you've been drinking. We're going to have to do a sobriety test. You insured?"

"Yeah, but—"

"We'll sort it out," Nate repeated. "Let's get out of the cold."

Nate drove back to town with Hawley and Ed sitting, stonily silent, in the back. He pulled off at the clinic, left Otto with them while they got patched up and went back to the station for a Breathalyzer.

While he was there, he called up the driving records of both parties. Working out the solution in his head, he carted the Breathalyzer back to the clinic.

There were a couple people in the waiting room. A young woman with a sleeping baby, an old man wearing dirt brown coveralls and gnawing on a pipe.

There was a woman sitting at a chair behind a low counter. She was reading a paperback novel with a mostly naked couple in passionate embrace on the cover. But she looked up when he entered.

"Chief Burke?"

"Yes."

"I'm Joanna. Doc said you could come on back when you got here, if you want. He's in exam room one doing Hawley. Nita's in two, stitching Ed."

"Otto?"

"He's using the office. Checking on Bing and the tow."

"I'll take Hawley. Which way's that?"

"I'll show you." She marked her book with a shiny foil tab, then got up to lead him to the door directly to her right. "Right in there." She gestured, then gave a quick knock. "Doc? Chief Burke's here."

"Come on in."

It was a standard exam room—table, little sink, rolling chair. The doctor wore an open flannel shirt over a thermal, and glanced over from his work on the cut over Hawley's eye.

He was young, mid-thirties, trim and fit-looking, with a sandy beard to go with the thatch of curly hair. He wore little round metal glasses over green eyes.

"Ken Darby," he said. "I'd shake hands, but they're busy."

"Nice to meet you. How's the patient?"

"Few cuts and bruises. You're a lucky bastard, Hawley."

"Say that when you see my truck, goddamn it. That damn Ed drives like an eighty-year-old city woman who lost her bifocals."

"I'm going to need you to blow into this."

Hawley eyed the Breathalyzer dubiously. "I ain't drunk."

"Then it won't be a problem, will it?"

Hawley grumbled but complied as Ken fixed a butter-fly bandage on the cut.

"Well, Hawley, you're right on the edge here. Makes this a judgment call for me as to whether or not I charge you with driving under the influence."

"Ah, crock of shit."

"But the fact is, since you're on the border here, and show no signs of being under the influence, particularly, I'm going to issue you a warning instead. Next time you go ice fishing and have a couple belts, you don't get behind the wheel."

"Ain't got no damn wheel to get behind."

"Since I can't write the moose a citation, your insurance company's going to have to battle it out with Ed's. You've got a couple of speeding tickets on your plate, Hawley."

"Speed traps. Anchorage bastards."

"Maybe. Once you get that wheel back, you keep your speed to the posted limit and get yourself a designated driver when you're drinking. We'll get along fine. Are you going to need a lift home?"

Hawley scratched his neck while Ken treated a scrape on his forehead. "Guess I will. I need to take a look at my truck, talk to Bing."

"Come by the station after you're done. We'll get you home."

"Guess that's fair as it gets."

ED WASN'T AS PLEASED with the decision. He sat on the exam table, the air bag burns scoring his cheeks, and his lip puffy from where he'd bitten into it on impact.

"He'd been *drinking*."

"He was under the legal limit. The fact is, the culprit here's a moose, and I can't give a ticket to the local

wildlife. It comes down to bad luck. Two vehicles meeting a moose on a stretch of road. You're both insured,
which is more than the moose is, I'd expect. Neither one
of you is seriously injured. Comes down to it, you both
got off lucky."

"I don't consider having my new car in a ditch and my
face smashed by an air bag lucky, Chief Burke."

"I guess it's a matter of perspective."

Ed slid off the table, jerked up his chin. "And is this
how we can expect you to handle law enforcement in Lunacy?"

"Pretty much."

"It seems to me we're paying you to do little more
than warm a seat in your office."

"I had to warm the seat in my vehicle to come out and
look at the wreck."

"I don't like your attitude. You can be sure I'm going
to discuss this incident and your behavior with the mayor."

"Okay. Do you need a ride home or to the bank?"

"I can get myself where I'm going."

"I'll let you get there, then."

He met up with Otto outside the exam room. Otto's
only sign of having heard the conversation was a lift of
eyebrows. But when they walked out together, he cleared
his throat.

"Didn't make a friend there."

"And I thought I was being so friendly." Nate shrugged.
"You can't expect a man to be in a cheery mood when his
car's smashed and he's getting his face sewn up."

"Guess not. Ed's a bit of a blowhard, and he likes to

throw his weight around. Got more money than anybody else in the borough and doesn't like you to forget it."

"Good to know."

"Hawley's all right. He's a good man in the bush, and he knows how to climb. Colorful enough to please the tourists who want to take on a mountain and keeps to himself most of the time. He drinks, but he doesn't drink himself drunk. My opinion? You handled that fair."

"That matters. Appreciate it. You write this up, Otto? I think I'll ride out, check on the tow."

Checking on the accident scene was an excuse, but nobody had to know but himself.

He found Bing with a gnarled plug of a man working on digging the SUV out of the ditch. Duty meant he had to stop, get out and walk over to ask if they needed any more help.

"We know what we're doing." Bing tossed a shovelful of snow on Nate's boots.

"Then I'll let you keep doing it."

"Asshole," Bing muttered under his breath as Nate walked back to his car.

Nate turned, considered briefly. "Is asshole a step up or step down from cheechako?"

The little man snorted out a laugh but only shoved the blade of his shovel into the snow, leaned on it as Bing measured Nate. "Same damn thing."

"Just checking."

Nate got back in the car and left Bing sneering after him.

He kept driving, away from town, around the sharp curve of the lake.

Meg lived out this way, he'd checked, and since he could see her plane resting on the frozen surface, he was in the right place.

He turned into what looked like it might be a road hacked out of the trees and bumped his way along it to a house.

He didn't know what he'd expected, but it wasn't this. The seclusion wasn't a surprise, nor were the heart-stopping views in all directions. Those went with the territory.

But the house was pretty, a kind of sophisticated cabin, he supposed. Wood and glass, covered porches, bright red shutters framing the windows.

A walkway had been dug through the snow from drive to front porch. He could see where other paths had been tramped down from the house to outbuildings. One of those buildings, midway from the house to the edge of the forest, rose on stilts.

On the porch was a neatly stacked mountain of split wood.

The sun was coming up now, gloriously, bathing the scene with that eerie dawn. Smoke pumped out of three stone chimneys into the lightening sky.

Fascinated, he shut off the engine.

And heard the music.

It filled the world. A strong, sweet female voice, twined around strings and pipes lifted with sunrise over the endless white.

It soared over him when he stepped out of the truck and seemed to come from the air or the earth or the sky.

Then he saw her—the sharp red of her parka, walking over the white, away from the frozen lake with two dogs trotting beside her.

He didn't call out to her, wasn't sure he could have. There was a picture here, and his mind clicked the shutter. The dark-haired woman in red, wading through the pristine white with two beautiful dogs flanking her, and the glory of the morning mountains at her back.

The dogs saw, or scented, him first. Barking cut the air, sliced through the soaring music. They shot toward him like two blurry gray bullets.

He considered leaping back into his truck and wondered if that would cement his status as cheechako asshole.

There was always the possibility that his outer gear was thick enough to protect his skin from canine teeth should it become an issue.

He stayed where he was, saying, good dogs, nice dogs, over and over in his head like a mantra.

He braced for a leap, hoped it wouldn't be at his throat. Both dogs spewed snow into the air, then stopped a foot in front of him, bodies quivering, teeth showing. Full alert.

Both pair of eyes were blue, ice crystal blue, like their mistress's.

Nate's breath streamed out, a cloud on the air. "Well, God," he murmured. "You're a couple of beauties."

"Rock! Bull!" Meg shouted out. "Friend."

The dogs relaxed immediately and moved forward to sniff at him.

"Will they take my hand off if I touch them?" he called.

"Not now."

Taking it on faith, he stroked a gloved hand over each head. Since they seemed to enjoy it, he crouched down and gave them both a good rub while they pressed against him.

"You got balls, Burke."

"I was hoping that wouldn't be the part they'd chomp on. Are they sled dogs?"

"No." Her cheeks were pink with cold when she reached him. "I'm not a musher, but they come from a good line of them. They just live the high life out here with me."

"They have your eyes."

"Maybe I was a husky in a former life. What're you doing out here?"

"I was just . . . what's that music?"

"Loreena McKennit. Like it?"

"It's amazing. It's like . . . God."

She laughed. "You're the first man I've met who'll admit She's a woman. Out for a holiday drive?"

He straightened. "Holiday?"

"New Year's Eve."

"Oh. No. Had a little vehicular out on Lake Drive. I'm looking for the primary witness. Maybe you've seen him. Big guy, four legs, funny hat." He made antlers out of his fingers.

Cutie, she wondered, why do your eyes look so sad even when you smile? "As it happens, I've seen a couple of guys like that in the vicinity."

"In that case, I should come in, take your statement."

"I might enjoy having you take my statement, but it'll have to wait. I've got to fly. I was just bringing the dogs back, about to shut off my music."

"Where you going?"

"I'm taking some supplies into a village in the bush. I've got to move if I want to get there and back before party time." She cocked her head. "Want to ride along?"

Nate glanced toward the plane and thought: In that? Not even for a chance to sniff at your neck. "I'm on duty. Maybe another time."

"Sure. Rock, Bull, home! Be right back," she told Nate.

The dogs raced off, and Nate realized one of the out-buildings was an elaborate doghouse, decorated with totem figures painted in a primitive-art folksy style.

High life, all right.

Meg disappeared into the cabin. A moment later, the music shut off.

She came out again with a pack slung over her shoulder.

"See you, Chief. We'll see about you taking my state-ment sometime."

"Looking forward to that. Fly safe."

She tossed her hair back, hiked down to the plane.

He stayed, watching her.

She tossed the pack inside, climbed up.

He heard the engine catch, the stunning roar of it bursting through the stillness. The prop whirled, and the plane began to skate over the ice, circling it, circling, tipping onto one ski and circling until it lifted off, nosed up and climbed.

He could see the red of her parka, the black of her hair, through the cockpit window, then she was just a blur.

He tipped his head back as she circled, in the air now, and dipped a wing in what he assumed was a salute.

Then she was spearing off, over the white, into the blue.

FIVE

NATE COULD HEAR the celebration getting under way. Music—a kind of jivey honky-tonk—piped up the stairs, even through the floor vents of his room. Voices hummed, seemed to press against the walls and floorboards. Laughter slapped out, as did the occasional thud he took as dancing feet.

He sat alone, in the dark.

The depression had crashed down over him, without warning, without a snicker. One minute he'd been sitting at his desk reading through files, and the next the smothering black weight had dropped down on him.

It had happened that way before, with no vague sense of unease, no creeping sadness. Just that swamping wave of black rolling him under. Just that harsh switch from light to dark.

It wasn't hopelessness. The concept of hope had to be a factor before you could embrace its absence. It wasn't grief or despair or anger. He could have handled or battled any of those emotions.

It was a void. Immeasurable, black, airless, and it sucked him in.

He could function through it; he'd learned how. If you didn't function, people wouldn't leave you alone and their concern and worry only drove you deeper into the pit.

He could walk, talk, exist. But he couldn't live. That's how it felt to him, when he was in the silky clutches of it. He felt like walking death.

The way he'd felt in the hospital after Jack, with the pain bubbling up under the drugs, and the awareness of what had happened smearing the path to oblivion.

But he could function.

He'd finished the day, locked up. He'd driven back to The Lodge, walked up to his room. He'd spoken to people. He couldn't remember what or who, but he knew his mouth had moved, words had come out.

He'd gone up to his room, locked the door. And sat in the winter black.

What the hell was he doing here, in this place? This cold, dark, empty place? Was he so obvious, so pathetic, that he'd chosen this town of perpetual winter because it so perfectly mirrored what was inside him?

What did he possibly expect to prove by coming here, pinning on a badge and pretending he still cared enough to do a job? Hiding, that was all he was doing. Hiding from what he was, what he'd been, what he'd lost. But you couldn't hide from what was with you, every minute of every day, just waiting to leap out and laugh in your face.

He had the pills, of course. He'd brought them with him. Pills for depression, pills for anxiety. Pills to help him sleep, down deep where the nightmares couldn't follow.

Pills he'd stopped taking because they made him feel less of who he was than the depression or anxiety or insomnia.

He couldn't go back, couldn't go forward, so why not

sink here? Deeper and deeper, until eventually he couldn't, wouldn't, crawl out of the void anymore. He knew, a part of him knew, he was comfortable there, all settled into the dark and the empty, wallowing in his own misery.

Hell, he could set up housekeeping there, like one of the crazies living in an empty refrigerator box under a bridge. Life was pretty simple in a cardboard box, and nobody expected you to do anything.

He thought of the old saw about a tree falling in the woods and twisted it around to suit himself. If he lost his mind in Lunacy, would he ever have had it to lose?

He hated the part of him that thought that way, the part of him that wanted to live there.

If he didn't go down, someone would come up. That would be worse. He cursed at the effort it took just to get to his feet. Had those little stirrings inside him, those quick sparks of life been a kind of mocking? Fate's way of showing him what it was to be alive, before it kicked him into the hole again?

Well, he still had enough anger to crawl out this time, this one more time. He'd get through this night, this last night of the year. And if there was nothing in the next, he sure as hell wasn't any worse off.

But tonight he was on duty. He closed a hand over the badge he'd yet to take off and knew it was ridiculous that a cheap piece of metal should steady him. But he'd taken even that, and he'd go through the motions.

The light burned his eyes when he switched it on, and he had to deliberately step away before he gave in to the temptation to just turn it off again. Just settle down in the dark again.

He went into the bath, ran the water cold. Then splashed it on his face to fool himself into believing it washed away the fatigue that snaked around the depression.

He studied himself in the mirror for a long time, searching for any tells. But he saw an average guy, no worries. A little tired around the eyes, maybe, a little hollow in the cheeks, but nothing major.

As long as everybody saw the same, that would be enough.

The noise washed over him when he opened his door. As with the light, he had to force himself to move forward instead of retreating back into his cave.

He'd given both Otto and Peter the night off. Eat, drink and be merry. They both had friends and family, people to sweep out the old with. Since Nate had been struggling to sweep out the old on his own for months, he didn't see why that should change tonight.

He carried the lead in his belly down the stairs.

The music was bright and better than he'd expected. And the place was packed. Tables were rearranged to make dancing room, and the patrons were taking advantage of it. Streamers and balloons festooned the ceiling, and the dress of the people was just as celebratory.

He saw some of the old-timers in what Peach had described for him as an Alaska tuxedo. They were sturdy work suits, cleaned up for the occasion. Some were worn with bolo ties and, oddly, paper party hats.

Many of the women had fancied things up with sparkly dresses or skirts, upswept hair, high heels. He saw Hopp, spruced up in a purple cocktail dress dancing—

fox-trot, two-step? Nate hadn't a clue—with a slicked-up Harry Miner. Rose sat on a high-backed stool behind the bar, with the man he concluded was her husband, David, standing beside her, gently rubbing the small of her back.

He saw her laugh at something the receptionist from the clinic said to her. And he saw the way she looked up, met her husband's eyes. He saw the warmth of love beat between them, and he felt cold, felt alone.

He'd never had a woman look at him like that. Even when he'd been married, the woman he'd thought was his had never looked at him with that open, unrestricted love.

He looked away from them.

His eyes scanned the crowd as cop's eyes do—measuring, detailing, filing. It was the sort of thing that kept him apart, and he knew it. It was the sort of thing he couldn't stop doing.

He saw Ed, and the allegedly snooty Arlene. Mitch of KLUN, with his streaky blond hair in a ponytail, and his arm around a girl who wasn't as pretty as he was. Ken was wearing a Hawaiian lei and having a lively discussion with The Professor, who wore his usual tweed.

Fellowship, Nate thought. Some of it drunken at this point, but it was still fellowship. And he was Outside.

He caught a hit of Charlene's perfume, but she followed up on it too fast for him to brace or evade. Curvy female was wrapped around him, warm, glossy lips were sliding silky over his, with a sly hint of tongue. His ass was stroked and squeezed, his bottom lip gently nipped.

Then Charlene slithered off, smiled sleepily at him.

"Happy New Year, Nate. That was just in case I can't get my hands on you at midnight."

He couldn't quite form a word and was half afraid he might be blushing. He wondered if her obvious, and inappropriate, come-on had pushed embarrassment through the black.

"Just where have you been hiding?" She laced her arms around his neck. "Party's been in gear more than an hour, and you haven't danced with me."

"I had . . . things."

"Work, work, work. Why don't you come play with me?"

"I need to speak with the mayor." Please, God, help me.

"Oh, this isn't the time for town politics. It's a *party*. Come on, dance with me. Then we'll have some champagne."

"I really need to deal with this." He put his hands on her hips, hoping to nudge her back out of intimacy range, and searched the crowd for Hopp—his savior. His gaze struck, and locked on to Meg's.

She gave him that slow, two-step smile, and lifted the glass she held in a mock toast.

Then dancing couples whirled in front of her, and she was gone.

"I'll take a rain check. I—" He spotted a familiar face, and latched on like a drowning man. "Otto. Charlene wants to dance."

Before either of them could speak, Nate was beating a fast retreat. He made it to the other side of the room before he risked taking a breath.

"Funny, you don't look like a coward."

Meg stepped up beside him. She held two glasses now.

"Then looks are deceiving. She scares me to death."

"I won't say Charlene's harmless, because she's anything but. Still, if you don't want her tongue down your throat, you're going to need to say so. Loud, clear, in words of one syllable. Here. Got you a drink."

"I'm on duty."

She snorted. "I don't think a glass of cheap champagne's going to change that. Hell, Burke. Just about every soul in Lunacy's right here."

"Got a point." He took the glass, but he didn't drink. He did, however, manage to focus on her. She was wearing a dress. He supposed the technical term was dress for the skin of hot red painted on her. It showed off that tight, athletic body he'd imagined in ways that might have been illegal in several jurisdictions. She'd left her hair down. Black rain to milk-white shoulders. Sky-high heels the same color as the dress showcased slim, muscular legs.

She smelled like cool, secret shadows.

"You look amazing."

"I clean up good if the occasion warrants it. You, on the other hand, look tired." And wounded, she thought. That's how he'd struck her when she'd seen him come down the stairs. Like a man who knew there was a huge, gaping wound somewhere on his body, but didn't have the energy to find it.

"Haven't got the sleep pattern down yet." He sipped the champagne. It tasted like flavored soda water.

"Did you come down to relax and party or to stand around looking dour and official?"

"Mostly door two."

Meg shook her head. "Try the first for a while. See what happens." She reached out, unpinned his badge.

"Hey."

"You need a shield, you can pull it out," she said as she tucked it into his front pocket. "Right now, let's dance."

"I don't know how to do what they're doing out there."

"That's okay. I'll lead."

She did just that and made him laugh. It felt rusty in his throat, but lightened some of the weight. "Is the band local?"

"Everybody's local. That's Mindy on the piano. She teaches in the elementary school. Pargo on the guitar. Works in the bank. Chuck's on fiddle. He's a ranger in Denali. A Fed, but Chuck's so affable we pretend he's got a real job. And Big Mike's on drums. He's the cook here. Are you committing all that to memory?"

"Sorry?"

"I can see you tucking those names and faces into a file in your head."

"Pays to remember."

"Sometimes it pays to forget." Her gaze flickered to the right. "I'm being signalled. Max and Carrie Hawbaker. They run *The Lunatic,* our weekly paper. They've been out of town most of the week. They want an interview with the new chief of police."

"I thought this was a party."

"They'll just hunt you down the minute the music stops anyway."

"Not if you sneak out with me, and we have our own party elsewhere."

She shifted, looked straight into his eyes. "I might be interested, if you meant that."

"Why wouldn't I mean it?"

"There's the question. I'll ask you sometime."

She didn't give him much choice as she angled around, waved. She was pulling him along with her, to the edge of the impromptu dance floor. Introductions were made, then she slipped away, leaving him trapped.

"Really good to meet you." Max gave Nate's hand an enthusiastic shake. "Carrie and I just got back into town, so we haven't had a chance to welcome you. I'm going to want a piece of your time for an interview for *The Lunatic*."

"We'll have to work that out."

"We could sit out in the lobby now, and—"

"Not now, Max." Carrie beamed a smile. "No work tonight. But before we get back to the party, I'd like to ask you, Chief Burke, if you'd have any problem with us running a police log in the paper. I think it would show the community what you do, how we handle things here. Now that we've got an official police department, we want *The Lunatic* to document it."

"You can get that information from Peach."

Meg wound her way back to the bar, got another glass of champagne before sliding onto a stool where she could watch the dancing while she drank.

Charlene slid onto the one beside her. "I saw him first."

Meg kept watching the dancers. "More who he sees, isn't it?"

"You're only looking at him because I want him."

"Charlene, if it's got a dick, you want it." Meg tossed back champagne. "And I'm not looking at him, particularly." She smiled into her glass. "Go ahead, make your play. It's no skin off mine."

"First *interesting* man who's come along in months." Feeling chatty now, Charlene leaned closer. "Do you know, he has breakfast with little Jesse every morning? Isn't that the sweetest thing? And you should've seen the way he handled the Mackies. Plus, he's got *mystery*." She sighed. "I'm a sucker for a man with mystery."

"You're a sucker for a man as long as he can still get it up."

Charlene's mouth twisted in disgust. "Why do you have to be so crude?"

"You sat down here to let me know you're hoping to fuck the new chief of police. You can put ribbons on it, Charlene, it's still crude. I just leave off the ribbons."

"You're just like your father."

"So you always say," Meg murmured as Charlene flounced away.

Hopp took Charlene's stool. "The two of you would fight about how much rain came down in the last shower."

"That's a little philosophical for us. What're you drinking?"

"I was going to get another glass of that lousy champagne."

"I'll get it." Meg walked around the bar, poured another glass and topped off her own. "She wants to take a nice, greedy bite out of Burke."

Hopp looked over at Nate, saw he'd managed to escape from the Hawbakers only to be caught by Joe and Lara Wise.

"Their business."

"Their business," Meg agreed, and clinked her glass to Hopp's.

"The fact that he looks to be more interested in taking one out of you isn't going to improve your relationship with your mother."

"Nope." Meg sipped, considering. "But it should make things exciting for a while." She saw Hopp cast her eyes to heaven and laughed. "I can't help it. I like trouble."

"He would be." Hopp turned on the stool when she saw Nate being pulled onto the floor again by Charlene. "All that business about still waters, blah blah. Those broody types can be hard to handle."

"He's about the saddest man I've ever seen. Sadder than that drifter stopped in here a couple of years ago. What was his name? McKinnon. Blew his brains out up in Hawley's cache."

"And wasn't that a mess? Ignatious might be sad enough to put the barrel of a .45 in his mouth, but he's got too much spine to pull the trigger. Think he's too polite, too."

"That's what you're banking on?"

"Yeah. That's what I'm banking on. Well, hell. I'm going to do my last good deed of the year and go save him from Charlene."

Sad, polite men were anything but her type, Meg told herself. She liked reckless men, careless men. Men who didn't expect to stay the night after. You could have a couple drinks with a man like that, tangle up the sheets if the mood struck, then move on.

No bumps, no bruises.

A man like Ignatious Burke? A roll with him was

bound to be bumpy, and it was bound to leave bruises. Still, it might be worth it.

In any case, she liked conversations with him, and that couldn't be overvalued in her opinion. She could happily go days, weeks without talking to another human being. So she appreciated interesting conversation. And she liked watching the sorrow that haunted his eyes come and go. She'd seen it lift a few times now. When he'd stood in front of her house that morning, listening to Loreena McKennit, and again for a few moments when they'd danced.

Sitting there now, with the music and the heat of humanity all around her, she realized she wanted to see it lift again. And that she had a good idea how to make it happen.

She went behind the bar, found an open bottle and two glasses. Holding them down at her side, she slipped out of the room.

Hopp tapped Charlene briskly on the shoulder. "Sorry, Charlene, I need an official moment with Chief Burke."

Charlene only pressed closer to Nate. He wondered if she'd just pop out the back of him. "Town Hall's closed, Hopp."

"Town Hall's never closed. Come on now, let the boy out of that stranglehold."

"Oh, all right. I expect you to finish this dance, handsome."

"Let's find ourselves a corner, Ignatious." Hopp waved people aside, cut a swatch through the crowd. She hunkered down at a table someone had pushed into the pool area. "Want a drink?"

"No, I think I want the back door."

"You can run, but you can't hide in a town this size. You're going to have to deal with her sooner or later."

"Let's go with later." He wanted to go upstairs, back to the dark. His head was pounding, his stomach queasy with the stress and effort of just being.

"I didn't just pull you away to break Charlene's head-lock. You've got my deputy mayor well and truly pissed."

"I know it. I handled that situation as seemed most prudent and within the confines of the law."

"I'm not questioning how you do your job, Ignatious." She waved that off as she'd waved off people. "I'm just giving you the facts. Ed's pompous, self-important and a pain in the ass more than half the time. Still, he's a good man and works hard for this town."

"Doesn't mean he can drive worth a damn."

She grinned at that. "He's always been a lousy driver. He's also powerful, rich and a grudge-holder. He won't forget you crossed him on this business. It might seem small potatoes to the type of thing you're used to dealing with, but in Lunacy, this was major."

"I can't be the first to cross him."

"You're not. Ed and I butt heads all the time. But the way he'd see that, he and I are on equal footing. I might even have a leg up. You're Outside, and he expects you to kowtow some. On the other hand, if you'd kowtowed, I'd have been very disappointed. Puts you between a rock and a hard place."

"I've been there before. Does kowtow really have anything to do with cows?"

She stared for a moment, then barked out a laugh. "A

polite and sneaky way to tell me to mind my own. Before I do, let me add something. Getting yourself caught between Charlene and Meg means that rock and hard place are both going to be very hot, very sticky, and mean as a demon from hell."

"Then I'd better not get caught."

"Good thinking." Her eyebrows lifted when his cell phone beeped.

"Calls to the station get transferred to my personal," he said as he pulled it out of his pocket. "Burke."

"Get your coat," Meg said. "Meet me out front in five minutes. I've got something I want to show you."

"Sure. Okay." He stuck the phone back in his pocket as Hopp watched him. "It's nothing. I think I'm going to duck out."

"Mmm-hmm. Use the door there, go through the kitchen."

"Thanks. And Happy New Year."

"Same to you." Hopp shook her head as he walked away. "Going to be trouble."

IT TOOK HIM more than five minutes to get to his room, pile on his gear, slip out, then walk around to the front of The Lodge. He was halfway there when he realized he hadn't been tempted to just lock the door behind him and burrow back in the dark.

Maybe it was progress. Or maybe lust was stronger than situational depression.

She was waiting, sitting on one of two folding chairs she'd set dead center of the street.

The bottle of champagne was screwed into the snow-pack. She sipped from her glass, and a thick blanket covered her lap.

"You can't sit out here in that dress even with your coat and the blanket—"

"I changed. I always carry extra clothes in my pack."

"Too bad. I was looking forward to seeing you in that dress again."

"Another time, another place. Have a seat."

"Okay. Why are we sitting outside in the street at . . . ten minutes to midnight?"

"Not much for crowds. You?"

"Not really."

"They can be fun for a while, on a special occasion. But it wears thin for me after a few hours. Besides," she handed him a glass, "this is better."

It amazed him the champagne wasn't frozen solid. "I think it would be better if we were inside, where frostbite isn't a factor."

"Not that cold out. No wind. Hovering around zero. Besides, you can't really see this from inside."

"See what?"

"Look up, Lower 48."

He looked where she pointed and lost his breath. "Holy God."

"Yeah, I always thought it was holy. A natural phenom caused by latitude, sunspots and so on. Scientific explanations don't make it less beautiful, or magical."

The lights in the sky were green with shimmers of gold, hints of red. The long, eerie streaks seemed to pulse and breathe, bathing the dark with life.

"The northern lights show best in the winter, but it's usually too damn cold to appreciate them. Figured this was a good night for the exception."

"I've heard of them. Seen pictures. It's not like the pictures."

"The best things never are. They show better out of town. Even better when you're camped up on one of the glaciers. One night when I was about seven, my father and I hiked up into the mountains and camped just so we could be up there to see. We lay on our backs for hours, damn near freezing, and just watched the sky."

The otherworldly green continued to shift, glow, expand, shimmer. It was raining liquid jewels of color. "What happened to him?"

"You could say one day he took another hike and decided to keep going. You got family?"

"Sort of."

"Well, we won't spoil this by telling our sad stories. We'll just enjoy the show."

They sat in silence in the middle of the street, spindly chairs balanced on the snowpack while the heavens flamed.

The flames sparked something inside him, stroked away the tension headache, settled him on the ridge of wonder where he could breathe.

She glanced toward The Lodge as the noise level grew. The shouts of countdown to midnight began. "Looks like it's just you and me, Burke."

"A better end to the year than I expected. You want me to pretend I'm kissing you because it's tradition?"

"Screw tradition." She grabbed his hair in two gloved hands, yanked him toward her.

Her lips were cold, and there was a strange, powerful thrill in feeling them warm against his. The full-throttle punch of the kiss jolted his sluggish system into drive, churned in his belly, snapped through his blood.

He heard the roar—but it was muffled, dim and distant—when midnight struck. Bells clanged, horns tooted, cheers sounded. And through them he heard, clear as a wish, his own heartbeat.

He dropped the glass in his hand, shoved the blanket away so he could reach her. The hum of frustration in his throat came from the barrier of thick layers of clothing. He wanted that strong, curvy body, the shape of it, the taste and scent of it.

Then the sound of gunshots had him jerking back.

"Celebration fire, that's all." Her breath streamed out in clouds as she tried to draw him back. This man could *kiss*, and she wanted to hold on to the punch-drunk sensation of having his lips, his tongue, his teeth ravish her.

Who needed cheap champagne?

"Maybe, but . . . I have to check."

She gave a half-laugh, then reached down to pick up their glasses. "Yeah, you would."

"Meg—"

"Go ahead, Chief." She gave his knee a friendly pat, smiled into those fascinating, and troubled, gray eyes. "A job's a job."

"It won't take long."

She was sure it wouldn't. A few shots in the air were

usual on holidays, at weddings, births—even at funerals, depending on the sentiments toward the dead.

But it didn't seem wise to wait. Instead, she left the chairs, the bottle, the glasses on the front porch. She carried the blanket back to her truck, tossed it in the cab.

Then she drove toward home while the green lights played across the sky. And she knew Hopp was right. Nate Burke was going to be trouble.

SIX

THE LUNATIC

Police Log
Monday, January 3

8:03 A.M. Report of snowshoes missing from porch, residence of Hans Finkle. Deputy Peter Notti responded. Finkle's statement "That [numerous colorful expletives deleted] Trilby's up to his old tricks" could not be verified. Snowshoes subsequently located in Finkle's truck.

9:22 A.M. Advised of vehicular accident Rancor Road. Chief of Police Burke and Deputy Otto Gruber responded. Brett Trooper and Virginia Mann involved. No injuries, other than the stubbed toe Trooper suffered as a result of repeatedly kicking his own mangled bumper. No charges filed.

11:56 A.M. Confrontation between Dexter Trilby and Hans Finkle reported at The Lodge. The argument, which included other various and colorful expletives, was apparently rooted in the earlier snowshoe incident. Chief Burke responded, and after some debate, it was suggested the altercation be settled through a checkers tournament. At press time, it was twelve games to ten, in favor of Trilby. No charges filed.

1:45 P.M. Report of loud music and speeding vehicles on Caribou. Chief Burke and Deputy Notti responded. James and William Mackie found to be racing snowmobiles and playing a recording of "Born to Be Wild" at a loud volume. After a brief, and according to witness reports, entertaining chase, a heated confrontation with the officers ensued, during which the CD containing the offending track was confiscated, and which included James Mackie's claim that "Lunacy's just no damn fun anymore." Both Mackies were ticketed for excessive speed.

3:12 P.M. Report of screaming in the vicinity of Rancor Wood, 2.1 miles from town post. Chief Burke and Deputy Gruber responded. Turned out to be a group of boys playing war, armed with popguns and a squirt bottle of ketchup. Chief Burke declared an immediate truce and escorted the soldiers—alive, dead and wounded—home.

4:58 P.M. Report of disturbance on Moose. Chief Burke and Deputy Notti responded. An argument between a sixteen-year-old female and a sixteen-year-old male involving an alleged flirtation with another sixteen-year-old male was settled. No charges filed.

5:18 P.M. Sixteen-year-old male ticketed for reckless driving and excessive horn blowing up and down Moose.

7:12 P.M. Responding to various requests, Chief
Burke removed Michael Sullivan from the curb at
the corner of Lunacy and Moose where he was
singing a loud and reportedly off-key rendition of
"Whiskey in the Jar." Sullivan spent the night in jail
for his own safety. No charges filed.

Nate read over the single day, then the rest of his second week in *The Lunatic*. He'd waited for the complaints
when the first issue that included the police log had come
out. But there'd been none. Apparently people didn't
mind having their names printed, even if it was in con-
junction with their indiscretions.

He slipped the newspaper into a desk drawer, with the
first issue. Two weeks down, he thought.

Still here.

SARRIE PARKER LEANED on the counter in The Corner
Store. She'd shed her bunny boots and parka at the door,
then plucked a pack of Black Jack gum from the point-of-
purchase display.

She was there to gossip, not to shop, and the gum was
the cheapest excuse at hand. She gave Cecil, Deb's King
Charles spaniel, a little pat on the head. He lounged, as
he did every day, in his cushioned basket on the counter.
"Don't see much of Chief Burke down at The Lodge."

Deb continued to shelve packs of smokes and chewing
tobacco. Her store was a clearinghouse for town news. If
she didn't know about it, it hadn't happened yet.

"Doesn't come around here much, either. Keeps to himself."

"Has breakfast there every day with Rose's boy and takes his dinner there most nights. Not much of an appetite, you ask me."

Since she had the pack of gum in her hand anyway, Sarrie opened it. "I pick up his room every morning, not that there's much to pick up. Man doesn't have anything but his clothes and shaving gear. Not a picture, not a book."

Since she did the majority of the housekeeping at The Lodge, Sarrie considered herself an expert on human behavior.

"Maybe he's having stuff sent."

"Don't think I didn't ask." Sarrie wagged a stick of gum before folding it into her mouth. "Made it a point to. I said to him, 'So, Chief Burke, you got the rest of your things coming up from the Lower 48?' And he says to me, 'I brought everything with me.' Doesn't make any phone calls, either, at least not from his room. Or get any. Far as I can see, the only thing he does up there is sleep."

Though there was no one else in the store at the moment, Sarrie dropped her voice, leaned in. "And despite Charlene's throwing herself at him, he's sleeping alone." She gave a sharp nod. "You change a man's sheets, you know what he's up to in the night."

"Maybe they do it in the shower or on the floor." Deb had the pleasure of seeing Sarrie's chipmunk-cheeked face register shock. "No law says you've got to do your screwing in bed."

Being a professional on the gossip circuit, Sarrie recovered quickly. "Charlene was getting any, she wouldn't still be chasing after him like a hound after a rabbit, would she?"

Pausing to scratch Cecil behind his silky ears, Deb had to concede the point. "Probably not."

"Man comes up here, hardly more than the clothes on his back, holes up hours on end in his room, steps around a willing woman *and* barely says more than boo unless you corner him, well, there's something strange about that man. If you ask me."

"He'd hardly be the first of that type to show up here."

"Maybe. But he's the first we made chief of police." She was still a little steamed he'd given her son a ticket the week before. Like twenty-five dollars grew on trees. "Man's hiding something."

"God's sake, Sarrie. Do you know anybody around here who isn't?"

"I don't care who's hiding what, unless he's got the authority to put me and mine in jail."

Impatient now, Deb jabbed keys on her cash register. "Unless you're planning on walking out of here without paying for that gum, you're not breaking any laws. So I wouldn't worry about it."

THE MAN UNDER DISCUSSION was still sitting at his desk. But now he'd been cornered. For two weeks, he'd managed to evade, sidestep or outrun Max Hawbaker. He didn't want to be interviewed. As far as Nate was concerned, the press was the press, whether it was a small-town weekly or *The Baltimore Sun.*

Maybe the citizens of Lunacy didn't mind their names in the paper, whatever the reason, but he'd yet to wash the bad taste out of his mouth that had coated it during his experience with reporters after the shootings.

And he'd known he'd have to swallow more when Hopp had marched into his office with Max at her side.

"Max needs an interview. The town needs to know something about the man we've got heading up our law and order. *The Lunatic* goes to press this time, I want this story in there. So . . . get to it."

She marched right out again, closing the door smartly behind her.

Max smiled gamely. "Ran into the mayor on my way over to see if you had a few minutes now to talk to me."

"Uh-huh." Since he'd been debating whiling away some time with computer solitaire or taking Peter up on his offer to give him another snowshoeing lesson, Nate couldn't claim not to have the time.

He'd pegged Max as an eager nerd, the sort that had spent most of his high school days being given wedgies. He had a round, pleasant face with light brown hair receding over it. He was carrying about ten extra pounds on a five-ten frame, most of it in the belly.

"Coffee?"

"Don't mind if I do."

Nate got up, poured two cups. "What do you take in it?"

"Couple of those creamers, couple of those sugars. Um, what do you think of our new feature? The police log?"

"It's all new to me. You've got the facts down. Seems thorough."

"Carrie really wanted to include it. I'm going to record this, if that's okay. I'll be taking notes, but I like to have a record."

"Fine." He doctored Max's coffee, brought it over. "What do you want to know?"

Settling in, Max took a small tape recorder out of his canvas sack. He set it on the desk, noted the time, turned it on. Then drew a pad and pencil out of his pocket. "I think our readers would like to know something about the man behind the badge."

"Sounds like a movie title. Sorry," he said when Max's brow creased. "There's not that much to know."

"Let's start with the basics. You mind giving me your age?"

"Thirty-two."

"And you were a detective with the Baltimore PD?"

"That's right."

"Married?"

"Divorced."

"Happens to the best of us. Kids?"

"No."

"Baltimore your hometown?"

"All my life, except these past couple weeks."

"So, how does a detective from Baltimore end up chief of police in Lunacy, Alaska?"

"I got hired."

Max's face stayed affable, his tone conversational. "Had to throw your hat into the ring to get hired."

"I wanted a change." A fresh start. A last chance.

"Some might consider this a pretty dramatic change."

"If you're going for something other than your usual,

why not make it big? I liked the sound of the job, the place. Now I've got the opportunity to do the job I know, but in a different setting, with a different rhythm."

"We just talked about the police log. This can't be anything like what you used to deal with. You're not concerned about being bored? Coming from the pace and action of a big city and into a community of less than seven hundred?"

Careful, Nate thought. Hadn't he just been sitting here, bored? Or depressed? It was hard to tell the difference. There were times he wasn't sure there was a difference since both left him with a heavy, useless feeling.

"Baltimore thinks of itself as a big small town. But the fact is, a lot of the time you're doing the job with a certain amount of anonymity. One cop's the same as another, one case piled on top of the next."

And you can never close them all, Nate thought. No matter how many hours you put in, you can't close them all and you end up with the Open and Actives haunting you.

"If someone calls here," he continued, "they know that either I or one of two deputies is going to come out and talk to them, to help resolve the situation. And I'm going to know, after some more time on the job, who needs assistance when the calls come in. It won't just be a name on a file, it'll be a person I know. I think this will add another level of satisfaction to the work I do."

It surprised him to realize he'd spoken the pure truth, without fully realizing it had been there.

"You hunt?"

"No."

"Fish?"

"Not so far."

Max pursed his lips. "Hockey? Skiing? Mountain climbing?"

"No. Peter's teaching me how to snowshoe. He says it'll come in handy."

"He's right about that. What about hobbies, leisure-time activities, interests?"

The job hadn't left him much room. Or, he corrected, he'd allowed the job to consume all his time. Isn't that why Rachel had looked elsewhere? "I'm keeping my options open there. We'll start with the snowshoeing, see what happens next. How'd you end up out here?"

"Me?"

"I'd like to know something about the guy asking the questions."

"That's fair," Max said after a moment. "Went to Berkeley in the sixties. Sex, drugs and rock and roll. There was a woman—as there should be—and we migrated north. Spent some time in Seattle. I hooked up with this guy there who was into climbing. I caught the bug. We kept migrating north, the woman and I. Anti-establishment, vegetarians, intellectuals."

He smiled, an overweight, balding, middle-aged man, who seemed amused by who he'd been, and who he was now. "She was going to paint; I was going to write novels that exposed man's underbelly, while we lived off the land. We got married, which screwed up everything. She ended up back in Seattle. I ended up here."

"Publishing a newspaper instead of writing novels."

"Oh, I'm still working on those novels." He didn't

smile now, but looked distant and a little disturbed. "Once in a while I pull them out. They're crap, but I'm still working on them. Still don't eat meat, and I'm still a greenie—environmentalist type—which irritates a lot of people. Met Carrie about fifteen years ago. We got married." His smile came back. "This one seems to be working out."

"Kids?"

"Girl and a boy. Twelve and ten. Now, let's get back to you. You were with the Baltimore PD for eleven years. When I spoke with Lieutenant Foster—"

"You spoke to my lieutenant?"

"Your former lieutenant. Getting some background. He described you as thorough and dogged, the kind of cop who closed cases and worked well under pressure. Not that any of us should mind having those qualities in our chief of police, but you seem overqualified for this job."

"That would be my problem," Nate said flatly. "That's about all the time I can give you."

"Just a couple more. You were on medical leave for two months after the incident last April during which your partner, Jack Behan, and a suspect were killed and yourself wounded. You returned to duty for another four months, then resigned. I have to assume the incident weighed heavily in your decision to take this position. Is that accurate?"

"I gave you my reasons for taking this position. My partner's death doesn't have anything to do with anyone in Lunacy."

Max's face was set, and Nate saw he'd underestimated

the man. A reporter was a reporter, he reminded himself, whatever the venue. And this one smelled a story.

"It has to do with you, Chief. Your experiences and motivations, your professional history."

"History would be the operative word."

"*The Lunatic* may be small-time, but as publisher I still have to do my homework, present an accurate story and a complete one. I know the shooting incident was investigated and it was found you fired your weapon justifiably. Still, you killed a man that night, and that has to weigh heavy."

"Do you think you pick up a badge and a gun for sport, Hawbaker? Do you think they're just for show? A cop knows, every day, when he picks up his weapon that it might be the day he has to use it. Yeah, it weighs heavy."

Temper licked at him, turned his voice as cold as the January wind that rattled against the windows. "It's supposed to weigh heavy—the weapon and what you might have to do with it. Do I regret deploying my weapon? I do not. I regret not being faster. If I'd been faster, a good man would still be alive. A woman wouldn't be a widow, and two children would still have their father."

Max had edged back in his seat, and he'd moistened his lips several times. But he stuck. "You blame yourself?"

"I'm the only one who came out of that alley alive." Temper died and left his eyes dull and tired. "Who else is there to blame? Turn off your recorder. We're done here."

Max leaned forward, shut off the machine. "I'm sorry to have hit a sore spot. There's not much public around here, but what there is has a right to know."

"So you guys always say. I need to get back to work."

Max picked up the recorder, tucked it away, then rose. "I, ah, need a picture to run with the story." Nate's silent stare had Max clearing his throat. "Carrie can come find you a little later. She's the photographer. Thanks for your time. And . . . good luck with the snowshoeing."

When he was alone, Nate sat very still. He waited for the rage, but it wouldn't come back. He'd have welcomed it, the wild, blinding heat of fury. But he stayed cold.

He knew what would happen if he stayed frozen. He got up, his movements slow and controlled. He stepped out, picked up a two-way.

"I've got to be out awhile," he told Peach. "Something comes up, you can reach me on the two-way or my cell."

"Weather's coming in," she told him. "Looks to be a bad one. You don't want to stray so far you're not tucked back in by dinnertime."

"I'll be back." He walked out into the entry, piled on his gear. He kept his mind a blank as he got into his car and drove. He pulled over again in front of Hopp's house, walked to her door and knocked.

She answered, wearing a pair of reading glasses on a chain over her thick corduroy shirt. "Ignatious. Come on in."

"No, thanks. Don't ever ambush me like that again."

Her fingers ran up and down her eyeglass chain as she studied his face. "Come in, we'll talk."

"That's all I have to say. All I'm going to say."

He turned, left her standing in the doorway.

He drove out of town, pulling over when he was clear

of houses. There were some people skating on the lake. He imagined they'd be coming in soon, as the light was already going. Farther out on the plate of ice was some-body's ramshackle ice-fishing house.

He didn't see Meg's plane. He hadn't seen her since they'd watched the northern lights.

He should go back, do what he was paid to do. Even if what he was paid to do wasn't a hell of a lot. Instead, he found himself driving on.

When he reached Meg's, her dogs were standing at alert, guarding the house. He climbed out, waited to see what their policy on unexpected company might be.

Their heads cocked, almost in unison, then they loped forward with a friendly edge to their barks. After some leaping and circling, one of them raced off toward the doghouse, bounded up the steps and through the door-way. And came back carrying a huge bone in its mouth.

"What's that from? A mastodon?"

It was gnarled and chewed and slobbered on, but Nate took it, deducing the game, and hurled it like a javelin.

They took off, bumping and bashing each other like a couple of football players racing for the pass. They dived into the snow, came up covered with it. The bone was clamped in both of their jaws now. After a quick and spir-ited tug-of-war, they pranced back as if they were har-nessed together.

"Teamwork, huh?" He took the bone again, hurled it again and watched the replay.

He was on his fourth pass when the dogs raced away from him, making beelines for the lake. Seconds later, he heard what they had. As the rumble of engine grew, Nate followed the path of the dogs down to the lake.

He saw the red flash and the dull glint of the lowering sun on the glass. To Nate's eye she seemed to be coming in too fast, too low. He expected her skis to catch on the treetops at best, for her nose to crash into the ice at worst.

The noise swallowed everything. With nerves dancing over his skin, he watched her circle, angle and slide down on the ice. Then there was silence so complete he thought he could hear the air she'd displaced sighing down again.

Beside him the dogs quivered, then bunched, then leaped from snow to ice. They sprawled and slid and barked in utter and obvious joy when the door opened. Meg jumped down, her boots ringing. She squatted, allowed herself to be licked while she energetically rubbed fur. When she straightened, she grabbed a pack out of the plane. And only then did she look at Nate.

"Somebody else crash fenders?" she called out.

"Not that I know of."

With the dogs dancing around her, she crossed the short span of ice, climbed up the slight slope of snow. "Been here long?"

"Few minutes."

"Your blood's still too thin to handle this cold. Let's go inside."

"Where were you?"

"Oh, here and there. Picked up a party a few days ago. They've been shooting caribou—photographically. Took them back to Anchorage today. Just in time," she added with a glance toward the sky. "Got a storm coming in. Air was getting very interesting."

"Do you get scared up there?"

"No. But I've gotten pretty interested from time to time." Inside the entry, she pulled off her parka.

"Ever crash?"

"I've had to, we'll say, put down abruptly." She yanked off her boots, then taking a towel out of a box, squatted down again to wipe off her dogs' feet. "Go on in. This'll take a minute, and it's crowded with the four of us in here."

He stepped inside, closing the inner door as he'd been taught to keep the heat in.

The windows were pulling in the last hints of sun of the short day, so the room was mixed with light and shadows. He could smell flowers—not roses, but something more primitive and earthy. It was mixed with dog and a hint of wood smoke in a strange and appealing combination.

He'd expected rustic and saw even in the half-light he'd been well off the mark.

In the spacious living area, the walls were a pale yellow. To mimic the sun, he supposed, and keep the dark at bay. The fireplace was built of polished stone in golden hues so that simmering logs glowed inside its frame. She had squat candles on the mantel in deeper yellows and dark blues. The long sofa picked up the blues and was decked with the toss pillows women insisted on having everywhere. A thick throw, with her key colors bleeding into each other, was draped over the back.

There were lamps with painted shades, gleaming tables, a patterned rug and two big chairs.

Watercolors, oil paintings, pastels, all of Alaskan scenes, decorated the walls.

To his left, stairs led up, and he found himself grinning at the newel post carved into a totem.

The door opened. The dogs led the way, each prancing over to the chairs and jumping up on one.

"Not what I expected," he commented.

"Too much expected leads to boredom." She crossed the room, opened a big carved box and hauled out split logs.

"Let me get that."

"Already got it." She bent, set the logs, then turned to him, keeping the fireplace at her back. "You want food?"

"No. No, thanks."

"Drink?"

"Not especially, no."

She crossed over, switched on one of the lamps. "Sex, then."

"I—"

"Why don't you go ahead up? Second door on the left. I just want to put out food and water for my dogs."

She strolled out, leaving him standing there with the dogs staring at him out of crystal eyes. He'd have sworn they were smirking.

When she came back, he was standing in exactly the same spot.

"Can't find the steps? Some detective you are."

"Listen, Meg . . . I just drove out to . . ." He dragged a hand through his hair, realizing he didn't have a clue.

He'd left town feeling that black hole gaping in front of him, and sometime during his game with the dogs, it had closed up again.

"You don't want sex?"

"I know a trick question when I hear one."

"Well, while you're thinking about how you're going to answer it, I'm going upstairs and getting naked." She shook her hair off her shoulders and behind her back. "I look really good naked, if you're wondering."

"I figured that."

"You're a little on the thin side, but I don't mind that." She walked to the steps, angled her head. Smiled and crooked her finger. "Come on, cutie."

"Just like that?"

"Why not? No law against it, yet anyway. Sex is simple, Nate. It's everything else that's complicated. So let's be simple for now."

She headed up the steps. Nate glanced back at the dogs, blew out a breath. "Let's see if I remember how to be simple."

He walked up, paused by the first door. The walls were a sizzling red, except the one that was mirrored. On the wall opposite the mirrors was a shelf unit holding a TV, DVD player, stereo components. Between them was what he recognized as state-of-the-art exercise equipment. An elliptical cross-trainer faced the TV, the Bowflex and rack of free weights lined up with the mirror.

He imagined the mini-fridge held bottles of water, maybe some sports drinks.

The room told him the body he was about to see naked got plenty of serious workouts.

She'd left the bedroom door open and was crouched in front of another fireplace, lighting the kindling. There was a big, whopping sleigh bed, all curves and dark wood. More art, more lamps accented the shades of green and ivory.

"I saw your equipment."

She sent a slow smile over her shoulder. "Not yet."

"Ha. I meant your personal fitness center next door."

"You work out, Chief?"

"Used to." Before Jack. "Not so much lately."

"I like the sweat, and the endorphin rush."

"So did I."

"Well, you'll have to get back to it."

"Yeah. This is some place you've got here."

"Took me four years to get it done. I need space, or I get twitchy. Lights on, lights off?" When he didn't answer, she straightened, glanced over her shoulder again. "Relax, Chief. I'm not going to hurt you—unless you ask for it."

She walked to the nightstand, pulled open a drawer. "Safety first," she announced and tossed him a condom in a foil pack.

"You're thinking too much," she decided when he stood, looking a bit bewildered. And, she thought, adorable with all that messy roasted-chestnut hair, those wounded-hero eyes. "I bet we can fix that. Maybe you need a little atmosphere. I don't mind that, either."

She lit a candle, wandered the room, lighting others. "A little music." Opening a cabinet, she switched on the CD player inside, adjusted the volume to low. It was Alanis Morissette this time, with her strangely appealing voice singing about the fear of bliss.

"Maybe I should've gotten you a little drunk first, but it's too late for that now."

"You're an original," Nate murmured.

"You bet your fine ass on that." She tugged her sweater over her head, tossed it into a chair. "Thermal underwear makes the striptease a little less than erotic, but the payoff should make up for it."

He was already brick hard.

"You plan to shed any of those clothes, or do you want me to take care of that for you?"

"I'm nervous. Saying that makes me feel like an idiot."

Oh, yeah, she thought again. Seriously adorable. Honesty in a man always was.

"You're only nervous because you're thinking." She dropped her trousers, stepped out of them. Sitting on the bed, she pulled off her socks. "If it hadn't been for the call of duty New Year's Eve, we'd have ended up in bed."

"You were gone when I came back."

"Because I started thinking. See, it's deadly." She pulled back the comforter and sheets.

He laid his shirt over her sweater. When he took his cell phone out of his pocket, set it down, he shrugged. "I'm on duty."

"Well, let's hope everyone behaves themselves." She pulled off her thermal top. Every muscle in his body bunched into a fist.

She was porcelain—delicate white skin carved into curves. But there was nothing fragile. Instead it was all drama and confidence, a photograph in black and white with light playing gold over it.

And he saw, with a surprised jolt of lust when she turned to switch off the light, to leave only the candles and fire burning, the little tattoo of spreading red wings at the small of her back.

"Half the thoughts in my head just evaporated."

She laughed. "Let's take care of the other half. Lose the pants, Burke."

"Yes, ma'am."

He unbuckled his belt, then his fingers went numb as she peeled off the rest of the thermal. His mouth was dry as dust. "You were right. You look really good naked."

"I'd like to say the same, if you ever get those clothes off." She slid onto the bed, stretched out. "Come on, cutie. Come get me."

She trailed a fingertip down her breast as he undressed. "Mmm, not bad, upper body wise. Nice muscle tone for somebody who hasn't been getting regular workouts. And . . ." She grinned, propped up on her elbows when he stripped off his pants. "Well, well, you really did stop thinking. Dress that soldier, and let's go to war."

He complied, but when he sat on the bed, he simply brushed his finger over her shoulder. "Give me a minute to plan my battle strategy first. I've never seen skin like yours. It's so pure."

"Can't judge a book by its cover."

Balancing herself, she reached up, grabbed a hank of his hair and dragged him down to her. "Give me that mouth. I didn't have nearly enough of it before."

It swept through him in a rush, all the needs, the desperation, the frantic urges that coalesced into blind lust. The taste of her exploded inside him, the ripe, greedy heat of her fired in his blood. His mouth bore down on hers, fed from hers until hungers he'd forgotten burst to life again.

He couldn't get enough, her mouth, her throat, her breasts. Her gasps and moans and cries were like lashes against his naked need, driving him to take more.

He clamped a hand between her thighs, crazed to feel the wet, the warmth, and pushed her so quickly, so violently to peak, they both shuddered.

It was like climbing a quiet, green hill and having it turn into a volcano. That was inside of him, she realized. The dangerous surprise under the injured calm. She'd wanted him, those sad eyes, that quiet manner. But she hadn't known what he would give her when the mask was yanked away.

She arched up, stunned, as he raked heat through her body. And when she cried out, it was with mindless pleasure. She rolled with him, digging with her nails, nipping with her teeth, her hands eager and possessive as they raced over slickened skin.

Her lungs burned with every panting breath.

He wanted to devour, to ravish and rule. He drove into her, would have buried his face in her hair, but her hands came up to his face. And she watched him, her eyes wild and blue as he thrust inside her, as he lost himself inside her. Watched him until he'd emptied himself inside her.

．．．

HE'D BEEN HULLED OUT until his skin was nothing but a husk with air inside it. He couldn't remember what it was to feel that dragging, drawing weight that closed down over his mind and so bloated his body it made just getting out of bed in the morning an exercise in will and control.

He was blind and deaf and replete. If he could have floated the rest of the way to oblivion, just as he was, he wouldn't have uttered a murmur of complaint.

"No falling asleep while still engaged."

"Huh? What?"

"Reverse thrusters, cutie."

He wasn't blind after all. He could see light, shadow, shape. None of it made any sense, but he could see it. Obviously he could hear, because the voice—her voice— was there drifting through the mild buzzing in his head.

And he could feel her, yielding under him—that soft, tight, curvy body, damp with the sweat they'd worked up, and smelling of soap and sex and female.

"Better give me a shove," he said after a moment. "I may be paralyzed."

"Not from where I'm sitting." But she planted her hand on his shoulder, and put some effort into pushing him over. Then took a long, whistling breath—in and out—and said, *"God!"*

"I think I saw Him, just a faint outline for a second. He was smiling."

"That was me."

"Oh."

She couldn't work up the energy to stretch, so yawned instead. "Somebody was *very* pent up. Mmmm. Lucky me."

The circuits in his brain were starting to connect again. He could almost hear them sizzle as contact was reestablished. "It's been a while for me."

Curious, she tipped onto her side. She saw the scars her fingers had played against. Puckers of wounds, bullet wounds, she knew, on his side, on his thigh.

"Define 'a while.' Like a month?" His eyes stayed closed, but his mouth curved. "Two months? Jesus, more? Three?"

"We'd be closing in on a year, I guess."

"Holy crap! No wonder I saw stars."

"Did I hurt you?"

"Don't be a jerk."

"Maybe not, but I sure as hell used you."

Deliberately, she traced a finger on the scar snaking down his side. He didn't flinch, but she felt him tighten and decided to keep it light for now.

"I'd say we used each other, and so well, so thoroughly, everyone in a hundred-mile radius of this bed is lying back right now, smoking a cigarette."

"You're okay with it?"

"You got short-term-memory syndrome, Burke?" Now, she stretched and gave him a quick jab with her elbow on the back end of the move. "Whose idea was this?"

He was quiet for a moment. "I was married for five years. I was faithful. The last two years of the marriage were rocky. Actually, the last year of it sucked completely.

Sex became an issue. A battleground. A weapon. Anything but a natural pleasure. So I'm rusty, and I'm not altogether sure what women are looking for in this area."

Not so light then, she mused. "I'm not women. I'm me. Sorry your ex jerked you around by the dick, but as I can attest that appendage is still in good working order, maybe it's time to get over it."

"Long past." He shifted, working his arm under her. He felt her stiffen a little, and the hesitation in her body before she relaxed again and let him settle her head on his shoulder. "I don't want this to be the end of it. Between us."

"We'll see what we think about that next time."

"I wish I could stay, but I have to get back. Sorry."

"I didn't ask you to stay."

He turned his head so he could see her face. Her cheeks were still flushed, her eyes still sleepy. But he was too good a cop to miss the wariness just under the ease. "I wish you'd ask me to stay, but since I'd have to say no, that's a waste of a wish. But I'd like to come back."

"You can't come back tonight. This storm hits and you make it out here—which you wouldn't—you'd be stuck. Could be days. That wouldn't suit me."

"If it's going to be that bad, come back into town with me."

"No. That *really* wouldn't suit me." Relaxed again, she walked her fingers up his chest, along his jawline and into his hair. "I'm fine here. Plenty of supplies, plenty of wood, my dogs. I like a good storm, the solitariness of it."

"And when it clears?"

She moved her shoulder, then rolled away. Rising, she

walked naked to the closet, the firelight playing over her white skin and that flashy spread of red wings, before she pulled out a thick flannel robe. "Maybe you'll give me a call, and if I'm around, you could bring me out a pizza."

She pulled on the robe, smiled as she belted it. "I'll give you a really good tip."

SEVEN

THE FIRST FLAKES FELL as he drove back to town. Fat and soft, they didn't look particularly threatening. In fact, he found them picturesque. They reminded him of the snows of his childhood, the ones that fell during the night and kept falling in the morning, so when you looked out your bedroom window, excitement sizzled in your blood.

No school!

It made him smile to think of it, to remember the days when snow was a thrill instead of a burden or a hazard. Maybe it would pay him to bring some of that childhood awe back inside himself.

To look around, see those oceans and rivers of white and consider the possibilities. He was learning to snow-shoe, so maybe he'd learn to ski. Cross-country skiing might be interesting. Besides, he'd lost too much weight over the last few months. That sort of exercise, added to the regular meals that were always being put in front of him, would help build him back up again.

Maybe he'd buy one of those Ski-doo things and race around in the snow for the hell of it. Have some fun, for Christ's sake. And he'd see some of the countryside from something other than a car.

He paused to watch a small herd of deer wind their

way through the trees to his left. Their coats were shaggy and dark against snow that came to their knees. If deer had knees.

It was a whole new world for the city boy, he decided, whose rural adventures until now had consisted of a couple of summer camping trips to western Maryland.

He parked in front of the station, remembered to plug his engine block heater into the outlet, then watched Otto and Pete string a knotted rope line along the sidewalk about waist high. Pulling his thick gloves back on, he walked over to join them.

"What's going on here?"

"Rope guide," Otto said, and wound it around a lamppost.

"For?"

"Man can lose himself a foot out the door in a whiteout."

"Doesn't look that bad." Nate glanced out at the street and missed the look Otto and Pete exchanged. "How much are they calling for?"

"Could get four feet."

Nate turned back sharply. "You're shitting me."

"Wind's coming with, so drifts could be two, three times that." There was obvious pleasure in Otto's tone as he worked the rope. "This ain't Lower 48 snow."

He thought of Baltimore, and how six inches of the white stuff could slow the city to a crawl. "I want these parked vehicles off the street and the snow removal equipment checked."

"People mostly leave their cars where they sit," Pete told him. "Dig them out after."

Nate considered following the when-in-Rome theory, then shook his head. They were paying him to establish order, so by God, he'd establish some order.

"Get them off the street. Anything still parked on this route in an hour gets towed. Alaska or Lower 48, it's still four feet of snow on the street. Until we're clear, we're on call twenty-four/seven. None of us leave the station without a two-way. What's the policy on out-of-towners?"

Otto scratched his chin. "Isn't any."

"We'll have Peach go down the list, contact all of them. We make arrangements for shelter for anyone who wants to come in."

This time, he caught the exchanged glance. Peter smiled gently. "Nobody's going to."

"Maybe not, but they'll have a choice." He thought of Meg, six miles out and essentially cut off. She wouldn't budge, that much he already knew of her. "How much of this rope do we have?"

"Plenty. People generally string their own guides."

"We'll make sure of it." He went inside to put Peach to work.

It took him an hour to organize procedure, and another ten minutes to deal with Carrie Hawbaker when she blew in with her digital camera. Unlike her husband, she seemed sharp and brisk, merely waving at him to go on about what he was doing so she could get candids.

He let her snap her pictures and talked to Peach about the in-progress snow emergency plans. He didn't have time to worry about it or to think about how his interview with Max had gone.

"Did you contact everyone outside of town?" he asked Peach.

"Twelve more to go."

"Anyone heading in?"

"Not so far." She ticked off her list. "People live out, Nate, because they like it out."

He nodded. "Contact them anyway. Then I want you to go on home and call me when you get there."

Her pudgy cheeks popped out with her smile. "Aren't you the mother hen."

"Public safety is my life."

"And chirpier than you've been." She took the pencil out of her bun, wagged it at him. "It's good to see."

"I guess a blizzard brings out my inner songbird."

He glanced toward the door, amazed when it opened again. Didn't anyone in Lunacy stay home in a snow-storm?

Hopp fluffed at her hair. "Pouring in now," she announced. "Heard you're clearing cars off the street, Chief."

"Snowplow'll be doing the first sweep of the mains shortly."

"It's going to take a lot of sweeps."

"I guess it will."

She nodded. "You got a minute?"

"Just about." He gestured toward his office. "You should be home, Mayor. If we get that four feet, you'll be wading in it up to your armpits."

"I'm short, but I'm hardy, and if I don't get out and about a bit during a storm, I get cabin fever. It's January, Ignatious. We expect to get hammered."

"Regardless, it's five above, dark as the inside of a dead dog and we're already heading toward the first foot, with winds gusting at thirty-five."

"Keeping your finger on the pulse."

"Lunacy Radio." He gestured toward the portable on his counter. "They promise to broadcast twenty-four hours a day while it blows."

"Always do. Speaking about media—"

"I gave the interview. Carrie took the pictures."

"And you're still pissed off." She bobbed her head at him. "Town gets its first official police department and brings in a chief from the Outside. It's news, Ignatious."

"No argument there."

"You were tap-dancing around Max."

"It was actually more of a two-step. I just learned how."

"Whatever the choreography, I stopped the dancing. And my method of doing so crossed a line. I apologize for it."

"Accepted."

When she held out her hand to shake on it, he surprised her by giving it a friendly squeeze. "Go home, Hopp."

"I'll say the same."

"Can't do it. First I get to live out a childhood dream. I'm going riding on a snowplow."

EVERY BREATH WAS LIKE inhaling splinters of ice. Those same splinters managed to spear around his goggles and into his eyes. Every inch of his body was double or triple wrapped, and he was still breathlessly cold.

It didn't seem real, any of it. The outrageous wind, the ear-pounding engine of the snowplow, the white wall the headlights could barely penetrate. Now and then he could see the glow of a lamp against a window, but most of the world had fined down to the half a foot of light jittering in front of the canary-yellow blade.

He didn't attempt conversation. He didn't think Bing wanted to talk to him anyway, but the noise made the subject moot.

He had to admit, Bing handled the machine with the precision and delicacy of a surgeon. It wasn't the swipe and dump Nate had expected. There were routes and disposal sites, curbside excavations, driveway detours, all executed in near whiteout conditions and at a speed that had Nate, continually, swallowing a protesting yelp.

He had no doubt Bing would love to hear him shriek like a girl, and so he gritted his teeth against any sound that could be mistaken as such.

After dumping another load, Bing took the brown bottle he'd wedged under the seat, unscrewed the cap and took a long pull. The smell that blew into Nate's face was potent enough to make his eyes water.

Since they were sitting, contemplating the growing mountain of snow, Nate decided to risk a comment. "I heard alcohol lowers body temperature," he shouted.

"Fucking propaganda." To prove it, Bing took another pull from the bottle.

Considering they were alone in the dark, in a blizzard, and that Bing outweighed him by around seventy pounds and would, Nate was sure, like nothing better than to bury him in the mountain of removed snow until his cold, dead body was found in the spring thaw, he decided not to argue the point. Or mention the law against carrying open containers of alcohol in a vehicle or the dangers of drinking while operating heavy machinery.

Bing turned his massive shoulders. Nate could see nothing but his eyes, squinting between watch cap and scarf. "See for yourself." He shoved the bottle into Nate's hand.

It didn't seem like the moment to mention he wasn't much of a drinker. More politic, he decided, and companionable to take a slug. When he did, his head exploded and his throat and stomach lining burned to cinders.

"Merciful Mother of God."

He choked and, when he inhaled, swallowed shards of flame rather than ice. Through the ringing in his ears he could hear laughing. Unless the sound was the howl of some giant, maniacal wolf.

"What the fucking fuck is that?" He continued to wheeze while tears streamed out of his eyes and froze on his face. "Battery acid? Plutonium? Liquid fire of hell?"

Bing took the bottle back, took a chug, and capped it. "Horse turd whiskey."

"Oh perfect."

"Man can't handle his whiskey ain't no man."

"If that's the criteria, I'll be a woman."

"I'll take you back, Mary. Done all can be done for now."

"Praise the tiny Baby Jesus."

There was a crinkling of the skin around Bing's eyes that could have indicated a smile. He reversed, turned around. "I got twenty in the pool says you'll be packing your bag before the end of the month."

Nate sat still, his throat burning, eyes stinging, his feet like icebergs despite two pair of thermal socks and boots. "Who holds the pool?"

"Skinny Jim, works the bar at The Lodge."

Nate merely nodded.

He didn't know where Bing got his sense of direction but decided the man could've guided Magellan. He zipped the machine along in the blinding snow and arrowed it straight to the curb at The Lodge.

Nate's knees and ankles wept when he jumped down. The snow on the sidewalk reached those frozen knees, and the wind blew it rudely in his face as he gripped the rope guide and pulled himself toward the door.

The heat inside was almost painful. Clint Black rolled out of the juke and replaced the humming in his ears. There were a dozen people seated at the bar or at tables, drinking, eating, holding conversations as if the wrath of God wasn't blowing on the other side of the door.

Lunatics, he thought. Every one of them.

He wanted coffee—blistering hot—and red meat. He'd cheerfully eat it raw.

He nodded as people called out to him and was fighting with snaps and zippers when Charlene hurried over to him.

"Why you poor thing! You must be frozen solid. Let me help you with that coat."

"I've got it. I—"

"Your fingers will be all stiff."

It was too weird, too surreal, to have the mother of the woman he'd bedded that afternoon undoing his snow-coated parka.

"I've got it, Charlene. Could use some coffee though. Appreciate that."

"I'll get it for you myself, right away." She patted his cold cheek. "You just sit right down."

But when he'd managed to strip off everything but his shirt and pants, he walked to the bar. He pulled out his wallet, signaled to the man they called Skinny Jim. "Here's a hundred," he said in a voice loud enough to carry. "Put it in the pool. It says I'm staying."

He stuck his wallet back in his pocket, then sat beside John. "Professor."

"Chief."

Nate angled his head to read the title of the current book. "*Cannery Row*. Good one. Thanks, Charlene."

"Don't you mention it." She set his coffee down. "We've got a nice stew tonight. Warm you right up. Unless you want me to take care of that for you."

"Stew would be great. Have you got rooms if some of these people need to stay here tonight?"

"We always got room at The Lodge. I'll dish you up that stew."

Nate swiveled on his stool, sipping coffee as he checked the room. Someone had plugged an old Springsteen into the juke, and The Boss was singing about his glory days while pool balls thudded into pockets. He recognized all the faces—regulars, people he saw nearly every night. He couldn't see the pool players from his angle but made out the voices. The Mackie brothers.

"Any of these people going to get drunk, then try to get home?" he asked John.

"Mackies might, but Charlene would talk them out of

it. Most will clear out in an hour or so, and the die-hards will still be here in the morning."

"Which camp would you be?"

"That depends on you." John lifted his beer.

"Meaning?"

"If you take Charlene up on her offer, I'll be heading on up to my room alone. If you don't, I'll be heading up to hers."

"I'm just here for the stew."

"Then I'll be staying in her room tonight."

"John. Doesn't it bother you?"

John contemplated his beer. "Having it bother me doesn't change the way things are. The way she is. The romantics like to say you don't have a choice who you love. I disagree. People pick and they choose. This is my choice."

Charlene brought out the stew, a basket with chunks of fresh bread, and a thick wedge of apple pie.

"Man works out in this weather, he needs to eat. You do justice by that now, Nate."

"I will. You hear from Meg?"

Charlene blinked as if translating the name from a foreign language. "No. Why?"

"Just thought you two might've gotten in touch with each other." To let the stew cool a little, he started with the bread. "Seeing as she's out there on her own in this."

"Nobody knows how to handle herself better than Meg. She doesn't need anyone. Not a man or a mother."

She walked away, letting the kitchen door slap shut behind her.

"Sore spot," Nate commented.

"Tender as they come. Bigger bruise yet if she thinks you're more interested in her daughter than in her."

"I'm sorry to be the cause of that, but I am." He sampled the stew. It was loaded with potatoes, carrots, beans and onions, and a strong, gamey meat that couldn't have come from cow.

It slid warm into his belly and made him forget about the cold.

"What's this meat in here?"

"That'd be moose."

Nate spooned up more, studied it. "Okay," he said, and ate.

IT SNOWED ALL NIGHT, and he slept like a stone through it. The view out his window when he woke was like the static on a television screen. He could hear the wind howling, feel it pressing against the windowpane.

The lights didn't work, so he lit candles, and they made him think of Meg.

He dressed, studying the phone. It was probably out, too. Besides, you didn't call a woman at six-thirty in the morning just because you'd had sex with her. There was no need to worry about her. She'd lived up here her entire life. She was tucked inside her house with her two dogs and plenty of firewood.

He worried anyway as he used his flashlight to guide himself downstairs.

It was the first time he'd seen the place empty. Tables were cleaned off, the bar was wiped down. There was no smell of coffee brewing, bacon frying. No morning clatter or conversation. No little boy sitting at a table looking up at him with a quick smile.

There was nothing but dark, the howl of the wind and . . . snoring. He followed the sound and shined his light over the Mackie brothers. They lay, toe to nose, on the pool table, snoring away under layers of blanket.

He worked his way into the kitchen and, after a hunt, found a muffin. Taking it with him, he pulled on his gear. With the muffin stuffed in his pocket, he pulled open the door.

The wind nearly knocked him over. The force of it, the shock of it, the bitter snow that flew into his eyes, his mouth, his nose as he fought his way through the door.

His flashlight was next to useless, but he aimed it out, followed the line of the rope in its beam. Then he stuffed the light in his pocket, gripped the rope with both hands and began to pull himself along.

On the sidewalk, the snow was up to his thighs. He thought a man could drown in it, soundlessly, even before he died of exposure.

He managed to fight his way to the street, where thanks to Bing's plow, and horse turd whiskey, the snow was no more than ankle deep, unless you ran into a drift.

He'd have to cross the street damn near blind, and without the guide, to get to the station. He closed his eyes, brought the image of the street, the location of the buildings into his head. Then lowering his shoulders to the wind, he let go of the rope, grabbed the flashlight again and started across.

He might as well have been in the wilderness instead of in a town with paved streets and sidewalks, with people sleeping behind board and brick. The wind was like a storm surf in his ears, one that kept trying to shove him back as he bulled his way through it.

People died crossing the street all the time, he reminded himself. Life was full of nasty risks, nastier surprises. A couple of guys could walk out of a bar and grill, and one of them could end up dead in an alley.

An idiot could walk into a blizzard, try to cross the street and end up wandering aimlessly for hours until he dropped dead of exposure three feet from shelter.

He was cursing when his boots bumped something solid. Picturing the curb, Nate waved his arms out like a blind man, and found the guide.

"For our next amazing feat," he muttered, hauling himself onto the buried sidewalk. He dragged himself along until he found the cross rope, then changed angles and plowed his way to the outer door of the station.

Wondering why he'd bothered to lock up, he fished out his keys, used his flashlight to help him find the locks. In the entry, he shook himself off, but kept his gear on. As he'd suspected, the station was frigid. Frigid enough, he noted, that the windows were frosted on the inside.

Someone with more forethought than he had stacked wood by the stove. He fired it up, stood holding his hands, still gloved, to the flame. When he had his breath back, he closed the stove door.

He got candles, a battery-operated lamp, and considered himself in business.

He found the battery radio, tuned in to the local station. As promised, they were on the air, and someone with a twisted sense of humor was spinning the Beach Boys.

Seated at his desk, he kept one ear on KLUN, the other on Peach's call radio and, mourning the lack of coffee, ate his muffin.

By eight-thirty, he was still on his own. A reasonable hour, he decided, and settled down at the ham radio. He'd gotten a basic lesson from Peach on operation and decided to take his first flight.

"This is KLPD calling KUNA. Come in, KUNA. Meg, you there? Pick up or sign on or whatever you call it." He got static, buzzing, a couple of squeals. "This is KLPD calling KUNA. Come on, Galloway."

"This is KUNA responding. You got a license to operate that radio, Burke? Over."

He knew it was ridiculous, but relief simply blew through him at the sound of her voice. Right on its heels was pleasure. "I'm C of P. Comes with the badge."

"Say over."

"Right, over. No, you okay out there? Over."

"That's affirmative. We're nice and cozy. Tucked up here listening to the taku. You? Over."

"I survived a hike across the street. What's taku? A rock group? Over."

"It's a mean bastard wind, Burke. The one shaking your windows right now. What the hell are you doing in the station? Over."

"I'm on duty." He glanced around the room, noted he could see his own breath. "Your power out?"

She waited a beat. "I'll say 'over' for you. In this, sure

it's out. Generator's up. We're fine, Chief. You don't have to worry. Over."

"Check in once in a while, and I won't. Hey, you know what I had yesterday? Over."

"Besides me? Over."

"Ha." God, this felt good, he thought. He didn't care if it was cold as the ice of hell. "Yeah, besides. I had horse turd whiskey and moose stew. Over."

She laughed, long and loud. "We'll make a sourdough out of you, Burke. Gotta go feed my dogs and my fire. See you around. Over and out."

"Over and out," he murmured.

It was warm enough now to shed the parka, though he kept on his hat and thermal vest. He was poking through the files, looking for busy work when Peach pushed through the door.

"Wondered if anyone was crazy enough to come in today," she said.

"Just me. How the hell did you get here?"

"Oh, Bing brought me in on the plow." She dusted one hand over the baby-blue fleece of her sweater.

"Snowplow as taxicab. Here, let me get that." He hurried over to take the big sack she carried. "You didn't have to come in."

"Job's a job."

"Yeah, but . . . coffee? Is this coffee?" He dug the thermos out of the sack.

"Wasn't sure you'd have the generator up yet."

"Not only don't I have it up, I don't know if I can find it. And since mechanics aren't my strong point, I wasn't sure I'd know what to do with it if I did find it. This *is* coffee. Marry me, have many, many children with me."

She giggled like a girl, slapped at him with her hand. "You be careful, throwing out offers like that. Just because I've been married three times already doesn't mean I won't go for four. You go ahead and have some coffee and a cinnamon bun."

"Maybe we could just live together in sin." He set the sack on the counter, and immediately poured coffee into a mug. The scent hit him like a beautiful fist. "Forever."

"You smile like that more often, I might just take you up on it. Well, look what the taku blew in," she added when Peter stumbled in.

"Holy cow. That's a whopper out there. Talked to Otto. He's on his way."

"Bing bring you in, too?"

"No, me and my dad mushed it."

"Mushed." Another world, Nate thought. But Peach was right, a job was a job. "All right then. Peter, let's get the generator going. Peach, get ahold of the fire department. Let's get a crew together and clear off the sidewalks as soon as it's light enough, so people can get around if they need to. Priorities are around the clinic and the station. When Otto gets here, tell him the Mackies are passed out on the pool table at The Lodge. Let's make sure they get home in one piece."

He pulled on his parka as he worked down his mental checklist. "Let's see if we can get an ETA on when power's going to be back on. People are going to want to know. Phones, too. When I get back in, we'll work up an announcement, have the radio run it, about what we know when we know it. I want people to know we're here if they need help."

And that, too, Nate discovered, felt good.

"Peter?"

"Right behind you, Chief."

JOURNAL ENTRY · *February 18, 1988*

Nearly lost Han in a crevice today. It happened so fast. We're climbing, pumped up, a few hours from the summit. Cold, hungry, edgy but pumped. Only a climber understands the juice of that combination. Darth's in the lead, the only way to keep him from pitching another shitfit, then Han, and I'm bringing up the flank.

But I forgot yesterday. The days are starting to blur now, one cold, white door opening to the next cold, white door.

I was lost in the rhythm of my own pounding head, in the spell of the climb, in the rise of white. We crawled and grunted our way up a rock pitch, moving well, aiming for heaven.

I heard Darth shout, *Rock!* And the cannonball of the boulder he'd dislodged spat out from that long chimney, whizzing by Han's head. I had an instant to think, no, I don't want to go this way, smashed by some fist of God, sucker punched off the mountain. It missed me, as it had Han, by inches, flying by in a finger snap of time, and crashing, bringing a quick and jagged rain of other rocks with it.

We cursed Darth, but then we curse one another over anything and everything now. Most of it in companionable good humor. It helps surge the adrenaline as we get higher, and the air's so thin that breathing is an exercise in pain and frustration.

I knew Han was flagging, but we pushed on. Pushed on, driven by obsession and Darth's relentless insults.

His eyes look mad behind his goggles. Mad and possessed. While I think of the mountain as a bitch when I'm driving into her belly with ax and frozen fingers, she's a bitch I love. I think for Darth she's a demon, and one he's hell-bent to conquer.

We bedded down that night by tying ourselves into pitons with the black world beneath us and the black sky above.

I watched the lights, a dazzle of liquid jade across that mirror of black.

Again today Darth took the lead. Being first seems to be another obsession, and arguing wastes time. In any case, I was concerned enough about Han to see the value of taking the flank, keeping the weakest of us in the middle.

So it was Darth's need to be first, and my position in the rear, that saved the life of one of our trio.

We'd packed the rope away. I'd said already that it was too cold for rope, didn't I? Again, we were moving well, moving up in the bright sparkle of the short day with even our curses whipped away by the roar of the wind.

Then I see Han stumble and start to slide. It was like the ground disappeared under him.

A moment's carelessness, a patch of windslab snow,

and he was tumbling toward me. I don't know, I swear, if I caught him or if he sprouted wings and flew. But our hands locked, and I slapped my ax into the ice, praying it would hold, praying the bitch wouldn't belch us both into the void. For eternity I was on my belly, holding his hands while he dangled over the edge of nothing. We're screaming, both of us, and I'm trying to dig in with my toes, but we're slipping, sliding. Another few seconds and it would've been let him go or both of us are gone.

Then Darth's ice ax cleaved into the ground beside me—an inch from my shoulder, and the pistoning of my heart cranked up to jackhammer. He used it for purchase, and reached down to grab Han's arm. Some of the weight lifted from my screaming muscles, and I was able to dig in, belly back. Bellying back, the two of us, pulling Han up with the blood boiling in our ears and our hearts slamming in our chests.

We rolled back from the edge, lay there on the snow, shaking under that cold, yellow sun. Shaking for what seemed hours, feet away from death and disaster.

We can't laugh about it. Even later none of us have the energy to make that short nightmare into a joke. We're too shaken up to climb, and Han's ankle is messed up. He'll never make the summit, and we all know it.

We have no choice but to chop out a platform and camp, divvy up food from our dwindling supplies while Han pops painkillers. He's weak, but not so weak his eyes don't roll with fear as the wind slams its killing fists at the thin walls of our tent.

We should go back.

We should go back. But when I floated that trial balloon, Darth went off, berating Han, shrieking at me in a voice shrill as a woman's. He looks half mad—maybe more than half—hulking in the dark, ice clinging to his stubbly beard and eyebrows, bitter lights in his eyes. Han's accident has cost us a day, and he'll be damned if it'll cost him the summit.

He has a point, I can't deny it. We are within striking distance of the goal. Han may be able to make it after a night's rest.

We'll climb tomorrow, and if Han can't manage, we'll leave him, do what we came to do, and pick him up on the way back.

It's insanity of course, and even with the drugs, Han looks wrecked and scared. But I'm caught in it. Past the point of no return.

The wind's howling like a hundred rabid dogs. That alone could drive a man mad.

EIGHT

FOR THIRTY HOURS, the snow fell and the wind howled. The world was a cold, white beast that rampaged day and night, fangs bared, claws extended to bite and rake at anyone brave or foolish enough to go out and face it.

Generators hummed or roared, and communications were reduced to radios. Travel was impossible as that beast stalked its way across the Interior and over southeast Alaska. Cars and trucks were buried, planes grounded. Even the sled dogs waited for it to pass.

The little town of Lunacy was cut off, a frozen island in the midst of a blind, white sea.

Too busy to brood, too astonished to curse, Nate dealt with emergencies—a child who'd toppled onto a table and needed to get to the clinic for stitches, a man who'd had a heart attack while trying to dig out his truck, a chimney fire, a family brawl.

He had Drunk Mike—as opposed to Big Mike the cook—in an unlocked cell sleeping off a bender, and Manny Ozenburger in a locked one, rethinking his position on driving his Tundra pickup over his neighbor's Ski-doo.

He kept crews hacking away at the snow on the main streets and pushed his way through the canyons of it to The Corner Store.

He found Harry and Deb sitting at a card table in front of the canned goods, playing gin while Cecil snuggled in his basket.

"Hell of a blow," Harry called out.

"No, it's just hell."

Nate pushed back the hood of his parka, stopped to give Cecil a quick rub. He was out of breath and vaguely surprised to still be alive. "I need some supplies. I'm going to bunk at the station until this is over."

Deb's eyes gleamed. "Oh? Something wrong at The Lodge?"

"No." Yanking off gloves, Nate began to hunt up basics to keep body and soul together. "Somebody needs to man the radio—and we've got a couple of guests."

"I heard Drunk Mike tied one on. Gin."

"Gin? Damn you, Harry."

"Tied one on," Nate agreed, dumping bread, lunch meat, chips on the counter. "And staggered around singing Bob Seger songs. Snow removal crew spotted him and hauled him up when he fell facedown in the middle of the damn street." Nate picked up a six-pack of Coke. "They hadn't seen him, brought him in, we might've found him by April, dead as Elvis."

"I'll just run a tab for these, Chief." Harry got out his book, noted down the purchases. "And I'm not convinced Elvis is dead. This going to be enough for you?"

"It'll have to be. Getting it back's going to be an adventure."

"Why don't you sit a minute, have some of this coffee?" Deb was already getting up. "Let me fix you a sandwich."

Nate stared at her. It wasn't the way people usually treated cops. "Thanks, but I need to get back. If you need anything, hell, send up a flare."

He pulled on his gloves, resecured his hood, then hefted his bag of supplies.

It wasn't any more hospitable out than it had been five minutes before. He felt the teeth and claws slice at him as he used the rope and instinct to drag his way toward the station.

He'd left every light burning, to give himself a beacon.

He could hear the muffled rumble of Bing's plow and hoped to sweet God that Bing didn't head his way, running over him accidentally—or purposely. The beast, as he thought of the storm, was doing its best to mock the efforts of the crews, but they'd made a difference.

Instead of swimming through the snow, he was wading through it.

He heard gunshots. Three quick reports. He paused, strained to make out the direction, then shook his head and kept going. He sincerely hoped no one was lying in the snow with a gunshot wound, because he couldn't do a damn thing about it.

He was about ten feet away from the station, concentrating on the haze of light, cheering himself on with the thought of heat, when Bing's plow rolled out of the white.

His heart stopped. He actually heard the thunder of it click off, and the swishing sensation of his blood draining. The plow looked enormous, a mountain of machine avalanching toward him.

It stopped, maybe a breathless foot from the toes of his boots.

Bing leaned out, his snow-caked beard making him resemble an insane Santa. "Out for a stroll?"

"Yeah. Can't get enough of it. You hear those gunshots?"

"Yeah. So?"

"Nothing. You need a break. The heat's on. We've got sandwich makings."

"Why you got Manny locked up? Tim Bower drives that damn pissant snowmobile around like a goddamn crazy teenager every chance he gets. Public fucking nuisance."

Since he was freezing, Nate decided to skip the part about destruction of private property and reckless driving. "Tim Bower was on the damn pissant snowmobile at the time Manny flattened it."

"Got off quick enough, didn't he?"

Despite everything, Nate found himself grinning. "Dived headfirst into a snowbank. Skinny Jim saw it. Said it looked like a double gainer."

Bing merely grunted, pulled his head in and backed the plow away.

Inside, Nate made sandwiches, took one to the disgruntled Manny and checked on Drunk Mike.

He decided to take his own meal at the radio. He liked hearing Meg's voice, feeling that strange, sexy connection. It had been a long time since he'd had anyone to talk to about his day, since he'd had anyone he'd wanted to talk to. The conversation added a little spice to his plain meal and some comfort to the solitude.

"Tim's wrecked that snowmobile more times than I can count," she said after he'd told her about its final destruction. "Manny did everyone a favor. Over."

"Maybe. I think I can talk Tim out of pressing charges if Manny pays for it. You planning on coming into town once this is cleared up? Over."

"I'm not big on plans. Over."

"Movie night's coming up. I was hoping to sample your popcorn. Over."

"It's a possibility. I've got some jobs lined up once I'm cleared to fly. But I like movies. Over."

He drank some Coke and pictured her sitting at the radio, the dogs at her feet and the fire glowing behind her. "Why don't we make it a date? Over."

"I don't make dates. Over."

"Ever? Over."

"Things happen if they happen. Since we both liked the sex, things will probably happen."

Since she didn't say "over," he assumed she was giving it some thought. He certainly was.

"Tell you what, Burke, next time things happen, you can tell me your long, sad story. Over."

He was imagining the red tattoo at the small of her back. "Why do you think I've got one? Over."

"Cutie, you're the saddest man I've ever seen. You tell me the story, and we'll see what happens next. Over."

"If we . . . damn it."

"What's that noise? Over."

"Sounds like Drunk Mike's awake and puking it up in the cell. Manny's finding that understandably objection-able," he added as the sounds of sickness and outrage spiked out of the cells. "I have to go. Over."

"Boy, a cop's life is fraught with danger. Over and out."

· · ·

UNDER THE CIRCUMSTANCES, Nate opted to let both of his prisoners hitch rides home on the plow. Braving the elements, he went out to dump more gas into the generator.

After a short debate, he carted one of the cots out, set it up near the radio. As an afterthought, he routed through Peach's drawer and found one of her paperback romance novels.

He settled in with the book—setting a mental alarm so he could put it, with its sexy cover, back where it came from with no one the wiser—a Coke, and the sounds of the storm.

The book was better than he'd imagined and took him away to the lush, green fields of Ireland in the days of castles and keeps. There was a hefty dose of magic and fantasy tossed in, so he followed the adventures of Moira the sorceress and Prince Liam with considerable interest.

The first love scene gave him pause as he thought about the maternal Peach reading about sex—between answering calls and handing out sticky buns. But he was caught up.

He fell asleep with the book open on his chest and the lights still blazing.

THE SORCERESS HAD Meg's face. Her hair, ink black, swirled into the air like wings. She stood on a white hill in brilliant sunlight that streamed through the thin red gown she wore.

She lifted her arms, slid the gown from her shoulders so that it slithered down her body. Naked, she walked to him. Her eyes were blue ice as she opened her arms and took him in.

He felt her lips on his, hot. Hungry. He was under her, surrounded by her. When she rose up, wild wind rushed through her hair. When she lowered, the heat of her all but burned him.

"What do you have to be sad about?"

Suddenly, through the pleasure was pain—abrupt, searing. He hissed against it, and his body stiffened. The burning insult of bullets into flesh.

But she smiled, only smiled. "You're alive, aren't you?" She lifted a hand, smeared with his blood. "If you bleed, you're alive."

"I'm shot. Jesus, I'm hit."

"And alive," she said as his blood dripped from her hand onto his face.

He was in the alley, smelling blood and cordite. Smelling garbage and death. Damp air from the rain. Cold, cold for April. Cold and wet and dark. It was all a blur, the shouts, the shots, the pain when the bullet dug into his leg.

He'd fallen behind, and Jack had gone in first.

Shouldn't be here. What the hell were they doing here?

More shots, flashes of light in the dark. Thuds. Was that steel hitting flesh? That stunning, obscene pain in the side that took him down again. So he'd had to crawl, crawl over the damp concrete to where his partner, his friend, lay dying.

But this time, Jack turned his head, and his eyes were red as the blood that pumped out of his chest. "You killed me. You stupid son of a bitch. Anybody should be dead, it's you. Now see if you can live with it."

HE WOKE IN A COLD SWEAT, his partner's dream voice still echoing in his head. Nate pushed himself up to sit on the side of the cot. He dropped his head in his hands.

So far, he thought, he was doing a lousy job of living with it.

He made himself get up, carry the bunk back to the cell. He thought of the pills he stowed in his desk drawer, but bypassed his office and made himself go out to pour the last of the gas into the generator.

It wasn't until he was heading back inside that he realized it had stopped snowing.

The air was perfectly still, perfectly quiet. There was a faint hint of moonlight sprinkling over the mounds and seas of snow, giving the white a pale blue hue. His breath clouded out as he stood, like a bug, he thought, trapped in crystal instead of amber.

The storm had passed, and he was still alive.

See if you can live with it. Well, he would. He'd keep seeing if he could live with it.

Inside, he brewed coffee, switched on the radio. A sleepy voice—who identified himself as Mitch Dauber, the voice of Lunacy—segued into local news, announcements and weather.

People started coming out, bears crawling out of their

caves. They shoveled and plowed. They gathered together for conversation, ate and walked and slept.

They lived.

THE LUNATIC

Police Log
Wednesday, January 12

9:12 A.M. A chimney fire in the residence of Bert
Myers was reported. Volunteer firefighter Manny
Ozenburger and Chief Ignatious Burke responded.
The fire was caused by a buildup of creosote. My-
ers suffered a minor burn on the hand while at-
tempting to grab burning logs out of the fireplace.
Ozenburger termed this action "dumbass."

12:15 P.M. Jay Finkle, age five, was injured in a fall
from his tricycle inside the bedroom of his residence. Chief Burke assisted Paul Finkle, Jay's
father, in transporting the injured boy to the Lunacy clinic. Jay received four stitches and a grape
lollipop. The Hot Wheels was undamaged, and Jay
states that he will drive more carefully in the future.

2:00 P.M. A complaint was lodged by Timothy
Bower against Manny Ozenburger. Witnesses
confirm that Ozenburger crashed his truck into
Bower's Ski-doo while Bower was operating same.
Though an informal poll indicates that 52 percent
believe Bower had it coming, Ozenburger was re-
manded to jail. Charges are pending. Members of

Lunacy's Volunteer Fire Department are organizing a Free Manny all-you-can-eat buffet.

2:55 P.M. Kate D. Igleberry reported being assaulted by her partner, David Bunch, at their residence on Rancor Road. At the same time, Bunch claims to have been assaulted by Igleberry. Chief Burke and Deputy Otto Gruber responded. Both complainants offered evidence of facial and bodily bruises, and in Bunch's case, a bite mark on the left buttock. No charges filed.

3:40 P.M. James and William Mackie were charged with reckless driving and excessive rates of speed on Ski-doos. William Mackie contends that "Ski-doos aren't damn cars." As recreational vehicles, he believes they should be exempt from posted limits and plans to bring this matter up at the next town meeting.

5:25 P.M. Snow removal crews discovered a man walking in a disoriented manner on the roadside near south Rancor Woods. He could be heard singing "A Nation Once Again." Subsequently identified as Michael Sullivan, the man was transported to Lunacy PD and turned over to Chief of Police Ignatious Burke.

ALONE IN THE STATION, Nate scanned the rest of the log. It continued, with reports of drunk and disorderlies, the loss and recovery of a missing dog, the call from one of the out-of-towners with a serious case of cabin fever claiming wolves were playing poker on his porch.

Names were printed on each and every item, no matter how embarrassing it might be for the individual. He wondered what it would've been like if *The Baltimore Sun,* for instance, had been so thorough and merciless in listing the calls, the names and the actions taken by the police force in Baltimore.

He had to admit, he found it endlessly entertaining.

Max and Carrie must have put the paper together and gone to print the minute the storm was over, he thought. Pictures of the storm and the aftermath were damn good, too. And the story on it, with Max's byline, was almost poetic.

He didn't mind the story on himself as much as he'd thought he would. In fact, he was going to keep his copy, along with his first two issues of *The Lunatic.*

Whenever he could get out to Meg's again, he'd take her one.

A week after the storm blew in, the roads were clear enough. Dropping by her place to take her a paper couldn't be considered a date.

Giving her a call just to make sure she was there and not flying around somewhere couldn't be considered plans.

It was just being practical.

Expecting his staff to come in any moment, Nate tucked the newspaper in a desk drawer and started out to put some fuel in the woodstove.

Hopp pushed through the outside door.

"We've got trouble," she said.

"Is it bigger than four and a half feet of snow?"

She shoved back her hood. Under it her face was bone white. "Three missing boys."

"Give me the details." He backed up. "Who, when and where they were last seen."

"Steven Wise, Joe and Lara's boy, his cousin Scott from Talkeetna and one of their college friends. Joe and Lara thought Steven and Scott were down in Prince William for winter break. Scott's parents thought the same. Lara and Scott's mother got together on the radio last night to pass the time and catch up, and it came out some of the things each of the boys had told them didn't jibe. They got suspicious, enough that Lara tried calling Steven at college. He's not back—neither is Scott."

"College where, Hopp?"

"Anchorage." She passed a hand over her face.

"Then they need to notify the Anchorage PD."

"No. No. Lara got hold of Steven's girlfriend. Those idiot boys are trying a winter climb up the south face of No Name."

"What's No Name?"

"It's a damn mountain, Ignatious." Fear was jumping in her eyes. "A goddamn big mountain. They've been gone six days. Lara's out of her mind."

Nate strode to his office, yanked out his map. "Show me the mountain."

"Here." She jabbed a finger. "It's a favorite with the locals, and a lot of climbers from Outside use it for entertainment or a kind of training ground for a try at Denali. But trying a climb in January's just bone stupid, especially for three inexperienced boys. We need to call Search and Rescue. Get planes in the air at first light."

"That gives us three hours. I'll contact S and R. Get on one of those two-ways, call Otto, Peter and Peach in here. Then I want to know who all the pilots are, other than Meg, in the area."

He scanned the phone numbers Peach had neatly listed. "What are the chances they're still alive?"

With a two-way in hand, Hopp sat heavily. "They need a miracle."

FIVE MINUTES AFTER she got the call, Meg was dressed and loading up gear. She was tempted to ignore the radio call from Lunacy PD, but decided it might be an update on the lost climbers.

"This is KUNA responding. Over."

"I'm going with you. Pick me up by the river on your way. Over."

Irritation rippled through her as she stuffed extra medical supplies in her bag. "I don't need a copilot, Burke. And I don't have time to waste showing you the sights. I'll contact you when I find them. Over."

"I'm going with you. Those boys deserve another pair of eyes, and mine are good. I'll be ready when you get here. Over and out."

"Damn it. I hate heroes." She hauled up the pack and, with the dogs beside her, went out. She grabbed the rest of the gear and, using the flashlight, trudged down to the lake in snowshoes.

She'd made two runs since the all clear to fly and

thanked God she didn't have to take an hour now to dig out her plane. She didn't think about the boys, dead or alive, on the mountain. She simply took the steps.

She pulled off the wing covers, stowed them. It was work, but less work than scraping the frost from uncovered wings. After draining the water traps in the bottoms of the wing tanks, she climbed up to check the gas level by eye. Topped off the fuel.

Making a circuit, she checked flaps, tail feathers, every part of the plane that moved to make certain everything was secure.

Lives had been lost, she knew, due to a loose bolt.

Her mind focused only on the safety check, she turned her prop several times to remove any pooled oil.

Swinging into the plane, she stowed the gear, then strapped in.

She hit the starter, switched on the engine. The prop turned, sluggishly at first, then the engine fired with a belch of exhaust. While the engine warmed, she checked gauges.

She was in control here, as much as she considered anyone was in control of anything.

It was still shy of dawn when she released the brakes.

She set the flaps, the trim tab for takeoff, gave the controls a shove and yank as she looked out to be sure the ailerons were moving, if the elevators responded. Satisfied, she straightened in her seat.

She kissed her fingers, touched them to the magnetized photo of Buddy Holly stuck to the control board. And rammed the throttle forward.

She hadn't yet decided whether to head to Lunacy or

not. As she circled the lake, building speed for takeoff, she let the decision hang.

Maybe she would, maybe she wouldn't.

She nosed up, rising into the air just as dawn began to break in the east. Then with a shrug, aimed that nose toward Lunacy.

He was where he'd said he'd be. Standing on the edge of the ice with a mountain of snow at his back. He had a pack slung over his shoulder. She could only hope someone had told the cheechako what to bring as emergency gear. She saw that Hopp was with him, and her stomach sank when she recognized the other figures as Joe and Lara.

It forced her to think of what might be. Of the bodies she'd transported before. Of the ones she might transport today.

She set down on the ribbon of ice, waited with the engines running for Nate to cross it.

The prop wash blew at his coat, his hair. Then he was climbing in, stowing his pack, strapping in.

"Hope you know what you're in for," she said.

"I haven't got a clue."

"Maybe that's better." She kissed her fingers, touched them to Buddy. Without looking at the terrified faces to her right, she pushed to take off.

Using the hand mike, she contacted control in Talkeetna and gave them her data. Then they were up, over the trees and veering east, northeast into the pale rising sun.

"You're eyes and ballast, Burke. If Jacob wasn't in

Nome visiting his son, I wouldn't have settled for you as either."

"Got it. Who's Jacob?"

"Jacob Itu. Best bush pilot I've ever known. He taught me."

"The man you shared your popcorn with at the town meeting?"

"That's right." They hit a pocket of air, and she saw his hand fist against the bumps. "You get airsick, I'm going to be really unhappy."

"No. I just hate flying."

"Why's that?"

"Gravity."

She grinned as they continued to bump. "Turbulence bothers you, you're going to have a really bad day. There's still time to take you back."

"Tell that to the three kids we're going after."

The grin vanished. She watched the mountains, the fierce rise of them, while the ground below blurred with speed and low-lying clouds. "Is that why you're a cop? Saving people's your mission?"

"No." He said nothing as they shuddered through another patch of rough air. "Why does a bush pilot have a picture of Buddy Holly in her cockpit?"

"To remind her shit happens." As the sun speared up, she took sunglasses out of her pocket and put them on. Below, she saw the snake of dogsled trails, spirals of chimney smoke, a wedge of trees, a rise of land. She used the landmarks as much as her gauges.

"Binoculars in the compartment there," she told him.

And made a small adjustment in the propeller pitch, eased the throttle forward.

"I brought my own." He unzipped his parka, pulled them out from where they hung around his neck. "Tell me where to look."

"If they attempted a climb up the south face, they'd've been dumped off on the Sun Glacier."

"Dumped off? By who?"

"That's a mystery, isn't it?" Her jaw set. "Some yahoo too interested in money to blow them off. A lot of people have planes, and a lot of people fly them. It doesn't make them pilots. Whoever it was didn't report them when the storm came through and sure as hell didn't pick them back up."

"Fucking crazy."

"It's all right to be crazy, it's not all right to be stupid. And that's the category this falls into. Air's going to get rougher when we hit the mountains."

"Don't say hit and mountain in the same sentence."

He looked down—a slice of trees, an ocean of snow, a plate of ice that was a lake, a huddle of perhaps six cabins all appearing, disappearing through clouds. It should have seemed barren, stark, and instead it was stunning. The sky was already going that deep, hard blue, with the cruel elegance of the mountains etched over it.

He thought of three boys trapped in that cruelty for six days.

She banked, sharp right, and he had to reach deep inside for the grit just to keep his eyes open. The mountains, blue and white and monstrous, swallowed the view.

She dipped through a gap, and all he could see, on either side, was rock and ice and death.

Over the whine of the engines, he heard something like thunder. And saw a tsunami of snow burst from the mountain.

"What the—"

"Avalanche." Her voice was utterly calm as the plane began to shake. "You're going to want to hold on."

It gushed, white over white over white, an iced volcano erupting, charging the air with the roar of a thousand runaway trains while the plane ping-ponged right, left, up, down.

He thought he heard Meg curse, and what sounded like antiaircraft fire beat against the plane. The storm that vomited out of the mountain spewed bits of debris over the windscreen. But it wasn't fear that rushed into him. It was awe.

Metal pinged and rang as bullets of ice and rock struck the plane. Wind dragged at it, yanked at it, pelted it until it seemed inevitable they would crash into the cliff face or simply be smashed apart by shrapnel.

Then they were cruising between walls of ice, over a narrow, frozen valley and into the blue.

"Kiss my ass!" She let out a whoop, threw her head back and laughed. "*That* was a ride."

"Awesome," Nate agreed, and twisted in his seat, trying to turn enough to see the rest of the show. "I've never seen anything like it."

"Mountains are moody. You never know when they're going to take a shot." She slid her gaze toward him. "You're pretty cool under fire, Chief."

"You, too." He settled back in his seat. And wondered if his pounding heart had broken any of his ribs. "So . . . come here often?"

"Every chance I get. You can start making use of those binocs. We've got a lot of area to cover, and we won't be the only ones covering it. Keep a sharp eye." She fixed on headphones. "I'll be in communication with control."

"Where do I aim my sharp eye?"

"There." She lifted her chin. "One o'clock."

Compared to Denali, it seemed almost tame, and its beauty somewhat ordinary beside The Mountain's magnificence. There were smaller peaks ranging between what they called No Name and Denali, and there were larger, rolling back, spearing up, all in a jagged, layered wall against the sky.

"How big is it?"

"Twelve thousand and change. A good, challenging climb in April or May, trickier, but not impossible in the winter. Unless you're a group of college kids on a lark, then it's next to suicide. We find out who transported three underage kids, dumped them out in January, there'll be hell to pay."

He knew that tone of voice—flat, emotionless. "You think they're dead."

"Oh, yeah."

"But you're here anyway."

"Won't be the first time I've looked for bodies—or found them." She thought of the supplies and gear in the plane. Emergency rations, medical supplies, thermal blankets. And prayed there would be cause to use them.

"Look for debris. Tents, equipment—bodies. There are a lot of crevices. I'll get as close as I can."

He wanted them to be alive. He'd had enough of death, enough of waste. He hadn't come to look for bodies, but for boys. Frightened, lost, possibly injured, but boys he could return to their terrified parents.

He scanned through his field glasses. He could see the bowel-loosening drops, the skinny ledges, the sheer walls of ice. There was no point in wondering why anyone would be compelled to risk limb or life, brave hideous conditions, starve and suffer to hack his way to the top. People did crazier things for sport.

He registered the buffeting winds, the uneasy proximity of the little plane to the unforgiving walls, and shut down the fear.

He searched until his eyes burned, then lowered the glasses to blink them clear. "Nothing yet."

"It's a big mountain."

She circled, he searched, while she continued to detail coordinates to control. He spotted another plane, a little yellow bird swooping to the west, and the sturdy bulk of a chopper. The mountain dwarfed everything. It no longer looked small to him, not with everything he had focused on it.

There were shapes that made its shape—plates of rippling ice, fields of snow, fists of black rock that were punched out of cliff walls and were streamed with somehow delicate rivers of more ice, like glossy icing.

He saw shadows he imagined the sun never found and vicious drops to nothing. From one a beam of light shot back at him, like sun bouncing off crystal.

"Something down there," he called out. "Metal or glass. Reflective. In that crevice."

"I'll circle around."

He lowered the binoculars to rub at his eyes, wishing he'd brought his own sunglasses. The glare was murderous.

She climbed, banked, and as she circled, Nate caught a flicker of color against the snow.

"Wait. There. What's that? About four o'clock? Jesus, Meg, four o'clock."

"Son of a bitch. One of them's alive."

He saw it now, the bright blue, the movement, the vaguely human shape, frantically windmilling arms to signal. She dipped the wings, right then left, right then left, as she arrowed back.

"This is Beaver-Niner-Zulu-Niner-Alfa-Tango. I've got one," she said into her headset. "Alive, just above Sun Glacier. I'm going in for him."

"You're going to land?" Burke asked when she'd repeated the call and relayed coordinates. "On that?"

"You're going one better," she told him. "You're going out on it. I can't leave the plane—crosswinds are too risky, and there's no place, and no time to tie down."

He stared down, saw the figure stumble, fall and roll, tumbling, sliding before it lay still, nearly invisible now in the white surf.

"Better give me a lesson and make it quick."

"I put down, you get out, climb up, get him, bring him back. Then we all go home and have a really big beer."

"Short lesson."

"No time for much more. Make him walk. If he can't, drag him. Grab some goggles. You'll need them. There's no fancy work here. It's just like crossing a pond and climbing a few rocks."

"Just doing it several thousand feet above sea level. No big deal."

She showed her teeth in a grin as she fought minor little wars to keep the plane steady. "That's the spirit."

The wind tore at the plane, and she fought back, dragging the nose back up, leveling the wings. She angled toward her approach, dropped the gear, cut back the throttle.

Nate decided not to hold his breath since inhaling and exhaling might not be an option very shortly. But she slid the plane onto the glacier, between the void and the wall.

"Move!" she ordered, but he was already yanking off his safety belt.

"It's probably twenty below out there, so you make it quick. Unless I have to take off again, don't try to give him any medical assistance until we've got him back in the plane. Just get him, haul him, dump him in."

"I've got it."

"One more thing," she shouted as he shoved open the door and the wind roared in. "If I do have to lift off, don't panic. I'll come back for you."

He leaped onto the mountain. It wasn't the time to question, to overthink. Cold cut into him like knives, and the air was so thin that it sliced his throat. There were hills rising up out of hills, rippling seas, acres of shadow, oceans of white.

He pushed himself across the glacier, settling for a lumbering jog instead of the sprint he'd hoped for.

When he hit rock, he went by instinct, pulling his way up, clattering like a goat, then sinking nearly to his knees when the short wall was scaled.

He heard engines, the wind and his own laboring breath.

He dropped down beside the boy and, despite Meg's instructions, felt for a pulse. The kid's face was gray, with rough patches of what looked like dried skin on his cheek, his chin.

But his eyes fluttered open. "Made it." He croaked out the words. "Made it."

"Yeah. Let's get the hell out of here."

"They're in the cave. Couldn't make it, couldn't make it down. Scott's sick, Brad—think his leg might be broken. I came for help. I came—"

"You've got it. You can show us where they are once we're back in the plane. Can you walk?"

"Don't know. Try."

Nate fought the boy up, took his weight. "Come on, Steven. One foot in front of the other. You've come this far."

"Can't feel my feet."

"Just lift your legs, one at a time. They'll follow. You've got to climb down." He could already feel the cold eating through his gloves and wished he'd thought to double up. "I'm not good enough at this to carry you. Hold on to me, and help me climb down. We've got to get down to help your friends."

"I had to leave them, to get help. Had to leave them with the dead man."

"It's all right. We're going back for them. We're climbing down now. Ready?"

"I can do it."

Nate went first. If the kid fell, fainted, slipped, he'd break the fall. He kept shouting at him as they picked their way down. Shouting to keep the boy steady and conscious, demanding answers to keep him alert.

"How long since you left your friends?"

"I don't know. Two days. Three? Hartborne didn't come back. Or . . . I think I saw, but then I didn't."

"Okay. Nearly there. You're going to show us where your friends are, in just a couple minutes."

"In the ice cave, with the dead man."

"Who's the dead man?" Nate dropped down on the glacier. "Who's the dead man?"

"Don't know." The voice was dreamy now as Steven slithered and slumped into Nate's hold. "Found him in the cave. Ice man, staring. Just staring. Got an ax in his chest. Spooky."

"I bet." He half dragged, half carried Steven toward the shuddering plane.

"He knows where the others are." He pushed, then climbed in to pull Steven into the plane. "He can show us."

"Get him in the back, under the blankets. First-aid kit's in the bag. Hot coffee in the thermos. Don't let him drink too much."

"Am I still alive?" The boy was shivering now, his body quaking from the cold.

"Yeah, you are."

Nate laid him on the floor between the seats, then covered him with blankets while Meg lifted off.

He heard the wind and engines screaming, and he wondered if they'd be ripped to pieces now after all.

"You need to tell us where your friends are."

"I can show you." With his teeth chattering, he tried to take the cup of coffee Nate poured.

"Here, let me do it. Just sip."

As he sipped, tears began to leak out of his eyes. "I didn't think I'd make it. They'd die up there because I couldn't make it down, to the plane."

"You did make it."

"Plane wasn't there. He wasn't there."

"We were. We were there." Doing his best to brace himself against the jolts of the plane, Nate carefully lifted the coffee again.

"We almost got to the top, but Scott was sick, and Brad fell. His leg's hurt. We got to the cave, we found the cave and got in before the storm hit. We stayed in there. There's a dead man."

"So you said."

"I'm not making it up."

Nate nodded. "You'll show us."

NINE

NATE HATED HOSPITALS. It was one of the triggers that shot him back into the dark. He'd spent too much time in one after he'd been wounded. Enough time for the pain and grief and guilt to coalesce into the gaping void of depression.

He hadn't been able to escape it. He'd longed for the emptiness of sleep, but sleep brought dreams, and dreams were worse than the black.

He'd hoped, passively, that he'd die. Just slide soundlessly away. He hadn't considered killing himself. That would have taken too much effort, too much activity.

No one had blamed him for Jack's death. He'd wanted them to, but instead they'd come with their flowers or sympathy, even their admiration. And it had weighed on him like lead.

Talk of therapy, counseling, antidepressants barely penetrated. He'd gone through the motions, just to get doctors and concerned friends off his back.

He'd gone through the motions for months.

Now he was back in a hospital and could feel the soft and sticky fingers of hopelessness plucking at him. Easier, so much easier to give in, to just let go and sink into the dark.

"Chief Burke?"

Nate stared down at the coffee in his hand. Black coffee. He didn't want it. Couldn't quite remember how it had gotten there. He was too tired for coffee. Too tired to get up and throw it away.

"Chief Burke?"

He glanced up, focused on a face. Female, mid-fifties, brown eyes behind small, black-framed glasses. He couldn't quite remember who she was.

"Yeah, sorry."

"Steven would like to see you. He's awake and lucid."

It swam back slowly, like thoughts oozing through mud. The three boys, the mountain. "How's he doing?"

"He's young and healthy. He was dehydrated, and he may lose a couple toes, but he may keep them all. So, he's lucky. The other two are on their way in. I'm hoping the same goes."

"They got them. Off the mountain."

"That's what I'm told. You can have a few minutes with Steven."

"Thanks."

As he followed her, the sounds and smells of the ER penetrated. The voices, the pings, the fretful crying of an infant.

He moved into an exam room and saw the boy on a bed. He had some color under the patches on his cheeks. His hair was matted and blond, his eyes clouded with worry.

"You got me off."

"Nate Burke. New chief of police in Lunacy." Since Steven held out a hand, Nate took it, careful to avoid pressing on the IV needle. "Your friends are on their way in."

"I heard. But nobody'll tell me how they are."

"We'll find out when they get here. They wouldn't be on their way if you hadn't given us the location, Steven. Nearly makes up for being stupid enough to go up there in the first place."

"Seemed like a good idea at the time." He tried a wan smile. "Everything went wrong. And I think something happened to Hartborne. We only gave him half the money, just to be sure he'd come back."

"We're checking into it. Why don't you give me his full name, any other information on him."

"Well, Brad knew him. Actually, Brad knew a guy who knew him."

"Okay. We'll talk to Brad."

"My parents are going to kill me."

Oh, to be twenty, Nate thought, and be as concerned with parental wrath as with a near-death experience. "Count on it. Tell me about the dead man in the cave, Steven."

"I didn't make it up."

"Not saying you did."

"We all saw him. We couldn't leave the cave, not with Brad's leg. We decided I'd go back down, meet Hartborne, get help. They had to stay in there with him. With The Ice Man. He was just sitting there, staring. The ax in his chest. I took pictures."

His eyes widened as he struggled to sit up straighter. "I took pictures," he repeated. "The camera. It—I think it's in the pocket of my insulated vest. I think it's still there. You can see."

"Hold on a minute." Nate moved over to the pile of

clothes, pawed through and came up with the vest. And in the inside zippered pocket was one of those small digital cameras, hardly bigger than a credit card.

"I don't know how to work this."

"I can show you. You have to turn it on, and then— see—the viewer here? You can call up pictures from the memory. The last ones I took were of the dead guy. I took like three, 'cause I wanted— there!"

Nate studied the facial close-up in the little viewer. The hair might've been black or brown, but it was covered with frost and ice that silvered it. Longish, nearly shoulder-length hair, with a dark watch cap pulled low over it. The face was narrow, white, slashed by ice-crusted brows. He'd seen death often enough to recognize it in the eyes. Wide and blue.

He recalled the previous picture.

There was the body of a man, age between—at his rough guess—twenty and forty. He sat with his back to the ice wall, legs splayed out. He wore a black and yellow parka and snow pants, climbing boots, heavy gloves.

What appeared to be a small ax was buried in his chest.

"Did you touch the body?"

"No. Well, I kinda poked at him—it. Frozen solid."

"Okay, Steven, I'm going to need to take your camera. I'll get it back to you."

"Sure. No problem. He could've been up there for years, you know? Decades or something. It creeped us out, let me tell you, but it sort of took our minds out of the shit we were in. Do you think they know anything about Brad and Scott?"

"I'll find out. I'll go get the doctor. I'm going to need to talk to you again."

"Anytime, man. Seriously, thanks for saving my life."

"Take better care of it."

He headed out, slipping the camera into his pocket. He'd have to contact the State Police, he thought. Homicide in the mountains was out of his jurisdiction. But that didn't mean he couldn't make some copies of the pictures for his own files.

Who was he? How had he gotten there? How long had he been there? Why was he dead? The questions got him through the ER and to the nurse's station just as the rescue team brought in the other two boys.

He decided the best place for him was out of the way, and when he spotted Meg swing in behind the team, he crossed to her.

"It's their lucky day," she said.

Nate caught a glimpse of one of the boy's faces, shook his head. "That's debatable."

"Any day the mountain doesn't kill you is lucky." And bringing them back alive when she'd expected to find bodies, pumped her. "They're probably going to lose a few digits, and the kid with the broken leg is in for some serious pain and physical therapy, but they're not dead. We've lost the light, and I don't see any reason to head out this late. We won't be flying back tonight. I'm going to get us a room at The Wayfarer. Rates are reasonable, and the food's good. You ready?"

"I've got a couple of things to do. I'll find you."

"You're longer than twenty minutes, you'll find me in

the bar. I want alcohol, food and sex." She gave him a suggestive smile. "More or less in that order."

"Sounds reasonable. I'll be there."

She zipped up her coat. "Oh, that reflection you caught? Plane wreck. Probably the guy who took those kids up. Mountain got one after all."

HE WAS CLOSER TO NINETY than twenty minutes, and he found Meg, as promised, in the bar.

It was wood-paneled, smoky and decorated with animal heads. She was passing the time at her table with a beer and a bump, and a plate of something that looked like nachos. She had her feet up on the second chair, but shifted them off when Nate stepped up to the table.

"There you are. Hey, Stu? Same for my friend."

"Just the beer," Nate corrected. "These any good?" he asked as he pried up a nacho.

"They fill the hole. When we're suitably buzzed, we'll go have a steak. Did you stay back to keep an eye on those boys?"

"That, and a couple of other things." He dragged off his hat, scooped a hand through his hair. "Rescue team didn't go into the cave?"

"Boys dragged themselves out when they heard the air support." She scooped up cheese, meat, salsa with a chip. "Priority was to get them down for medical assistance. Somebody'll go up, eventually, for the gear they left behind."

"And the dead guy."

She lifted her eyebrows. "You bought that story?"

"Yeah, I did. Added to that, the kid took pictures."

She pursed her lips, then pried up another loaded chip. "No shit?"

"Beer's up," came the call from the bar.

"Hold on," she said to Nate. "I'll get it."

"You want another round, Meg?" Stu asked her.

"We'll let him catch up some first." She snagged the brown bottle, brought it back to the table.

"He took pictures?"

Nate nodded, took a gulp of beer. "Digital camera, which he had in his pocket. I talked this guy at the hospital into printing them out for me." He tapped his fingers on the manila envelope he'd tossed on the table. "I had to turn the camera over to the State boys. Maybe they'll keep me in the loop, maybe not." He shrugged.

"You want to be in the loop?"

"I don't know." He shrugged again, tapped his fingers again. "I don't know."

Oh, he wanted to be in the loop, she thought. She could all but see him making some sort of mental list. Some sort of cop list. If that's what it took to turn those sad, gray eyes sharp, she hoped the State boys let him play.

"He probably hasn't been up there very long."

She lifted her glass. "Why do you say that?"

"Somebody would've found him."

She shook her head, sipped whiskey. "Not necessarily. Cave like that can get buried in a storm, drowned under in an avalanche or overlooked by climbers. Another avalanche, oh look, there's a cave. Then it depends on where he was in the cave. How deep. Could've been up there for a season or for fifty years."

"They'll get forensics either way. They'll be able to date him, hopefully ID him."

"Already working on solving the case." Amused, she gestured toward the envelope. "Let me see. Maybe we'll be like Nick and Nora Charles."

"It's not the movies, and it's not pretty, Meg."

"Neither is gutting a moose." She chomped another nacho, then drew the envelope over to open it. "If he's a local, maybe somebody'll recognize him. Though you get plenty of Outsiders on No Name in any given year. The kind of gear he's wearing should . . ."

He saw her color drain, her eyes glaze—and cursed himself. But when he started to take the printout from her, she jerked back, shoved at his arm with her free hand.

"You don't need to look at that. Let's just put it away."

She needed to look. Maybe the air was trapped in her lungs, and maybe her stomach had pitched down to her feet. But she needed to look. Deliberately she took the rest of the photos out, lined them up on the table. Then she picked up the whiskey, downed it.

"I know who this is."

"You recognize him?" Without thinking, Nate scooted his chair closer to hers so they stared at the photos together. "You're sure?"

"Oh, yeah. I'm sure. It's my father."

She shoved away from the table. Her face was very pale, but she didn't quiver. "Pay for the drinks, will you, Chief? I'm going to have to put a hold on that steak dinner."

He moved fast, scooping the printouts back in the envelope, digging out bills to drop on the table, but she was already through the lobby and at the top of the steps when he caught up.

"Meg."

"Back off a minute."

"You need to talk to me."

"Come up in an hour. Room 232. Go away, Ignatious."

She kept climbing, didn't allow herself to think, didn't allow herself to feel. Not yet, not until she was behind a locked door. There were things she didn't believe in sharing.

He didn't follow. Part of her brain registered that, and gave him points for restraint and maybe sensitivity. She went into the room where she'd already dumped spare gear, locked the door, added the chain.

Then she walked directly into the bathroom and was miserably and violently ill.

When she was done, she sat on the chilly floor, her forehead braced on her knees. She didn't weep. She hoped she would, hoped she could cry at some point. But not now. Now she felt raw and shaken and—thank God—angry.

Someone had killed her father and left him alone. For years. For years when she'd lived without him. When she'd believed he'd walked away from her without a second thought. That she wasn't good enough or important enough. Smart enough, pretty enough. Whatever enough seemed to fit at any given time when the missing of him was a hole in her belly.

But he hadn't walked away from her. He'd gone to the mountain, something as natural for him as breathing. And died there. The mountain hadn't killed him. She could have accepted that as fate, as destiny. A man had killed him, and that couldn't be accepted. Or forgiven. Or left unpunished.

She rose, stripped, and running the water cold, stepped into the shower. She let it stream over her until the fuzziness in her head cleared. Then she dressed again to lie down on the bed, in the dark, and think about the last time she'd seen her father.

He'd come into her room where she'd been pretending to study for a history test. As long as she was pretending to study, she didn't have to do her chores. She'd been sick of chores.

She remembered, even now, that quick lift in the heart when she saw it was her father rather than her mother coming to check on her. He *never* nagged about chores or studying.

She thought he was the most handsome man in the world, with his long dark hair and his fast grins. He'd taught her everything she believed really important. About the stars and climbing, about survival in the wild. How to build a campfire, how to fish—and clean and cook the catch.

He'd taken her flying with Jacob, and it was their secret that Jacob was teaching her to fly.

He looked at the book open on her bed where she was flopped on her belly. And rolled his eyes. "Boring."

"I *hate* history. I have a test tomorrow."

"Bummer. You'll do okay. You always do." He sat on

the bed, gave her ribs a quick tickle. "Hey, kid, I gotta take off for a while."

"How come?"

He lifted a hand, rubbed his thumb and forefinger together.

"How come we need money now?"

"Your mom says we do. She's the one who knows."

"I heard you fighting this morning."

"No big deal. We like to fight. I'll pick up a couple of jobs, make some moola. Everybody'll be happy. A couple of weeks, Meg. Maybe three."

"I don't have anything to *do* when you're gone."

"You'll find something."

And she could tell, even as a girl of thirteen she could tell, he was already gone in his head. His pat on the head was absent, like an uncle's. "We'll go ice fishing when I get back."

"Sure." And she was sulking, ready to shrug him off before he could shrug her off.

"See you later, cupcake."

She had to force herself not to spring up, to rush after him, hold tight before he strolled away.

A hundred times since that afternoon, she'd wished she'd given in, given them both that one last contact.

She wished it now, even as she rode that last memory in the dark.

She stayed where she was until she heard the knock on the door. Resigned, she got up, switched on lights, ran her hand through the hair that hadn't quite dried from the shower.

When she opened the door to Nate, he was carrying a

tray and had another sitting on the floor outside the door.

"We need to eat." Maybe he'd hated it when people had pushed food or whatever cure or comfort on him during the worst of his own misery. But it worked, and that was the bottom line.

"Fine." She gestured toward the bed, the only surface big enough in the room to double as a dining table. Then she bent and hefted the second tray.

"If you want to be alone after, I can get another room."

"No point." She sat cross-legged on the bed and, ignoring the salad on her tray, cut into the steak.

"That one's mine." He switched trays. "They said you went for bloody. I don't."

"Don't miss a trick, do you? Except you brought up coffee instead of whiskey."

"You need a bottle, I'll get you one."

She sighed, cut into the meat. "Bet you would. How'd I end up sharing a steak dinner in Anchorage with a nice guy?"

"I'm not, particularly. I gave you an hour so you could pull yourself together. I brought you food so you'd keep yourself together while you tell me about your father. I'm sorry, Meg, it's a hard hit. After you talk to me, we're going to have to take this to the detective in charge."

She cut another bite, forked down into one of the soggy steak fries. "Tell me something. Back where you came from, you were a good cop?"

"It's about the only thing I was ever good at."

"You handle murders?"

"Yeah."

"I'll talk to whoever's in charge, but I want you looking into this for me."

"There's not that much I can do."

"There's always something. I'll pay you."

He ate contemplatively. "A hard hit," he repeated. "Which is why I'm not going to slap at you for that insult."

"I don't know that many people who find money insulting. But fine. I want someone I know looking for the son of a bitch who killed my father."

"You barely know me."

"I know you're good in bed." She smiled a little. "Okay, a guy can be an asshole and still be a stallion. But I also know that you keep your head under pressure and are dedicated or stupid enough to climb out on a glacier to save a kid you've never met. And you think ahead enough to remember to ask down in the restaurant how Meg likes her steak. My dogs like you. Help me out here, Chief."

He reached out and touched her hair, a little stroke over the damp black. "When's the last time you saw him?"

"February 1988. February sixth."

"Do you know where he was going?"

"He said to pick up some work. Here in Anchorage, I figured, or up in Fairbanks. He and my mother had been fighting about money and a variety of other things. That was typical. He said he'd be gone a couple weeks or so. He never came back."

"Your mother file a missing person's report?"

"No." Then her brow creased. "At least I don't think so. We assumed, everyone assumed, he'd just taken a hike. They'd been fighting," she continued, "maybe more than usual. He was restless. Even I could see it. He wasn't the salt of the earth, Nate. He wasn't a responsible sort, though he was always good to me, and we never went without anything important. It wasn't enough for Charlene, and they argued."

She steadied herself, kept eating because it was there. "He drank, he smoked dope, he gambled when he felt like it, worked when he felt like it and fucked off when he felt like it. I loved him—maybe because of all that. He was thirty-three when he left that afternoon—and using the wisdom of hindsight and maturity, I can see it was freaking him out to be thirty-three. To be the father of a half-grown girl and hooked up with the same woman year after year. Maybe he was at a kind of crossroads, you know? Maybe he decided to take that winter climb as a kind of last idiocy of youth—or maybe he was never coming back anyway. But somebody made the decision for him."

"He have enemies?"

"Probably, but nobody I could say would cause him harm. He'd piss people off, but nothing major."

"What about your stepfather?"

She gave her salad a couple of pokes with her fork. "What about him?"

"How soon after your father disappeared did Charlene get married? How'd she work the divorce?"

"First, she didn't need a divorce. She and my father weren't married. He didn't believe in the legal boundaries of marriage, and blah blah. She married Old Man

Hidel about a year after—a little less. If you're thinking Karl Hidel climbed up No Name and carved an ice ax in my father's chest, you can forget it. He was sixty-eight and fifty pounds overweight when Charlene hooked him."

As an afterthought she picked up the salad bowl and ate. "Smoked like a chimney. He could barely climb the stairs much less a mountain."

"Who would have climbed with your father?"

"Jesus, Nate, anybody. Anybody who wanted the rush. You know those kids today? Give them a little time, and they'll talk about what happened up there as if it was one of the most exciting events of their lives. Climbers are crazier than bush pilots."

When he said nothing, she let out a little breath, ate some more salad. "He was a good climber, had a solid rep there. Maybe he had taken a job guiding a group up on a winter climb. Or he hooked up with a couple of buddies and like-minded morons and decided to fart into the face of death."

"He ever do anything stronger than pot?"

"Maybe. Probably. Charlene would know." She rubbed her eyes. "Shit. I have to tell her."

"Meg, were either one of them involved with anyone else while they were together?"

"If that's a delicate way of asking if they screwed around, I don't know. Ask her."

He was losing her. Her anger and impatience would make questioning impossible in another minute or two. "You said he gambled. Seriously?"

"No. I don't know. Not that I've ever heard. He'd

blow a paycheck if he had one. Or pile up some IOUs, because he didn't win very often. But nothing heavy. At least not locally. I never heard about him being into anything illegal other than recreational drugs. And there are plenty of people who'd be happy to tell me if he had been. Not because they didn't like him. People did. Just because people like to tell you that kind of thing."

"Okay." He rubbed a hand on her thigh. "I'll ask some questions, and I'll make nice with whoever catches the case so they'll keep me updated."

"Well. Let's get out of here." She rolled off the bed, leaving her half-eaten dinner. Her hands rapped a beat against her legs. "I know this place. The music's good. We can have a couple of drinks, then we'll come back and have some chandelier-swinging sex."

Instead of commenting on her change of mood, he merely glanced up at the old and dingy ceiling light. "That doesn't look all that sturdy."

It made her laugh. "We'll live dangerously."

TEN

WHEN HE WOKE, the dream was fading, leaving only a bitter, salty taste in his throat. As if he'd swallowed tears. He could hear Meg breathing beside him, soft and steady. Some part of him, struggling under the weight of despair, wanted to turn to her. For the comfort and oblivion of sex.

She'd be warm, and she'd come to life around him.

Instead, he turned away. And he knew, he *knew* it was indulgent; it was self-defeating to choose to embrace the misery. But he got out of bed alone in the dark, found his clothes. He dressed and left her sleeping.

In the dream, he'd been climbing the mountain. He'd fought his way up ice and rock, thousands of feet above the world. In the airless sky, where every breath was agony. He had to go up, was compelled to claw his way up another inch, another foot, while below him was nothing but a swirling, white sea. If he fell he would drown in it, soundlessly.

So he climbed until his fingers bled and left red smears on the ice-sheathed rock.

Exhausted, exhilarated, he dragged himself onto a ledge. And saw the mouth of the cave. Light pulsed from it and lit hope in him as he crawled inside.

It opened, it towered, like some mythical ice palace. Huge formations speared down from the roof, up from the floor to form pillars and archways of white and ghostly blue where ice glinted like a thousand diamonds. The walls, smooth and polished, gleamed like mirrors, tossing his reflection back at him a hundred times.

He gained his feet, circling the splendor of it, dazzled by the sheen and the space and the sparkle.

He could live here, alone. His own fortress of solitude. He could find his peace here, in the quiet and the beauty and the alone.

Then he saw he was not alone.

The body slumped against the gleaming wall, fused to it by years of relentless cold. The ax handle protruded from its chest, and the frozen blood shone red, red, red, over the black parka.

And his heart tipped when he understood he hadn't come for peace after all, but for duty.

How would he carry the body down? How could he bear the weight of it on that long, vicious journey back to the world? He didn't know the way. He didn't have the skill or the tools or the strength.

As he walked toward the body, the walls and columns of the cave hurled the reflections at him. A hundred of him, a hundred dead. Everywhere he looked, death joined him.

The ice began to crackle. The walls began to shake. A thunderous sound roared as he pitched to his knees at the foot of the body. The dead face of Galloway turned up to his, teeth bared in a bloody grimace.

And it was Jack's face—and Jack's voice that spoke as the ice columns tumbled, and the floor of the cave heaved. "There's no way out, for either of us. We're all dead here."

He'd wakened as the cave swallowed him.

MEG WASN'T SURPRISED to find Nate gone. It was after eight when she surfaced, so she imagined he'd gotten bored or hungry waiting for her to wake up.

She was grateful to him, for the companionship and the straightforward manner wrapped around compassion. He'd let her deal with shock and grief—and whatever else she was feeling—on her own terms. She considered that a valuable asset in a friend or a lover.

She was pretty sure they were both.

She was going to have to keep dealing—with herself, her mother, with everyone in town. With the cops.

She didn't see the point in dwelling on it now. There'd be enough dwelling when she got back to Lunacy.

She figured she'd find Nate or he'd find her before it was time to head back. Meanwhile, she wanted coffee.

The dining room was set for breakfast, with plenty of takers. Cheap lodgings, good food appealed to a lot of the pilots and guides who used Anchorage as a launch pad. She saw a scatter of familiar faces.

Then she saw Nate.

He sat alone at a rear corner booth. Since that was a prized spot, it told her he'd been there for some time. He had a mug of coffee and a newspaper. But he wasn't drinking; he wasn't reading. He was off somewhere, in his own thoughts. Bleak and sorrowful thoughts.

Looking at him from across the busy room, she knew she'd never seen anyone so alone.

Whatever his long, sad story was, she thought, it was going to be a killer.

As she started toward him, someone called her name. While she answered it with a wave, she saw Nate draw in. She watched him bring himself back, deliberately pick up his coffee and settle himself before he looked over. Smiled at her.

An easy smile, secret eyes.

"You got a good night's sleep."

"Good enough." She slid in across from him. "You eat?"

"Not yet. Did you know people used to commute from Montana to work in the canneries around here?"

She glanced down at the newspaper and the article. "Actually, I did. It's good pay."

"Yeah, but not exactly a daily battle with rush hour. I figured you lived in Montana because you wanted to raise horses or cattle. Or maybe start a paramilitary camp. Okay, gross generalization, but still."

"You're a real East Coast boy. Hey, Wanda."

"Meg." The waitress, who looked to be about twenty, and perky, set down another mug of coffee, pulled out her pad. "What can I get you?"

"Couple eggs, over easy, Canadian bacon, hash browns, wheat toast. Jocko?"

"Ditched him."

"Told you he was a loser. What do you want, Burke?"

"Ah . . ." He searched around for his appetite, then decided the sight and smell of food might help him locate it. "Ham-and-cheese omelette, and the wheat toast."

"Gotcha. I'm dating this guy named Byron," she told Meg. "He writes poetry."

"Can only be an improvement." Meg turned back to Nate as Wanda walked away. "Wanda's parents were one of the seasonals when she was a kid. Used to spend her summers here when they worked in the canneries. She liked it, moved up permanently last year. Habitually dates assholes, but other than that, she's okay. What were you thinking about before I came over?"

"Nothing, really. Just passing the time with the paper."

"No, you weren't. But since you did me a favor last night, I won't push it."

He didn't deny; she didn't press. And she didn't, though the urge scraped at her, reach over and stroke his cheek. When she had a brood going, she didn't want comfort. So she gave him the same courtesy she expected for herself.

"Is there anything else we have to do here before we head back? If we're going to be a while, I want to have someone go out and check on my dogs."

"I called the State cops. A Sergeant Coben's in charge of the case, for now anyway. He'll probably want to talk to you—and your mother at some point. There's not likely to be much movement on this until they can get a team up there and bring him back down. I called the hospital. All three boys are in satisfactory condition."

"You've been busy. Tell me, Chief, do you take care of everybody?"

"No. I just handle details."

She'd heard bigger bullshit in her life, but then she lived in Lunacy. "She do a number on you? The ex-wife?"

He shifted. "Probably."

"Want to spew? Trash her over breakfast?"

"Not so much."

She waited while Wanda served the meal, topped off the coffee. Meg cut into the eggs, letting the yolk run where it liked. "So I slept with this guy in college," she began. "Great looker. Kind of stupid, but he had tremendous staying power. He started playing this head game on me. How I should think about wearing more makeup, dressing better, maybe I shouldn't argue with people so much. Blah blah. Not," she said with a wag of her fork, "that I wasn't gorgeous and sexy and smart, oh no, but if I just fixed up a little more, went along a little more."

"You're not gorgeous."

She laughed, her eyes dancing, and bit into her toast. "Shut up. This is my story."

"You're better than gorgeous. Gorgeous is just lucky DNA. You're . . . vivid," he decided. "Compelling. That's the sort of thing that comes from inside spaces, so it's better than gorgeous. If you want my opinion."

"Wow." She sat back, surprised enough to forget her breakfast. "If I was anybody else, I'd be speechless after a comment like that. As it is, I've lost my trend. What the hell was I talking about?"

This time when he smiled, it reached his eyes, warmed up the gray. "Asshole college boy you slept with."

"Right. Right." She dived into the hash browns. "There was more than one, but anyway, I was twenty and this dude's passive-aggressive insults were starting to get under my skin—especially when I found out he was boffing this brain-dead bimbo with pots of money and breast implants."

She fell silent, concentrating on her breakfast.

"So, what did you do?"

"What did I do?" She drank some coffee. "Next time we went to bed, I screwed his brains out, then slipped him a couple of sleeping pills."

"You drugged him?"

"Yeah, so?"

"Nothing. Nothing."

"I paid a couple of guys to carry him down to one of the lecture halls. And I dressed his sorry ass in sexy women's underwear—bra, garter belt, black hose. That was challenging. I made up his face, curled his hair. Took some pictures to put up on the Internet. He was still sleeping when the first class started piling in at eight." She ate some eggs. "It was a hell of a show—especially when he woke up, got a clue and started screaming like a girl."

Enjoying her, appreciating the single-mindedness as much as the creativity of her revenge, Nate toasted her with his coffee. "You can bet I won't be commenting on your wardrobe."

"Point of the story. I believe in payback. For the little things, for the big ones. For everything in between. Letting people screw you over is just lazy and uncreative."

"You didn't love him."

"Hell, no. If I had, I wouldn't have just embarrassed him. I'd have caused him intense physical pain in addition."

He toyed with the rest of his omelette. "Let me ask you something. Are we exclusive?"

"I consider myself very exclusive, in every way."

"What we have going on together," he said patiently. "Is this an exclusive arrangement?"

"Is that what you're looking for?"

"I wasn't looking for anything. Then there you were."

"Uh-oh." She let out a long breath. "Good one. Seems like you've got a whole big pot of good ones. I don't have a problem limiting myself to swinging from the chandelier with just you, for as long as we're both enjoying it."

"Fair enough."

"She cheat on you, Burke?"

"Yeah. Yeah, she did."

Meg nodded, continued to eat. "I don't cheat. Okay, sometimes I cheat at cards, but just for the hell of it. And sometimes I lie when it's expedient. Or when the lie's just more fun than the truth. I can be mean if it suits me, which is a lot."

She paused, reaching across to touch his hand for a moment so there was a connection between them. "But I don't kick a man when he's down, unless I'm the one who put him down in the first place. I don't put him down unless he deserves it. And I don't break my word if I give it. So I'll give you my word. I won't cheat on you."

"Except at cards."

"Well, yeah. It's going to be light soon. We should get going."

SHE DIDN'T KNOW how she was going to handle it with Charlene. Any angle she picked, the result was going to be the same. Hysteria, accusations, rage, tears. It was always messy with Charlene.

Maybe Nate read her mind, because he stopped Meg outside the door of The Lodge. "Maybe I should break this to her. I've had to give family members this kind of news before."

"You've had to tell people their lover's been dead in an ice cave for fifteen years?"

"The means don't change the impact that much."

His voice was gentle, in direct contrast to the jagged edge of hers. It calmed her. More than calmed her, she realized. It made her want to lean on him.

"Much as I'd like to pass this plate to you, I'd better handle it. You're welcome to pick up the pieces after I'm done."

They went inside. A few people were loitering over coffee or eating an early lunch. Meg flipped open her coat as she signalled to Rose.

"Charlene?"

"Office. We heard Steven and his friends are going to be okay. Roads were still too bad, but Jerk swung in to fly Joe and Lara down this morning. Get you some coffee?"

Nate watched Meg walk through a doorway. "Sure."

· · · ·

SHE WENT STRAIGHT THROUGH the lobby area, skirted the counter and entered the office without knocking.

Charlene was at her desk, on the phone. She gave Meg an impatient, back-fingered wave.

"Now, Billy, if I'm going to get screwed like that, I expect to be taken out to dinner first."

Meg turned away. If her mother was haggling over the price of supplies, she had to let it run through. The office didn't look efficient. It looked like Charlene—female and obvious and foolish. Lots of cotton-candy pink in the fabrics, armies of silly dust catchers. Paintings of flowers in gold frames on the walls, silk pillows mounded on the velvet settee.

It smelled of roses, from the room spray Charlene spritzed every time she entered the room. The desk itself was an ornate reproduction antique she'd bought from a catalog and paid too much money for. Curvy legs and lots of carving.

The desk set was pink, as were all her personal stationery and Post-its. All of them were topped with *Charlene* in fancy, nearly illegible script.

There was a pole lamp beside the settee—a gold wash with a pink beaded shade more suitable, in Meg's mind, to a bordello than an office.

She wondered, as she often did, how she could have come from anyone whose tastes, whose mind, whose ways, were so directly opposed to her own. Then again,

maybe her own life was nothing more than an endless re-
bellion against the womb.

Meg turned back when she heard Charlene purr her
good-byes.

"Trying a price hike on me." With a short laugh,
Charlene poured herself another glass of water from the
pitcher on her desk.

Didn't look efficient, Meg thought, but looks were
deceiving. When it came to business, Charlene could cal-
culate her profit and loss to the penny, any time of the
day or night.

"I hear you're a hero." Charlene watched her daughter as she sipped. "You and the sexy chief. You stay over
in Anchorage to celebrate?"

"We lost the light."

"Sure. Just a word of advice. A man like Nate's got
baggage and plenty of it. You're used to traveling fast and
light. It's not a good match."

"I'll keep that in mind. I need to talk to you."

"I've got calls and paperwork. You know this is my
busy time of day."

"It's about my father."

Charlene lowered her water glass. Her face went very
still, very pale, then the color erupted in her cheeks.
Candy pink to match the room.

"Did you hear from him? Did you see him in Anchorage? That son of a bitch. He'd better not think for one
minute he can come back here and pick things up. He's
not getting anything out of me, and if you've got any
sense, you'll say the same."

She shoved away from the desk and stood, her color rising from pink to hot and red. "Nobody, *nobody* walks away from me then walks back. Not ever. Pat Galloway can go fuck himself."

"He's dead."

"Probably had some sob story to tell. He was always good with . . . What do you mean he's dead?" Looking more annoyed than shocked, she flipped back her curly hair. "That's ridiculous. Who told you such a stupid lie?"

"He's been dead. It looks like he's been dead a long time. Maybe only days after he left here."

"Why would you say something like that? Why would you say something like that to me?" The angry red color had drained, turning her face white, white and drawn and suddenly old. "You can't hate me that much."

"I don't hate you. You've always been wrong about that. Maybe I'm ambivalent toward you most of the time, but I don't hate you. Those boys found an ice cave. It's where they took shelter part of the time they were on the mountain. He was in there. He's been in there."

"That's crazy talk. I want you to get out." Her voice rose to a hoarse shriek. "Get the hell out of here right now."

"They took pictures," Meg continued, even as Charlene grabbed one of her paperweights and heaved it against the wall. "I saw them. I recognized him."

"You did *not!*" She whirled, grabbed a trinket off a shelf, threw it. "You're making this up to get back at me."

"For what?" Meg ignored the statuary and glassware that smashed into walls, onto the floor, even when a shard nicked her cheek. It was Charlene's usual method of venting temper.

Break it, destroy it. Then have someone sweep it up. And buy new.

"For being a lousy mother? For being a big ho? For sleeping with the same guy I was sleeping with to prove you weren't too old to steal him from me? Maybe for telling me, most of my life, what a disappointment I am as a daughter. Which offense am I pulling out of my hat?"

"I raised you by myself. I made sacrifices for you so you could have what you wanted."

"Too bad you never gave me violin lessons. I could use one about now. And guess what, Charlene. This isn't about you or me. It's about him. He's dead."

"I don't believe you."

"Somebody killed him. Murdered him. Somebody hacked an ice ax into his chest and left him on the mountain."

"No. No, no, no, no." Her face was frozen now, as still and cold as the sky behind her. Then it collapsed as she slid down to the floor to sit among the broken china and glass. "Oh, my God, no. Pat. Pat."

"Get up, for God's sake. You're cutting yourself." Still angry, Meg marched around the desk, grabbed Charlene by the arms to haul her up.

"Meg. Megan." Charlene's breath hitched in and out, in and out. Her big, blue eyes swam. "He's dead?"

"Yes."

The tears spilled over, flooded her cheeks. On a wail, she dropped her head on Meg's shoulder and clung.

Meg fought her first instinct to pull away. She let her mother weep, hold on and weep. And she realized it was the first sincere embrace they'd shared in more years than she could count.

WHEN THE STORM PASSED, she took Charlene up the back way to her room. It was like undressing a doll, she thought, as she took off her mother's clothes. She doctored the minor cuts, slid a nightgown over Charlene's head.

"He didn't leave me."

"No." Meg walked into the bath, scanned her mother's medicine cabinet. There were always plenty of pills. She found some Xanax, filled a glass of water.

"I hated him for leaving me."

"I know."

"You hated me for it."

"Maybe. Take this."

"Murdered?"

"Yes."

"Why?"

"I don't know." She set the glass aside after Charlene took the pill. "Lie down."

"I loved him."

"Maybe you did."

"I loved him," Charlene repeated as Meg pulled the covers over her. "I hated him for leaving me alone. I can't stand to be alone."

"Go to sleep for a while."

"Will you stay?"

"No." Meg pulled the drapes, spoke into the shadows. "I don't hate being alone. And I need to be. You won't want me when you wake up anyway."

But she stayed until Charlene slept.

She passed Sarrie Parker on the stairs on the way down. "Let her sleep. Her office is a mess."

"I heard." Sarrie raised her eyebrows. "Must've said something that put her into a hell of a temper."

"Just try to get it cleaned up before she goes back in there."

She kept walking and grabbed her coat as she swung into the restaurant. "I have to go," she said to Nate.

He pushed away from the bar, caught up with her at the door. "Where?"

"Home. I need to be home." She welcomed the cold, the light slap of the wind.

"How is she?"

"I gave her a tranquilizer. She comes out of it, she's going to crash down on you. Sorry." She pulled on her gloves, then pressed her hands to her eyes. "God. God. It was what I was expecting. Hysterics, rage, why do you hate me. The usual."

"Your face is cut."

"Just a scratch. China-poodle shrapnel. She throws things." She breathed carefully as they walked toward the river. She watched the ghost of her breath fly and fade. "But when it sank in, when she understood I wasn't messing with her, she fell apart. I didn't expect what I saw then. I didn't expect what I saw on her face. She loved him. I never considered that. I never thought she did."

"It doesn't seem like the best time for either one of you to be alone."

"She won't be. I need to be. Give me a few days, Burke. You're going to have your hands full around here anyway. Few days, this will settle in some. Come out and see me. I'll fix you a meal, take you to bed."

"Phones are back up. You could call me if you need anything."

"Yeah, I could. I won't. Don't try to save me, Chief." She slid her sunglasses on. "Just handle the details."

She turned, pulled his head down to hers and indulged them both in a hot, seeking kiss. And drew back, patted his cheek with her gloved hand.

"Just a few days," she repeated, then crossed to her plane.

She didn't look back, but she knew he stood by the river, knew he watched her fly away. She blanked it out of her mind, all of it, and let herself soar over the tops of the trees, on the edge of the sky.

It wasn't until she saw the drift of smoke from her own chimney and the silky bullets that were her dogs race across the snow toward the lake that she felt her throat slam shut on her.

It wasn't until she saw the figure step out of her house, slowly follow the path of the dogs, that she felt the tears well up in her eyes.

Her hands began to shake so she had to fight to steady them and land. He was waiting for her, the man who'd stepped in as her father when her own had stepped away.

She got out, struggled to keep her voice even. "Didn't think you were coming back for another day or two."

"Something told me to come now." He studied her face. "Something's happened."

"Yes." She nodded, bent to greet her delighted dogs. "Something happened."

"Come inside and tell me."

It wasn't until she was inside, in the warmth, when he'd brewed her tea and watered her dogs, when he listened without comment, that she broke down and wept.

ELEVEN

I stood above the clouds. This, for me, is the defining moment of any climb. All the exhaustion, the pain, the sheer
misery of the cold washes out of you, when you stand at
the summit. You're reborn. In that innocence, there is no
fear of death or of life. There is no anger, no sorrow, no
history and no future. There is only the moment.

You've done it. You lived.

We danced on the virgin snow, nearly thirteen thousand feet above the ground with the sun beaming in our
eyes and the wind playing our mad tune. Our shouts
slammed and echoed against the sky, and our giddiness
swirled into the rippling ocean of clouds.

When Darth said we should jump, I nearly took the
leap. What the hell. We were gods here.

He meant it. It gave me a jolt—not quite fear—to realize he was serious. Let's jump. Let's fly! A little too
much Dex in my buddy here. A little too much speed to
pump him up for the fight to the finish.

He actually grabbed my arm, daring me. I had to pull
myself, and him, away from the edge. He cursed me for
it, but he was laughing. We both were. Insanely.

He said something a little weird, but it was the place

for it, I'd say. Rambling bitching, with that bubbling laughter, about my luck. Bagged myself the sexiest woman in Lunacy and got to sit around pissing away the days while she did the work. Get to take off, free as I please, and not only bang a whore, not only hit it big in the backroom, but I'm standing on the top of the world just because I fucking wanted to.

Now I won't even jump.

Things are going to change, that's what he told me. Things are going to turn around. He's going to get a woman other men want, he's going to hit it big. He's going to live large.

I let him stand and stew about it. It was too fine a moment for pettiness.

I passed through insane joy into the peace—utter and complete. We're not gods here, but only men who've struggled their way to one more peak. I know a thousand things I've done might be insignificant. But not this. This marks me.

We haven't conquered the mountain, but have joined with it.

I think, because I've done this, I might be a better man. A better partner, a better father. I know some of Darth's ramblings are truth. I haven't earned all that I have, not the way I earned this moment. I know the desire to be more strikes me as I stand in the battering wind above a world full of pain and beauty, curtained now by the clouds that tempt me to dive through them, to hurry back to that pain and that beauty.

Strange that I should stand here, where I so desperately wanted to be, and ache for what I left behind.

. . .

NATE STUDIED THE PHOTOGRAPHS from the ice cave. There was nothing new to see, and as he'd studied them every spare moment for the last three days, he had every detail imprinted on his brain.

He had a few stingy notes from the State Police. Weather permitting, they'd send up a forensics and re-covery team within the next forty-eight hours. He knew they'd interviewed the three boys extensively, but most of what had been asked and answered he'd gotten through the grapevine rather than official channels.

He wanted to set up a case board, but it wasn't his case.

He wasn't going to be allowed to examine the cave, to sit in on the autopsy once the body was brought down. Any data passed to him would be at the investigation team's discretion.

Maybe, once the body had been positively identified as Patrick Galloway, he'd have a little more edge. But he wasn't going to be in the loop.

It surprised him how much he wanted to be. It had been a year since his juices had been stirred by a case. He wanted to work it. Maybe it was partially because Meg was connected, but for the most part it was the photo-graphs. It was the man he saw in them.

Frozen in that moment, seventeen years before. Pre-served, and all those details of his death preserved with him. The dead had the answers, if you just knew where to look.

Had he fought? Been taken by surprise? Had he known his killer? Killers?

Why was he dead?

He slid the file he'd started into a drawer when he heard the knock on his office door.

Peach stuck her head in. "Deb caught a couple of kids shoplifting over at the store. Peter's free. You want him to go round them up?"

"All right. Notify the parents, get them down here, too. What did they take?"

"Tried to get some comic books, candy bars and a six-pack of Miller. Ought to know better. Deb's got an eye like a hawk. Jacob Itu's just come in. He'd like a minute, if you've got one."

"Sure, send him back."

Nate rose, wandered to his coffeemaker. Another hour of sunlight, he calculated, though what there was of it today was gloomy and dank. He looked out his window, picked out No Name, and studied it as he sipped his coffee.

He turned when he heard Jacob approach. The man was an emblem for the classic Native Alaskan with his raw-boned face and dark, intense eyes. His hair was silvered, worn in a single braid. His boots were sturdy, his clothes work-rough, with a long brown vest over flannel and wool.

Nate judged his age at somewhere on the high side of fifty, with a look of health and fitness, and ropy strength.

"Mr. Itu." Nate gestured to a chair. "What can I do for you?"

"Patrick Galloway was my friend."

Nate nodded. "You want coffee?"

"No. Thank you."

"The body hasn't yet been recovered, examined or positively identified." Nate sat behind his desk. It was the same spiel he'd been giving everyone who'd come in or caught him on the street, at The Lodge, over the past couple of days. "The State Police are in charge of the investigation. They'll notify next-of-kin, officially, when the identification's verified."

"Meg would not mistake her father."

"No. I agree."

"You can't leave justice to others."

That had been his creed once. The creed that had sent both him and his partner into an alley in Baltimore.

"It's not my case. It's not my jurisdiction or my province."

"He was one of us, as his daughter is. You stood in front of the people of this place when you came and promised to do your duty to them."

"I did. I will. I'm not letting it go, but I'm well down the feeding chain on this."

Jacob stepped closer, his only movement since coming into the room. "When you were Outside, murder was your business."

"It was. I'm not Outside anymore. Have you seen Meg?"

"Yes. She's strong. She'll use her grief. She won't let it use her."

As I do? Nate thought. But this man with his intense eyes and ruthlessly controlled anger couldn't see what was inside of him.

"Tell me about Galloway. Who would he have gone climbing with?"

"He'd know them."

"Them?"

"A winter climb on No Name would need at least three. He was reckless, impulsive, but he wouldn't have attempted it with less than three. He wouldn't have climbed with strangers. Or not only strangers." Jacob smiled slightly. "But he made friends easily."

"And enemies?"

"A man who has what others covet makes enemies."

"What did he have?"

"A beautiful woman. A quick-witted child. An ease of manner and lack of ambition that allowed him to do as he pleased most of the time."

Coveting another man's woman was often a motive for murder between friends. "Was Charlene involved with anyone else?"

"I don't think so."

"Was he?"

"He may have enjoyed another woman from time to time when he was away from home, as some men will. If he enjoyed one in town, he didn't tell me of it."

"He wouldn't have had to tell you," Nate responded. "You'd have known."

"Yes."

"And so would others. A place like this may have secrets, but that's not the kind that stays buried for long." He considered another moment. "Drugs?"

"He grew a little marijuana. He didn't deal."

Nate lifted his eyebrows. "Just grass?" When Jacob hesitated, Nate leaned back. "Nobody's going to bust him for it now."

"Primarily grass, but he wasn't likely to turn down anything that came to hand."

"Did he have a dealer? In Anchorage, say?"

"I don't think so. He rarely had the money to spend on that sort of indulgence. Charlene held the purse, and she held it tight. He liked to climb and to fish and to hike. He liked to fly but had no interest in learning to pilot. He'd work when he needed money. He disliked restrictions, laws, rules. Many do who come here. He wouldn't have understood you."

The important thing, as Nate saw it, was for him to understand Patrick Galloway.

He asked more questions, then filed away the notes he'd made after Jacob left.

Then it was time to deal with the more mundane matter of a couple of adolescent shoplifters.

With that, a pair of missing skis and a fender bender, he stayed busy until the end of shift.

He was taking the evening off, leaving Otto and Pete on call. Unless there was a mass murder, he was off the clock until morning.

He'd given Meg her few days. He hoped she was ready for him.

It was his own fault, he decided, that he'd gone back to The Lodge to pick up a change of clothes—in case he stayed out at Meg's.

Charlene caught him while he was still in his room.

"I need to talk to you." She scooted around him at the door and walked over to sit on the bed. She wore all black—a snug sweater and snugger pants and those skinny heels she liked to teeter around in.

"Sure. Why don't we go down and have some coffee?"

"This is private. Would you close the door?"

"Okay." But he stood by it, just in case.

"I need you to do something. I need you to go to Anchorage and tell those people they have to release Pat's body to me."

"Charlene, they haven't recovered the body yet."

"I *know* that. Haven't I been on the phone with those bureaucrats and insensitive bastards every day? They're just leaving him up there."

When her eyes filled, Nate's stomach sank.

"Charlene." He looked around, a little desperately for some tissue, a towel, an old T-shirt, and ended up going into the bath. He came out with a roll of toilet paper and pushed it into her hand. "Getting people up there, and making the recovery, is a complicated business."

He didn't want to add that a few days, one way or the other, wasn't going to make a damn bit of difference. "There've been storms up there and high winds. But I talked with Sergeant Coben myself today. If it's clear, they hope to send a team up in the morning."

"They said I'm not next-of-kin, because we weren't legally married." She yanked off several sheets of tissue, buried her face in the wad.

"Oh." He puffed out his cheeks, blew out a breath. "Meg—"

"She's not legitimate." Voice cracking, Charlene waved the soggy wad. "Why should they give him to her? They'll send him back to his parents, back east. And that's not *fair!* That's not *right!* He left them, didn't he?

He didn't leave me. Not on purpose. But they hate me, and they'll never let me have him."

He'd seen people squabble over the dead before, and it was never pretty. "Have you talked to them?"

"No, I haven't talked to them," she snapped, and her eyes dried up cold. "They don't even acknowledge me. Oh, they've talked to Meg a few times, and they gave her some money when she turned twenty-one. Little enough when they've got *piles* of it. They didn't bother with Pat when he was alive, but you can bet your ass they'll want him now that he's dead. I want him back. I want him back."

"Okay, why don't we take this one step at a time." He saw no choice, so he sat down beside her, draped an arm over her shoulder so she could cry on his. "I'll keep in touch with Coben. I'm going to tell you the body's not going to be released for a while anyway. It could be some time. And it seems to me that as his daughter Meg has as much right as his parents."

"She won't fight for him. She doesn't care about things like that."

"I'll talk to Meg."

"Why would anybody kill Pat? He never hurt anybody. But me." She gave a watery laugh, the sort that sounded both sad and wistful. "And he never meant to. He never meant to make you cry or make you mad."

"He make a lot of people mad?"

"Me, mostly. He made me crazy." She sighed. "I loved him like crazy."

"If I asked you to think back, really think back, to the weeks around the time he left, could you? The details of it, even the little ones."

"I guess I could try. It was so long ago, it barely seems real anymore."

"I want you to try, take a couple of days and really think back. Write things down when they come to you. Things he said, did, the people he was with, anything that seemed different. We'll talk about it."

"He's been up there all this time," she whispered. "Alone in the cold. How many times have I looked at that mountain over the years? Now, every time I do, I'll see Pat. It was easier when I hated him, you know?"

"Yeah, I guess I do."

She sniffled, straightened. "I want his body brought here. I want to bury him here. That's what he'd have wanted."

"We'll do everything we can to make that happen." Since she was softened up with the tears, and not currently hitting on him, it might be the time to press for information. "Charlene, tell me about Jacob Itu."

She dabbed at her eyelashes. "What about him?"

"What's his story? How did he hook up with Pat? It helps me to have a picture."

"So you can find out what happened to Pat?"

"Exactly. He and Jacob were friends?"

"Yeah." She sniffled again, a bit more delicately. "Jacob's sort of . . . mysterious. At least *I've* never understood him."

Judging from the sulky look, that meant she'd never been able to get him into bed. Interesting, Nate decided. "He strikes me as a loner."

"I guess." She shrugged now. "He and Pat hit it off. I think he was sort of, I don't know, *amused* by Pat mostly.

But they liked all that hunting and fishing and hiking crap. Pat was good at all the outdoorsy stuff. He and Jacob used to go out into the bush for days while I was back here dealing with a baby and work and—"

"So that was the bond, the connection," Nate interrupted.

"Well, and they both hated the government, but so does everybody else around here. He and Pat liked doing the living-off-the-land stuff together, but under it, it was Meg."

"What was Meg?"

"Well . . ."

She shifted toward him into what Nate recognized as gossip mode. He stayed where he was, sitting intimately on the bed with her, unwilling to change the dynamics until he'd gotten what he was after.

"Jacob used to be married."

"Is that so?'

"Ages ago. Eons. Back when he was like eighteen, nineteen, living in this little village in the bush outside of Nome." Her face was animated now as she gave her little hair toss and settled in to give him the dish. "I got all this from Pat—and here and there. Jacob never has much to say to me."

She started to sulk again, to poker up. "So he was married," Nate prompted.

"Some young thing, same tribe. They grew up together and everything—one of those soul mates deals. She died in childbirth. Her and the baby—the girl. She went into labor too early, a couple of months early, and there were complications. Whatever, I can't remember exactly what went wrong, but they couldn't get her to a hospital, not in time anyway. It's sad," she said after a beat, and her eyes, her face, her voice softened with genuine sympathy. "It's really sad."

"Yes, it is."

"Pat said that's why he became a bush pilot. If he'd had a plane, or they'd been able to get one in time, maybe . . . So he moved out here, said he couldn't stay there because there his life was over. Or something like that. Anyway, when we came around, when he saw Meg, Jacob said her spirit spoke to his. He wasn't even high," she said with a roll of her eyes. "Jacob didn't get high. He says that sort of thing. He told Pat that Meg was his spirit child, and Pat thought that was cool. It seemed weird to me, but Pat was okay with it. He figured it made him and Jacob brothers."

"Did he and Pat ever argue about anything? About Meg, for instance?"

"Not that I ever heard of. Of course, Jacob doesn't argue. He just freezes you with those long—what do you call it?—inscrutable," she decided. "Those inscrutable stares. I guess he stepped up with Meg when Pat left. But Pat didn't leave." Tears welled in her eyes again. "He died."

"I'm sorry. I appreciate the information. It always helps to get a picture."

"You talk to Meg." Charlene got to her feet. "You talk to her about making those Boston people see Pat belongs here. You make *her* see. She won't listen to me. Never did, never will. I'm counting on you, Nate."

"I'll do what I can."

She seemed to be satisfied with that, and left Nate sitting on the side of the bed, picturing himself being squeezed flat by two difficult females.

HE DIDN'T CALL HER. She might put him off or just not answer the phone. The worst she could do if he showed up on her doorstep was send him away again, and at least he'd have seen for himself if she was okay.

He drove along the tunnel of road with the walls of snow on either side. The sky had cleared some, as predicted, so there was a faint glimmer of moon and starlight. It drizzled on the mountains that filled his view, glinted off his glimpses of the river.

He heard the music before he made the turn to her house. It filled the dark, soared through it and swallowed it. Just as the lights beat back the night. She had them on, all of them, so the house, the grounds, the near trees were lit like fire. And through it, the music streamed and flew.

He thought it was some sort of opera, though that kind of music wasn't his strong point. It was wrenching, the sort of thing that broke the heart even as it, somehow, lifted the soul.

She'd cleared a walkway, a good three feet wide. He could imagine the time and effort that had taken. Her porch was clear of snow, and a wood box beside the door was full.

He started to knock, then decided nobody could hear a knock over the music. He tried the door, found it unlocked, eased it open.

The dogs, who'd been sleeping despite the music, leaped up from the rug. After a few quick, warning barks, tails wagged. To Nate's relief, they appeared to remember him and pranced over to greet him.

"Good, great. Where's your mom?"

He tried a couple of shouts, then made his way through the first floor. There were cheery fires burning in both the living room and kitchen—and something simmering on the stove that smelled like dinner.

He started to take a peak—maybe a sample—when he caught a movement through the window.

He moved closer. He could see her now, clearly in the flood of lights. She was bundled head to foot, trudging back through the snow on the fat, round snowshoes they called bear claws. As he watched she stopped, lifted her head to the sky. She stood, staring up, music pouring over her. Then she threw her arms back to the sides and fell backward.

He was at the door in one bounding leap. Wrenching it open, he shot out, jumped the steps, skidded on the frosty path she'd cleared.

She popped up when he shouted her name.

"What? Hi, where'd you come from?"

"What happened? Are you hurt?"

"No. I just wanted to lie in the snow for a minute. Sky's clearing up. Well, give me a hand up since you're here."

Even as he reached out, the dogs flew out and leaped on both of them.

"Left the door open," Meg managed as one of the huskies rolled with her in the snow.

"Sorry. Closing it slipped my mind when I thought

you had a seizure." He hauled her up. "What are you do-ing out here?"

"I was in the shed, working on this old snowmobile I picked up a few months ago. Every now and then I go in and give it a few whacks."

"You know how to fix a snowmobile?"

"My talents are endless and varied."

"I bet they are." Looking at her, he forgot all the lit-tle irritations of the day. "I was thinking I might buy a snowmobile."

"Really. Well, once I get this one up and running, I'll make you a deal. Let's go in. I'm ready for a drink." She sent him a sidelong look as they started for the house. "So, were you just in the neighborhood?"

"No."

"Checking up on me?"

"Yeah, and hoping for that free meal."

"That all you're hoping for?"

"No."

"Good. Because I'm ready for that, too." She picked up a broom cocked by the door. "Brush me off some, will you?"

When he'd done his best, she took off the bear claws. "Take your coat off, stay awhile," she invited and began to strip off her own.

"Hey. Your hair."

She rubbed a hand over it as she hung up her parka and hat. "What about it?"

"There's a lot less of it."

It came to just below her jaw now, straight and full and thick—and a little crazed from her hands.

"I wanted a change. So I changed." She walked over, got a bottle from the pantry. Getting down glasses, she glanced back and saw him grinning at her. "What?"

"I like it. It makes you look, I don't know, young and cute."

She angled her head. "Young and cute like you want me to dress in a pinafore and Mary Janes and call you Daddy?"

"I don't know what a pinafore is, but you can wear one if you want. I'd as soon skip the Daddy part."

"Whatever blows up your skirt." She shrugged, poured deep-red wine into two glasses. "It's good to see you, Burke."

He walked over, took the glasses out of her hands and set them down on the counter. And using his hands to skim back that thick hair, leaned down, slow, eyes open, and kissed her. Soft and quiet until the warmth sparked with licks of heat. And he watched her watch him through the kiss, saw those perfect blue eyes of hers flicker once.

When he eased her back, he lifted the wineglasses again, gave one to her.

"It's good to kiss you, too."

She rubbed her lips together and was surprised the heat that had pumped into them didn't spark from the friction. "Hard to argue with that."

"I worried about you. You don't want to hear that, puts your back up. But that's the way it is. We don't have to talk about any of it if you're not ready."

She took a drink, then another. A lot of patience inside there, she decided. And the kissing cousin to patience was tenacity.

"Might as well deal with it. Do you know how to make a salad?"

"Ah . . . You open one of those bags of salad stuff you buy at the store and dump it into a bowl?"

"Not a guy for the kitchen, huh?"

"No."

"Still, at this point in our relationship, when you're hot for me, you'll learn to chop vegetables without complaining about it. Ever peel a carrot?" she asked as she walked to the refrigerator.

"Yes, yes, I have."

"There, that's a start." She piled produce on the counter, handed him a carrot and a peeler. "Do that."

While he did, she began to wash lettuce. "In some cultures, women hack off their hair as a sign of mourning. That's not why I did it, altogether. He's been gone a long time, and I adjusted to that—in my own way. But it's different now."

"Murder changes everything."

"More than death does," she agreed. "Death's natural. It's a pisser because, hey, who wants to, but there's a cycle and nobody gets to jump off the wheel."

She dried the lettuce, those long fingers with their short, blunt nails working briskly. "I could've accepted his death. I'm not going to accept his murder. So I'll push at the State cops, and I'll push at you until I'm satisfied. This may cool off your hotness for me, but that's the breaks."

"I don't think it will. I haven't felt hot for a woman in a while, so I'm due."

"Why not?"

He handed her the carrot for inspection. "Why not what?"

"Why haven't you been hot for a woman?"

"I . . . hmm."

"Performance issues?"

He blinked, managed a strangled laugh. "Well, Jesus. That's a question. But this is just too weird a conversation to have over lettuce."

"Back to murder, then," she replied.

"Who took them up?" he questioned.

"What?"

"They'd have needed a pilot, right? Who flew them to the base camp or whatever you call it."

"Oh." She paused, tapped her knife on the cutting board. "You *are* a cop, aren't you? I don't know, and it may be tricky to find out after all this time. But between me and Jacob, we should be able to do it."

"Whoever it is took down at least one less man than he dropped off. But he didn't report it. Why?"

"And those are the things we need to find out. Good. A direction."

"The investigators in charge will be asking those questions, heading in that direction. You might want to give yourself some time to deal with the more personal business."

"You mean the custody battle and funeral Charlene's planning." She began to slice interesting ribbons from a hunk of red cabbage. "I've already had an earful, which is why I stopped answering the phone yesterday. Fighting over a dead body's just a little too stupid for me. Especially when she has no idea if his family will object to her burying him here in the first place."

"Have you met them?"

She got out a pot and began to fill it with water for the pasta. "Yeah. His mother contacted me a few times, and when she offered to fly me out there to meet his family, I was curious enough to go. I was eighteen. Charlene was supremely pissed, which only made me want to go more."

After the pot was on a burner, she gave the sauce a little stir, then came back to finish the salad. "They're okay. Snooty, highbrowed, not the sort of people I'd hang out with, or who'd want me hanging around for long. But they were decent to me. They gave me money, which has to earn them some points."

Reaching for the bottle, she topped off her glass, held it up, eyebrows raised to Nate.

"No, I'm good."

"It was enough money for me to put a down payment on my plane and this place, so I owe them."

She paused to sip her wine contemplatively. "I don't think they're going to fight Charlene and insist on dragging him back east. She wants to think so, because she likes to hate them. Just like they enjoy disregarding her. That way they can all make more out of my father than he was."

She got out plates, passed them off to Nate for the table. "Is staying quiet an interrogation technique?"

"It can be. It can also be called listening."

"There's only one person I know—well, that I'm willing to spend appreciable time with—who listens like you.

That's Jacob. It's a good, strong quality. My father would listen to me, sometimes. But you could see him start to drift if it went on too long to suit him. He'd sit it out, but he wasn't hearing you. Jacob always heard me.

"Anyway," she said after a huffed-out sigh. "Patrick Galloway. He was an inconsiderate bastard. I loved him, and he was never really inconsiderate to me. But he was to his family, who, whatever their faults, didn't deserve to have their son take off without a word before his eighteenth birthday. And he was to Charlene, leaving her to earn most of the coin and take care of the bulk of the messy stuff.

"I think she probably loved him, which was—maybe is—her cross to bear. I don't know if he loved her."

She pulled a clear glass container of rotini out of a cabinet, dumped some into the boiling water, continued to speak while she adjusted the heat and stirred.

"And I don't think he'd have stuck it out with us if someone hadn't killed him before he'd had a chance to take off anyway. But now I can't know, and he never got the chance to make his choice. That's what counts. What counts is someone ended him. So that's my focus on this. Not where he ends up being put in the ground."

"Sensible."

"I'm not a sensible woman, Burke. I'm a selfish one. You'll figure that out for yourself soon enough." She got a plastic container out of the fridge, shook it, then drizzled the contents over the salad. "There's a baguette in that drawer there. Fresh from this morning."

He opened the drawer, found the bread. "I didn't know you'd been into town."

"I haven't. I took a couple days off to burrow." After unwrapping the bread, she cut a few thick slabs. "Baking's one of the things I do when I'm burrowing, which prevents it from becoming wallowing."

"You bake bread." He sniffed at it. "I've never known anybody who bakes bread. Or flies a plane. Or can fix a snowmobile engine."

"As I said, a woman of strange and varied talents. I'll show you some more of them after dinner. In bed. Top off the wine, will you? We're about ready here."

MAYBE IT WAS THE ATMOSPHERE, maybe it was the woman, but he couldn't remember a more relaxed meal.

She'd said she wasn't sensible, but he saw good, clear sense in the way she lived, took care of her home. In how she dealt with shock and grief, even anger.

Jacob had said she was strong. Nate was beginning to believe she was the strongest person he'd ever met.

And the most comfortable with herself.

She asked about his day. It took him a while to get his rhythm there. He'd been so accustomed through his marriage to leaving the job outside.

But she wanted to hear about it, to comment, to gossip, to laugh.

Still, under the ease he felt with her was a frisson of excitement, anticipation, that sexual buzz that heated his blood whenever he was around her.

He wanted to get his hands in her hair, to get his teeth on the nape that shorter length exposed. He could think of that, imagine that, have his belly tighten even as he felt the weight of the day slide off his shoulders.

At one point, she stretched out, laying her feet in his lap as she leaned back to drink more wine. And his mouth went dry, his mind fuzzy.

"I used to shoplift." She tossed a chunk of bread to each dog and it immediately made him think of how such an action would have caused his own mother to freak.

And how much he liked watching the dogs field the bread, like a couple of outfielders shagging pop flies.

"You . . . used to steal."

"I don't really equate shoplifting with stealing."

"Taking things, not paying for them."

"Okay, okay." She rolled her eyes. "But it was really more of a rite of passage, at least for me. And I was too slick to get caught like those kids you bagged today. I never took anything I had any use for. It was more: Hmm, wonder if I can get away with this. Then I'd hide the booty in my room and take it all out at night and gloat over it. I'd take it all back within a couple of days, which was nearly as dangerous and thrilling. I think I'd have been a good criminal if I lived somewhere else, because I got that it's not so much what you get as the getting of it."

"You don't still . . ."

"No, but now that you mention it, it might be fun to see if I still have the knack. And if I get busted, I have this in with the chief of police." She dropped her feet, leaned over to pat his thigh while he studied her with those serious, gray eyes. "Don't look so worried. Everybody in town knows I'm crazy and wouldn't hold it against me."

She rose. "Let's get these dishes out of the way. Why don't you let the dogs out? They like a good run this time of day."

Once the kitchen was tidied to her specifications and the dogs settled down on the floor with a couple of tibia-sized rawhide bones, she wandered into the living room to flip through her CD list.

"I don't think Puccini sets the right tone for the next portion of our evening."

"Is that what that was? The opera stuff?"

"Well, I guess that answers the question of your opinion on that area of music."

"I just don't know anything about it. I liked the way it sounded outside when I drove up. Sort of full and strange and heart-wrecking."

"There may be hope for you. Hmm, could pull out Barry White, but it seems pretty obvious. What do you think of Billie Holiday?"

"Ah, dead blues singer?"

She turned to him. "Okay, what *do* you know about music?"

"I know stuff. What's on the radio or, you know, VH1." Her amused stare had him stuffing his hands in his pockets. "I like Norah Jones."

"Norah Jones it is, then." She found a number, then programmed her unit to select it.

"And Black Crowes," he continued in his own defense. "And actually, Jewel's new stuff is pretty hot. Springsteen's still The Boss. And there's—"

"Don't sweat it." She laughed and grabbed his hand. "Jones works fine for me." She began drawing him up the stairs. "If you do me right, I'll hear my own music anyway."

"But no pressure."

"Bet you can handle it." At the top of the stairs, she turned into him, backed him through a doorway. "Handle me, Chief. I've been wanting you to."

"I think about you all the time. At inappropriate moments."

She hooked her arms around his waist. She'd been needing him, she'd been wanting him. So strange, so new for her to need and want so very specifically. "Such as?"

"Like picturing you naked when I was going over the weekly rotation with Peach. It can be disconcerting."

"I like you picturing me naked, especially at inappropriate times." She grazed her teeth over his jaw. "Why don't you get me that way now?"

"I like you dressed, too. Just FYI," he said as he tugged her sweater up.

He liked the feel of her body under his hands and how he had to go layer by layer before he reached skin. And how warm that skin was, how smooth. And despite the fleece and wool and cotton, despite all that practicality, there was the secret, sexy scent of her under it.

She touched him, easily and eagerly, stripping those layers from him as he did from her. And she lit something inside him, something more than lust. Something that had been hibernating far too long.

He could lose himself in her without feeling lost. Let himself go without worrying if he'd find his way back. When his mouth closed over hers, tasted both surrender and demand, he had all he needed.

They circled toward the bed, lowered to it. He heard her sigh and wondered if she could be as relieved or as needy as he. She drew him down, arched and offered when his mouth roamed her throat, when his teeth nipped their way to her nape. He felt her heart kick lightly against his and the firm, welcoming stroke of her hands on his back.

She wanted him to take what he needed. That was rare for her, a woman who preferred seeing to her own needs first—and often last as well. But she wanted to give to him, to ease away that smudge of sorrow that haunted his eyes. And she knew, somehow, she could give, and he would never leave her wanting.

There was more to the heat of his lips, the greed of his hands than a search for satisfaction. If some part of her worried over it, she brushed it aside. She knew there was always plenty of later for worries and regrets.

So she rose to him, found his face with her hands, with her lips, and let the tender mix with the heady.

He moved over her, stirring little quivers, lighting little fires, and finally clasped her hands with his to keep her from arousing him too much, too soon.

He wanted to taste her. Those shoulders, breasts, that wonderful lean line of her. As his lips roamed over her, she shuddered, her breath catching on a moan as her fingers flexed in his.

He stroked his tongue over her, into her, and set her wild.

She came on a gallop, her body going hot and damp as pleasure flooded her. Her system screamed with release, then churned in a desperate quest for more.

He gave her more, shockingly, until she would have clawed and bit to have him, until her body went lax and dazed with the drug he'd sent swimming into her blood.

"Meg." He pressed his mouth to her belly, under her heart, over it.

As her freed hands gripped his hips, he lifted hers.

He was inside her, at last. Linked. Mated. Dropping his forehead to hers, he fought for breath and waited for his head to clear so he would know every second, every movement, every thrill.

She held him, held him close as bodies merged and minds blurred. He said her name again, an instant before he emptied.

SHADOW

Follow a shadow, it still flies you;
Seem to fly it, it will pursue.

BEN JONSON

And coming events cast their
shadows before.

THOMAS CAMPBELL

TWELVE

SHE DIDN'T MIND lying quiet in the dark. In fact, she liked it, especially when her body was loose from sex.

She heard the dogs come in and settle in their usual tangle on the floor at the foot of the bed.

The grandmother clock from her office down the hall bonged nine.

Too early to sleep, she thought. And too relaxed to stir.

The perfect time, then, to satisfy some of her curiosity about the man beside her.

"Why did she cheat on you?"

"What?"

"Your wife. Why did she cheat on you?"

She felt him shift, moving his body slightly apart from hers. A shrink, she supposed, would have theories on that.

"I guess I wasn't giving her what she was looking for."

"You're good in bed. Better than good. Hold on a minute."

She rolled out of bed and, since she was determined to ferret out some information, dug out a robe. "Be right back," she said, and headed down to get the wine and fresh glasses.

When she came back, he was up, had pulled on his

pants and was tossing a fresh log on her bedroom fire. "Maybe I should—"

"If *go* is the next word, forget it. I'm not done with you." She sat back on the bed, poured the glasses. "It's time for that long, sad story, Burke. You might as well start with her, since she's probably the root."

"I don't know that she is."

"You were married," Meg prompted. "She was unfaithful."

"That about wraps it up."

But she only cocked her head, held out a glass. He hesitated, but walked back. Accepting the wine, he sat on the bed with her. "I didn't make her happy, that's all. It's not easy being married to a cop."

"Why not?"

"Because . . ." Let me count the ways, he thought. "The job pulls at you all the damn time. The hours suck. Every second time you make plans, you have to cancel. You get home late, and your head's still in the case. When you work homicides, you can drag death around with you even when you don't want to."

"Sounds true enough." She sipped her wine. "Tell me this. Were you a cop when she married you?"

"Yeah, but—"

"No, no, I'm asking the questions here. How long did you know each other before you took the leap?"

"I don't know. A year." He took a slow sip of wine and watched the fire. "Closer to two, I guess."

"Was she slow? Stupid?"

"No. Jesus, Meg."

"Just pointing out that you'd have to be one or the other to be involved with a cop for a year or more and not clue in to the rules of the road."

"Yeah, maybe. That doesn't mean you have to like the rules or want to live with them."

"Sure, people are entitled to change their minds, whenever. No law against it. I'm saying she married you knowing the package. So using the package as an excuse to cheat or cast blame in your direction if things weren't working doesn't wash."

"She married the son of a bitch she was cheating with, so I guess that plays into it."

"Okay, she fell for somebody else. Shit happens. But that's on her. Pushing the blame for her actions on you is just bitchy and cheap."

He looked at her now. "How do you know she did?"

"Because I'm looking at you, cutie. Am I wrong?"

He took a gulp of wine. "No."

"And you let her."

"I loved her."

Those wonderful eyes clouded with sympathy as she touched his cheek, brushed her hand through his messy mass of hair. "Poor Nate. So she broke your heart and kicked you in the balls. What happened?"

"I knew things weren't right. I ignored it, so that's on me. Figured it'd smooth out. I should've worked at it harder."

"Coulda, shoulda, woulda."

He gave a half-laugh. "You're tough."

Easing over, she kissed his cheek. "How's that? So

you didn't pay enough attention to the cracks in the ice as you should have, in your opinion. What then?"

"Bigger cracks. I thought I could take some time off, and we could get out of town, rediscover. Whatever. She wasn't interested. I wanted kids. We'd talked about it before we got married, but she'd chilled to the idea. We had some rounds about that. We had some rounds about a lot of things. It's not all her fault, Meg."

"It never is."

"I came home one day. Bad day. Caught a case, drive-by shooting. A woman and her two kids. She's waiting for me. Tells me she wants a divorce, that she's sick of waiting around until I decide to come home. Sick of having her needs and wants and plans take a backseat to mine, and so on. I blew, she blew, and it comes out she's in love with somebody else—who happens to be our frigging lawyer—and she's been seeing him for months. She lays it all out. I've emotionally deserted her, never consider her needs or desires, expect her to alter her plans at the drop of a hat. I'm not there for her anyway, so she wants me out. And has considerately packed up most of my stuff."

"What did you do?"

"I left. I'd just come in from dealing with the useless slaughter of a twenty-six-year-old woman, her ten- and eight-year-old kids. And after Rachel and I yelled at each other for an hour, I didn't have anything left. I packed up my car, drove around awhile and landed at my partner's. Slept on his couch for a few nights."

To Meg's mind, the woman—Rachel—should've been the one sleeping on a friend's couch, after Nate had de-

livered a good kick in her ass to help her out the door.
But she let it pass.

"Meanwhile?"

"She served me with papers; I went to talk to her. But
she was done and made it clear. She didn't want to be
married to me. We'd divide up the assets and walk away.
I was married to the job, anyway, so she was superfluous.
That's what she said. End of story."

"I don't think so. A guy like you might get his heart
cracked, and he might mope about it for a while. Then he
gets pissed off. Why haven't you?"

"Who says I didn't?" He got up, set his wine aside,
walked to the fire. To the window. "Look, it was a bad
year. A long, bad year. Or two. My mother got wind of
the divorce in progress and that was lots of fun. She came
down on me like bricks."

"Why's that?"

"She liked Rachel. She never wanted me to be a cop
in the first place. My father died, line of duty, when I was
seventeen; she never got over it. She'd handled, pretty
well, being a cop's wife. But she couldn't handle being a
cop's widow. And she never forgave me for wanting to be
what he was. Somewhere in her head she thought that
Rachel, that marriage, would turn me into something
else. It didn't, and as far as she was concerned, I'd
wrecked it. That pissed me off for a while, so I buried
myself in the job and got through."

"And then?"

He turned away from the window, came back to sit.
"Rachel got married. I don't know why it was such a kick
in the gut, but it hit me pretty hard, and I guess it

showed. Jack, my partner, said we were going out, have a couple drinks. Jack was a family man. He'd go home to his wife and kids, but I was down, he was my partner, so he sat with me over a couple of beers and let me vent. He should've been home, instead of walking out of a bar with me in the middle of the night. He should've been home in bed with his wife. But he wasn't. And we come out, and we see it, half a block up. Drug deal going south. Guy starts shooting, and we pursue. Down the alley, and I'm hit."

Shot, she thought. "The scars on your leg and right side."

"I go down with the leg shot, but I tell Jack I'm okay. I'm calling for backup on my cell. And I'm pulling myself up, and he shoots Jack. Chest, gut. Jesus. I can't get to him. Can't, and the shooter's coming back. Crazy, hyped up. Fucking crazy to come back instead of run. He hits me again, not much more than a graze really. Just this hot arrow under the ribs. And I emptied my clip in him. I don't remember, but that's what they told me. I remember crawling to Jack, watching him die. I remember the way he looked at me, how he gripped my hand and said my name—like what the hell? And how he said his wife's name, when he knew. I remember that, every night."

"And blame yourself."

"He wouldn't have been there."

"I don't see things that way." She wanted to gather him up, rock him like a child. A mistake for him, she knew, an indulgence for her. So she sat beside him, only laid her hand on his thigh. "Every choice a person makes takes them somewhere. You wouldn't have been there either if your wife had been waiting at home for you. So you could just as easily blame her and the guy she'd been seeing. Or you could just blame the man who shot him, because you know, somewhere you know, he's the one to blame."

"I know all that. Heard it all before. It doesn't change how I feel at three in the morning or three in the afternoon. Or whenever it wants to slap me down."

Might as well say it all, tell her all, whatever it cost.

"I went into a hole, Meg, a big, black, nasty hole. I've been trying to climb out, and sometimes I'm almost there, right at the edge. Then something from below reaches up and drags me back down again."

"You have therapy?"

"The department arranged it."

"Meds?"

He shifted again. "I don't like them."

"Better living through chemistry," she said, but he didn't smile.

"They make me edgy or jumpy or out of myself. I can't do the job on meds, and if I couldn't do the job, the whole thing was pointless. But I couldn't stay in Baltimore, either. Couldn't face it every day. Another body, another case—trying to close the ones Jack and I caught together before. Seeing somebody else at his desk. Knowing he left a wife and kids who loved him, and there was nobody who'd have been left if it'd been me instead."

"So you came here."

"To bury myself. But things happened. I saw the mountains. I saw the lights. Northern lights."

He looked at her and realized by the faint smile on her face she understood. He didn't have to say more. So he could say more.

"And I saw you. Similar reaction to all. Something inside me wanted to come back to life. I don't know how it'll be or if I'm any good for you. I'm not a sure bet."

"I like long odds. Let's just see how it plays."

"I should go."

"Didn't I say I wasn't done with you? I'll tell you what we should do. We should go out and jump in the hot tub for a while, then we should come back up here and roll around naked again."

"Go out? As in outside? Get in a tub of water outside where it's about ten degrees?"

"Not in the tub, it isn't. Come on, Burke, get hardy. Get stimulated." And soak away some of those blues, she thought.

"We could stay right here in bed and get stimulated."

But she rolled away. "You'll like it," she promised, and yanked him out of bed.

She was right: He did like it. The insanity of the rushing cold, the painful plunge into hot water, the absurdly sexy sensation of being naked with her under a sky now mad with stars and those magical, shifting lights.

Steam pumped and plumed off the surface, and the dogs once again raced like maniacs. The only downside he could see was having to heave himself out again, race through the bitter air to the house—and the possibility of a heart attack.

"Do you do this a lot?"

"A couple times a week. Gets the blood moving."

"I'll say."

Sinking a little lower, he tipped back his head. And the northern lights filled his vision. "Oh, man. Do you ever get tired of it? Even used to it?"

She mirrored his pose, enjoying the way the cold streamed into her face while the heat saturated her body. "Used to it in a way that makes you proprietary. Like they belong to me, and I just share them with a few lucky others.

"I go out most nights, just to look. There's nobody out, and everything's quiet. And yeah, then they belong to me."

There were shimmers of lavender tonight, swirls of deep blue, hints of red. The music she'd chosen this time had Michelle Branch singing passionately about the light shining in the dark.

Stirred, he found her hand in the heat of the water, linked fingers. "I guess this is perfect," he murmured.

"Seems like."

He soaked himself in the lights and the music, in the heat and the music. "Are you going to get weirded out if I fall in love with you?"

She didn't speak for a moment. "I don't know. I might."

"I might. That's a revelation for me. That I'd have enough left inside to head in that direction."

"I'd say you've got plenty left. On the other hand, I don't know as I have enough to begin with to walk that way."

He looked at her then, smiled. "Guess we'll find out."

"Maybe you should just focus on the moment, enjoy it for what it is. Live that."

"Is that what you do? Live for the moment?"

The red was deepening, overpowering the softer, sweeter lavender. "Sure."

"I don't buy it. You can't run your own business without looking ahead, building for the future."

The movement of her shoulders rippled the water. "Business is business. Life is life."

"Uh-uh. Not for people like you and me. Work is life. That's part of our problem or one of our virtues. Depending on how you look at it."

She was studying his face now, frowning. "Well, that's some hot-tub philosophy."

He glanced over as she did, toward the sound of the dogs barking fiercely in the woods. "They always carry on like that?"

"No. Might be they flushed a fox or a moose." But her brow remained creased until the dogs quieted. "Too early in the season for bear. And Rock and Bull can handle almost anything. I'll call them back in a minute."

HE'D BROUGHT A COUPLE of hunks of fresh meat. The dogs knew him, so he wasn't worried. But it was best to be prepared. He was here, surveying the house from the shelter of the trees because he believed in being prepared.

He wasn't sure what it meant that the cop and the daughter of his old friend were frolicking in the hot tub.

Maybe it was good. An affair would keep them both occupied.

In any case, he didn't think much of the cop. Just a kind of figurehead who hauled in drunks or broke up fights. Nothing much to worry about there.

Then again, he'd stopped worrying the body would be found. He'd stopped thinking about it and had put the whole ugly business out of his mind years ago. It had happened to someone else. It had never happened.

It would never be a problem.

But now it was.

He would deal with it.

He was older now, calmer now. He was more careful now.

Loose ends to snip. If one of them turned out to be Meg Galloway, he'd be sorry. But he had to protect himself.

He supposed it was best if he began to do so right away.

He shouldered his rifle and left the dogs gobbling up the last of the meat.

HE'D PREPARED EVERYTHING. Standing in the darkened office, he saw nothing, thought of nothing he'd missed. They'd need to talk, of course. It was only right, only fair. He was a fair man.

Still, it was dangerous for him to be here at this time of night. If he was seen, he'd need reasons, excuses. Plausible deniability, he thought with a half smile.

It had been so long since he'd done anything danger-ous. So long since he'd been the man who climbed mountains and lived large. The taste of it awakened that old excitement.

That's why they'd called him Darth once. For his ruthlessness and love of dark deeds. It's what had pushed him to do the reckless and the sublime. It's what had urged him to kill a friend.

But that had been a different man, he reminded him-self. He'd remade himself. What he did now wasn't for pleasure or for curiosity. It was to protect the innocent man he'd become.

He had the right to do that.

So when his old friend came through the back door, he was waiting quietly. Calm as ice.

Max Hawbaker jolted when he saw the man sitting behind the desk. "How'd you get in?"

"You know you leave the back open half the time." He rose, movements relaxed and easy. "I couldn't stand around outside waiting for you. Someone might have seen me."

"All right, all right." Max dragged off his coat, tossed it aside. "It's crazy meeting here at the paper in the middle of the damn night. You could have come to the house."

"Carrie might hear. You never told her any of this. You swore."

"No, I never told her." Max swiped a hand over his face. "Mother of God, you said he'd fallen. You said he went crazy and cut the rope. That he'd gone down in a crevice."

"I know what I said. I couldn't tell you the truth. It

was horrible enough, wasn't it? You were banged up and delirious when I got back to you. I saved your life, Max. I got you down."

"But—"

"I saved your life."

"Yes. All right, yes."

"I'll explain everything. Get out that bottle you keep in your drawer. We need a drink."

"All these years. All these years, he's been up there. Like that." He *did* need a drink and grabbed two coffee mugs, then the bottle of Paddy's out of his drawer. "What am I supposed to think? What am I supposed to do?"

"He tried to kill me. I can still hardly believe it." Plausible deniability, he thought again.

"Pat? Pat tried to—"

"Luke—remember? Skywalker, the Jedi knight. The more drugs he took, the crazier he got. It stopped being a game. When he reached the summit, he wanted to jump, and damned near dragged us both off."

"My God. My God."

"He said it was a joke, after, but I knew it wasn't. We were coming down, rappelling down the face, and he took out his knife. Christ God, he started sawing at my rope and laughing. I barely got to the ledge when he cut it through. I took off."

"I can't believe it." Max swallowed whiskey, poured more. "I can't believe any of this."

"I couldn't believe it when it was happening. He'd lost his mind. The drugs, the altitude, hell, I don't know. I got to the ice cave. I was panicked. I was furious. He came after me."

"Why didn't you tell me any of this before?"

"I didn't think you'd believe me. I took the easy way out. You'd've done the same."

"I don't know." Max dragged a hand through his thinning hair.

"You *did* take the easy way. When you thought he'd fallen, you agreed to keep your mouth shut. You agreed not to say anything at all, to anyone. Patrick Galloway took off, parts unknown. End of story."

"I don't know why I did it."

"Three thousand came in handy for your paper, didn't it?"

Max flushed, stared into his glass. "Maybe it was wrong to take it. Maybe it was. I just wanted to put it all behind me. I was trying to start something here. I didn't know him that well, not really, and he was gone. We couldn't change that, so it didn't seem to matter. And you said, you said how there'd be an investigation if we told anyone we'd been up there, that he'd died up there."

"There would've been. The drugs would've come out, Max, you know it. You couldn't afford another drug bust. You couldn't afford to have the cops wondering if you—if either of us—had been responsible for his death. However he died, that's still true, isn't it?"

"Yes. But now—"

"I had to defend myself. He came at me with the knife. He came at me. He said the mountain needed a sacrifice. I tried to get away; I couldn't. I grabbed the ax and . . ." He cupped his hands around the mug, pretended to drink. "Oh, God."

"It was self-defense. I'll back you up."

"How? You weren't there."

Max gulped down whiskey as a bead of sweat trickled down his temple. "They're bound to find out we went up there. There's an investigation. Cops are involved now, and we can't avoid it. They'll backtrack. Maybe they'll find the pilot who took us up."

"I don't think so."

"It looks like murder, and they'll dig. Dig enough and they'll identify us. People saw us with him in Anchorage. They might remember. It's better to come forward now, to give them the whole story, explain what happened. Before they charge one or both of us with murder. We've got reputations, positions, professions. Jesus, I've got Carrie and the kids to think of. I need to tell Carrie, to explain all this to her before we go to the police."

"What do you think will happen to our reputations, our positions if this comes out?"

"We can weather it, if we go to the police and tell them everything."

"That's the way you want to play it?"

"It's the way we *have* to play it. I've been thinking about this since they found him. I've been working it all out. We need to go to the cops before the cops come looking for us."

"Maybe you're right. Maybe you are." He set the mug down, rose as if to pace back and forth behind Max's chair. He drew a glove out of his pocket, slid it onto his right hand. "I need a little more time. To think. To put things in order in case . . ."

"Let's take another day." Max reached for the bottle

again. "Give us both time. We'll go to Chief Burke first, get him behind us."

"You think that'll work?" His voice was soft now, with a hint of amusement in it.

"I do. I really do."

"This works better for me." From behind, he grabbed Max's right hand, clamped his own over it on the butt of the gun. And hooking his left around Max's throat, jammed the barrel to his temple. His old friend reared back in shock, gulped for air. And he pulled the trigger.

The explosion was huge in the small room and sent his hand to shaking. But he made sure to press Max's limp finger to the trigger. Fingerprints, he thought, his mind bell-clear even as he shuddered. Gunpowder residue. He released his hold so Max's head fell to the desk and the gun clattered to the floor beside the chair.

Carefully, with his gloved hand, he turned on the computer, and brought up the document he'd written while waiting for his friend to meet him.

I can't live with it any longer. His ghost has come back to haunt me. I'm sorry for what I did, for everyone I hurt.

Forgive me.

I killed Patrick Galloway. And now I'll join him in Hell.

Maxwell Hawbaker

Simple, clear-cut. He approved it and left the computer on. The light from the screen and the flare from the desk lamp shone on blood and gray matter.

He stuffed the soiled glove in a plastic bag, pushed that into the pocket of his coat before putting it on. He donned fresh gloves, his hat, scarf, then picked up the coffee mug—the only thing in the room he'd touched without gloves.

Walking into the bathroom, he poured the whiskey down the sink, rinsed the sink with water. He wiped the mug clean, then carried it back to the office and set it down again.

Max's eyes stared at him, and something about it forced bile up into his throat. But he swallowed it down, forced himself to stand and study the details. Satisfied he'd overlooked nothing, he left the way he'd come in.

He took the side streets, making sure his scarf was over his face, his hat low on his head in case some insomniac looked out a window.

Above him, the sky streamed with the northern lights.

He'd done what he'd had to do, he told himself. Now it was over.

When he got home, washed away the scent of cordite and blood that clung to him, he had a single short whiskey as he watched the old glove burn up in the fire.

There was nothing left now, so he put it all cleanly out of his mind.

And slept the sleep of the innocent.

THIRTEEN

CARRIE STOPPED BY The Lodge on the way to the paper to pick up a couple of bacon-and-egg sandwiches. She'd been surprised, then a little annoyed to find Max gone when she'd wakened. Not that it was the first time he'd gone back to the paper at night, and ended up sleeping there. Or left early in the morning before either she or the kids were awake.

But he always left her some sweet or silly note on his pillow when he did.

There'd been no note that morning, and no answer when she'd called the paper.

It wasn't like him. But then, he hadn't been himself for the last several days. That was starting to annoy her, too.

There was a *huge* story brewing, what with Patrick Galloway's body being discovered. *Allegedly* Pat Galloway's body, she reminded herself. They needed to decide how to handle the story, how much space they'd want to devote to it—and if they should get their butts down to Anchorage when the body was finally brought down.

She'd already dug through her old snapshots and had culled several of Pat. They'd want to run his picture along with the story.

And pictures of the three boys who'd found him. She wanted to interview them, certainly Steven Wise, who was a hometown boy. Rather she wanted Max to do so, as he was better at interviewing than she was.

Max wouldn't talk about it. Why, he'd even snapped at her once when she'd brought it up.

Time for him to go in to the clinic and get himself a physical. He tended to get a delicate stomach when he wasn't eating or sleeping right. Which he hadn't been, come to think of it, since news came down about the Galloway business.

Maybe it was because they were of an age, she mused as she pulled up at the curb in front of *The Lunatic*. And that he'd known the man a little. They'd struck up a friendship in the few months Max had been in Lunacy before Pat ... . left. Best to leave it at *left* until they had all the facts.

But she didn't see why Max should take out his middle-aged blues or whatever on her.

She'd actually known Pat longer than Max had, and she wasn't going into a funk. She was sorry, of course, for Charlene and Meg—they'd have to be interviewed, too—and she intended to give them both her condolences in person as soon as she could.

But it was *news*. The sort she and Max should be investigating and writing about for the paper. For God's sake, they had the hometown advantage here. It could mean having their articles picked up by the wire services.

Well, she was going to make that doctor's appointment for him herself, then nag him into keeping it. They had a hell of a lot to do, what with the Galloway story and their plans to cover the Iditarod. Lord, it was already almost February, and March first nearly on them. They needed to get started if they were going to get any color on the race before deadline.

She needed her man in tip-top shape—and she'd remind him of it at the top of her lungs if need be.

She climbed out of the car with the take-out bag steaming fragrance and already spotted with grease. And shook her head when she saw the faint wash of light from the rear of their storefront operation. Max had fallen asleep at his desk again, she'd bet the bank.

"Carrie."

"Hi, Jim." She stopped on the sidewalk to talk to the bartender. "Early for you."

"Need some supplies." He nodded toward The Corner Store. "Weather's supposed to stay clear, so I thought I'd do a little fishing." He glanced in the paper's window at the light. "Somebody else is starting early."

"You know Max."

"Nose for news," he said, tapping his own. "Hey, Professor. Time for school?"

John stopped to make it a trio. "Just about. Thought I'd walk it while I have the chance. Radio said we might break thirty today."

"Spring's coming," Carrie announced. "And this breakfast is getting cold. I'd better get in and give Max a shove off his desk."

"Got anything on the Galloway story?" John asked her.

She dragged out her keys. "If there's anything to get, we'll have it for the next edition. Have a good one."

After letting herself in, she flipped on the lights. "Max! Rise and shine!" She clamped the take-out bag between her teeth to free her hands. She stripped off her coat, hung it on a peg. She stuffed her gloves in one pocket, her hat in the other.

As a matter of habit, she finger-fluffed her flattened hair.

"Max!" she called again, stopping by her desk to turn on her computer. "I got breakfast, though I don't know why I'm so good to you seeing as you've been cranky as a constipated bear lately."

Setting the bag down, she moved to the coffeemaker and carried the carafe into the bathroom to fill. "Bacon-and-egg sandwiches. I just saw Skinny Jim and The Professor out on the street. Well, I saw The Professor at The Lodge first, finishing up his oatmeal before school. Looks pretty chipper for a change. I wonder if he's thinking, now that Charlene knows her old flame's dead, she's going to settle down with him. Poor slob."

She started the coffee, then dug out paper plates and napkins for the sandwiches. Under her breath she was humming "Tiny Dancer," the Elton John number that had been playing on her favorite classic rock station on the drive in.

"Maxwell Hawbaker, I don't know why I put up with you. If you're going to be sullen and sulky much longer, I'm going hunting for a happier, younger man. See if I don't."

With a plated sandwich in each hand, she started back to Max's little office. "But before I leave you for my wild, sexual affair with a twenty-five-year-old stud, I'm hauling your dumpy ass to the clinic for . . ."

She stopped in the doorway, and her limp hands folded out at the wrists. The sandwiches plopped, one-two, onto the floor. Through the roar in her ears, she heard the screaming.

NATE HAD HIS SECOND CUP of coffee while he discussed the LEGO castle he and Jesse were building as their morning project. He'd had the first at Meg's, and most of his mind was still back there with her.

She'd be flying north today, delivering supplies, then stopping off at Fairbanks to buy items for the locals here. For her fee of five percent tacked on to the purchase price, they could save themselves the round trip to one of the cities—a choice that wasn't always possible in winter—and have her do the shopping, the transporting and the delivery.

It was, she'd told him, a small but steady portion of her business.

He'd gotten a look at her office that morning, too. It was just as bold and stylish as the rest of the place, and set up for comfort and efficiency.

A sturdy, crate-style desk, a tough-looking black computer with a wide, flat screen. Leather executive chair, he remembered, an old-fashioned freestanding clock and a lot of black-framed, arty pencil sketches on the wall.

There'd been a huge plant, something that had looked like long, green tongues—in a glossy, red pot, snow-white file cabinets and a star-shaped crystal suncatcher hanging from a chain in front of the window.

He'd found it both practical and female.

They'd made no plans for later. She shook off the notion of plans, and he thought that was just as well. He needed some time to think. About what direction they were or might be taking.

His scorecard with women was pitifully low. Maybe he had a chance to change that with her. Or maybe it was just the moment, an interim sort of thing. There was a lot waking up inside him after a long, dark sleep. How did he know what was real? Or if it was real, if he could keep it that way.

If he wanted to.

Better, for now, to drink his coffee, eat his breakfast and build a plastic castle with a kid who was just happy to have the company.

"It should have a bridge," Jesse said. "The up-and-down bridge."

"Drawbridge?" Nate pulled his attention back. "We might be able to work that. We could get some fishing wire."

The boy looked up at him and beamed. "Okay!"

"Here you go, Chief."

He caught Rose's wince when she set his plate down. "Okay?"

"Back's a little stiff. Had the same thing with this one." She ruffled her son's hair.

"Maybe you ought to see the doctor."

"I've got a checkup today. Jesse, you let Chief Burke eat his breakfast while it's hot."

"We need fishing wire for the bridge."

She left her hand on his head another moment. "We'll get you some."

She looked over as Skinny Jim stumbled in the door. "Jim?"

"Chief. Chief. You gotta come. Come quick. At the paper. It's Max. Oh, my God."

"What happened?" But he held up a hand even as he said it. He could see from the ghost-white pallor of Jim's face, the wide, glazed eyes that it was bad. And beside him the little boy was watching with his rosebud mouth opened in a stunned O. "Wait."

He got up fast, grabbed his coat. "Outside." And he gripped the man's trembling arm, pulling him out the door. "What is it?"

"He's dead. Sweet Jesus God. Max is dead, shot dead. Half his head—half his head's gone."

Nate yanked Jim up when the man's legs buckled. "Max Hawbaker? You found him?"

"Yes. No. I mean, yes, it's Max. Carrie. Carrie found him. We heard her screaming. She went inside, and The Professor and I were standing there talking for a minute, and she started screaming like somebody was killing her. We ran in, and . . . and . . ."

Nate continued to drag him down the street. "You touch anything?"

"What? I don't think. No. The Professor said to go get you, to go to The Lodge and get you. That's what I did." He was swallowing fast and often. "Think I'm going to be sick."

"No, you're not. You're going to go to the station house, get Otto. You're going to tell him what you just told me and that I need a camera, some evidence bags, some plastic gloves, the crime scene tape. Just tell him I need crime scene equipment. Can you remember that?"

"I—yeah. I'll do it. I'll do it right now."

"Then stay there. You stay at the station until I come to talk to you. Don't talk to anybody else. Go."

Nate angled toward the paper and quickened his pace. His brain had gone on auto, and preserving the scene was key. Right now, as far as he knew, there were two civilians in there, which meant it was already compromised.

He yanked open the door, and saw John kneeling on the floor in front of a sobbing Carrie. John was still wearing his outdoor gear, minus his gloves, and was pressing a glass of water to Carrie's lips. He looked up at Nate, and a shadow of relief moved across his shocked face.

"Thank God. Max. Back there."

"Stay here. Keep her here."

He started toward the back office. He could smell it. You could always smell it. No, he corrected, not true. There would be no smell of death in the ice cave where Galloway waited. Nature would have covered it.

But he could smell Max Hawbaker's death even before he saw it. As he could smell, beneath it, the fried eggs and bacon from the two sandwiches on the floor just over the threshold.

His gaze scanned the room from the doorway, the placement of the body, the gun, the nature of the wound. It said suicide. But he knew the first murmur from a crime scene was often a lie.

He moved in, keeping to the edges of the room, noting the pattern of the blood spatter on the chair, the computer screen, the keyboard. And the pool of it from the head wound that had soaked the desk and dripped onto the floor before death had turned off the pump.

Powder burns, he noted. The barrel of the .22 had probably been directly against the temple. No exit wound. And unlike Jim's babbling statement, the insult to the face was minor. The bullet had left a relatively neat hole before it entered the brain and bounced around gleefully, like a pinball hitting top score.

Dead, most likely, before his head had hit the desk.

Noting the swirling pattern of color from the screen saver, Nate drew a pen out of his pocket and moved in close enough to tap the mouse.

The document sprang on-screen.

His eyes narrowed as he read it, stayed narrowed as he looked down at the body of the man who claimed to have killed Patrick Galloway.

He moved back to the doorway, then signaled for Otto to wait when the deputy rushed in the front. Nate walked to Carrie, and like John, crouched down.

"Carrie."

"Max. Max." She raised red, horrified eyes to his. "Max is dead. Somebody—"

"I know. I'm so sorry." He clasped his hands over hers. "I'm going to help him now. I need you to go over to the station and wait for me."

"But Max. I can't leave Max."

"You can leave him with me. I'm going to take care of him. John's going to help you get into your coat. And in a minute, he and Otto will take you over. I'm going to be there as soon as I can. So you go over there, and you wait for me."

She stared dully, shock still glazing her eyes. "Wait for you."

"That's right." She'd do what he said. The shock and the horror would make her obedient. For a while. "Otto?"

He rose, moved toward the back again.

"Merciful God," Otto said under his breath.

"I need you to take both of them over. Jim's still there?"

"Yeah." He swallowed audibly. "Jesus, Chief."

"Keep them there, and keep them separated. Let Peach take care of Carrie for now. I want you to call Peter in, tell him to come straight here."

"I'm here now. Peter can ride herd over at the station while—"

"I need you to start taking statements. You'll handle that better than Peter. Start with Jim. I want the doctor here, too. You get in touch with Ken and tell him to come straight here. I want him standing in. I don't want any mistakes on this, and I want it kept quiet until we have this scene secured and the statements on file. Use a tape recorder. Get the time and the date on it and take notes as a backup. Keep everyone there, everyone in separate places until I get back. You got that?"

"Yeah." He swiped a hand over his mouth. "Why the hell would Max kill himself? That's what it is, isn't it? Suicide?"

"Let's work the scene and the witnesses, Otto. Let's take it a step at a time."

When he was alone, he picked up the camera Otto had brought in to record the scene. He went through one pack of film, reloaded and shot a second.

Then taking out a notebook, he wrote down details. The fact that the rear door was unlocked, the make and caliber of the gun, the exact wording of the note on-screen. He did a rough sketch of the room, adding in the position of the body, the gun, the lamp, the bottle of whiskey and the single mug.

He had on his gloves and was sniffing at both bottle and mug when Peter came in.

"Take the crime scene tape, Peter. I want you to use it on the front and back doors."

"I got here as soon as I could—" Peter broke off when he reached the doorway.

When Peter's skin tinged with green, Nate snapped at him. "You don't get sick in here. You have to puke, you do it outside and take that tape with you."

Peter angled his body away, looked hard at the wall and breathed through his mouth. "Otto said Max killed himself, but I didn't think—"

"We haven't determined that. What we have determined is Max is dead. Right now, this is a crime scene, and I want it secured. Nobody gets in here but the doctor. Clear?"

"Yes, sir." Peter fumbled the yellow tape out of the box Otto had thrown together and then staggered back outside.

"State boys are going to want you, Max," he murmured. "It looks like you're going to tie things up for them, with a fucking bow on top. Maybe that's just what you did. But I'm not a big believer in bows."

He walked out and, with his hands still gloved, called Sergeant Coben in Anchorage.

"I'm not leaving this body sitting here until you can fly in from Anchorage," he said after he'd given Coben the essentials. "You've run me by now. You know I'm qualified. I've secured and recorded the scene, and I've got a doctor on the way in. I'm gathering the evidence and having the body moved to the clinic. Everything I've got's at your disposal once you get here."

He waved Ken inside when the doctor came to the door. "And I expect the same cooperation regarding the Galloway investigation. This is my town, Sergeant. We both want to nail this down, but we're going to have to share the hammer. I'll be expecting you."

He hung up. "I need you to look at the body. Can you give me an approximate time of death?"

"So it's true. Max is dead." Ken slipped his fingers under his glasses, pressed them to his eyes. "I've never had to do this sort of thing before, but I should be able to give you a ballpark."

"Good enough. Put these on." Nate handed him a pair of gloves. "It's not pretty," he added.

Ken stepped in, then took a moment to visibly steady himself. "I've dealt with gunshot wounds. But nothing quite like this, not when I knew the victim. Why the hell'd he do this to himself? The winters can prey on people, but he's been through them before. Worse than this. He wasn't suffering from depression. Carrie would've told me, or I'd've seen it myself." He flicked a quick glance at Nate.

"I never thought about killing myself. Too much effort. If I change my mind, I'll try to let you know first."

"Feeling better these days?"

"Some days. Ready now?"

Ken squared his shoulders. "Yeah, thanks." He stepped over. "Can I touch him? Move him at all?"

He had the photographs and had outlined the body in crime scene tape for lack of something better. So he nodded.

Leaning down, Ken lifted one of Max's hands. Pinched the skin. "I'd do better if I could get him to the clinic, strip the body, do a more thorough exam."

"You'll get your chance. Give me an approximation."

"Well, digging back into my student days, and figuring the temperature of the room, the state of rigor, I'd guess between eight and twelve hours. That's really rough, Nate."

"So, that would be somewhere between nine P.M and one A.M. Good enough. We might be able to close that in some with Carrie's statement. I'm going to send Peter for a body bag. I need you to put the body somewhere secure—and cold."

"I've got the area we use as a makeshift morgue when we have a death."

"That'll work. I don't want you talking about this to anyone. Keep him under wraps until I get there."

He supervised the transfer of the body, made a print-out of the note on the computer before shutting it down. Once he'd locked the doors, he started back to the station.

Hopp ran him down.

"I need to know what the holy hell is going on."

"I'm still working that out. What I can tell you is that Max Hawbaker was found dead at his desk at the paper, apparently from a gunshot wound to the head. Possibly self-inflicted."

"Oh, God. Oh, god*damn* it. Possibly?" She trotted to keep up with him and plucked at his sleeve when he outdistanced her. "What do you mean possibly? You think he was murdered?"

"I didn't say that. I'm looking into it, Hopp. The State Police have been notified and will be here in a few hours. When I have answers, I'll let you know. Let me do my job." He hauled open the door of the station. And shut it in her face.

He took the time in the Arctic entry to pull off his gear and try to clear his mind. The sun was up now, and the day as clear as the forecasters had promised.

They'd be heading up to retrieve Galloway today, he thought. And maybe, they'd be flying in to pick up the body of his killer. Two for one.

He'd see about that.

He opened the inner door and found John sitting in one of the wait chairs, reading a paperback copy of *Watership Down*. John got to his feet, stuffed the book in his back pocket without marking his place. "Peach has Carrie back in your office. Otto's with Jim back in a cell. Not locked up," he added quickly. Then sighed. "Hard to think."

"Otto get your statement?"

"Yes. There wasn't that much to tell. I left The Lodge, took a walk, heading to school. I saw Jim and

Carrie, stopped for a minute to talk to them. Carrie had breakfast in a bag—and the light was on in Max's office. You could see the backwash of it through the window. She went in, and Jim and I stood there another couple minutes talking. He was going to pick up some bait. Going fishing. He likes to rib me about it because I don't hunt or fish."

He began to rub the left side of his jaw as if it ached. "Next thing we knew, Carrie's screaming. We ran in, and we saw him. Saw Max."

He closed his eyes, drew a couple of breaths. "I'm sorry. I've never seen anyone dead before—not until they were . . . prepared for viewing."

"Take your time."

"I, ah, I pulled Carrie back. Didn't know what else to do. Yanked her away, and I said, 'Jim, the Chief's at The Lodge. Go get him.' Carrie was hysterical. I sat her down, held her down at first because she wanted to go back to Max. Then I got her some water and just stayed there until you came in. That's it."

"Any of you go in the room?"

"No. Well, Carrie was just inside the room. She was standing maybe, I don't know, a step or two inside. She was holding a paper plate in each hand. She'd dropped the sandwiches and was just standing there screaming, with a plate in each hand."

"How long between the time you heard her screaming and the time you reached her?"

"Maybe thirty seconds. Nate, she sounded like someone was carving her up with a knife. We both reacted. We were through the door fast. Probably less than thirty."

"Okay. I may need to talk to you again, and the State cop who's coming in will want to. Stay reachable. And I'd like to keep this quiet. Not much chance of it, but I'd like to."

"I'm going to go on into school." He checked his watch in an absent gesture. "Already late, but maybe it'll keep my mind off it. I'll be there most of the day."

"Appreciate the help."

"He always seemed so harmless," John said as he reached for his coat. "Benign, if you know what I mean. Always looking for a story in a place like this. Town gossip, local color, births. Deaths. I'd have said he was a contented man, running his little paper, raising his children."

"Hard to see under the surface sometimes."

"No doubt about it."

He went in to see Jim next, corroborated John's story. Once he'd sent the man on his way, Nate sat down on the bunk next to Otto.

"I've got Peter down at the clinic. I'm going to leave him there for now. He's a little shaken, and I was hard on him. I need you to start a canvass. Work your way out from the paper, talk to people who live nearby. Ask if anyone heard a gunshot last night. We're working on between nine P.M. and one A.M. right now. I want to know if anyone saw Max or anyone else around the building. When, where, who. If they heard a car, if they heard voices, if they heard or saw any damn thing, I want to know."

"State coming in?"

"Yeah."

Otto's face settled into bulldog lines. "I don't think that's right."

"Right or not, that's the way it is. Give Peter an hour, then pull him in to work the canvass with you. Ken can be trusted to keep the body locked away. Did you talk to Carrie?"

"Tried to. Didn't get much."

"It's all right. I'll talk to her now." He rose. "Otto, did Max know Patrick Galloway?"

"I don't know." He frowned. "Yeah, sure he did. It's hard remembering back that far. But it seems to me Max came along the summer before Pat disappeared. Was murdered," he corrected. "Max worked for a paper in Anchorage and decided he wanted his own rag, small-town deal. That's the story, anyway."

"Okay. Start the canvass."

As Nate approached his office door, he thought he heard singing. Crooning, he corrected, the way you might croon to a baby. Opening his door, he saw Carrie stretched out on a blanket on the floor, her head pillowed in Peach's ample lap. Peach stroked her hair and crooned.

She looked up when Nate entered. "Best I could do," she murmured. "Poor thing's broken to bits. Sleeping now. I, ah, happened to find some Xanax in your desk drawer. I cut one in half for her."

He had to ignore the twist of embarrassment. "I need to talk to her."

"Hate to wake her up. Still, she should be a little calmer than she was when Otto tried. You want me to stay?"

"No, but don't go far."

When he sat on the floor, Peach closed a hand over his

wrist. "I guess I don't have to tell you to be gentle. You'd know, and you've got that in you. But all the same . . ." She trailed off, stroked Carrie's cheek. "Carrie? Sweetie, you need to wake up now."

Carrie opened her eyes, and they were unfocused and dull. "What is it?"

"Nate's got to talk to you, baby. Can you sit up?"

"I don't understand." She rubbed her eyes like a child. "I had a dream . . ." She focused on Nate now, and those eyes filled. "Not a dream. Max. My Max." When her voice broke, Nate took her hand.

"I'm sorry, Carrie. I know this is hard, and I'm sorry. You want some water? Anything?"

"No. No. There's nothing." She pushed herself up, buried her face in her hands. "There's nothing."

Nate rose, helped Peach struggle her way to her feet. "I'll be right outside if you need me," she said and went out, closing the door quietly behind her.

"Do you want a chair, or do you want to stay where you are?"

"I feel like I'm still in a dream. Everything's floating inside my head."

He decided the floor would do, and he sat again. "Carrie, I need to ask you some questions. Look at me. What time did Max leave the house last night?"

"I don't know. I didn't know he was gone until I got up this morning. I was annoyed. He always leaves me a note on the pillow when he goes in to work at night or early in the morning."

"When did you see him last?"

"I saw—this morning—I saw—"

"No." He took her hand again, tried to lead her away from that image. "Before. Was he home for dinner?"

"Yes. We had chili. Max made it. He likes to brag about his chili. We all had dinner together."

"What did you do then?"

"We watched TV. Or I did. The kids watched a little, then Stella got on the phone with one of her friends, and Alex got on his computer. Max was restless. He said he was going to read a book, but he wasn't. I asked him what was up, and he was irritable with me."

A tear spilled over, tracked a lonely line down her cheek. "He said he was working something out, and couldn't I leave him the hell alone for five minutes. We got snappy with each other. Later, when the kids were in bed, he said he was sorry. He had something on his mind. But I was still mad and shrugged him off. We hardly spoke to each other when we went to bed."

"What time was that?"

"About ten-thirty, I guess. But no, that's not right. I went up to bed then, and he muttered something about staying up to watch CNN or something. I didn't pay attention because I was annoyed. I went up to bed early because I was mad and didn't want to be with him. Now he's gone."

"He was still home at ten-thirty. You didn't hear him leave?"

"I just went straight to bed. I fell asleep. When I got up this morning, I knew he hadn't come to bed. He always pulls the sheets out from the bottom of the mattress. Drives me crazy. I thought maybe he'd been sulky and slept on the couch, but he wasn't there. I got the kids off to Ginny's. It was her turn to drive them in. Oh, my God. My God, the kids."

"Don't worry. They're being looked after. I'm going to get all of you home once we're done here. You went into town."

"I decided to forgive him. You can't stay mad at Max. And I was going to make him an appointment for a checkup. He's been off his feed for the last few days. I stopped to get us some breakfast, then I drove to the paper. I saw Jim and John, then I went in and found him. I found him. How could anybody hurt Max that way?"

"Carrie, did he ever leave the back door of the paper unlocked?"

"All the time. He never remembered to lock up. Why bother, he'd say. If somebody really wanted to get in, they'd just kick the door in anyway."

"Did he own a handgun?"

"Sure. A few of them. Everybody does."

"A .22? A .22 Browning pistol."

"Yes. Yes. I need to get my kids."

"In a minute. Where did he keep that gun?"

"That one? In the glove compartment of his truck. He liked to use it to target shoot, mostly. Sometimes he'd like to stop on the way home from work and shoot a few cans. Working out a story idea, he'd say."

"Did he ever say anything to you about Patrick Galloway?"

"Of course. Everybody's talking about Galloway these days."

"I mean specifically. About himself and Galloway."

"Why would he? They only knew each other for a little while before Pat left."

Nate weighed his options. She was next-of-kin and had to be told. It might as well be now. "There was a note written on his computer."

She knuckled at tears. "What kind of a note?"

Nate rose again, opened the file he'd put on his desk. "I'm going to let you read a copy of it. It's not going to be easy, Carrie."

"I want to see it now."

Nate handed it to her, waited. He saw what little color that had come back into her face drain off again. But her eyes, rather than going dull with shock, went hot.

"This is wrong. This is crazy. This is a *lie!*" As if to prove it, she sprang to her feet and ripped the printout into shreds. "This is a terrible lie, and you should be ashamed. My Max never hurt a living soul in his life. How dare you? How dare you try to say he killed someone and killed *himself*."

"I'm just showing you what was on his computer."

"And I'm telling you it's a lie. Somebody killed my husband, and you'd better do your job and find out who did this. Whoever hurt my Max put this lie on there, and if you believe it for one second, you can go to hell."

She ran out of the room, and seconds later, he heard her fractured weeping.

He slipped out, saw her enveloped in Peach's arms. "See that she and her kids get home," he said quietly, then eased back into his office.

For a time he just stood, studying the torn shreds of paper on the floor.

FOURTEEN

HOPP KEPT AN OFFICE at Town Hall. It wasn't much bigger than a broom closet and was furnished in that same haphazard style, but since Nate wanted to keep the meeting formal, he arranged to meet her there.

As she was wearing full makeup and a dark suit, he figured they were on the same page.

"Chief Burke." The words were two quick bites, the gesture of her hand toward a chair a short jab.

He could smell the coffee from the mug on her desk, and the pot behind her on the short counter was nearly full. He wasn't asked to help himself.

"I'm going to apologize for being abrupt with you this morning," he began, "but you got in my way at the wrong time."

"I'll remind you that you work for me."

"I work for the people of this town. And one of them's stretched out on a table in our part-time morgue. That means he's my priority, Mayor. You're not."

The mouth she'd painted a bold crimson tightened. He heard her long, hissing inhale, and the slow expulsion of air. "Be that as it may, I *am* mayor of this town, which makes its residents my chief concern as well. I was hardly sniffing around for gossip and resent being treated as if I were."

"And be that as *it* may, I had a job to do. Part of that was the full intention of giving you a report once I'd completed my preliminary. Which I'm prepared to do now."

"I don't like your snippy attitude."

"Right back at you."

This time her mouth dropped open, her eyes flared. "Obviously your mother didn't teach you to respect your elders."

"Guess it didn't take. Then again, she doesn't like me, either."

She drummed her fingers on her desk—short, practical and unpainted nails that didn't go with the red mouth or business suit. "You know what pisses me off right now?"

"I'm sure you're going to tell me."

"The fact that I'm not mad at you anymore. I like holding on to a good mad. But you had a point earlier about the people of this town being your priority. I respect that, because I know you mean it. Max was a friend, Ignatious. A good one. I'm upset about this."

"I know. I'm sorry for that, and I'll apologize again for not being more . . ."

"Sensitive, courteous, forthcoming?"

"Take your pick."

"All right, let's move on." She pulled out a tissue, blew her nose enthusiastically. "Get yourself some coffee, and tell me what's what."

"Thanks, but I've already downed about a gallon. As far as I can piece together, Max left his house sometime after ten-thirty last night. He'd had a spat with his wife—nothing too serious, but she claims he'd been off the last few days. She pinpoints it to the time the news hit about the discovery of Patrick Galloway's body."

Hopp's forehead wrinkled; the lines around her mouth deepened. "Why would that be, I wonder. I don't recall they knew each other all that well. Seems to me they hit it off well enough, but Max hadn't been here long when Patrick went missing."

"I don't have any evidence, as yet, that points to Max making any stops before going to his office at the paper. Sometime, if the doc's estimate is correct, before one A.M., he—or person or persons unknown—put a bullet in his brain through his right temple."

"Why would anybody—" She caught herself, waved him on. "Sorry. Go ahead and finish."

"From the on-scene evidence, the deceased was sitting at his desk at the time. The back door was unlocked, which I'm told was fairly habitual. His computer was on, as was the desk light. He had a partial bottle of Paddy's whiskey on the desk and a coffee mug with about a fingerful of whiskey left in it. It'll be analyzed, but I didn't detect any other substance in the mug."

"God. I just saw him yesterday morning."

"Did he seem off to you?"

"I don't know. Can't say I was paying attention." She pressed steepled hands to the bridge of her nose, held them there a moment, then dropped them. "Now that you mention it, maybe he was distracted. But I can't think of any reason he'd do this to himself. He and

Carrie had a good marriage. His kids aren't in any more trouble than kids that age are. He loved running the paper. Maybe he was sick? Maybe he'd found out he had cancer or something and couldn't face it."

"Clean bill of health last checkup at the clinic. Six months ago. The weapon found on scene was his, duly registered. According to his wife it was one he most often kept in the glove compartment of his truck. For target shooting. There was no sign of struggle."

"Poor Max." She grabbed another tissue, but rather than use it, just balled it in her fist. "What could have driven him to end his own life, to do that not just to himself, but his family?"

"There was a note on his computer. It claimed he'd killed Patrick Galloway."

"What?" The coffee she'd just lifted lapped at the top of the mug as she set it down again. "Ignatious, that's crazy. Max? That's just crazy."

"He used to climb, didn't he? More fifteen, sixteen years ago than now?"

"Well, yes. Yes. But half the people in town do or did some climbing." She laid the flat of her hands on the desk. "I will not believe that Max killed anyone."

"You were prepared to believe he killed himself."

"Because he's *dead*. Because everything I've heard points to it. But murder? That's nonsense."

"There'll be tests run to verify the .22 in evidence was used. Fingerprints, powder residue. I'm going to tell you that I believe the tests will substantiate what appears to be a suicide, and that in all likelihood his death will be of-

ficially ruled same—just as the Galloway homicide will be
closed."

"I can't believe this."

"I'm also going to tell you I'm not convinced."

"Ignatious." She pressed her hand to her temple.
"You're confusing me."

"Awfully neat, isn't it? A computer note? Anybody
can tap a few keys. Guilt kills him after all these years?
Well, he lived with it pretty well up to now. Carrie said
he left her a note on his pillow whenever he decided to
go into work late or early. A man does that, but he
doesn't leave a personal note for her when he decides to
kill himself?"

"You're saying . . ."

"Easy to get a gun out of a glove compartment, if you
know it's there. Not that hard to stage a suicide if you
think it through and keep your blood cool."

"You think . . . God, you think Max was murdered?"

"I didn't say that, either. I said I'm not convinced this
is what it looks like on the surface. So, if this is ruled a
suicide and the Galloway case is closed before I am convinced, I'm going to keep looking into it. You're paying
me, so you ought to know if I'm spending official time
chasing a wild goose."

She stared at him, then he heard her take another of
those long, audible breaths. "What can I do to help?"

SERGEANT ROLAND COBEN struck Nate as a solid cop,
a twenty-year man with a lot of cases under his belt. He

was about six feet, a little thick through the middle, a little tired around the eyes. He had a crisp white-blond crew cut, a regulation shine on his boots and a wad of cherry-scented gum in his mouth.

He'd brought a two-man crime scene unit with him, and both officers were busy combing Max's office while Coben studied the photographs Nate had taken.

"Who's been on this scene since the body was discovered?"

"Me, the town doctor and one of my deputies. Before I let them in, I took the pictures, ran the outline, bagged evidence. Everyone gloved up. The scene's secure, Sergeant."

Coben looked over at the grease stains on the rug just inside the inner door. Nate had dutifully bagged the sandwiches as well. "That as far as the wife got?"

"According to her and the two witnesses, yes. And no one but me touched anything but the body."

Coben made some sound of assent and studied the note on the computer screen. "We'll take the computer with us, along with the evidence you gathered. Let's have a look at the body."

Nate led him out the back.

"Worked Homicide Outside, didn't you?"

"I did."

Coben climbed easily into Nate's four-wheel. "That's handy. Lost your partner, I hear."

"That's right."

"Took a couple of hits yourself."

"I'm still standing."

Coben dutifully hooked his seat belt. "A lot of medical leave, on and off, your last year with Baltimore."

Nate leveled one quiet look. "I'm not on medical leave now."

"Your lieutenant says you're a good cop and maybe you lost some of your edge, some of your confidence, after your partner went down. Turned in your badge down there last fall and broke off with the department shrink."

Nate stopped in front of the clinic. "You ever lose a partner?"

"No." Coben waited a minute. "But I've lost a couple of friends, line of duty. Just trying to get a feel for you, Chief Burke. City cop from Outside, one with your experience, might get his back up when he has to pass a big case on to State authorities."

"He might. And a State cop might not have the same investment in this town, and what goes on here, as its chief of police."

"You haven't been chief very long." He stepped out of the car. "Maybe we both got a point. The department's been able to handle the press on The Ice Man—they just love to name these violent-crime victims."

"Always do."

"Well, they're holding the line on the media now, but that changes once the team brings him down. It's going to be big, fat news, Chief Burke. The sort the national media loves to cover. Now you've got the body of the man claiming to be his killer, and there's more news. Quicker we wrap this up, the better it is for everybody. The neater we wrap it, the better."

Nate stayed on the opposite side of the car. "Are you worried about me going to the media, stirring up publicity for myself, for the town?"

"Just a comment, that's all. There was a lot of press out of that shooting in Baltimore. A lot of it focused on you."

Nate felt the heat rising in him, the long, slow simmer of anger that bubbled from gut to throat. "So you figure I must like seeing my name in print, seeing my face on TV, and a couple of dead men give me the opportunity to tune that up."

"You could earn yourself some points, seems to me, if you're planning on going back to Baltimore."

"Then it's pretty lucky for me that I happened to come here just in time for all this to go down."

"Doesn't hurt to be in the right place at the right time."

"Are you trying to provoke me, or are you just a natural asshole?"

Coben's lips quirked. "Could be both. Mostly I'm just trying to get a feel for things."

"Then let's clear this up. This is your investigation. That's procedure. But this is still my town; these are still my people. That's a fact. And whether or not you trust me, like me, or want to take me to dinner and a movie, I'm going to do my job."

"Then we'd better take a look at the body."

Coben headed inside, and fighting off temper, Nate followed.

There was only one person in the waiting area. Bing looked embarrassed, then irritated to have been found sitting on one of the plastic chairs.

"Bing," Nate said with a nod, and the man grunted before jerking the ancient copy of *Alaska* in front of his face.

"Doc's with a patient," Joanna said, giving Coben a good once-over. "Sal Cushaw cut her hand on a hacksaw, and he's stitching her up. She needs a tetanus shot, too."

"We need the keys to the morgue," Nate told her, and her eyes darted between him and Coben.

"Doc's got them, said nobody could go in there but you."

"This is Sergeant Coben, with the State Police. Would you go get the keys?"

"Sure. Okay."

She scurried away just as Bing began to mutter. "Don't need no storm troopers in Lunacy. Take care of our own."

Nate simply shook his head as Coben glanced over his shoulder. "Don't bother," he murmured.

"You sick, Bing?" Nate leaned back on the counter. "Or just passing the time?"

"My business is my business. Just like if a man wants to blow his head off, that's his business. Cops can't leave well enough alone."

"You're right about that. We're just pains in the ass with badges. When's the last time you talked to Max?"

"Never had much to say to him. Pip-squeak."

"I heard he bitched at you about plowing in his driveway, so you plowed it out and dumped the snow on top of his car."

Bing's grin spread in the mass of his beard. "Maybe. Don't think he blew his head off over it, though."

"You're a mean bastard, Bing."

"Damn right."

"Chief?" Joanna came back to the counter, held out the keys. "It's the one with the yellow mark. Doc said he'd come back as soon as he's finished with Sal."

"Hey! I'm next in line here." Bing rattled his magazine. "Hawbaker's not going to get any deader."

Joanna folded her lips. "You ought to have some respect, Bing."

"What I got is hemorrhoids."

"Tell the doc to finish with all his patients," Nate said. "Where is it?"

"Oh, sorry. Straight back, then the first door on the left."

They walked back in silence, and Nate used the key to unlock the door. They stepped into a room with a wall of metal shelves and two metal tables. Nate switched on the overhead and noted both tables were the style used for autopsies or funeral parlor prep rooms.

"I'm told they use this as a part-time morgue. There's no funeral parlor in town, no undertaker. They bring one in when they need one, and he'll prep a body for burial here."

He walked to the table where Max was laid out, uncovered to preserve any possible trace evidence, as per Nate's orders. The body's hands were bagged.

"Nails are chewed down below the quick on his right hand," Nate pointed out. "Cut on his bottom lip. Looks like he bit it."

"No defensive wounds evident. Powder burns around the wound. Can we confirm he was right-handed?"

"We can. We have."

Sealing the hands meant preserving them for residue testing. There were photographs of the body, of the scene, even of the outer door from every possible angle. Witness statements had been taken and typed up while the witnesses were fresh, and the building locked tight and sealed with police tape.

Burke had run a clean scene, Coben thought, and had saved him considerable work.

"We'll go over him here to see if we can find any trace evidence. Did you go through his pockets?"

"Wallet, open roll of Tums, loose change, book of matches, notebook, pencil. He had his driver's license, credit cards, about thirty in cash, family pictures in his wallet. Cell phone, another book of matches and a pair of wool gloves in the pockets of the coat in his office."

Nate slipped his hands into his own pockets, continued to study the body. "I went through the truck parked outside the scene. Registration in the name of the vic and his spouse. Maps, operator's manual for the truck, an open pack of ammo for the .22, a roll of breath mints, several pens and pencils and another notebook in the glove compartment. A lot of hand-scribbled notes in the books—reminders, ideas for articles for the paper, observations, phone numbers. First-aid and emergency kits in the back of the cab. The truck was unlocked, keys in the ignition."

"Keys in the ignition?"

"Yeah. Statements from acquaintances indicate he had a habit of leaving the keys in there and rarely remembered or thought to lock up. All removed items are bagged, labeled, listed. I've got them locked up back at the station."

"We'll take them, and him, in. Let the ME make his determinations. But it looks like suicide. I'm going to want to talk to the wife, the two witnesses, and anyone who might be aware of his relationship with Patrick Galloway."

"He didn't leave his wife a note."

"Sorry?"

"Nothing personal. Nothing detailed in the computer note, either."

Irritation flickered in Coben's eyes. "Look, Burke, you and I both know that suicide notes aren't nearly as typical as Hollywood makes them. The ME will make the call, but from where I'm standing this is suicide. The note links him to Galloway. We'll pursue that, see if we can find a trail back to confirm. I'm not going to cut corners on this, or on Galloway, but I'm not going to kick, either, if it turns out both cases fall closed in my lap."

"It doesn't add up for me."

"Check your math."

"Do you have a problem with me pursuing this, *quietly*," he added with emphasis, "from a different angle?"

"It's your time to waste. But don't step on my toes."

"I still remember how to dance, Coben."

IT WAS HARD TO KNOCK on Carrie's front door. The intrusion on her grief seemed impossibly callous. He remembered, too well, how Beth had crumbled when he'd first seen her after Jack's death.

And he'd been helpless, bound to a hospital bed, dopey from surgery, drowning in grief and guilt and rage.

There was no grief now, he reminded himself. A little guilt for the way he'd had to handle her earlier. But no rage. Now he was just a cop.

"She's going to resent me," Nate told Coben. "If you play on that, you might get more out of her."

He knocked on the front door of the two-story cabin. When the redhead opened it, he had to flip through his mental files.

"Ginny Mann," she said quickly. "I'm a friend of the family. A neighbor. Carrie's upstairs, resting."

"Sergeant Coben, ma'am." Coben took out his identification. "I'd really like to speak with Mrs. Hawbaker."

"We'll try not to take long." Artist, Nate remembered now. Painted landscapes and wildlife studies that were sold in galleries here, and in the Lower 48. Taught art at the school, three days a week.

"Arlene Woolcott and I have the kids back in the kitchen. We're trying to keep them busy. I guess I could go upstairs and see if Carrie's up to it."

"We'd appreciate it." Coben stepped in. "We'll just wait here."

"Nice place," Coben said when Ginny went upstairs. "Homey."

Comfortable sofa, Nate noted, a couple of roomy chairs, colorful throws. A painting of a spring meadow, backed by the white mountains and blue sky that he imagined was the redhead's work. Framed pictures of the kids, and other family shots, on the tables, along with the everyday mess from an average home.

"They were married about fifteen years, I think. He used to work for a paper in Anchorage but relocated and started his weekly here. She worked with him. It was pretty much a two-man operation, with some—what do you call it—stringers? They published articles from locals, some photographs, and picked up stories from the wire services. Older kid's about twelve, a girl. She plays the piccolo. Younger son, ten, is a hockey freak."

"You've picked up a lot in the few weeks you've been here."

"I picked up more since this morning. First marriage for her, second for him. She's been here a couple of years longer than him. Moved up on one of those teacher programs. Gave it up to work with him when he got the paper started, but she still substitutes if they call her in."

"Why'd he move here?"

"I'm working on that." He shut down when Ginny started back down, her arm draped around Carrie's shoulder.

"Mrs. Hawbaker." Coben stepped forward, voice sober. "I'm Sergeant Coben with the State Police. I'm very sorry for your loss."

"What do you want?" Her gaze riveted, hard and bright, on Nate's face. "We're in mourning."

"I know this is a difficult time, but I need to ask you some questions." Coben glanced at Ginny. "Would you like your friend to stay with you?"

Carrie shook her head. "Ginny, would you stay with the kids? Would you keep them back there, away from this?"

"Of course. You just call me if you want me."

Carrie went into the living room, sank into one of the chairs. "Ask what you need to ask, then go. I don't want you here."

"First I want to tell you we'll be taking your husband's body back to Anchorage, for autopsy. He'll be released to you again as soon as possible."

"Good. Then you'll find out he didn't kill himself. Whatever he says," she added with a quick, resentful glance at Nate. "I know my husband. He'd never do that to me or his children."

"May I sit down?"

She shrugged.

Coben sat on the couch facing her, his body angled slightly in her direction. It was good, Nate thought. He was keeping it between the two of them, keeping it sympathetic. He started her on the standard questions. After the first few, she drew back.

"I told *him* all this already. Why do you have to ask me again? The answers aren't going to be any different. Why don't you go out there and find out who did this to my Max?"

"Do you know anyone who wished your husband harm?"

"Yes." Her face lit up with a kind of horrible pleasure. "Whoever killed Patrick Galloway. I'll tell you exactly what happened. Max must have found something out. Just because he ran a small-town weekly didn't mean he wasn't a good reporter. He dug something up, and someone killed him before he could decide what to do."

"Did he discuss any of this with you?"

"No, but he was upset. Worried. He wasn't himself. But that doesn't mean he killed himself, and it doesn't mean he killed anyone else. He was a good man." Tears began to track down her cheeks. "I slept beside him for almost sixteen years. I worked beside him every day. I had two children with him. Don't you think I'd *know* if he was capable of this?"

Coben changed tacts. "Are you sure about the time he left the house last night?"

She sighed, flicked at tears. "I know he was here at ten-thirty. I know he was gone in the morning. What more do you want?"

"You stated that he kept the gun in the glove compartment of his truck. Who else would have known that?"

"Everybody."

"Did he keep the glove compartment locked? The truck locked?"

"Max couldn't remember to close the bathroom door half the time, much less lock anything. I keep the guns we have in the house locked up, and I keep the key because he was absentminded about that sort of thing. Anybody could have taken that gun. Somebody *did*."

"Do you know the last time he used it?"

"No. Not for certain."

"Mrs. Hawbaker, did your husband keep a diary or a journal?"

"No. He just wrote things down when they came to him on whatever was handy. I want you to go now. I'm tired, and I want to be with my children."

OUTSIDE, COBEN PAUSED beside the car. "Still some loose ends there I'd like tied up. Be a good idea to take a look through his things, his papers, see if there's anything regarding Galloway."

"Such as motive?"

"Such as," Coben agreed. "Any reason you couldn't work on tying up those ends?"

"No."

"I want to get the body back to Anchorage, start the tests. And I want to be there when they recover Galloway's body."

"I'd appreciate a call on that when you have him. His daughter's going to want to see him. And her mother's going to be pretty insistent about taking custody of the body."

"Yeah, I've already heard from her. Once he's down, and positively ID'd, we'll let the family fight that end out. His daughter can come down for a visual, but his prints are on file. A couple of minor drug busts. We'll know if it's Galloway once we have the body."

"I'll bring her in, I'll tie up your loose ends and I'll do what I can to play mediator with the deceased's family. In return I want copies of every piece of paperwork on both these cases. That includes case notes."

Coben looked back at the neat house on its blanket of

snow. "You seriously think somebody staged this suicide to cover up a sixteen-year-old crime?"

"I want the copies."

"Fine." Coben pulled open the passenger door. "Your lieutenant said you had good instincts."

Nate sat behind the wheel. "And?"

"Good doesn't always mean right."

FIFTEEN

HE HAD TO WORK with what he had, and that included his two deputies and his dispatcher. He pulled them all into his office, along with the necessary extra chairs.

There was a plate of peanut-butter cookies and a pot of fresh coffee on his desk, courtesy of Peach. And he thought: Why the hell not?

He took a cookie, gestured with it toward his deputies before biting in. "First, the results of the canvass."

"Pierre Letreck thinks he might've heard what sounded like a gunshot." Otto pulled out his notebook and made a business out of flipping through pages. "He says he watched a movie on cable. Claimed at first it was *The English Patient,* and I said, 'Pierre, don't hand me that shit, you never watched anything of the kind.' And he said, 'How the hell do you know what I watch in the privacy of my own home, Otto?' To which I responded—"

"Just give me the bottom line, Otto."

Otto scowled, looked up from the notebook and his careful reading. "Just trying to be thorough. What he watched, which he told me after considerable interrogation, was some skin flick called *Alien Blondes.* He thought it went off around midnight, and he was in the bathroom taking a . . . relieving his bladder," he amended after a loud throat-clearing from Peach. "He heard what he thought was a gunshot and, being of a curious nature, looked out the bathroom window. At that time he saw no one, but did notice Max's—the deceased's—truck parked in back of the paper. He then completed his business and retired for the night."

"He thinks somewhere in the vicinity of midnight?"

"Chief?" Peter raised his hand. "I checked the listings, and the movie ended at twelve-fifteen. According to Mr. Letreck's statement, he went straight from his living room to the bathroom and heard the single shot almost immediately."

"Did he notice anything else? Any other vehicles?"

"No, sir. Otto made him go through it a couple of times, but he stuck with the statement."

"Anybody else hear anything, see anything?"

"Jennifer Welch thinks she might have." Otto flipped more pages. "She and Larry, her husband, were sleeping, and she says she thinks she might've been wakened by a noise. They've got an eight-month-old baby, and she says she sleeps pretty light. As soon as she woke up, the baby started crying, so she doesn't know, for sure, if it was the baby or a noise that woke her up. But the timing's about the same as Pierre's. Said she looked at the clock when she got up to get the baby, and it was about twelve-twenty."

"Where are these two houses in reference to *The Lunatic*'s back office?" Nate gestured to the chalkboard he'd picked up at The Corner Store and hung on his wall. "Draw it out for me, Otto."

"I'll do it." Peach hauled herself to her feet. "Neither of these two can draw worth a damn."

"Thanks, Peach." Nate looked back at his deputies. "Were these the only two you could find who heard anything?"

"That's it," Otto confirmed. "We got Hans Finkle, who said his dog started barking sometime in the night, but he just threw a boot at it and didn't notice the time. Fact is, most people aren't going to pay any mind to a gunshot."

"Are any of you aware of Max having words with anybody lately?"

At the negative responses, Nate looked over at the blackboard. Peach was taking him literally, he noted. Rather than just drawing a diagram, she was busily sketching buildings, adding trees. There was even the silhouette of the mountains in the background.

"Nate?" Otto shifted in his seat. "Not criticizing or anything, but this seems like a lot of official fuss for a suicide, especially since the State's got the body and will be in charge of closing it up."

"Maybe." He opened a file. "What's said in this room stays in this room, until I tell you otherwise. Understood? This was written on Max's computer." He read the note, was met with shocked silence. "Comments?"

"That doesn't seem right." Peach spoke softly, the chalk still in her hand. "I know I'm just a glorified secretary around here, but that doesn't seem right."

"Why?"

"I can't see Max hurting anybody, not in my wildest

dreams. And, as I recall, he admired Pat, sort of had a little hero-worship going there."

"Is that so? People I've talked to are saying they barely knew each other."

"That's true enough, and I'm not saying they were the best of friends, but Pat had a way about him. He was good-looking, and charming when he wanted to be, which was most of the time. He played the guitar and drove a motorcycle, he climbed mountains and went off into the bush for days at a time if the mood struck him. He had the sexiest woman in town warming his bed. Had that pretty little daughter who adored him."

She set the chalk aside, brushed the dust from it off her hands. "And he didn't give a damn about much of anything. Plus he could write. I know Max wanted to get him to write for the paper—adventure stuff. I know because Carrie told me about it. She and Max were just getting serious about each other, and she was a little worried because Pat was wild."

When Nate gestured for her to keep going, she walked over, poured herself some coffee. "I was going through the last spin of that bad cycle with my third husband. So with me she had a sympathetic ear and gave me one back. We talked a lot in those days. She was worried Pat might talk Max into going off to do something crazy. According to her, Max said Pat was what Alaska was all about. Living large, living your own way, bucking whatever system tried to stop you."

"Sometimes admiration becomes envy. Sometimes envy kills."

"Maybe it does." Absently, Peach picked up a cookie,

nibbled. "But it's hard for me to see it. I know you said this stays here, but Carrie's going to need friends now. I want to go see her."

"That's fine, but you keep what we discuss here out of it." He rose, walked to the board.

She'd drawn in the road running behind the paper, had even put in the street sign and labeled it Moose Lane. The Letreck house was mostly garage, he remembered it now. Pierre ran a small appliance-repair business out of it, and his living quarters were an afterthought attached to his workshop. It sat across from the back of the paper and two lots to the east.

The Welch house, a bungalow style, stood directly across from the rear door of the paper. Hans Finkle's second-story apartment was above Letreck's garage.

She'd sketched in other houses, other businesses, and written the appropriate names across the buildings in her careful script.

"Good work, Peach. What we're going to do now is set up a case board." He picked up his file and walked to the freestanding corkboard he'd borrowed from Town Hall. "Anything we get that applies to Galloway or Hawbaker gets copied. A copy gets pinned up to this board. The State's already gone through the paper, but, Otto, you and I are going over there and go through everything again, in case they missed something. Peach, I'm going to want to get inside the Hawbakers', go through Max's things there. Carrie's not going to be receptive to that, not for a while. Maybe you can try to smooth that way for me."

"All right. It's sounding like you don't believe what it said in that note. And if you don't believe that—"

"Best not to believe anything until you have all the details lined up," he interrupted. "Peter, I want you to contact the paper in Anchorage where Max worked. I want you to find out what he did there, who he did it for and with, and why he left. Then you type it all up in a report. Two copies. I want one on my desk before you leave today."

"Yes, sir."

"And all three of you have homework. You were here when Pat Galloway disappeared; I wasn't. So you're going to spend some time thinking back to the weeks before and after that event. Write down everything you remember, no matter how irrelevant it might seem. What you heard, what you saw, what you thought. Peter, I know you were a kid, but people don't always see kids, and they say things, do things around them without thinking."

He finished pinning up the photographs, Galloway on one side of the board, Hawbaker on the other. "There's one vital piece of information I want. Where was Max Hawbaker when Galloway left town?"

"Not that easy to pin that down, after all this time," Otto said. "And the fact is Galloway could've been killed a week after he left. Or a month. Or six damn months."

"One step at a time."

"Hard as it is to take when you've drunk beer and fished out of the same hole with somebody, if Max confessed to murder, then shot himself, what are we trying to prove?" Otto pressed.

"That's supposition, Otto. It isn't fact. The facts are we've got two dead men, some sixteen years apart. Let's just work from there."

. . .

NATE DIDN'T EVEN STOP by his room on the way out of town. There would be too many questions he couldn't, or wouldn't, answer waiting at The Lodge. Better to evade them until he'd worked out an official line.

In any case, he wanted the open space, the frosty dark and the icy shine of the stars. The dark was beginning to suit him, he thought. He couldn't remember what it was like to begin or end his workday with any hint of the sun.

He didn't want the sun. He wanted Meg.

He had to be the one to tell her, the one to shake her world a second time. If, once he had, she tried to shut him out, he'd have to push to stay inside.

He'd managed, with little effort, to close people out for months. He wasn't quite sure if the ease of his solitude had been because he'd been unable to hear people trying to break down the walls, or if there'd simply been no one who'd cared enough to try.

Either way, he knew how painful it was to come back. How all those atrophied emotions and sensations burned and twisted as they struggled back to life. And he knew he cared enough to do whatever it took to spare her from that.

And there was more. He could admit that as he drove alone, with only the rumble of the heater breaking the silence. He needed her knowledge, her memories of her father to fill in gaps in the picture he was creating.

Because he needed the work, the headachy, exhausting, frustrating buzz of police work. Those muscles were flexing again, painfully. He wanted that pain. Needed it.

Without it, he was afraid, very afraid, he'd just slide silently back into the numbness again.

Lights were on in her house, but her plane wasn't there. He recognized the truck outside as Jacob's. A whip of worry slapped down his spine as he pushed out of his car.

The door of the house opened. He saw Jacob in the stream of light an instant before the dogs flew out. Over their noisy greeting, he called out: "Meg?"

"Picked up another job. She'll be camping out tonight in the bush with a hunting party she took in."

"That typical?" Nate asked when he reached the porch.

"Yes. I came to see to her dogs, and check the heat block on her car. That, too, is typical."

"She called you then?"

"Radioed. There's stew if you're hungry."

"Wouldn't mind."

Jacob walked back to the kitchen leaving Nate to close the door. The radio was on, tuned to KLUN. The DJ announced a round of Buffy Sainte-Marie as Nate tossed his coat over the arm of a chair.

"You've had a long day," Jacob commented as he spooned up stew.

"You've heard, then."

"Nothing travels swifter than bad news. A selfish last act, to take his own life so brutally, leaving his wife to find the shell. The stew's hot, the bread's good."

"Thanks." Nate sat. "Was Max a selfish man?"

"We all are, and most selfish when we despair."

"Despair's personal, that's not necessarily the same as

selfish. So, do you remember when Max came here to start the paper?"

"He was young and eager. Persistent," Jacob added, and poured coffee for both of them.

"Came here by himself."

"Many do."

"But he made friends."

"Some do," Jacob said with a smile. "I wasn't one of them, particularly, though we weren't enemies. Carrie courted him. She set her sights on him and pursued. He wasn't handsome or rich or brilliant of mind, but she saw something and wanted it. Women often see what doesn't show."

"Guy friends?"

Jacob raised his eyebrows as he slowly sipped his coffee. "He seemed to be comfortable with many."

"I heard he used to climb. You ever take him up?"

"Yes. Summer climbs on Denali and Deborah, if I remember, when he first came. He was a fair climber. And once or twice I flew him and others into the bush for hunting parties, though he didn't hunt. He wrote in his book or took photographs. Other flights for other stories and photographs. I flew him and Carrie to Anchorage both times she was ready to deliver their children. Why?"

"Curious. He ever climb with Galloway?"

"I never took them together." Jacob's eyes were intense now. "Why would it matter?"

"Curious, that's all. And since I'm curious, would you say Patrick Galloway was a selfish man?"

"Yes."

"Just yes?" Nate said after a moment. "No qualifications?"

Jacob continued to drink his coffee. "You didn't ask for qualifications."

"How'd he rate as a husband, a father?"

"He was, at best, a poor husband." Jacob finished his coffee, turned to the sink to wash the mug. "But some would say he had a difficult wife."

"Would you?"

"I would say they were two people with a strong bond, who pulled and twisted that bond in their individual pursuits of opposing desires."

"Would Meg be that bond?"

Carefully, Jacob laid a cloth on the counter and the cup on it to dry. "A child is. They were no match for her."

"Which means?"

"She was brighter, stronger, more resilient, more generous than either of them."

"More yours?"

Jacob turned back, and there was nothing to read in his eyes. "Meg is her own. I'll leave you now."

"Does Meg know what happened with Max?"

"She didn't mention it. Neither did I."

"She say when she thought she'd be back?"

"She'll fly the party out the day after tomorrow, weather permitting."

"You got any problem with me staying out here tonight?"

"Would Meg?"

"I don't think so."

"Then why would I?"

· · · ·

HE KEPT COMPANY with her dogs and made use of her fitness equipment. It felt good, better than he'd imagined, to pump iron again.

He didn't intend to pry into her things, but when he was alone, Nate found himself wandering the house, poking into closets, peeking into drawers.

He knew what he was looking for—pictures, letters, mementos that pertained to her father. He told himself if Meg had been there, she'd have given them to him.

He found the photograph albums on the top shelf of her bedroom closet. Above a wardrobe that fascinated him with its mix of flannel and silk. Beside the album was a shoe box crammed with loose pictures she'd yet to organize.

He sat down with them on the spare bed, opened the red cover of an album first.

He recognized Patrick Galloway immediately in the snapshots behind the clear, sticky plastic. A younger Galloway than the one he'd seen in the digitals. Long-haired, bearded, dressed in the uniform of bell-bottom jeans, T-shirt and headband of the late sixties and early seventies.

Nate studied one where Galloway leaned against a burly motorcycle, an ocean behind him, a palm tree to his right—and his hand lifted, fingers veed in the peace sign.

Pre-Alaska, Nate thought. California, maybe.

There were others of him alone, one with his face dreamy and lit by a campfire while he strummed an acoustic guitar. More of him with a very young Charlene. Her hair was long and blond and curling crazily, her eyes laughing behind blue-tinted sunglasses.

She was beautiful, he realized. Seriously beautiful, with a streamlined body, soft, smooth cheeks, a full and sensual mouth. And couldn't have reached her eighteenth birthday by his estimation.

There were several others—traveling photos, camping shots. Some were of one or both of them with other young people. A few urban pictures where he thought he recognized Seattle. Some, where Galloway was clean-shaven again, were taken inside an apartment or small house.

Then he came across one with Galloway. The beard was back and he was leaning against a road sign.

WELCOME TO ALASKA

He could track their trail by the photos. Their time in the southeast of the state, working the canneries, he supposed.

And he got his first glimpse of Meg—so to speak— with the photo of a hugely pregnant Charlene.

She wore a skimpy halter and jeans cut below her enormous and naked belly. Her hands were cupped on the mound, protectively. She had the sweetest look on her face, a painfully young face, Nate thought, that radiated hope and happiness.

There were photos of Patrick painting a room—the nursery—others of him building what looked like a cradle.

Then, to Nate's shock, there were three pages of photos detailing labor and delivery.

He'd worked Homicide and had seen, he considered, just about all there was to see. But the sight of those up-close images had the stew rolling dangerously in his belly.

He flipped past them.

The sight of baby Meg settled his stomach and made him grin. He wasted time skimming through those—or maybe not, he thought, as he could study the tender or joyful way one or both of the new parents held the child. The way they held each other.

He could watch the seasons change, the years pass, as he moved to the next album. And he saw the young, pretty face of Charlene grow harder, leaner, the eyes less full of light.

Photos per year began to diminish into those taken more on holidays, birthdays, special occasions. A very young Meg grinning gleefully as she hugged a puppy with a red bow around its neck. She and her father sitting under a straggly Christmas tree, or Meg by a river, arms full of a fish almost as big as she.

There was one of Patrick and Jacob, arms slung around each other's shoulders. The shot was fuzzy and badly cropped, making Nate wonder if Meg had been behind the camera.

He dumped the shoe box and began to sort through the loose snapshots. He found a series of group shots, all of which obviously were taken the same day.

Summer, he thought, because there was green instead of snow. Did it get that green here? he wondered. That warm and bright? The mountains were in the distance, their peaks gleaming white under the sun, the lower reaches silver and blue and dotted with green.

Someone's backyard cookout, he thought. Or a town picnic. He could see picnic tables, benches, folding chairs, a couple of grills. Platters of food, kegs of beer.

He picked out Galloway. The beard was gone again, and the hair was shorter, though it still nearly reached his shoulders. He looked tough and fit and handsome. Meg had his eyes, Nate thought, his cheekbones, his mouth.

He found Charlene, dressed in a tight shirt that showed off her breasts, brief shorts that showed off her legs. Even in the photo he could see her face was carefully made-up. Gone was the fresh, lovely young girl laughing out of tinted lenses. This was a woman, beautiful and sharp and aware.

But happy? She was laughing or smiling in every shot, and posed as well. In one she sat provocatively on the lap of an older man who looked both surprised and overwhelmed by the armful of her.

He saw Hopp sitting beside a gangly, silver-haired man. They were both drinking beers and holding hands.

He found Ed Woolcott, banker and deputy mayor—leaner, sporting a moustache and short beard, mugging for the camera with the silver-haired man Nate took as Hopp's dead husband.

One by one, he identified people he knew. Bing, looking just as burly and sour as he did today, but about fifteen pounds lighter. Rose, that had to be beautiful Rose, fresh and young as the flower she was named for, holding the hand of a handsome little Peter.

Max, with more hair and less belly, sitting beside Galloway, and both of them about to bite into enormous slices of watermelon.

Deb, Harry and—jeez, a fifty-pounds-lighter Peach—arms linked, hips cocked, smiles blazing for the camera.

He went back through them again, concentrating on Galloway. He was in nearly every shot. Eating, drinking, talking, laughing, playing his guitar, sprawled on the grass with kids.

He culled shots of the men. Some were strangers to him, others looked too old, even then, to have made that arduous winter climb. And some had been too young.

But he wondered as he scanned from face to face, if it would be one of them. Had one of the men who'd celebrated that bright, shiny day, who had eaten and laughed with Patrick Galloway and Max Hawbaker, killed both of them?

More loose shots were individuals, groups, holidays. He found Christmas again, and again a picture or two of Max with Galloway. Jacob with them, or Ed or Bing or Harry or Mr. Hopp.

Ed Woolcott, still with a moustache and beard, a fuming bottle of champagne, Harry in a Hawaiian shirt, Max draped in Mardi Gras beads. He spent another hour with the pictures before putting them back, exactly as he'd found them.

He would have to find a way to confess to Meg that he'd invaded her privacy. Or find a way to have her show him the photos without letting her know he'd already seen them.

He'd decide which later.

Now it was time to let the restless dogs out for a last run. And since he was just as restless, it seemed a good time to practice his snowshoeing.

He went out with the dogs. Instead of racing off, they trotted along beside him as he walked out to get his snowshoes out of the car.

Peter had shown him the basics and had proven to be a patient teacher. Nate still fell on his face—or ass—now and then and sometimes got the shoes bogged down, but he was making progress.

He strapped them on, took a few testing strides. "Still feel like an idiot," he confided to the dogs. "So let's keep tonight's practice session between us."

As if in challenge, the dogs bounded off toward the woods. It would be a hell of a hike, Nate decided as he pushed a flashlight into his pocket, but exercise helped beat back depression. And, if he was lucky, would tire him out enough to let him sleep through any dreams that wanted to haunt him.

He used the house lights and the stars to reach the edge of the woods. His progress was slow and not particularly graceful. But he made it and was pleased he was only slightly out of breath.

"Getting back in shape. Some. Still talking to myself, though. But that doesn't mean anything."

He looked up so that he could see the northern lights, could watch them spread their magic. Here he was, Ignatious Burke of Baltimore, snowshoeing in Alaska under the northern lights.

And pretty much enjoying it.

He could hear the dogs thrashing around, letting loose with the occasional bark. "Right behind you, boys."

He pulled out the flashlight. "Too early for bear," he

reminded himself. "Unless, of course, we've got an in-somniac in the area."

To reassure himself, he patted his side and felt the shape of his service weapon under the parka.

He set off, trying to get into an easy rhythm instead of the awkward step-clomp-step he fell into if he wasn't pay-ing attention. The dogs raced back, danced around him, and he was pretty sure they were grinning.

"Keep it up and there'll be no dog biscuits for you. Go do whatever dog business you've got to do. This is thinking time for me."

Keeping the lights of the house visible through the trees to his left, he followed the dog tracks. He could smell the trees—the hemlock he'd learned to identify—and the snow.

Not that many miles west, or north, there would be no trees, so he'd been told. Just seas of ice and snow, rolling forever. Places where no roads cut through that sea.

But here, with the smell of the forest, he couldn't imagine it. Could hardly conceive that Meg, who had a sexy red dress in her closet and baked bread when she brooded, was out there, somewhere in that sea even now.

He wondered if she'd looked up at the northern lights, as he had. And thought of him.

With his head down, the flashlight beam shining ahead, he pushed his body into the steady pace and let his mind wander back to the photos of that sunny day.

How long after that summer picnic had Patrick Gal-loway died in ice? Six months? Seven?

Were those pictures with Christmas lights from his last holiday?

Had one of those men who'd smiled or mugged for the camera been wearing a mask, even then?

Or had it been impulse, insanity, the momentary madness of temper that had brought that ax down?

But it had been none of those things that had left a man in that cave for all these years, preserved in the ice and permafrost.

That took calculation. That took balls.

Just as it took both calculation and balls to carefully stage a suicide.

Or it could all be bullshit, he admitted, and the note left could be God's own truth.

A man could hide things from his wife, from his friends. A man could hide things from himself. At least until that despair, that guilt, that fear wrapped around his throat and choked him off.

Wasn't he chasing this case for the same reason he was out here in the dark, in the cold, tromping around on oversized tennis rackets? Because he needed to be normal again. He needed to find who he'd been before his world had caved in on him. He needed to break out of his own cocoon of ice and live again.

Everything pointed to suicide. All that was arguing against it were his own instincts. And how could he trust them after letting them lie stagnant so long?

He hadn't worked a murder in close to a year, hadn't done much more than ride a desk for his last months with BPD. And now he wanted to turn a suicide into a homicide because, what, it made him feel useful?

He could feel the weight bearing down on him as he thought of the way he'd pushed his opinions onto

Coben, the way he'd issued orders despite the doubts in his deputies' eyes. He'd invaded Meg's privacy, for no good reason.

He could barely run a little cop shop that dealt mainly with traffic violations and breaking up shoving matches, and suddenly he was the big, bad cop who was going to close the books on a murder that took place sixteen years ago and disprove a nearly textbook suicide?

Yeah, sure, then he'd track down this nameless, faceless killer, sweat a confession out of him and hand him over to Coben, all tied up in a big pink ribbon.

"What bullshit. You can barely pass for a cop now, what makes you think . . ."

He trailed off, staring dully down at the snow that gleamed under the beam of his light. And the tracks that marred its surface.

"Funny. Must've circled around somehow."

Not that he gave a good damn. He could wander around aimlessly all night, just like he wandered around aimlessly most days.

"No." He closed his eyes, broke into a light sweat at the physical effort it took to push away from that void. "Not going back there. That's the bullshit. Not going back down in that hole."

He'd take the antidepressants if he had to. Do yoga. Lift weights. Whatever it took, but he couldn't go back down there again. He'd never crawl his way free if he went back down this time.

So he just breathed, opening his eyes, watching his breath stream out white and vanish. "Still standing," he murmured, then looked down at the snow again.

Snowshoe tracks. Curious, and using the curiosity to hold back the dark, he stepped back, compared those tracks with the ones in front of him. They looked the same, but it was a little tough to gauge any difference in the beam of his flashlight—and considering the fact he wasn't some wilderness tracker.

But he was sure enough he hadn't tromped around in the woods, circled, and somehow ended up walking over his own path—coming in the opposite direction.

"Could be Meg's," he murmured. "She might've walked out here anytime, just like I'm doing now."

The dogs ran back, zoomed over the tracks and toward the lights of the house. To satisfy himself, Nate changed his direction, which almost set him on his ass, and followed the tracks.

But they didn't go all the way through the woods. A fist balled in his belly as he followed the way they'd stopped, where someone had obviously stood, looking through the trees toward the rear of the house—and the hot tub where he and Meg had relaxed the night before.

And the dogs had set up a racket in the woods, he remembered now.

He followed their trail, backtracking now. He saw other tracks. Moose, maybe, or deer? How would he know? But he decided, on the spot, he would damn well learn.

He saw depressions in the snow and imagined the dogs had lain there, rolled there—and again the tracks he followed indicated someone had stood, feet slightly apart, as if watching the dogs.

As he circled around with the trail, he could see where

it would lead him now. To the road, several yards from Meg's house.

He was well out of breath by the time he'd followed it to the bitter end. But he knew what he was looking at. Someone had walked, or driven, on that road. Entered the woods well out of sight of the house, then had hiked through those woods—purposely, he thought, directly to Meg's.

Hardly a neighbor paying a call, or someone looking for help due to a breakdown or accident. This was surveillance.

What time had they gone out to the tub the night before? Ten, he thought. No later than ten.

He stood on the side of the road, with the dogs snuffling along the snow-packed ground behind him.

How long, he wondered, to walk back to the road? It had taken him more than twenty minutes, but he imagined you could halve that if you knew what you were doing. Another ten, tops, to get to Max's house, take the gun from the glove compartment. Five more to get into town.

Plenty of time, he thought, plenty to get into the unlocked door, type a note on the computer.

Plenty of time to do murder.

SIXTEEN

NATE WASN'T SURPRISED to find Bing Karlovski had a
sheet. It wasn't a big shock to his system to find charges
of assault and battery, simple assault, aggravated assault,
resisting arrest, drunk and disorderly, on that sheet.

Running names, whether or not he *officially* had a
case, was basic procedure. Patrick Galloway might have
died while Nate was still learning to handle his first sec-
ondhand car, but Max Hawbaker had died on his watch.

So he ran Bing. He ran Patrick Galloway and printed
out his record of minor drug pops, loitering, trespassing.

He worked steadily down his list, discovering that
Harry Miner had a disorderly conduct and injury to
property. Ed Woolcott had a sealed juvie, a DUI. Max
had racked up a few trespassing, disorderly conducts and
two possession pops.

John Malmont, two D&Ds. Jacob Itu came out clean
and Mackie Sr. had a fistful of D&Ds, simple and aggravated assaults, and injuries to property.

He didn't spare his deputies and saw that Otto had
mixed it up a few times in his younger days with disorderly conducts, assault and battery—charges dropped.
Peter, as he'd suspected, was as clean as fresh snow.

He made lists, notes, and added them to his file.

He played it by the book, as much as he was able. The

problem was, as he saw it, he hadn't read the book star-
ring the small-town chief of police nipping his way up the
investigative food chain behind a State cop.

He considered it wise, or at least politic, to filter all his
inquiries through Coben. Hardly mattered, Nate decided when he hung up the phone, as none of those inquiries could be answered. Yet.

Anchorage was urban, which meant it had all the
bogging red tape and backups of an urban area. Autopsy
results, not yet in. Lab results, not yet in.

The fact that the chief of police of Lunacy knew in his
gut Maxwell Hawbaker had been murdered didn't carry
much weight.

He could take the easy way and let it drag him down.
Nate figured he'd taken the easy way for a long time now.
Or he could use his underdog status to rise to the occa-
sion.

Sitting at his desk, with the snow falling soft and
steady outside his window, Nate couldn't quite see the
way to rise.

He had little to no resources, little to no autonomy, a
force that was green as a shamrock and an evidentiary
trail that pointed its bony finger straight to suicide.

Didn't mean he was helpless, he reminded himself as
he got up to pace. To study his case board. To stare hard
into the crystal eyes of Patrick Galloway.

"You know who did you," he murmured. "So let's
find out what you can tell me."

Parallel investigations, he decided. That's the way he
was going to proceed. As if he and Coben were running
separate investigations that ran along the same lines.

Rather than sticking his head out the door, he went back and made use of the intercom. "Peach, call over to The Lodge and tell Charlene I want to talk to her."

"You want her to come over here?"

"That's right, I want her to come over here."

"Well, it's still breakfast time, and Charlene sent Rose home. Ken thinks the baby might come a little earlier than expected."

"Tell her I want her to come over as soon as possible, and that I shouldn't have to keep her long."

"Sure, Nate, but it might be easier if you just went over and—"

"Peach. I want her here, before lunchtime. Got that?"

"All right, all right. No need to get snippy."

"And let me know when Peter gets back from patrol. I need to talk to him, too."

"Awful chatty today."

She cut off before he could comment.

He wished he'd gotten better pictures of the snow-shoe prints. By the time he'd driven into town, picked up the camera, driven back to Meg's, fresh snow had been falling. He didn't know what the hell a bunch of snow-shoe tracks was going to tell him, and he hesitated to pin them up.

But it was *his* case board, for what it was worth.

He was tromping around in the dark, just as he'd been tromping around in the woods the night before. But if you kept going, you got somewhere eventually. He grabbed a few tacks and pinned up his shots.

"Chief Burke." Apparently Peach had taken a cue

from him, as her formal tones came through his intercom. "Judge Royce is here, and he'd like to see you if
you're not too busy."

"Sure." He grabbed the buffalo plaid blanket he'd
brought in as a makeshift drape for his board. "Send him
back," he said, and tossed the red-and-black checks over
the board.

Judge Royce was mostly bald, but wore the thin
fringe that circled his dome long and white. He had
Coke-bottle glasses perched on a nose as sharp and
curved as a meat hook. He had what the polite might call
a prosperous build, with a wide chest and a heavy belly.
His voice, at seventy-nine, resounded with the same
power and impact as it had in his decades on the bench.

His thick, dung-colored corduroy pants swished as he
walked into Nate's office. With them he wore a matching
corduroy vest over a tan shirt. And the off-key adorn-
ment of a gold loop in his right ear.

"Judge. Coffee?"

"Never say no." He settled himself in a chair with a
windy sigh. "Got a mess on your hands."

"Seems it's on the hands of the State authorities."

"Don't shit a shitter. Two sugars in that coffee. No
cream. Carrie Hawbaker was by to see me last night."

"She's going through a bad time."

"Your husband ends up with a bullet in his brain, yep,
it's a bad time. Pissed at you."

Nate handed the coffee over. "I didn't put the bullet
in his brain."

"Nope, don't figure you did. But a woman in Carrie's

state doesn't quibble at taking a shot at the messenger. She wants me to use my influence to have you removed from office, and, hopefully, run out of town on a rail."

Nate sat, contemplated his own coffee. "You got that much influence?"

"Might. If I pressed the matter. Been here twenty-six years. Could say I was among the first lunatics in Lunacy." He blew once on the steaming surface of his coffee, sipped. "Never in my life had a decent cup of cop coffee."

"Me, either. Are you here to ask me to resign?"

"I'm cantankerous. You get to be when you hit eighty, so I'm practicing. But I'm not stupid. Not your fault Max is dead, poor slob. Not your fault there was a note on his computer claiming he killed Pat Galloway."

His eyes were very alert behind those thick lenses as he nodded at Nate. "Yeah, she told me that one, and she's trying to talk herself into you making that up, so you can tie things up neat and tidy. She'll get past that. She's a sensible woman."

"And you're telling me this because?"

"It might take her a little while to remember how to be sensible. Meanwhile, she might try to make trouble for you. It'll help her through the grief. I'm going to smoke this cigar." He pulled a fat one out of his shirt pocket. "You can fine me for it once I have, if you've a mind to."

Nate pulled open a desk drawer, dumped out the contents of a tin of pushpins. Rising, he walked over, handed it to the judge as an ashtray.

"You knew Galloway?"

"Sure." The judge puffed the cigar to life and filled the air with its subtle stink. "Liked him well enough. People did. Not everybody, as it turns out." He glanced toward the draping blanket. "That your dead board under there?"

When Nate didn't respond, he puffed and sipped, puffed and sipped. "I tried capital cases, back in the dark ages. Presided over them when I was wearing robes. Now unless you think I climbed up No Name when I was past sixty and put an end to a man half my age, you should be able to cross me off your list of suspects."

Nate leaned back. "You had a couple of simple assault pops."

Royce pursed his lips. "Been doing your homework. A man who's lived as long as I have, lived up here as long as I have and hasn't gotten into a tangle couldn't be a very interesting man."

"That may be. A man who's lived here as long as you could probably handle the climb if he put his mind to it. And an ax against an unarmed man makes up for any age difference. Theoretically."

Royce grinned around his cigar. "You got a point. I like to hunt and spent some time with Pat out in the bush a time or two, but I don't climb. Never did. You can verify that if you ask around."

It only took once, Nate thought, but filed the statement away. "Who did? Who did climb with him?"

"Max did, as I recall, first season he was here. Ed most likely did, and Hopp—both of them once or twice, on easy, summer climbs, I'd say. Harry and Deb. They both like to climb. Bing's been up a few times. Jacob and Pat did a lot of climbing, a lot of hiking and camping together—or working as a team to guide paying customers. Hell, more than half the people in Lunacy take a whack at the mountains. More than that who've been here and gone. He was a good climber, from what I'm told. Made some of his living—such as it was—taking people up."

"A winter climb. Who around here would've been capable of a winter climb on that mountain?"

"Don't have to be capable so much as willing to challenge the elements." He puffed and sipped some more. "You going to show me the board?"

Since he could find no reason not to, Nate got up and removed the blanket. The judge sat where he was a moment, lips pursed. Then he pushed his bulk out of the chair and moved closer.

"Death robs youth, most times. You don't expect it to preserve it. He had potential. Wasted most of it, but Pat still had enough potential to make something of himself. He had that pretty, ambitious woman, a smart, charming child. Had brains, had talent. Problem was he liked to play the rebel so he pissed most of that away. A man would have to get fairly close in to dig an ax into another man's chest that way, wouldn't he?"

"Seems to me."

"Pat wasn't much of a scrapper. Peace, love and rock and roll. You're too young to know the era, but Pat was the sort who embraced all that crap. Make love, not war, flowers in your hair and a roach clip in your pocket." The judge sniffed. "Still, I can't see him standing there quoting Dylan or whatever when somebody came at him with an ice ax."

"If he knew who it was, trusted him, didn't take it seriously. There are a lot of possibilities."

"Max being one of them." The judge shook his head as he shifted his attention to the photographs of Max Hawbaker. "I wouldn't have thought so. Get to be my age, nothing much surprises you, but I wouldn't have thought it of Max. Physically, Pat could have swatted him down like a fly. Which you've thought of," the judge said after a moment.

"Harder to swat flies armed with deadly weapons."

"Point. Max was a decent enough climber, but I wonder if he was good enough to get down that mountain, in February, without the help of someone with Pat's skill. I wonder how he managed that and how he lived with settling down here, marrying Carrie, raising his kids, knowing Pat was up there—that he was responsible for killing him."

"The argument's going to be he couldn't live with it."

"Sure is handy, isn't it? Pat's body's found through more luck than sense, and a few days later, Max confesses and kills himself. Doesn't explain, doesn't spell it all out. Just I did it, I'm sorry. Bang."

"Handy," Nate agreed.

"But you're not buying it."

"I'll be saving my money for the time being."

WHEN THE JUDGE LEFT, Nate made additional notes. He'd need to talk to several more people now, including the mayor, the deputy mayor and some of the town's most prominent citizens.

He wrote PILOT on his pad. Circled it.

Galloway had gone, reportedly, to Anchorage to pick up some winter work. Had he found any?

If Galloway had been playing it straight with Charlene, had fully intended to come back after a few weeks, that would narrow the time of the murder to February.

A big if, but working with that theory, it would be possible—with time and legwork, to verify that Max had been out of Lunacy during that time frame.

If so, for what purpose?

If so, had he gone alone? How long had he been gone? Had he come back alone, or with a companion?

He was going to have to pick his way through Carrie's memories for the answers. She wasn't going to be amenable just now. Maybe she'd talk to Coben, but if the ME ruled suicide, would Coben bother to follow up?

There was a knock, and even as Nate rose to cover the board again, Peter stepped in. "You wanted to see me?"

"Yeah. Close the door. Question."

"Yes, sir, Chief."

"You know any reason somebody would be out snowshoeing in the woods by Meg's place, in the dark?"

"Sorry?"

"I'm just guessing here, but I don't think most people would go out shoeing around in the woods, in the dark, for sport."

"Well, I guess you could, if you were going to visit someone or something, or couldn't sleep. I don't get it."

He gestured to the board. "I found those tracks last night, when I was out practicing, giving the dogs a last run. I followed them from the road, about fifty yards up from Meg's place, and to the edge of the woods by the back of her house."

"Sure they weren't yours?"

"I'm sure."

"How do you know they were made at night? Somebody, most anybody, might have taken a hike there any time. Wanted to do some hunting or take a walk across from the lake."

Good points, Nate conceded. "Meg and I were out there the night Max died. Took a dip in her hot tub."

Peter looked politely at the wall, cleared his throat. "Well."

"While we were out there, the dogs got antsy. Took off into the woods. They were barking like they'd scented something, carried on long enough that Meg was on the point of calling them back, but they settled down. Now before you point out they could have treed a squirrel or chased down a moose, I found a spot where it looked like they'd rolled around in the snow, and the tracks, the snowshoe tracks, indicated somebody stopped and stood there. I'm not Daniel frigging Boone, Peter, but I can follow the dots."

He tapped a finger on the photographs. "Somebody entered the woods, far enough from Meg's as not to be seen. Then walked in a reasonably direct line—as someone would who knew the layout and had a purpose—toward the back of her house. The dogs' behavior indicates they recognized this individual and considered him or her friendly. This individual then stopped at the edge of the screen of trees."

"If, um, I was hiking around and happened to spot

you and Meg . . . taking a dip in her hot tub, I'd probably be, you could say, hesitant to make myself known. I'd
probably back off and leave, with the sincere hope you
didn't spot me. It'd be embarrassing otherwise."

"Seems to me it'd be less embarrassing altogether not
to go sneaking around by her house in the dark."

"It would." Studying the pictures, Peter pulled on his
bottom lip. "Maybe it was somebody setting or checking
traps. It's really Meg's property, right there by her house,
I mean, but a little poaching maybe. She wouldn't like it,
because of her dogs. I bet she had the music going."

"She did."

"So, somebody might've headed toward the house,
just to see, especially if he was checking traps."

"Okay." It was reasonable. "How about you and Otto
taking a run out there, see if you can find any traps. If
you do, I'd like to know who set them. I don't want to
see one of the dogs hurt."

"We'll get right on that." He glanced back toward the
board. He might've been green, but he wasn't slow.
"You think somebody was spying on her? Somebody
who's involved in all this?"

"I think it's worth finding out."

"Rock and Bull wouldn't let anybody hurt her. Even
if they considered the . . . individual friendly, anybody
made any kind of threatening move on her, they'd attack."

"That's good to know. Let me know about those
traps, one way or the other, as soon as you can."

"Ah, Chief? I think you should know Carrie Hawbaker's been making a lot of calls, talking to a lot of

people. She's saying you're trying to smear Max's character so you can puff yourself up. Mostly people know she's just upset and a little crazy right now, but, well, some of them, maybe some who didn't much like the idea of bringing in someone from Outside, are stewing about it."

"I'll handle it, but I appreciate the heads-up."

There was concern in his dark eyes and a hint of anger on his face. "If people knew you were working so hard to try to find out the whole truth, they might settle."

"Let's just do the job for now, Peter. Cops never win popularity contests."

HE WASN'T GOING TO WIN one with Charlene, either, Nate decided, when she stormed into his office an hour later.

"I'm up to my ears over at The Lodge," she began. "Rose isn't in any shape to wait tables or anything else. And I don't appreciate you calling me over here like I'm some criminal. I'm in mourning, goddamn it, and you should have some respect."

"I've got nothing but respect, Charlene. If it'll help any, you can cross my room off the housekeeping schedule until things get back to routine. I can deal with it myself."

"That's hardly going to make a difference, with every other person in town coming in to gossip and sniff around about my Pat and about poor Carrie. You think because Max went and killed himself she's got more grief than I do?"

"I don't think it's a contest."

She tossed her head, jutted up her chin. Nate figured she'd stomp her foot next, but she folded her arms instead.

"If you talk to me that way, I don't have a thing to say to you. Don't think I'm going to tolerate you taking that attitude with me just because you're banging Meg."

"You're going to want to sit down and shut up."

Her mouth dropped open, her cheeks flamed. "Who the hell do you think you are?"

"I think I'm the chief of police, and if you don't stop being a pain in my ass and cooperate, I'm going to put yours in a cell until you do."

Her mouth, painted Caribbean coral, opened and closed like a guppy's. "You can't do that."

Probably not, Nate thought, but he was past playing with her. "You want to sit around sulking and playing the injured party? I know that tune, and it gets old and boring for everybody who has to hear it. Or do you want to do something about it? Do you want to help me find out who killed the man you say you loved?"

"I *did* love him! The stupid, selfish bastard." She dropped into a chair, burst into tears.

He debated for five seconds on how to handle her. He walked out, grabbed the box of tissues Peach kept on her desk and ignored his dispatcher's wide eyes. Back in the office, he dropped the box on Charlene's lap.

"Go ahead, have a jag. Then mop yourself up, pull it together and answer some questions."

"I don't know why you have to be mean to me. If you

treated Carrie like this, no wonder she's saying terrible things about you. I wish you'd never come to Lunacy."

"You won't be the only one to wish it, once I find the man who killed Patrick Galloway."

She lifted her swimming eyes at that. "You're not even in charge."

"I'm in charge of this office. I'm in charge of this town." The anger that was stirring inside him felt good; it felt just. Cop juice, he realized. He'd missed it.

"And right now, I'm in charge of you. Did Pat Galloway leave town alone?"

"You're nothing but a bully. You're—"

"Answer the damn question."

"Yes! He packed a bag, tossed it in the truck and left. And I never, ever saw him again. I raised our child alone, and she's never once been grateful for—"

"Did he have plans to meet up with anyone?"

"I don't know. He didn't say. He was supposed to get some work. We were about tapped. I was *tired* of living hand to mouth. His family had money, but he wouldn't even consider—"

"Charlene. How long did he plan to be gone?"

She sighed, began to shred the damp tissue. Winding down, Nate thought.

"Couple of weeks, maybe a month."

"He never called, never got in touch."

"No, and I was mad about that, too. He should've called after a week or two, to let me know what was going on."

"You try to get in touch with him?"

"How?" she demanded, but the tears were dried up now. "I badgered Jacob. Pat always talked to him more than to me, but he said he didn't know where he was. He could've been covering for him for all I know."

"Jacob was still flying regularly then?"

"So?"

"Making regular runs, the way Meg does now." Her answer was a shrug, so Nate kept probing. "Was he, or anyone else you can think of, out of town for, let's say, a week or ten days during February of that year?"

"How the hell am I supposed to know that? I don't keep tabs on people, and it was sixteen years ago. This month," she added, and he could see that the fact it was a kind of anniversary had just occurred to her.

"Sixteen years ago Pat Galloway disappeared. I bet if you put your mind to it, you could remember a lot of details about those weeks."

"I was scrambling to pay the rent, just like I was more than half the time. I had to ask Karl for more hours work at The Lodge. I was a hell of a lot more worried about myself than what other people were up to."

But she leaned back, closed her eyes. "I don't know. Jacob left about the same time. I remember because he came by to see Pat, the day Pat left, and said he'd have flown him into Anchorage if he'd known he was going. He was flying Max down, and a couple others, I think. Harry. Harry was hitching a ride to Anchorage to look into a new supplier or something. Or maybe that was the year after, or before. I don't know for sure, but I think it was then."

"Good." He made notes on his yellow legal pad. "Anyone else?"

"It was a slow winter. Hard and slow. That's why I wanted Pat to find some work. Town was dead; we couldn't get the tourists in. The Lodge was damn near empty, and Karl gave me busy work just to tide me over, help me out. He was a sweet man; he looked out for me. Some people went hunting, some holed up and waited for spring. Max was trying to get the paper off the ground and was hunting up advertisers, pestering people for stories. Nobody took him seriously back then."

"Was he in town the whole month?"

"I don't know. Ask Carrie. She was chasing him like a hound chases a rabbit, back then. Why do you care?"

"Because I'm in charge of this office, of this town, of you."

"You didn't even know Pat. Maybe it's like some people are saying. You just want to make a big stir, get some press before you go back where you came from."

"I'm from here now."

HE ANSWERED A COUPLE OF CALLS, including another residential chimney fire and a complaint about the Mackie brothers blocking the road with an overturned Jeep Cherokee.

"It wasn't like we did it on purpose." Jim Mackie stood in the thickly falling snow, scratching his chin and scowling at the Jeep that lay on its side like a tired old man taking a nap. "We got it cheap, and we were hauling it home. Gonna rebuild the engine, paint her up and sell her again."

"'Less we decided to keep her," his brother put in, "hook a plow up to her and give Bing some competition."

Nate stood in the snow, in the miserable cold, and studied the mess. "You don't have a trailer hitch, a tow bar or any of the standard towing equipment. You just figured you'd haul this heap twenty miles with a couple of rusted chains hooked on to your truck with, what is this, baling wire?"

"It was working." Bill furrowed his brow. "Till we hit that rut and she rolled over like a dog playing dead, it was working fine."

"We were working out how to get her up again. No cause for everybody to go crazy about it."

He heard the howl of what had to be a wolf, eerie and primal in the ghostly gloom. It served to remind him he was standing on a snowy, rural road on the edge of the Alaskan Interior with a couple of lamebrains.

"You're blocking traffic and obstructing the town plow from clearing the road for people who have enough sense to drive responsibly. If this had happened five miles the other way, you'd have hampered the fire department on a call. Bing's going to get this thing upright and tow it to your place. You're going to pay his standard fee—"

"Son of a bitch!"

"And the fine for towing a vehicle without proper equipment or signage."

Bill looked so pained that Nate wouldn't have been surprised to see tears run from his eyes. "How the hell are we supposed to make a profit on this if you go around fining us and making us pay that penny-pinching Bing's towing fee?"

"That's a puzzle, all right."

"Hell." Jim kicked the bald rear tire of the Jeep. "Seemed like a good idea at the time." Then he grinned. "We'll fix her up good. Maybe you'll want to buy her for the police department. Hook a plow to her cheap enough. Be useful."

"Take it up with the mayor. Let's get this off the road."

It took Bing, his helper Pargo, both Mackies and Nate to get the job done. When it was over, and Bing was towing the Jeep away, Nate tried to roll the kinks out of his back.

"How much you pay for it?"

"Two thousand." Bill got a gleam in his eye. "Cash."

He calculated, loosely, what it would cost to make it roadworthy, how much Bing would skin them for over the towing. "I'm going to let this go with a warning. Next time you boys decide to be enterprising, get a tow bar."

"You're all right, Chief." Both Mackies slapped him on the back and nearly sent him pitching face-first in the snow. "Pain having cops around, but you're all right."

"Appreciate that."

He drove the short distance back to town and swung to the curb when he saw David helping Rose out of their truck in front of the clinic.

"Everything okay?" he called out.

"Baby's coming," David yelled back.

Nate jumped out and took Rose's other arm. She

continued to take slow, steady breaths, but she smiled at him with those melted chocolate eyes.

"It's okay. Everything's fine." She leaned against her husband as Nate opened the door. "I didn't want to go to the hospital in Anchorage. I wanted Doc Ken to deliver. Everything's fine."

"My mother has Jesse," David told him. He was looking a little pale, Nate thought. And he felt considerably pale himself.

"Do you want me to stay, do anything?" Please say no. "Call anyone?"

"My mother's coming." Rose let David help her out of her coat. "Doc said I could go anytime when I saw him last checkup. Looks like he was right. Four minutes apart," she told Joanna, who hurried over. "Steady and strong now. My water broke about twenty minutes ago."

And that, Nate decided, was about all a man, even one with a badge, needed to hear.

"I'll let you get to it." He took Rose's coat from David, hung it up. "Call if . . . whatever. Peter's out doing something for me, but I'll call him in if you want."

"Thank you."

They disappeared into the back, to do things he didn't care to think about. But he dug out his phone. It rang in his hand.

"Burke."

"Chief? It's Peter. We didn't find any traps, any sign of them either. If you want, we can extend the search, um, widen the parameters."

"No, that'll do. Head on back. Your sister's in the process of making you an uncle again."

"Rose? Now? Is she okay? Is she—"

"She looked fine to me. She's here at the clinic now. David's with her. His mom has Jesse, and your mom's on her way."

"So am I."

Nate stuffed the phone back in his pocket. He should probably stand by, at least until more of the family arrived. The waiting room of the clinic was as good a place as any to sit and think about tracks in the snow.

And what he would tell Meg when she returned to Lunacy.

SEVENTEEN

IT WAS A GIRL, eight full pounds of one, with the requisite complement of digits and a thatch of black hair. Her name was Willow Louise, and she was beautiful. This information came from Peter, who rushed into the station four hours after he'd rushed into the clinic.

Knowing his job, Nate had stopped by The Corner Store and picked up cigars. And while he was there found a sturdy five-ring binder. It was army green rather than the black he would have preferred but he bought it, charged it to the Lunacy PD account.

It would hold his notes, copies of all the reports and photos. It would be his murder book.

He passed the cigars out with some ceremony to Peter, Otto and an amused Peach. The gesture warmed the cold shoulder she'd given him since he'd snapped at her that morning.

After some backslapping and smelly smoke, he gave Peter the rest of the day off.

Nate hunkered back in his office, spent some time with the hole punch and the copier. He put his murder book in order. Having it and the board gave him that tangible foundation. It was cop work.

It was his work.

He intended to spend the next part of his shift harassing Anchorage with more calls, but Peach came in. She shut the door, sat down and folded her hands in her lap.

"Problem?"

"You think those tracks back at Meg's place are something to worry about?"

"Well . . ."

"Otto told me, since you didn't."

"I, ah—"

"If you told me what's what around here, I wouldn't get irritable."

"Yes, ma'am."

Her lips twitched at that. "And don't think I'm not on to you, Ignatious. You use that agreeable tone when you want to change the subject or make someone *think* you're agreeable when you're not."

"Busted. I thought it was worth checking out, that's all."

"And you don't mention it to your dispatcher because maybe you don't think she's smart enough to know you're spending as much free time as you can manage out there snuggled up with Megan Galloway?"

"No." Watching her, he tapped the corner of his murder book right, tapped it left. "But maybe I didn't want to discuss said snuggling with the woman who brings me sticky buns. Because she might get the wrong idea."

"And Peter and Otto wouldn't?"

"They're guys. Mostly guys only have one idea about . . . snuggling, so it didn't apply. I'm sorry I was short with you this morning, and I'm sorry I didn't keep my valued and respected dispatcher in the loop."

"You've got a smooth way about you," she said after a minute. "You worried about Meg?"

"I'm wondering what business anybody had sneaking around there, that's all."

"She'd be the first to tell you she can handle herself and always could. But I'm of the opinion it never hurts a woman to have a good man looking out. People around here, they don't hurt each other. Oh, some fistfights now and then or some backbiting, what have you. But it's a place you feel safe, where you know if you had trouble, somebody'd lend a hand."

She drew the pencil out of her bun, ran it through her fingers. "Now this happens, and you wonder if feeling safe was just an illusion. People get worked up. Get scared and spooked."

"And a lot of those people are armed and territorial."

"And a little bit crazy," she added with a nod. "You're going to want to be careful."

"Who did Max trust enough to let get that close, Peach? Close enough to put a bullet in his head?"

She played with the pencil another moment, then stuck it firmly back in her bun. "You're not going to let it be suicide."

"I'm not going to let it be what it's not."

She sighed, twice. "Can't think of anybody he wouldn't have trusted. Same goes for me, and just about everyone in Lunacy. We're a community. We may argue and disagree and kick some ass now and then, but we're still a community. And that's next door to family."

"Put it this way: Who would Max have climbed with

back when Galloway went missing that he'd trust well enough today?"

"God Almighty." Staring at him, she pressed a fist to her heart. "You're scaring me some. Putting it that way, you're making me think which one of my neighbors, my friends, might be a cold-blooded killer."

"I don't know that it's cold."

But you are, she realized suddenly. When it comes down to this, you are. "Bing, Jacob, Harry or Deb. Lord God. Ah, Hopp or Ed, though Hopp was never too keen on climbing. Mackie Sr., Drunk Mike if he was sober enough. Even The Professor went up a couple times. Short, summer climbs as far as I know."

"John always had a thing for Charlene."

"Holy hell, Nate."

"Just getting a picture, Peach."

"I guess so. Long as I can remember anyway. Not that she looked twice at him—well, any more than she looked twice or three times at any man when she was with Pat. Then she married Karl Hidel, what, about six months after Pat left. Everybody knew, including Old Man Hidel, that she married him for his money, for The Lodge, but she was good to him."

"Okay."

Her gaze flicked to his board, away again. "How am I going to look at these people straight on now?"

"Downside of being a cop."

She looked a little dazzled, and a little chagrined, at being termed a cop. "Guess it is." She pushed to her feet, stood in her red sweater with pink Valentine hearts around the hem. "I want you to know before I say this last thing that I like Meg. I've got a lot of affection and respect for her. But I've got a lot of affection and respect for you, too, and I'm hoping she doesn't break your heart."

"Noted."

He waited until she'd gone out to swivel around in his chair and stare out at the snow. A few weeks before, he hadn't thought there was enough left of his heart to break. Now he didn't know whether to be pleased or annoyed to realize there was.

Recovery? he wondered. Or stupidity? Maybe they were the same thing.

He swiveled back and made the calls.

SHE DIDN'T COME BACK that night. Nate spent it at her place, with her dogs. He worked off some frustration, and a growing anger, in her weight room. In the morning, when the snow had slowed to a thin drizzle, he drove back to Lunacy and the job.

SHE HADN'T CONTACTED HIM, and that was deliberate. Inconsiderate, Meg admitted when she settled back in the cab at Anchorage Airport. He'd probably worry some. He had worry-about-the-woman genes if she was any judge. He'd be hurt and he'd be mad, and that was also deliberate on her part.

The man had spooked her.

There'd been a look in his eye when he'd watched her climb into her plane. More than that was the sensation that look had caused to roll around inside her.

She wasn't after that sort of depth and feeling and *contact*. Why the hell couldn't people just enjoy some good, simple sex without mucking it up with . . . whatever. Loyalty was one thing, and she'd give and get that—as long as the blood ran hot. She wasn't her mother, ready to roll with whoever came along. But she wasn't a woman looking to share home and hearth for the long term, either.

That's what he was about, and she'd known it. She'd known what was behind those sad, wounded eyes the first time she'd looked into them. She'd had no business sleeping with a man who'd want or expect more than sex.

Wasn't her life complicated enough right now without feeling obliged to make adjustments for anybody else? For a man, for God's sake.

She'd been smart to take the extra jobs, and she loved the feeling of being flush. She'd been smarter yet to stay away from him and Lunacy for a couple extra days. Settle herself down.

God knew she needed to be settled for what she was about to do.

She hadn't contacted Nate, but she'd contacted Coben.

The body had been recovered and brought to the facilities in Anchorage.

Now she was on her way to the morgue to identify her father.

Alone. Another deliberate act. She'd been living her life, handling her affairs, dealing with her own details alone nearly as long as she could remember.

She had no intention of changing that now.

If it was her father in the morgue—and she knew in her gut it was—then *he* was her responsibility, her grief and, in a strange way, her release.

This she wouldn't share, even with Jacob. The only person she loved absolutely.

What she was doing was a formality, more a courtesy. Coben had made certain, in his flat and polite way, she knew that. Patrick Galloway had a record, and his prints were on file. Officially, he'd already been identified.

But she was next of kin and permitted to see him, to confirm the identity, to sign papers, give her statement. Deal with it.

When she arrived, she paid off the cab. Steeled herself.

Coben was there, waiting.

"Ms. Galloway."

"Sergeant." She offered her hand, found his cool and dry.

"I know this is difficult and want to thank you for coming."

"What do I have to do?"

"There's some paperwork to clear. We'll streamline it, make this as quick as we can."

He led her through it. She signed where she needed to sign, accepted her visitor's badge and hooked it on her shirt.

She kept her mind blank as he led her down a wide,

white corridor and did her best to ignore the vague and persistent odors that snuck into the air.

He took her into a little room with a couple of chairs and a wall-mounted TV. There was a window, covered on the other side by tight, white blinds. Bracing herself, she walked to it.

"Ms. Galloway." He touched her shoulder, lightly. "If you'll look at the monitor."

"Monitor?" Confused, she turned, stared at the dull, gray screen. "The television? You're going to show him to me on television. Christ, don't you think that's more ghoulish than just letting me . . ."

"It's procedure. It's best. When you're ready."

Her mouth had gone dry, with a sandy coating that tasted foul. She was afraid to try to swallow it, afraid that it would simply come up again, erupt out of her in ripe sickness before she'd even begun.

"I'm ready."

He lifted a phone from the wall, murmured something. Then, picking up a remote, aimed it at the screen and clicked.

She saw him only from the tops of his shoulders. They hadn't closed his eyes, was her first, panicked thought. Shouldn't they have closed his eyes? Instead, they were staring, the icy blue she remembered filmed over. His hair, moustache, the stubbly beard were all the pure, dark black she remembered.

There was no ice now to silver them, to sheen like glass over his face. Was he still frozen? she thought dully. Internally? How long did it take for heart and liver and kidneys to thaw out when a hundred-and-seventy-pound man had been frozen solid?

Did it matter?

Her stomach shuddered, and she felt a tingling in the tips of her fingers, the tips of her toes.

"Can you identify the deceased, Ms. Galloway?"

"Yes." There was an echo in the room—or in her head. Her voice seemed to go on forever, shimmering back, tinny and soft. "That's Patrick Galloway. That's my father."

Coben clicked off the screen. "I'm very sorry."

"I'm not finished. Turn it back on."

"Ms. Galloway—"

"Turn it back on."

After a brief hesitation, Coben complied. "I should warn you, Ms. Galloway, the media—"

"I'm not worried about the media. They're going to splash his name around whether I worry about it or not. Besides, he might've enjoyed that."

She wanted to touch him, had prepared herself for that. She couldn't say why she'd wanted that contact— her skin against his skin. But she could wait, wait until they'd done what they needed to do to the shell of him. When they had, she'd give him that last touch, the touch she'd denied herself in childish pique so many years ago.

"All right. You can turn it off."

"Would you like a minute? Would you like some water?"

"No. I'd like information. I want information." But her legs betrayed her, going loose at the knees so she had to let herself fold into a chair. "I want to know what happens now, how you intend to find the person who killed him."

"It might be best if we discussed this elsewhere. If you come back with me to—"

He broke off when Nate stepped into the room. "Chief Burke."

"Sergeant. Meg, you should come with me. Jacob's waiting upstairs."

"Jacob?"

"Yeah, he flew me in." Without waiting for assent, Nate took her arm. He pulled her up, led her from the room. "I'll get Ms. Galloway to the station, Sergeant."

Her vision was blurry. Not tears, but shock, she realized. It was seeing her father dead on that screen, dead on TV, as if his life, the end of it, had been some sort of episode.

A cliffhanger, she thought giddily. One hell of a cliffhanger.

So she let him guide her and said nothing to him, nothing to Jacob, nothing at all until they walked outside.

"I need some air. I need a minute." Pulling her arm free, she walked half a block. She could hear the traffic, busy, city traffic, and could see out of her periphery the smears and blurs of color from people passing her on the sidewalk.

She could feel the cold on her cheeks, and the thin winter sunlight that filtered through those thickly overcast skies on her exposed skin.

She drew on her gloves, put on her sunglasses and walked back.

"Coben contacted you?" she asked Nate.

"That's right. Since you've been out of touch, there are some things you need to know before we talk to him again."

"What things?"

"Things I don't want to discuss on the damn sidewalk. I'll get the car."

"Car?" she said to Jacob when Nate strode away.

"He rented one at the airport. He didn't want you in a cab. He wanted you to have some privacy."

"Considerate. Which I'm not. You don't have to say it," she went on when Jacob stood in silence. "I can see it in your eyes."

"He tended your dogs while you were gone."

"Did I ask him to?" She heard the bitchiness in her voice and swore. "Damn it, *damn it,* Jacob, I'm not going to feel crappy for living my life the way I've always lived it."

"Did I ask you to?" He smiled a little, and the pat of his hand on her arm nearly broke the wall she'd built viciously against tears.

"They put him on a television screen. I couldn't even look at him, not really."

She walked to the curb when Nate pulled up in a Chevy Blazer. And climbing in, squared her shoulders. "What do I need to know?"

He told her of Max in the detached, straightforward style he would have used to inform any civilian with a need to know in regards to a case. He continued to speak, continued to drive with his eyes on the road, even when she turned her head to stare at him.

"Max is dead? Max killed my father?"

"Max is dead. That's a fact. The medical examiner ruled it suicide. The note left on his computer claimed responsibility for the murder of Patrick Galloway."

"I don't believe it." There was too much churning inside her, too much beating against that defensive wall. "You're saying Max Hawbaker went homicidal all of a damn sudden, stuck an ice ax in my father's chest, then climbed down the mountain and strolled back into Lunacy? That's just bullshit. That's stupid cop tie-it-up-and-forget-it *bullshit*."

"I'm saying that Max Hawbaker is dead, that the ME ruled it a suicide, determining same from physical evidence, and that there was a note written on the computer—which was decorated with some of Max's blood and brains—that claimed responsibility. If you'd bothered to contact anyone over the last few days, you would have been apprised and updated."

His voice was flat, and so, she noted, were his eyes. Nothing there, nothing that showed. She wasn't the only one with walls. "You're being awfully careful not to express your opinion, Chief Burke."

"It's Coben's case."

He left it at that and pulled into a visitor's slot at the parking lot of the State Police.

"HAWBAKER'S DEATH has been ruled a suicide," Coben stated. They gathered in a small conference room. Coben had his hands folded on a file on the table. "The weapon was his, and his prints—only his prints—were found on it. Gunpowder residue was found on his right hand. There was no sign of break-in or struggle. A whiskey bottle and a mug thereof were on his desk. Autopsy results prove he'd consumed just over five ounces of whiskey prior to his death. His prints—and only his— were on the keyboard of the computer. The wound, the position of the body, the position of the weapon, all indicate self-infliction."

Coben paused. "Hawbaker was acquainted with your father, Ms. Galloway?"

"Yes."

"And you're aware he had occasion to climb with your father from time to time?"

"Yes."

"Were you aware of any friction between them?"

"No."

"You may also be unaware that Hawbaker was fired from the paper in Anchorage for drug use. My investigation indicates that Patrick Galloway was known to use recreational drugs. As yet, I've found no evidence that your father sought or had gainful employment in Anchorage, or elsewhere, after he left Lunacy, purportedly to seek same."

She spared him a glance. "Not everyone works on the books."

"True. It would appear that Hawbaker, whose whereabouts during the first and second week of February of that year cannot as yet be determined, met Patrick Galloway and together they sought to climb the south face of No Name. Supposition would be that during that climb, perhaps influenced by drugs and physical distress,

Hawbaker murdered his companion and left the body in the ice cave."

"It could be supposed that pink pigs fly," Meg returned. "My father could have snapped Max in two without breaking a sweat."

"Physical superiority wouldn't hold up against an ax, particularly in a surprise attack. There was nothing in the cave that indicated a fight. We will, of course, continue to study and evaluate all evidence, but sometimes, Ms. Galloway, the obvious is the obvious because it's truth."

"And sometimes crap floats." She got to her feet. "People always say suicide's a coward's way. Maybe that's valid. But it seems to me it takes a certain amount of guts and determination to put the barrel of a gun to your head and pull the trigger. Either way, Max doesn't fit the bill for me. Because either way is extreme, and he just wasn't. What he was, Sergeant Coben, was ordinary."

"Ordinary people do the unspeakable every single day. I'm sorry about your father, Ms. Galloway, and I give you my word that I'll continue to work the case to its conclusion. But at this time, I have nothing more to tell you."

"Another minute, Sergeant?" Nate turned to Jacob and Meg. "I'll meet you outside." He closed the door behind them himself. "What else do you have? What aren't you telling her?"

"Do you have a personal connection with Megan Galloway?"

"Undetermined at this particular time and irrelevant. Give and take, Coben. I can tell you that there are a good half dozen people still living in Lunacy who could have climbed with Galloway that winter, people Max knew as friends and neighbors and who could have sat in that office with him on the night of his death. The ME's determination was made on facts, but he doesn't know the town, the people. He didn't know Max Hawbaker."

"And you barely did." Coben held up a hand. "But, I have evidence there were three people on that mountain at the probable time of Galloway's death. Evidence that only two of them were in that cave. Evidence I believe was written by Galloway's own hand."

He pushed the file toward Nate. "He kept a journal of the climb. There were three of them up there, Burke, and I'm dead sure Hawbaker was one of them. I'm not sure he was the second man in that cave. There's a copy of the journal in the file. I'm having an expert verify it's Galloway's writing from another sample, but eyeballing it, I'd say it is. It's up to you if you want to share that with his daughter."

"You wouldn't."

"Against the grain some to share it with you. Just like it is to admit you've got more Homicide experience than I do and a better handle on the people of that town. Lunacy fits, Burke, because I'd say you've got at least one certifiable lunatic living under your nose."

HE FLEW BACK WITH MEG, with the file tucked under his parka. After he'd read it, he'd decide if he'd tell her about it. Decide if he'd tell anyone.

Since he couldn't quite pull off the denial that he was in the air, he did what he could to enjoy the view.

Snow. More snow. Frozen water. Icy beauty with dangerous pockets. Not unlike his current pilot.

"Is Coben an asshole?" she asked abruptly.

"I wouldn't say so."

"Is that because you cops stick together, or is it an objective opinion?"

"Some of both, maybe. Following the evidence doesn't an asshole make."

"It does if either of you seriously believes Max whacked my father with an ax. I expected better from you."

"See where expectations get you?"

She took the plane into a deep, left dip that had his stomach sloshing toward his throat. Before he could object, she dipped right.

"You want me puking in your cockpit, you just keep it up."

"Cop ought to have a stronger stomach." She nosed down with such speed he could see nothing but that white world hurtling toward them—and his own mangled body in twisted, burning wreckage.

His vicious, violent cursing had her laughing as she shot the plane up again.

"You got a death wish?" he shot out.

"No. You?"

"I did, but I got over it. You pull that again, Galloway, and when we're on the ground, I'm going to knock you on your crazy ass."

"You wouldn't. Guys like you don't hit women."

"Oh, just try me."

She was tempted, was feeling just crazed enough to be tempted. "You ever knock the cheating Rachel around?"

He looked over. There was a wildness about her, in her eyes, vivid on her face. "Never even considered it, but I'm forging new territory every day."

"You're pissed off at me. All mopey and hurt because I didn't radio in every hour to make kissy noises."

"Just fly the plane. My ride's at your place. That's where Jacob picked me up."

"I didn't need you there. I didn't need you coming in to hold my hand."

"I don't believe I offered to hold your hand." He waited a beat. "Rose and David had a girl. Eight pounds. Named her Willow."

"Oh?" Some of that wild temper eased out of her face. "A girl? They're okay?"

"Fine and dandy. Peach says she's beautiful, but when I went to see, she looked like a really irritated guppy with black hair."

"Why are you talking to me conversationally when you're mad enough to pop me between the eyes?"

"I prefer to keep things neutral as Switzerland until you land the damn plane."

"Fair enough."

Once she had, she grabbed gear, hopped out. Slinging what she could over her shoulders, she bent to greet her excited dogs. "There you are, there's my guys. Miss me?" She shot a glance up at Nate. "Going to deck me now?"

"If I did, your dogs would rip my throat out."

"Sensible. You're a sensible man."

"Not always," he said under his breath as he followed her to the house.

Inside, she tossed her gear aside then went directly to the fire to stack logs and kindling. She needed to deal with the plane. Drain the oil and haul it to the shed to keep it warm. Cover the wings.

But she wasn't feeling practical and efficient. She wasn't feeling quite sane.

"Appreciate you looking out for Rock and Bull while I was gone."

"No problem." He turned his back, carefully laying the file under his parka. "Busy were you?"

"Making hay." She got the fire started. "Jobs fall into my lap, I take them. Now I've got a couple of nice fat fees to bank."

"Good for you."

She dropped into a chair, hooked a leg over the arm. All insolence now. "Back now, and it's good to see you, lover. You got time, we can go upstairs for some welcome-home sex." She smiled as she began unbuttoning her shirt. "Bet I could get you up for it."

"That's a poor imitation of Charlene, Meg."

It wiped the smile off her face. "You don't want to fuck, fine. No need to insult me."

"But there seems to be a need for you to hurt me, make me mad. What is it?"

"Your problem." She pushed up, started to shove by him, but he gripped her arm, swung her back.

"Nope," he said and ignored the warning growl from the dogs. "It appears to be yours. I want to know what it is."

"I don't *know!*" The distress in her tone turned the

growls into snarls. "Rock, Bull, relax. Relax," she said more calmly. "Friend."

She knelt down, hooked an arm around each of them, nuzzled. "Damn it. Why don't you yell or storm out or tell me I'm a cold, heartless bitch? Why don't you give me a damn break?"

"Why didn't you bother to contact me? Why have you been spoiling for a fight since you saw me?"

"Hold on a minute." She got up, snapped her fingers for the dogs to follow her into the kitchen. After digging out Milk Bones, she tossed one to each dog. Then she leaned back against the counter and looked at Nate.

Not quite gaunt anymore, she thought. He'd put on a little weight in the last month or so. The kind that looked good on a man, the sort that spoke of muscles toning. His hair looked wild and sexy and a little past trimming time. And those eyes, calm and wrenchingly sad and irresistible, stayed level and patient on hers.

"I don't like being accountable to anyone. I'm not used to it. I built this place, built my business, built my life a certain way because they suit me."

"Are you worried I'm going to start holding you accountable? Expecting you to change the order of things for me?"

"Aren't you?"

"I don't know. Maybe I see a difference between accountability and caring. I was worried about you. For you. And your dogs weren't the only ones who missed you. As to the order of things, I'm still working on my own. A day at a time."

"Tell me something. No bullshit. Are you falling in love with me?"

"Feels like it."

"What does it feel like?"

"Like something coming back inside me. Warming up and trying to find its rhythm. It feels scary," he said, crossing to her. "And good. Good and scary."

"I don't know if I want it. I don't know if I've got it."

"Me, either. But I do know I'm tired of being tired, and empty, and just going through the motions so I can get by. I feel when I'm with you, Meg. I feel, and some of that's painful. But I'll take it."

He cupped her face in his hands. "Maybe you should try that for now, too. Just take it."

She closed her hands over his wrists. "Maybe."

EIGHTEEN

He's gone crazy. Out of his freaking mind. Too much Dex, and Christ knows what else. Too much altitude. I don't know. I think I've calmed him down. Storm came up so we've taken shelter in an ice cave. Hell of a place. Like some sort of miniature magic castle with ice columns and arches and sudden drops. Wish all of us had gotten here. I could use a little help bringing old Darth back to earth.

He's got some whacked-out idea that I tried to kill him. We had some trouble on the rappel, and he's screaming at me, into the wind, that I want to kill him. Came at me like a maniac, and I had to knock him flat. Calmed him down though. Got him calm. He apologized, laughed about it.

We'll just take a breather here, pull ourselves together. We've been playing the first-thing-I'll-do-when-I'm-back-in-the-world game. He wants a steak; I want a woman. Then we both agreed we wanted both.

He's still jittery; I can see it. But hell, the mountain does that to you. We need to get back to Han, get moving down. Get back to Lunacy.

Weather's clearing, but there's a feeling in the air. Something's coming down. It's time to get the hell off the mountain.

IN HIS OFFICE, with the door shut, Nate read the last entry in Patrick Galloway's climbing journal.

Took you another sixteen years to get off the mountain, Pat, he thought. Because something sure as hell came down.

Three went up, he thought, and two came down. And two kept silent for sixteen years.

But there were only two in that cave, Galloway and his killer. Nate was more certain than ever that the killer hadn't been Max.

Why had the killer let Max live for so long?

If Han equaled Max, Max had been injured, not seriously, but enough to make the descent difficult. He'd been the least experienced and hardy of the three if he was reading correctly between the lines of Galloway's journal.

But the killer had brought him down, let him live another sixteen years.

And Max had kept the secret.

Why?

Ambition, blackmail, loyalty? Fear?

The pilot, Nate decided. Find the pilot and the story he had to tell.

He locked the copy of the journal in a desk drawer along with his murder book, pocketed the keys.

When he went out, he found Otto just coming in from patrol. "Ed Woolcott said somebody broke the lock on his ice-fishing shack and took off with two of his rods, his power auger, a bottle of single-malt scotch, and defaced the shack with paint."

His face pink from the cold, Otto headed straight to the coffeepot. "Kids most likely. I told him he's the only one around here who locks his shack, and that just makes kids want to break in."

"How much is it worth. Altogether?"

"*He* says about eight hundred. StrikeMaster power auger runs about four hundred." Both disgust and derision covered his face. "That's Ed for you. You can pick up a good hand auger for maybe forty, but he's gotta fly first class."

"We have a description of the property?"

"Yeah, yeah. Any kid stupid enough to show off a rod that has Ed's name brass-plated on it deserves to get busted. Scotch? They likely drank themselves sick on it. Probably just drilled a hole through the ice somewhere with the auger, did a little fishing and drinking. I expect they'll ditch the gear somewhere or try to sneak it back to the shack."

"It's still breaking and entering and theft, so let's follow it through."

"You can bet they're insured, and for more than he paid for them. You know he talked to a lawyer about suing Hawley for running him off the road back around the first of the year? A lawyer. Jesus H. Christ."

"I'll talk to him."

"Good luck." Otto sat at his desk with his coffee and scowled at his computer screen. "Gotta write this up."

"I'm heading out, doing a follow-up on something." He paused. "You do much climbing these days?"

"What do I want to go up a damn mountain for? I can see them fine from here."

"But you used to."

"Used to tango with loose women, too."

"Yeah?" Amused, Nate sat on the corner of Otto's desk. "You're a deep pool, Otto. These women wear tight dresses and skinny high heels?"

Humor battled grouchiness. "They did."

"With those sexy slits in the skirt, on the side so their legs slid out like a slice of heaven when they moved?"

Otto's glower lost its war with a smile. "Those were the days."

"Bet they were. I never learned to tango, or climb. Maybe I should."

"Stick with the tango, Chief. Surer to live through that."

"The way some people talk about climbing, it's like a religion. Why'd you give it up?"

"Got tired of flirting with frostbite and broken bones." His eyes darkened as he looked down into his coffee. "Last time I went up was on a rescue. Party of six, avalanche took them. We found two. The bodies. You've never seen a man taken out by an avalanche."

"No, I haven't."

"Count your blessings. That was nine years back next month. I never went up again. Never will."

"You ever climb with Galloway?"

"Couple times. He was a good climber. Damn good for an asshole."

"You didn't like him?"

Otto began to play hunt-and-peck with the keyboard. "If I disliked every asshole I met, there wouldn't be many left. Guy got himself stuck in the sixties. Peace, love, drugs. Easy way out, you ask me."

In the sixties, Nate thought, Otto had been sweating in a jungle in Nam. That sort of friction—soldier and hippy—could blow up under less stress than a winter climb.

"You yammer about living the natural life and save the frigging whales," Otto went on as he jabbed at keys, "and what you're doing is sitting on your ass living on the government you bitch about all the time. Got no respect for that."

"I guess you wouldn't have had a lot in common, what with you coming from the military."

"We weren't drinking buddies." He stopped typing, looked up at Nate. "What's all this about?"

"Just trying to get a full picture of the man." As he rose, he asked, casually, "When you did climb, who'd you use as a pilot?"

"Mostly Jacob. He was right here."

"I thought Jacob did some climbing, too. You ever go up with him?"

"Sure. Get Hank Fielding maybe, out of Talkeetna to fly us, or Two-Toes out of Anchorage, Stokey Loukes if he was sober." He shrugged. "Plenty of pilots around to take up a party if you got the money to pool. If you're really thinking of going up, you get Meg to take you and get yourself a professional guide, not some yahoo."

"I'll do that, but I think I might settle for the view from my office."

"Smarter."

Interrogating his own deputy didn't give him any pleasure, but he'd write up the conversation in his notes. He couldn't picture Otto going berserk on speed and attacking a man with an ax. But he couldn't picture him doing the tango with a woman in a tight dress, either.

People did a lot of changing in sixteen years.

He went to The Lodge and found Charlene and Cissy serving the early dinner crowd. Skinny Jim worked the bar. And The Professor manned his stool, nursing a whiskey and reading Trollope.

"Got a pool starting on the Iditarod," Jim told him. "You want in?"

Nate sat at the bar. "Who do you like?"

"I'm leaning toward this young guy, Triplehorn. An Aleut."

"He's gorgeous," Cissy commented when she stopped by with empties.

"Doesn't matter what he looks like, Cissy."

"Does to me. Need a Moosehead and a double vodka rocks."

"Sentimental money's on this Canadian, Tony Keeton."

"We're sentimental over Canadians?" Nate wondered as Jim poured the vodka.

"Nah. The dogs. Walt Notti bred his dogs."

"Twenty then, on the Canadian."

"Beer?"

"Coffee, thanks, Jim." While Jim and Cissy dealt with drinks and continued to argue over their favored mushers, Nate turned to the man beside him. "How you doing, John?"

"Not sleeping very well. Yet." John marked his page, set the book down. "Can't get the image out of my head."

"It's tough. You knew Max pretty well. Wrote some articles for his paper."

"Monthly book reviews, the occasional color piece. Didn't pay much, but I enjoyed it. I don't know if Carrie will keep the paper going. I hope she does."

"Somebody told me Galloway wrote some pieces for *The Lunatic*. Back in its early days."

"He was a good writer. He'd have been a better one if he'd focused on it."

"I guess that's true of anything."

"He had a lot of raw talent, in several areas." John glanced over his shoulder, toward Charlene. "But he never buckled it down. Wasted what he had."

"Including his woman?"

"I'd be biased on that subject. In my opinion, he didn't put much effort into his relationship or much of anything else. He had a couple of chapters of several novels, dozens of half-written songs, any number of abandoned woodworking projects. The man was good with his hands, had a creative mind, but no discipline or ambition."

Nate weighed the possibilities. Three men, drawn together by location, avocation—the writing—and the climb. And two of the three in love with the same woman.

"Maybe he'd have turned that around, if he'd had the chance."

John signaled for Jim to refill his glass. "Maybe."

"You read his stuff?"

"I did. We'd sit around over a beer, or two, or some other recreational drug," John added with a half smile. "And discuss philosophies and politics, writing and the human condition. Young intellectuals." John lifted his glass in toast. "Who were going absolutely nowhere."

"You climbed with him?"

"Ah, adventure. Young intellectuals don't come to Alaska without needing to have them. I enjoyed those days and wouldn't have them back for a Pulitzer." Smiling the way a man does over past glories, he sipped at the fresh whiskey.

"The two of you were friendly?"

"Yes. We were friends, on that intellectual level, in any case. I envied him his woman; that was no secret. I think it amused him and made him feel a bit superior to me. I was the educated one. He'd tossed the prospect of a superior education away, yet look what he had."

John brooded into his drink. "I imagine he'd still be amused that I continue to envy him his woman."

Nate let that sit a minute, drank coffee. "Did you two climb with a group, or alone?"

"Hmm." John blinked, like a man coming out of a dream. Memories, Nate thought, were just another kind of dream. Or nightmare. "Groups. There's camaraderie in the insanity. The best I remember was a summer climb on Denali. Groups and solos picking their way up that monster like ants on a giant cake. Base camp was like a little town all of its own and a crazed little party."

"You and Pat?"

"Mmm, along with Jacob, Otto, Deb and Harry, Ed, Bing, Max, the Hopps, Sam Beaver, who died two years ago from a pulmonary embolism. Ah, let's see, Mackie Sr. was there, as I recall. He and Bing started to beat the snot out of each other for something, and Hopp—the deceased Hopp—broke it up. Hawley was there, but he fell over drunk and cracked his head. We wouldn't let him climb. And there was Missy Jacobson, a freelance photographer with whom I had a short, intense affair before she moved back to Portland and married a plumber."

He smiled at that. "Oh yes, Missy, with her big, brown eyes and clever hands. Those of us from Lunacy had put our party together like a holiday. We even had a little flag we were going to stick on the summit for photo ops for the paper. But none of us made it to the top."

"None of you?"

"No, not then. Pat did later, as I recall, but on that climb we were plagued with bad luck. Still, that night at base camp we were full of possibilities and goodwill. Singing, screwing, dancing under that wonderful, endless sunlight. As alive as I think any of us had ever been."

"What happened?"

"Harry was sick. Didn't know it, but by morning he was running a fever. Flu. He said he was fine, and nobody wanted to argue. He didn't make it five hours. Deb and Hopp got him back down. Sam fell, broke his arm. Missy was getting sick. Another group coming down took her back to base. The weather turned, and those of us who were left pitched tents and huddled down praying for it to pass. It didn't; got worse. Ed got sick, then I got sick. One thing after another until we had to call it and go back. Miserable end to our little town holiday."

"Who got you back to town?"

"Sorry?"

"You have a pilot?"

"Oh. I remember being stuffed into that plane, everyone sick or pissed or sullen. Can't remember the pilot. Some friend of Jacob's, I think. I was dog sick, that I recall vividly. I wrote about it at some point. Tried for a little humor in a piece for *The Lunatic*."

He polished off the whiskey. "I always regretted not hoisting that flag."

Nate let it go and wandered to Charlene. "Can you take a break?"

"Sure. When Rose is back on her feet."

"Five minutes. You're not that crowded yet."

She shoved her order pad in her pocket. "Five. We don't keep things moving in here, people will start going to The Italian Place. I can't afford to lose my regulars."

She clipped her way out of the restaurant into the empty lobby. The sound of her heels made Nate think of the tango, and he wondered what sort of vanity would overcome a woman's need for comfort when she was going to be hopping on her feet for a few hours.

"To your knowledge, Patrick Galloway was going to Anchorage to look for work."

"We've been through this."

"Indulge me. If he went there, and got a wild hair to do a climb, who would he most likely hire to fly him to Sun Glacier?"

"How the hell am I supposed to know? He wasn't supposed to be climbing, he was supposed to be looking for a job."

"You lived with him for close to fourteen years, Charlene. You knew him."

"If it wasn't Jacob, and he was in Anchorage, it would probably have been Two-Toes or Stokey. Unless he got that hair when neither of them were around, then he'd have hired whoever was handy. Or more likely have bartered something for the flight. He didn't have any money to spare. I only gave him a hundred out of my household fund. Any more, I knew he'd piss it away."

"You know where I can find either of those pilots?"

"Ask Jacob or Meg. They run in that world; I don't. You should have told me they brought him back down, Nate. You should have told me and taken me to see him."

"There was no point in putting you through that. No," he said before she could object. "There wasn't."

He nudged her into a chair, sat beside her. "Listen to me. It won't help you to see him that way. It won't help him."

"Meg saw him."

"And it ripped her up. I was there; I know it. You want to do something for him, for yourself? You want to find your closure? Make time to go see your daughter. Be her mother, Charlene. Give her some comfort."

"She doesn't want comfort from me. She doesn't want anything from me."

"Maybe not. But offering it might help you." He got to his feet. "I'm going out to see her now. Anything you want me to tell her?"

"You could tell her I could use a hand around here for the next couple of days, unless she's got something more important to do."

"Okay."

IT WAS FULL DARK when he got back to Meg's. He could see she looked calmer, steadier and more rested. The position of the pillows and throw on the sofa told him she'd had a nap in front of the fire at some point.

He'd figured out the best way to handle things and handed her a bouquet of mixed mums and daisies he'd picked up at The Corner Store. They weren't particularly fresh, but they were flowers.

"What's this for?"

"See, I realized we were working backward, in the traditional sense. I got you into bed, or you got me, so that pressure's off. Now I'm romancing you."

"Is that right?" She sniffed at them. Maybe it was a cliché, but she had a weakness for flowers, and men who thought to offer them. "Then the next step would be what, a pickup at a bar?"

"I was thinking more of a date, dinner, say. But you could pick me up in a bar. That works for me, too. Meanwhile, I'd like you to pack some things and come back with me to The Lodge for the night."

"Oh, so we can still have sex during this romancing period?"

"You could get your own room, but I'd rather have the sex. You could bring the flowers, too. And the dogs."

"And why would I leave the comfort of my own home to have sex with you in a hotel room?" She twirled the flowers, watched him over them. "Oh, for the thrill factor in our backward relationship. It's stupid enough to appeal to me, Burke, but I'd as soon stay here, and we can pretend we're in some cheap motel room. We can even see if there's any porn on cable."

"That sounds really good, but I'd like you to come back with me. Someone was skulking around in your woods the other night."

"What are you talking about?"

He told her about the tracks.

"Why the hell didn't you tell me about this when it was light, so I could see for myself?" She tossed the flowers down on the table and headed for her parka.

"Hold on. It snowed a good six inches. You won't be able to see anything. Otto and Peter already tromped around in there anyway. I didn't tell you before because you had enough on your plate. This way you had a nap and some quiet time. Pack what you need, Meg."

"I'm not going to be driven out of my house because somebody walked around in the woods. Even if I want to take a page out of your book of paranoia and conclude he or she was spying or up to some nefarious plan, I wouldn't be driven out. I can—"

"Handle yourself. Yes, I know."

"You think I can't?" She spun on her heel, marched into the kitchen.

When he came in behind her she was yanking a rifle out of the broom closet.

"Meg."

"Just shut up." She checked the chamber. To his distress, he saw it was fully loaded.

"Do you know how many accidents go down because people keep loaded weapons in the household?"

"I don't shoot anything by accident. Come out here."

She pulled open the door.

It was dark, it was cold and he had an irritated woman with a loaded rifle on his hands. "Why don't we just go inside and—"

"That branch, two o'clock, seven feet up, forty feet out."

"Meg—"

She shouldered the rifle, got her bead and fired. The blast of it boomed in his head. The branch exploded, six inches in.

"Okay, you can shoot a rifle. Gold medal for you. Come inside."

She fired again, and the six inches of branch jumped on the snow like a rabbit.

Her breath steamed out as she fired again and obliterated what was left.

Then she picked up her spent shells, walked back inside and replaced the rifle.

"A plus on marksmanship," Nate commented. "And though I have no intention of letting it come to that, I will point out that blasting the shit out of a tree branch isn't anywhere near the same level as putting a bullet into flesh and bone."

"I'm not one of your dainty Lower 48 women. I've taken down moose, buffalo, caribou, bear—"

"Ever shot a human being? It's not the same, Meg. Believe me, it's not. I'm not saying you're not smart or capable or strong. But I am asking you to come back with me tonight. If you won't, I'll stay here. But your mother could use some help at The Lodge with Rose out. She's overworked and churned up about your father."

"Charlene and I—"

"I can't connect with mine, you know. My mother. She barely speaks to me, and my sister stays away from both of us because she just wants to have a nice, normal life. Can't blame her."

"I didn't know you had a sister."

"She's two years older. Lives in Kentucky now. I haven't seen her in . . . five years, I guess. The Burkes aren't big on family gatherings."

"She didn't come to see you when you were shot?"

"She called. We didn't have a lot to say to each other. When Jack was killed and I was shot up, my mother came to see me in the hospital. I thought, as much as I was thinking, that maybe, just maybe, something would come out of all that horror. I thought we'd work our way back to each other. But she asked me if I'd stop now. If I'd resign from the force before she had to visit my grave instead of my hospital bed. I told her no, that it was all I had left. She walked out without another word. I don't think we've exchanged more than a dozen words since.

"The job cost me my best friend, my wife, my family."

"No, it didn't." She couldn't stop herself from taking

his hand, lifting it to her cheek. Rubbing it there. "You know it didn't."

"Depends how you turn it, that's all. But I didn't give it up. I'm here because even at the bottom, it was the one thing I kept. Maybe it's what stopped me from sinking all the way down, I don't know. But I do know you've got a chance to make some sort of peace with your mother. You ought to take it."

"She could've asked me to give her a hand."

"She did. I'm just the filter."

On a sigh, she turned around and gave the under-the-sink cabinet a testy little kick. "I'll chip in some time, but don't look for happy-ever-after on this, Nate."

"Ever after's too long to worry about anyway."

HE DROPPED HER OFF at The Lodge, then went back to the station.

He spent some time writing up notes from his conversations with Otto and John, then began a search-and-run on the names of the pilots Otto had given him.

He found no criminal on Stokey Loukes, nothing more than a few traffic violations. He lived in Fairbanks now and was employed as a pilot for a tour organization called Alaska Wild. Their web page promised to show clients the real Alaska, and help them bag game, reel in enormous fish and capture scenes of The Great Alone all for various package prices. Group rates available.

Fielding moved to Australia in '93 and died of natural causes four years later.

Thomas Kijinski, aka Two-Toes, was a different story. Nate found several pops for possession of controlled substances, intent to distribute, D&D, petty larceny. He'd been kicked out of Canada, and his pilot's license had been suspended twice.

On March 8, 1988, his body had been found stuffed in a trash bin on a dock in Anchorage, multiple stab wounds. His wallet and watch had been missing. Conclusion: mugging. The perpetrator or perpetrators had never been identified.

Shine a light on it another way, Nate thought as he printed out the data, and you have a cleanup rather than a mugging. Pilot takes three, brings back two. Couple weeks later, the pilot's stabbed and stuffed in the garbage.

Made a man stop and think.

With the station quiet around him, Nate uncovered his case board. He brewed more coffee and dug up a can of processed ham from the storeroom to make himself what passed for a sandwich.

Then he sat at his desk, studying the board, reading his notes, reading Patrick Galloway's last journal entry.

And spent the long evening hours thinking.

NINETEEN

HE DIDN'T TELL HER about the journal. When a woman ended the day tired and irritable, it seemed unwise to give her one more thing to add to the mix.

He had to give Meg points for shoving up her sleeves and pitching in at The Lodge, and bonus points for rolling out of bed the next morning and handling the breakfast crowd. Especially since the tension between her and Charlene was thick enough to slice up and fry alongside the bacon.

Still, when he took a table, she walked over, coffeepot at the ready. "Hi. I'm Meg, and I'll be your server this morning. Since I'm looking for a really big tip, I'm going to wait until after you eat to bash this pot over Charlene's head."

"I appreciate that. How long before Rose comes back on?"

"Another week or two anyway, and then Charlene's going to let her set her own schedule until she feels ready for full-time."

"You gotta say, that's obliging."

"Oh, she's plenty obliging with Rose." She shot a

short and bitter look over her shoulder in Charlene's direction. "She loves her. It's me she can't tolerate. What'll it be, handsome?"

"If I say the two of you are probably after the same things, in different ways, are you going to bash me over the head with that coffeepot?"

"I might."

"Then I'll have the oatmeal."

"You eat oatmeal?" She wrinkled her sexily crooked nose. "Without somebody holding a knife to your throat?"

"It sticks with you."

"Yeah, for weeks."

With a shrug, she walked off to take more orders, top off mugs of coffee.

He liked watching her move. Quick, but not rushed, sexy, but not obvious. She wore the ubiquitous flannel shirt, open over a white thermal. A silver pendant bounced lightly from its chain between her breasts.

She'd slapped some makeup on—he knew because he'd watched her, and *slapped* was the operative word. Fast, efficient, absent, quick brushes of color on the cheeks, shadowy stuff on the eyes, then careless flicks of mascara on those long, dark lashes.

And when a man noticed how a woman handled mascara, Nate mused, he was sunk.

Charlene came out with an order; Meg went back with her pad. They didn't acknowledge each other, except for the sudden dip in temperature.

He picked up his coffee, pulled out his notebook to use it as a shield when Charlene headed in his direction.

Even a man who was sunk had enough self-preservation to stay out of the middle of two sniping women.

"Want me to top that off for you? She get your order? I don't know why she can't be more pleasant to the customers."

"No, thanks. Yes, she did. And she was pleasant."

"To you, maybe, because you're balling her."

"Charlene." He caught the unmuffled snickers from the booth where Hans and Dexter habitually sat. "God."

"Well, it's no secret, is it?"

"Not anymore," he muttered.

"Spent the night in your room, didn't she?"

He set his coffee down. "If that's a problem for you, I can take my things to her place."

"Why should it be a problem for me?" Despite his no, thanks, she topped off his coffee in an automatic gesture. "Why should anything be a problem for me?"

To his utter terror, her eyes filled with tears. Before he could think how to handle it, or her, she rushed out of the room, coffee sloshing in her pot.

"Women," Bing said from the booth behind him. "Nothing but trouble."

Nate shifted around. Bing was plowing through a plate of eggs, sausage and home fries. There was a sneaky grin on his face, but if Nate didn't mistake it, a little gleam of sympathy in his eyes.

"You ever been married, Bing?"

"Was once. Didn't stick."

"Can't imagine why."

"Thought about doing it again. Maybe I'll get myself

one of those Russian mail-order women, like Johnny Trivani's doing."

"He's going through with that?"

"Sure. Got it down to two, last I heard. Thought I'd see how it works out for him, then look into it."

"Uh-huh." Since they were having what passed as a conversation, Nate decided to probe. "Do you do any climbing, Bing?"

"Used to some. Don't like it much. I got free time, I'd rather go hunting. You looking to recreate?"

"Might be. Days are getting longer."

"You got city all over you, and a skinny build. Stick with town, Chief, that's my advice. Take up knitting or some shit."

"I've always wanted to macramé." At Bing's blank look, Nate only smiled. "How come you don't have a plane, Bing? Guy like you, likes his independence, knows his machines. Seems like a natural."

"Too much work. I'm gonna work, it's gonna be on the ground. Besides, you have to be half crazy to pilot."

"So I hear. Somebody mentioned some pilot to me, funny name. Six-Toes something."

"That'd be Two-Toes. Lost three of them on one foot to frostbite or some shit. Now that was one crazy bastard. Dead now."

"That so? Crashed?"

"Nah. Got himself beat up in a fight. Or no . . ." Bing's brow wrinkled. "Stabbed. City crime. Teach you to live with that many other people."

"There you go. Did you ever go up with him?"

"Once. Crazy bastard. Flew a bunch of us out to the bush for caribou. Didn't know he was higher than the frigging moon until he damn near killed us. Blackened his eye for it," Bing said with relish. "Crazy bastard."

Nate started to respond, but Meg came out of the kitchen—and the front door opened.

"Chief Nate!" Jesse flew in, steps ahead of David. "You're here."

"You, too." Nate flicked a finger down the boy's nose. "David. How's Rose, and the baby?"

"Good. Really good. We're giving her a break, having a man's breakfast here."

"Can we sit with you?" Jesse asked. "'Cause we're all men."

"You bet."

"And the best-looking men in Lunacy." Meg slid the oatmeal, a plate of wheat toast and a bowl of mixed fruit in front of Nate. "You driving yet, Jesse?"

He laughed and scooted into the booth beside Nate. "No." He bounced. "Can I fly your plane?"

"When your feet reach the pedals. Coffee, David?"

"Thanks. You sure this is all right?" he asked Nate.

"Sure. I've missed my usual breakfast buddy here. How's it feel to be the big brother?"

"I dunno. She cries. Loud. And then she sleeps. A lot. But she held my finger. She sucks on Mom's boobie to get milk."

"Really," was all Nate could think to say.

"Why don't I get you some milk, in a glass?" Meg poured coffee for David.

"Rose heard you were pitching in for her." David added sugar to his coffee. "She wanted you to know she appreciates it. We all do."

"No problem." Meg glanced over when Charlene came back in. "I'll get that milk while you decide what to have for your manly breakfast."

Nate left his truck for Meg and walked to the station. The sunlight was weak, but it was light. The mountains were misted by clouds, the kind he now knew carried snow with them. But the bitter wind and the cold it whipped up had mellowed. The walk warmed his muscles, cleared his head.

He passed familiar faces, exchanged greetings in the absent way people who saw each other almost every day were wont to do.

And he thought, with some surprise, that he was making a place for himself. Not just an escape, a refuge or a stopgap, but a place.

He couldn't remember the last time he'd thought about leaving or just drifting to some other town, some other job. It had been days since he'd had to force himself out of bed in the morning or since he'd sat in the dark for hours, afraid to face sleep and the nightmares that ran with it.

The weight could still come back, into his head, his shoulders, his gut, but it wasn't as heavy, wasn't as often.

He looked to the mountains again and knew he owed Patrick Galloway. Owed him enough for cracking open that dark so that he couldn't and wouldn't give up trying to find him justice.

He stopped when Hopp swung her four-wheel over.

She rolled down her window. "I'm on my way to see Rose and the baby."

"Give them my best."

"You ought to pay a call yourself. Meanwhile, couple of things. Feds'll be setting off a controlled avalanche the day after tomorrow so the road between here and Anchorage is going to be blocked."

"Say that again?"

"Feds set off an avalanche from time to time, clear the mountain. Got one scheduled for about ten o'clock A.M., day after tomorrow. Peach just got the dispatch and told me when I stopped in. You'll need to get a bulletin out."

"I'll take care of it."

"And there's a damn bull moose wandering around the school yard, and when a couple of kids decided to chase it, it bashed into a couple of parked cars, then chased back. They've got the kids inside now, but that moose is *pissed*. What're you grinning at?" she demanded. "You ever see a pissed-off moose?"

"No, ma'am, but I guess I'm going to."

"If you can't head it out of town, you're going to have to take it down." She nodded when he stopped grinning. "Somebody's going to get hurt."

"I'll take care of it."

He quickened his pace. Damn if he was going to shoot some stupid moose, especially on school grounds. Maybe that labeled him an Outsider, but that's the way it was.

He pushed into the station and saw his staff, and Ed Woolcott. Otto's face was flushed with temper, and his nose and Ed's were all but bumping.

Avalanches, a pissed-off moose, pissed-off deputy, pissed-off banker. A well-rounded morning.

"It's about damn time," Ed began. "I need a word with you, Chief. In your office."

"You'll have to wait. Peach, get the information on the scheduled avalanche to KLUN. I want it announced every half hour through the day. And make up some fliers, get them posted around town. Peter, I want you to ride out, personally inform anyone residing south of Wolverine Cut that this is coming and they'll be cut off until the roads are cleared."

"Yes, sir."

"Chief Burke."

"Just a minute," he said to Ed. "Otto, we've got an angry moose down at the school. Already some vehicular damage." He strode to the weapon cabinet as he spoke. "I need you to come with me, see if we can herd it out."

He unlocked the cabinet, chose a shotgun with the sincere prayer he wasn't going to have to use it.

"I've been waiting ten minutes," Ed complained. "Your deputies are capable of handling a simple wildlife situation."

"You can wait here, or I'll come by the bank as soon as this situation is under control."

"As deputy mayor—"

"You're being a real pain in the ass," Nate finished. "Otto, we'll need your car. Mine's back at The Lodge. Let's go."

"Looked like a landed trout, gulping," Otto said when they were outside. "He's going to want to fry you for that, Nate, sure as God made little green apples. Ed doesn't take to being stonewalled."

"He's outranked. The mayor told me to deal with the moose; I'm dealing with the moose." He climbed in Otto's car. "We're not shooting it."

"Why do you have the shotgun?"

"I plan to intimidate him."

The town's schools were a connected trio of small, low-slung buildings with a pretty grove of trees on one side and a little squared-off field on the other. He knew the younger kids were allowed out into the field twice a day for a kind of recess—weather permitting.

Since most of the kids had been born there, it took some pretty serious weather to cancel recess.

The high schoolers liked to use the grove to hang out—maybe smoke or fool around—before and after classes.

There was a flagpole, and at this time of day both the U.S. and the Alaskan flag should have been up and waving. Instead, they were a little under half-mast and flicking fitfully in the disinterested wind.

"Kids must've been hoisting the flags when they spotted it," Nate muttered. "Decided to chase after it."

"Just going to irritate it doing that."

Nate glanced at the two smashed-up cars in the tiny lot. "Looks like."

He spotted the moose now, at the edge of the grove, rubbing his antlers on bark. He also saw a light trail of blood. Since no one had reported an injury, he assumed it was moose blood.

"Doesn't look like he's causing any trouble now."

"Looks like he cut himself up bashing those cars, so he's not going to be in a good mood. If he decides to stay around, he'll be trouble, especially if some idiot kid slips by a teacher and decides to chase it again or runs home to get a gun and shoots at it."

"Well, shit. Get as close as you can, and maybe it'll move off."

"Charge, more likely."

"I'm not shooting some moose while it's scratching itself on a tree, Otto."

"Somebody else will, if he sticks close to town. Moose meat's a good meal."

"It's not going to be me, and it's not going to be within town limits, damn it."

He saw the moose turn as they edged closer and saw to his consternation a look more fierce than dumb in those dark eyes. "Hell. Shit, damn, fuck. Blast the horn."

Moose weren't slow. Where had he gotten the idea they were? It galloped toward them, apparently more challenged by the sound of the engine and horn than intimidated. Still cursing, Nate hitched himself out of the window, aimed the gun toward the sky and fired. The moose kept coming, and adding his own oaths to the mix; Otto swerved to avoid collision.

Nate pumped, fired into the air again.

"Shoot the son of a bitch," Otto demanded as he whipped the wheel and nearly dumped Nate out of the window.

"I'm not doing it." Pumping the shotgun again, Nate fired into the snowy ground, a foot in front of the moose.

This time it was the moose that veered off and, with his ungainly trot, headed into the trees.

Nate fired, twice more, to keep it going.

Then he dropped back on the seat, huffed out two breaths. From behind them came the sounds of hoots and cheers and laughter as kids popped out of the school doors.

"You're crazy." Otto pulled off his cap to scrub a hand over his crew cut. "You've got to be crazy. I know you shot a man dead back in Baltimore and sent him to hell. And you can't put some buckshot into a moose?"

Nate took another deep breath and pushed the image of the alley out of his mind. "The moose was unarmed. Let's go, Otto. I need to deal with the deputy mayor. You can come back and take the reports."

THE DEPUTY MAYOR had not deigned to wait. In fact, Peach told Nate, he'd stormed out after a short diatribe on why it had been a mistake to hire some lazy, puffed-up Outsider.

Taking it in stride, Nate passed the shotgun to Otto, snagged a two-way and set out to walk to the bank.

Somewhere in the wide, wide world, Nate imagined there was a place colder than Lunacy, Alaska, in February. And he hoped to God he never paid a visit there.

The sky had cleared, which meant any stingy heat had lifted up and away. But the sun streamed, so with luck they might hit a sweaty twenty degrees by midafternoon. And the sun, Nate saw, was ringed by a rainbow circle, a colorful halo of reds and blues and golds. What Peter had told him was called a sun dog.

People were out and about, taking advantage of the bright morning to do their business. Some of them called out greetings to him or flipped waves.

He saw Johnny Trivani, the hopeful groom, chatting on the sidewalk with Bess Mackie, and Deb outside the store washing windows as if it had been a fine spring day.

He lifted a hand to Mitch Dauber, who sat in the window of KLUN spinning records and observing life in Lunacy. He expected Mitch would have something philosophical to say about the moose before the end of the day.

February. It struck him as he stood on the corner of Lunatic and Denali. Somehow it had gotten to be so far into February they were nearly to March. He was coming right up on the line of his sixty days, his own point of re-turn. And was still here.

More than here, he thought. Settling into being here.

Thoughtful, he crossed over and into the bank.

There were two customers doing business at the bank counter, and another picking up mail from the post office. From the way they and the tellers eyeballed him, Nate imagined Ed had still been in a temper when he'd come in.

In the silence that fell, he nodded, then stepped through the short, swinging gate that separated the bank lobby from the offices.

It didn't boast a drive-through, and there were no ATMs lurking outside, but the bank had a nice carpet, a few local paintings on the wall and a general air of efficiency.

He walked to the door that had Ed Woolcott's name on a shiny brass plaque, and knocked.

Ed opened it himself, sniffed. "You'll have to wait. I'm on the phone."

"Fine." When the door shut in his face, Nate simply slipped his hands into his pockets and studied the paintings.

He noted one of a totem in a snowy woods was signed by Ernest Notti. One of Peter's relatives? he wondered. He still had a lot to learn about his Lunatics.

He glanced around. There was no protective glass between teller and customers, but there were security cameras. He'd checked the place out already, before he'd opened his own accounts.

Now that conversation had started up again, he tuned in to snatches. Movie night, an upcoming bake sale to benefit the school band, the weather, the Iditarod. Small-town small talk, and nothing like what he would have heard if he'd walked into one of the branches of his bank in Baltimore.

Ed kept him waiting ten minutes, a little power flex, and was stone-faced, with a little flush on his cheekbones, when he opened the door.

"I want you to be aware I've made a formal complaint to the mayor."

"Okay."

"I don't like your attitude, Chief Burke."

"Noted, Mr. Woolcott. If that's all you want to tell me, I need to get back to the station."

"What I want is to know just what you're doing about the theft of my property."

"Otto's handling that."

"My property was vandalized and damaged. Expensive

fishing gear has been stolen. I believe I'm entitled to the attention of the chief of police."

"And you've got it. A report has been duly filed, and the officer in charge is pursuing the matter. The theft isn't being taken lightly by me or my staff. We have a detailed description of the stolen property, and if the thief is dumb enough to use it, talk about it or try to sell it within my jurisdiction, we'll make an arrest and recover your property."

Ed's eyes were slits in his rawhide face. "Maybe if I was female, you'd take more interest."

"Actually, I don't think you'd be my type. Mr. Woolcott," he continued, "you're upset, and you're angry. You've got a right to be. You were violated. The fact that it was, most likely, kids being stupid doesn't lessen that violation. We'll do everything we can to get your property back. If it helps, I'll apologize for being abrupt with you earlier. I was concerned that children might be injured, and that took priority. You have two children in that school. I assume their safety would take precedence over an update on your stolen property."

The flush had died down, and a long huff told Nate the crisis had passed. "Be that as it may, you were rude."

"I was. And distracted. To be frank, I've got a lot on my mind just now. Patrick Galloway's murder, Max's apparent suicide." He shook his head, as if overwhelmed. "When I signed on for this job, I expected to be handling, well, at worst the sort of theft you've experienced."

"Tragic." Ed sat now and was gracious enough to gesture Nate to a chair. "It's so damn tragic and shocking. Max was a friend, a good one."

He rubbed the back of his neck with his hand. "I thought I knew him and had no idea, no clue, that he was contemplating suicide. Leaving his wife, his kids that way." He held up his hands, a kind of silent apology. "I guess I'm more upset about it than I've wanted to admit, and it's been eating at me. I owe you an apology, too."

"Not necessary."

"I've let this theft build up. Defense mechanism. It's easier to get riled about that than think about Max. I've been trying to help Carrie with the details on his memorial and some of the finances. A lot of paperwork comes along with death. It's hard. It's hard to deal with it."

"Nothing harder than burying a friend. You knew him a long time."

"A long time. Good times. Our kids have grown up together. And this on top of finding out about Pat . . ."

"You knew him, too."

He smiled a little. "Before I married Arlene. Or as she'd say, before she tamed me. I wasn't always the solid citizen and family man I am now. Pat was . . . an adventure. Those were good times, too. In their way."

He looked around his office as if it belonged to someone else, and he couldn't quite remember how he'd come to be there. "It doesn't seem possible. None of it."

"It's been a shock for everyone to find out about Galloway."

"I thought he'd taken off—everyone did—and it didn't surprise me. Not really. He was restless, reckless. That's what made him so appealing."

"You climbed with him."

"God." Ed sat back now. "I used to love to climb.

The thrill and the misery. Still do love it, but I rarely have, or take, the time. I've been teaching my son."

"I've heard Galloway was good."

"Very good. Though that recklessness was there. A little too much of it for comfort for me, even when I was thirty."

"Do you have any thoughts on who would've been climbing with him that February?"

"None, and believe me, I have thought about it since we heard the news. I suspect he might have picked up someone, or a group, and taken them up for a winter climb. It was the sort of thing he might do on impulse, to earn a little money, and for the buzz. And one of them killed him, God knows why." He shook his head. "But aren't the State Police handling that investigation?"

"They are. I'm just curious, unofficially."

"I doubt they'll ever find out who it was, or why. Sixteen years. God, how things change," he murmured. "You hardly notice as they do. You know I ran the bank singlehanded at one time, lived here, too. Kept the money in that safe right over there."

He gestured to a black floor safe.

"I didn't know that."

"I was twenty-seven when I landed here. Going to carve my place out of the wilderness, civilize it to my liking." He smiled now. "Guess I did just that. You know, the Hopps and Judge Royce were my first customers. Took a lot of faith for them to put their money in my hands. I never forgot it. But we had a vision, and we built this town out of it."

"It's a good town."

"Yes, it is, and I'm proud of my part in making it. Old Man Hidel was here, with the original Lodge. He banked with me, too, after a while. Other people came along. Peach with her third, no it was her second husband. They lived out in the bush awhile, came here for supplies and company from time to time. She came back for good when he died. Otto, Bing, Deb and Harry. Takes strength of character and vision to make a life here."

"Yes, it does."

"Well . . ." He drew air in through his nose. "Pat had vision, of his own kind, and he was a character. I don't know about that strength. He was an entertaining bastard, though. I hope this will all be put to rest properly. Do you think we'll ever know, for certain, what happened up there?"

"Odds aren't favorable. But I think Coben will give it the proper time and effort. He'll look for the pilot, and anyone who might have seen Galloway in the days before he went up. They might want to talk to you, about who he used as a pilot on his climbs."

"It would've been Jacob, most usually. But surely if Jacob had taken him up, he'd have reported it when Pat didn't come back." He lifted his shoulders. "So, logically, it would have to have been someone else. Let me think . . ."

He picked up a silver pen, tapped it absently against his desk blotter. "When we climbed with Jacob, as I recall, he sometimes used—what was his name—Vietnam vet, Lakes . . . Loukes. That's it. Then there was this maniac. Two-Toes, they called him. Do you think I should call this Coben and tell him?"

"Couldn't hurt. I should get back." He rose, held out a hand. "I hope we're square now, Mr. Woolcott."

"Ed. And we are. Damn auger. I paid too much for it, so it's a double annoyance. It's insured, so are the rods, but it's the principle."

"Understood. Listen, I'll take a ride out to your ice shack, take a look around."

Satisfaction settled over Ed's face. "Now, I appreciate that. I put a new lock on. Let me get you the keys."

SINCE MOOSE AND APOPLECTIC deputy mayors had been dealt with, Nate swung by to see Rose. He made what he hoped were appropriate noises over the baby, who looked like a black-headed turtle swaddled in a pink blanket.

He called in, let Peach know he was taking a run out to the lake to run another check of Ed's ice shack. On impulse, he stopped by the dog run at The Lodge, sprang Rock and Bull, and took them with him so they could have an hour of free rein.

It was a nice ride, with the radio turned from Otto's choice of country-western to Nate's preference for alternative rock. He drove to the lake to the bouncy beat of blink-182.

Ed's shack sat alone on a rippled plate of ice. It was, Nate estimated, about the size of two generous outhouses stuck together and was fashioned out of what he thought might be cedar shakes. A little more upscale than he'd expected, with the sides silvered by weather and topped by a peaked roof.

And set well apart from the huddle of other shacks.

He decided it looked like the manor house and the peasant village, amusing himself.

The dogs raced over the ice like a couple of kids on school holiday, while Nate slipped and slithered his way across.

The quiet was amazing—like a church—with a kind of musical hush from that light wind through the snow-drenched trees. The sun dog shimmered in the icy blue sky and had the frozen lake gleaming.

The sense of silence and solitude was so strong that he jumped, reached for his weapon when he heard the long, echoing call overhead.

The eagle circled, gold-brown and gorgeous against the heavy sky. The dogs bumped each other playfully, then dived into the bank of snow at the edge of the lake.

He could see Meg's plane from here, he realized. The red flash of it just at the long curve of the frozen water. And other little snips of civilization if he cared to look. There, a stream of smoke from a chimney, a glimpse of a house through the thick trees, his own breath stream-ing out.

He let out a short laugh. Maybe he should give this ice-fishing business a shot. There had to be something to be said for the primitive rush of dropping a line through a hole in the ice and sitting in the quiet on a plate of frozen water.

He crossed to the shack and saw the sloppy spray-painted DICK SHIT! spewed across the door in virulent yellow.

Another sign of civilization, Nate thought as he fished out the keys.

Ed had bolted on two new padlocks, each with a fat, shiny chain.

He dealt with them, stepped in.

The graffiti artists had been at work inside. Obscenities squirreled around the walls. He adjusted his annoyance with Ed. He'd have been royally pissed, too, to find this sort of thing in one of his sanctuaries.

He could see the rack where the rods had been, as well as the utter tidiness under the disorder the vandals had caused.

The tackle, the Coleman stove, the chairs hadn't been touched, but a cabinet he suspected had held the scotch—Glenfiddich, according to Otto's report—and some food supplies was empty and open.

He found cleats that snapped on boots and made a mental note to buy some for himself. He found a first-aid kit, extra gloves, hat, an old, worn parka, snowshoes and a couple of thermal blankets.

The snowshoes were hung on the wall, just over a screaming yellow ASSHOLE. If they'd been used recently, Nate couldn't tell.

There was fuel for the stove, a fish scaler and a couple of wicked-looking knives. A number of magazines, a portable radio. Extra batteries.

Nothing, he supposed, that you wouldn't expect to find in an ice-fishing shack in Alaska.

When he walked out again, he circled around. He looked down toward Meg's plane, then across where her woods began.

He tried to picture Ed Woolcott—pompous, but tough—skulking around the woods on snowshoes.

TWENTY

THE MOOSE WAS the hot topic for most of the week. Nate was razzed or congratulated on his moose dispersing technique, depending on the source.

Nate considered the moose a kind of blessing. It took people's minds off murder and death, at least for a little while.

He'd considered going back to speak with Carrie, and some strategies for getting past the probability she'd slam the door in his face and refuse to see him. The notification that the body had been released and cremated—and that Meg was flying Carrie into Anchorage to pick up the ashes—decided him.

"I'm going to need to come with you," he told Meg.

"Look, Chief, it's going to be hard enough to deal with coming and going without you there to rub the circumstances in her face."

"I don't intend to do any rubbing. I'm going to go see her now. We'll meet you at the river."

"Nate." She finished dragging on her boots. "Maybe you think the Lunacy PD has to be represented here, for whatever cop reason, but send Otto or Peter. Fair or not, you're the last person Carrie wants to see today."

"We'll meet you at the river." He was halfway to the

door of the room they were temporarily sharing, when it struck. He turned, grinned. "Rock and Bull. I'm slow, but I just got it. Must be all the moose talk. Rocky and Bullwinkle."

"You are slow. Or you had a deprived childhood."

"No. I just figured they were macho names, like, I don't know, boxers. The Rock, Raging Bull, whatever."

Her lips tipped up at the corners. Why was it he could charm her even when she was annoyed with him? "The Rock's a wrestler."

"Close enough. See you in an hour."

He'd already informed his staff—who had the same pessimistic attitude as Meg—that he'd be making the trip to Anchorage that morning. So he drove straight to Carrie's.

The door swung open before he was halfway up the walk. She stood in a black sweater and pants, blocking the door. "You can just turn around and go back to your car. I don't have to talk to you, and I don't have to let you into my house."

"I'd like five minutes, Carrie. I sure as hell don't want to stand out here shouting what I have to say to you through a closed door. I don't think you'd like that, either. It'd be easier on both of us if you give me that five minutes inside, especially since I'm going to be on the plane with you in an hour."

"I don't want you with me."

"I know that. If you still feel that way after you hear what I have to say, I'll send Peter instead."

He could see the struggle on her face. Then she

turned, walked away, leaving the door open to him and the brisk cold.

He walked in, shut the door. She stood in her living room, her back to him, her arms folded against her chest tight enough that he saw her knuckles whiten against her own biceps.

"Are your kids here?"

"No, I sent them to school. They're better off with the routine, with their friends. They need some normal. How can you come here like this?" She whirled around. "How can you come here and harass me on the day I'm going to bring my husband's ashes home? Don't you have any heart, any compassion?"

"I'm here officially, and what I'm going to say to you is confidential."

"Officially." She all but spat it. "What do you want? My husband's dead. He's dead and he can't defend himself against the terrible things you say about him. You won't say those things in his house. This is Max's house, and you won't say those horrible lies about him here."

"You loved him. Did you love him enough to give me your word that what I do say here won't be repeated? To anyone. Anyone, Carrie."

"You'd dare ask me if I loved—"

"Just yes or no. I need your word."

"I've got no interest in repeating your lies. Say whatever you have to say and get out. I'll promise to forget you were even here."

It would have to do. "I believe Max was on the mountain with Patrick Galloway at the time of Galloway's death."

"Go to hell."

"I also believe there was a third person with them."

Her mouth trembled open. "What do you mean, a third person?"

"Three of them went up, two of them came down. I believe that third person is responsible for Galloway's murder. And I believe he killed Max or induced Max to kill himself."

While she stared, her hand groped out, fumbled its way to the back of a chair. Her body seemed to sink into it. "I can't understand you."

"I can't give you all the details, but I need your cooperation . . . I need your help," he amended, "to prove what I believe. There was a third man, Carrie. Who was it?"

"I don't know. God, I don't know. I—I told you someone killed Max. I told you he didn't kill himself. I told Sergeant Coben. I keep telling him."

"I know. I believe you."

"You believe me." Tears gushed out of her eyes, rained down her cheeks. "You believe me."

"I do. But the fact is the ME's ruled it suicide. Coben may have his doubts, and he may have his instincts, even a certain amount of circumstantial evidence, but he doesn't have the investment we do. He doesn't have the room or the time to push on this the way I do. We're going to need to go back, a long time. You're going to need to try to remember details, feelings, conversations. It's not easy. And you're going to need to keep this to yourself. I'm asking you to take a risk."

She brushed at tears. "I don't understand."

"If we're right, and someone killed Max because of what happened on that mountain, that someone may be watching you. He may wonder what you know, what you remember, what Max might have told you."

"You think I could be in danger?"

"I think I want you to be very careful. I don't want you discussing this with anyone, not even your kids. Not your best friend, not your priest. No one. I want you to let me go through Max's things, his personal papers. Everything—here and at the paper. And I don't want anyone to know about it. I want you to go back and think about that February. What you did, what Max did, who he spent time with, how he behaved. Write it down."

She stared at him with something that looked like hope fighting through the grief. "You're going to find out who did this to him? To us?"

"I'm going to do everything I can."

She mopped at her cheeks. "I said terrible things about you to—to anyone who'd listen."

"Some of them were probably true."

"No, they weren't." She pressed her fingers to her eyes now. "I'm so confused. I'm sick, sick in my heart, in my head. I made myself hire Meg to take me, to bring us back, because I needed to prove I didn't believe . . . that I wasn't ashamed. But part of me was." She dropped her hands, and her eyes were shattered. "If he was up there, he must have known . . ."

"We're going to work all that out. Some of the answers may be hard, Carrie, but it's better than just having questions."

"I hope you're right." She got to her feet. "I need to fix myself up a little." She started out, then stopped and turned around. "That business with the moose, out at the school? Max would've loved that. He would have loved writing that up. 'Troublemaking Moose Expelled from Lunacy High,' or something like that. That sort of story just tickled him. A man like that, a man who could find such pleasure in something so foolish, he couldn't have done what was done to Pat Galloway."

"I WANTED TO MARRY HIM almost as soon as I met him. I liked the way he'd talk and talk about starting up a town paper, how it was important to record the little things, just as much as the big ones."

Carrie looked out the window in her seat beside Meg, and Nate could see her gaze was on the mountains. "I came here to teach, and I stayed because it got inside me. I wasn't a very good teacher, really, but I wanted to stay. And I liked the odds—a lot more men than women. I was looking for a man." She slid a sideways glance at Meg.

"Who isn't?"

Carrie laughed a little, but the sound was hoarse. "I wanted to get married and have kids. One look at Max and I decided he'd fit the bill. He was smart, but not too smart, cute, but not so handsome I'd worry other women would be after him. A little wild—more that he wanted to be wild—but the sort you knew you could fix up with some time and effort."

She broke off, and her hitching breaths were an obvious fight against tears.

"Do women make checklists of stuff like that? You know, like you do on a house you're thinking of buying. Fixer-upper. Solid foundation but needs new trim. That kind of thing?" Nate asked.

Carrie let out a watery giggle, pressed her hand to her lips.

"We do. Or I sure did the closer I got to thirty. I didn't love him right off, I mean not like some huge, hot burst. But I got him into bed, and that part was good. Another check in the plus column."

There was another beat of silence, then Nate cleared his throat. "Ah, are those particular checks size-specific or color-coded?"

"Don't worry, Burke, you get a nice fat check in that column, too," Meg interjected. She flipped him a glance that was full of appreciation and understanding. He was keeping it light and easy for the widow. As much as he could. She looked over at Carrie. "You always looked good together. Like a team."

"We were a good team. Maybe I never got that big, hot burst, but I'll tell you when I fell in love with him—really, absolutely, no-going-back in love with him. It was when he held our daughter for the first time. The look on his face when he lifted her up that first time, the way he looked at me when he did. All that shock and wonder, the thrill and the terror, all of it on his face. So I didn't get an explosion, but what I got was warm and steady and real.

"He didn't kill your father, Meg." She looked out the window again. "The man who held that baby the way he did, he couldn't have killed anyone. I know you have reason to think different, and I want you to know how much I value and appreciate your . . . kindness in taking me today."

"We both lost someone we loved. It wouldn't prove anything if we slapped each other about it."

Women, Nate thought, were tougher and more resilient than any man he knew. Including himself.

HE TRACKED DOWN COBEN as soon as they landed, and though it felt callous, he left Meg with Carrie to deal with the arrangements and release of Max's ashes.

"Thomas Kijinski aka Two-Toes. He looks like the best bet. There's a pilot, Loukes, works out of Fairbanks now, and a couple others Galloway used occasionally." He set the list he'd made on Coben's desk. "But Kijinski pops for me. He ends up dead, a couple of weeks after Galloway."

"Stabbing, investigated and deemed a mugging." Coben drew in a breath. "Kijinski played with some bad boys. He gambled pretty heavy, was suspected of running drugs. Time of his death he had markers out for somewhere in the neighborhood of ten large. Investigating officer believed one of his IOUs was collected in flesh, but he couldn't prove it."

"And you're buying that kind of coincidence?"

"I'm not buying anything. The fact is, Kijinski lived a

bad life and met a bad end. If he happened to be the pilot who took Galloway on his last climb, he isn't going to
tell us about it."

"Then it shouldn't be a problem for you to give me a
copy of the file on him."

Coben sucked air through his nose again. "I've got
the press on my ass on this, Burke."

"Yeah, I've caught some of the reports. I've given
some reporters an official statement."

"You've seen crap like this?" He yanked a copy of a
tabloid out of a drawer, tossed it down. The headline
screamed:

ICE MAN RECOVERED
FROM FROZEN GRAVE

There was a picture of Galloway, as he'd been in the cave,
in lurid color under the boldface type.

"You had to expect shit like this," Nate began.

"One of the recovery team had to take that shot. One
of them cashed in, made a few bucks by selling it to the
tabloids. My lieutenant's breathing down my neck. I
don't need you doing the same."

"There was a third man on the mountain."

"Yeah, there was, according to Galloway's journal. Of
course, we can't prove he died after that last journal entry. With sixteen years between, we've got a lot of room
on time of death. Could've been then, or a month after.
Six months after."

"You know better than that."

"What I know." Coben lifted one hand. "What I can

prove." Then the other. "ME ruled suicide, and my lieu-tenant likes it. Too damn bad Hawbaker didn't name names in his note."

"Give me the file, and I'll get names. You can smell it the same as I can, Coben. If you want to close the lid on the stink, that's up to you. But I've got a memorial to go to and a woman with two kids who deserves to know the truth, so she can learn to live with it. I can take a few days and go hunting for information here in Anchorage, or you can give me the file and let me get back to Lunacy."

"If I'd wanted to close the lid, I wouldn't have given you Galloway's journal." Frustration rippled around him in nearly visible waves. "I've got brass to answer to, and they want the lid closed. The prevailing theory is that Hawbaker killed Galloway, and the third man—the one who was injured according to the journal. And if you look at this straight on, that's what plays. Why would Galloway's killer spare an injured man, a potential wit-ness? Hawbaker does them both. Then fear of exposure, remorse, and he offs himself."

"That's tidy."

Coben flattened his lips. "Some like it tidy. I'll get you the file, Burke, but you keep your personal investigation low-key. The lowest. The press, my lieutenant, anybody gets wind you're poking around, and I'm helping you, it comes down on me."

"Done."

MEG WAS SO SATURATED with Carrie's grief that she didn't mind spending another evening waiting tables.

Given a choice, she'd have preferred to load up her dogs and fly out to the bush. Somewhere. Anywhere she could spend a couple of days completely alone, away from the pulls and tugs of people and all their needs.

That, she thought as she swung into the overheated kitchen at The Lodge, was the Galloway gene. Take off, flip it off, shrug it off. Life's too short for hassles.

But there was enough of something else in her— Christ, she hoped it wasn't Charlene—to make her stay and see it through.

She hooked her orders on the turntable for Big Mike. Two meat loafs, a vegetarian special and the salmon surprise.

She picked up the completed orders from her last trip in, balanced them with such ease it made her wince. Nothing against waitpersons the world over, she thought as she carried the food out, but she wished she wasn't so good at it. It wasn't on the scope for her, even as a fall-back career.

God, she wanted the air, some silence. Her dogs. Her music. Some sex.

She was ready to pop.

She worked another two hours, through the clatter, the complaints, the gossip, the bad jokes. She could feel the pressure building up inside her, the desperate need to get out, get away. When the crowd thinned out, she caught Charlene at the kitchen door.

"That's all you get for tonight. I'm taking off."

"I need you to—"

"You're going to have to need somebody else. Shouldn't be hard for you." She headed for the stairs.

She wanted a shower, and by God, she was packing up her things and going home.

This time it was Charlene who caught her.

"We're going to have another rush in an hour. People coming in to drink, to—"

"Oddly enough, I don't care." She'd have closed the door in Charlene's face, but her mother was through the door and slamming it behind her.

"You never did. I don't *care* that you don't care, but you owe me."

Forget the shower, she'd just pack. "Bill me."

"I need help, Megan. Why can't you ever just help me out without being so bitchy about it?"

"I inherited the bitch from you. Not my fault." She ripped open a drawer and dragged whatever was in it out, tossed it on the bed.

"I built something here. You benefited from that."

"I don't give a rat's ugly ass about your money."

"I'm not talking about money." Charlene grabbed clothes from the bed and hurled them into the air. "I'm talking about this place. It means something. You never cared. You couldn't wait to get away from it and from me, but it means something. We've been written up in the paper, in magazines, in tour guides. I got people working here who depend on their paycheck to put food on their table and clothes on their kids' backs. I've got customers who come in here every damn night because it means something."

"You've got," Megan agreed. "It's nothing to do with me."

"That's what he always said, too." Enraged, she

kicked at a pair of jeans on the floor. "You look like him, you sound like him."

"That's not my fault, either."

"Nothing was ever his fault. Bad run of luck playing poker, gee, guess there's no money this week. Need a little space, Charley, you know how it goes. I'll be back in a couple of days. Something'll turn up; stop nagging at me. Somebody had to pay the bills, didn't they?" Charlene demanded. "Somebody had to pay for medicine when you got sick or come up with the cash to get you shoes. He could bring me all the wildflowers he could pick in the summer or write me pretty songs and poems, but they didn't put food on the table."

"I put food on my table. I buy my own shoes." But she'd calmed a little. "I'm not saying you didn't work. You did plenty of scheming on top of it, but it's your life. You got what you wanted."

"I wanted him. Goddamn it. I wanted him."

"So did I, so we both lost out there. Nothing we can do about it." She'd come back for her things, Meg thought. Right now she just needed out. She walked to the door, hesitated.

"I called Boston, talked to his mother. She's . . . she won't block you from claiming his body, from burying him here."

"You called her?"

"Yeah, it's done." She opened the door.

"Meg. Megan, please. Wait a minute." Charlene sat on the side of the bed, clothes strewn on the floor around her. "Thank you."

Hell. Oh, hell. "It was just a phone call."

"It matters." Charlene gripped her hands together in her lap and stared at them. "It matters so much to me. I was so mad at you for going to Anchorage to . . . to see him. For cutting me out."

Meg closed the door, leaned back against it. "That's not what I was doing."

"I wasn't a good mother. I wanted to be at first. Tried to be. But there was always so much to do. I didn't know there'd be so much to do."

"You were pretty young."

"Too young, I guess. He wanted more." She looked up then, shrugged. "He just loved you to pieces, and he wanted more kids. I wouldn't let it happen. I just didn't want to go through it all again, getting fat and tired, going through that *pain*. Then having all that to do. And the money that was never there when you needed it or just wanted it. He pushed for it, and I pushed back with other things, until it seemed we spent half the time pushing each other. And I was jealous because he doted on you, and I was always the outsider, always the one saying no."

"I guess somebody had to."

"I don't know if we'd have made it. If he'd come back, I don't know if we'd have stuck it out. We started wanting such different things. But I know if we'd split, I know he'd have taken you."

As if to keep her hands busy, she smoothed the bed-spread on either side of her. "He'd have taken you," she repeated. "I'd've let him. You should know that. He loved you more than I could."

It was hard, harder than anything she could remember, to walk to the bed and sit. "Enough to scrape the money together to buy me shoes?"

"Maybe not, but enough to take you camping so you could look at the stars. Enough to sit at the fire and tell you stories."

"I like to think you'd have made it if he'd come back."

Charlene looked over, blinked. "Really?"

"Yeah. I like to think you'd have found a way to make it work. You'd already stuck together a long time. Longer than a lot of people do. I want to ask you something."

"This seems like the time."

"Was there a big, hot blast the first time you met him? When you fell for him?"

"Oh God, yes. Nearly burned me up. And it never stopped. I'd think it was dead, cold and dead, when I got mad enough or tired enough. But then he'd look at me, and it was back. I never had that with anyone else. I keep waiting for it, but I never get it."

"Maybe you should be looking for something else this time. Somebody told me recently about the benefits of a good, steady warmth."

She rose, picked up scattered clothes. "I can't go back down there and work tonight."

"Okay."

"I'll work breakfast for you, but I need you to get somebody else to cover for Rose. I've got to get back to my place, my life."

Charlene nodded, pushed to her feet. "You gonna take the sexy cop with you?"

"Up to him."

SHE PACKED UP, tidied the room. Meg considered leaving Nate a note but decided that was a little too rude, a little too wrong, even for her.

Didn't have her car anyway, she remembered, not that she was above "borrowing" his. Or someone else's. And telling them about it later.

In the end, she slung her knapsack over her shoulder and hoofed it to the station, after a detour by The Italian Place.

He'd said he'd be working late, covering the desk. Whatever. Since his car was locked, she debated briefly. She could dig out her handy set of keys, probably find one that would work. But he wouldn't appreciate it if he'd set the car alarm.

Which, being city bred, he might have done.

She carried her pack, and the large pizza, into the station.

Awfully damn quiet, was her first thought. How did the man work without music? She tossed her pack aside, started to call out, but he appeared in the doorway.

If she hadn't been looking, she wouldn't have seen the way his hand rested on the butt of his holstered weapon—or the way it drifted away when he smiled at her.

"I smell food—and woman. Gets my caveman instinct going."

"Pizza, pepperoni. Figured you could use something hot, which includes me, about this time."

"That's a big affirmative to both. What's the knapsack for?"

She hadn't seen him look at it. "I'm running away. Want to come with?"

"Fight with Charlene?"

"Yes, but that's not why. We sort of made up, actually. I just have to get the hell out of here, Burke. Too many people for too long. Gets me edgy. I thought pizza, then some sex back in my place would scratch that itch before I hurt someone and you had to arrest me."

"That's a plan."

"I was going to just go, but I didn't. I want the points for doing it this way."

"Scoreboard's adjusted. Why don't you bring that back? I'll dig up something to wash it down with."

"Got that." She dug one-handed into her duffel, pulled out a bottle of red. "Liberated it from the bar at The Lodge. We'll have to drink it all, to dispose of the evidence."

She passed him the bottle as she walked past him, then turned into his office and set the pizza on his desk.

He'd closed his files, both hard copy and computer, and had tossed the blanket over the board when he heard the outer door open.

"Napkins?" she asked.

It wasn't gentlemanly, but he couldn't leave her alone in the office. "Under Peach's counter." He pulled out his Swiss Army knife, levered out the corkscrew. "Never ac-

tually used this one before. Lot of damn work, but hey."
He muscled out the cork as she came back in. "Success."

She tossed down the napkins, got two mugs from beside his coffeemaker. "What's this?" she tugged the side
edge of the blanket with a finger.

"Don't." At her look of surprise, he shook his head.
"Just don't. Let's eat."

They sat, divvied up wine and pizza. "Why are you
working so late, and alone? Are you killing time until I
finish my moonlighting for the night?"

"That's one part. But tell me, what did you fight with
Charlene about?"

"You're changing the subject."

"Yes, I am."

"Her being demanding, me being ungrateful, and so on
and so forth. Then we came around to my father, and . . .
other things, and some of it made sense to me. Enough
for me to be able to admit he wasn't the easiest guy to be
with, as a partner, and that she, in her own strange and
annoying way, probably did the best she could. That we
both loved him, more than we can love each other."

She poured more wine, deliberately picked up a second slice of pizza though her stomach had gone knotty.
"Under that blanket's about my father, isn't it? I've seen
enough cop movies, enough cop TV, Burke, to know you
people stick up photographs and reports and what have
you when you're investigating."

"I'm not investigating anything, officially. Yes, it has
to do with your father, and I want you to leave that blanket where it is."

"I told you before, I'm not delicate."

"And I'm telling you now, there are some things I don't share. Won't ever."

She was silent, studying her pizza. "That the sort of statement that had your wife doing another man?"

"No," he said evenly. "She couldn't have cared less about my work."

She closed her eyes a moment, then made herself open them and meet his. "That was a cheap shot. I'm not above a cheap shot." She tossed the pizza down. "I don't like myself very much tonight. That's why I have to get out, get away, get back to who I am when I like me."

"But you came here first, to bring me pizza and wine."

"You've got a little hook in me somewhere. I don't know if it's going to stick, but it's there for now."

"I love you, Megan."

"Oh, Jesus, don't say that *now!*" She sprang up, pulling at her hair as she paced. "When I'm in this pissy, bitching mood. Do you *look* to be kicked in the face by women, Ignatious? Are you just itching for somebody else to smack your heart around?"

"It was that big blast for me," he went on calmly. "It took a big blast to break through, I'd guess, since I've been pretty busy wallowing for the last year. Most of the time, lately, it banks down to a nice simmer. Easier to live with the simmer than the blast. Now and then it kicks up again though. Goes right through me like a fireball."

She stopped, dropped down again because her knotty stomach was busy doing flips. "God help you."

"Yeah, I thought the same myself. But I do love you, and it's different than it was with Rachel. I had all this stuff planned out then, a nice, steady, sensible, normal kind of step and stage."

"And you're not looking for sensible and normal with me."

"Be a waste of time."

"Don't give me that. You've got home and hearth tattooed on your butt."

"Do not. You're the one with the tattoo, which I find incredibly erotic, by the way. Maybe when you decide you're in love with me, we can think about what happens next, but for now—"

"When I decide."

"Yeah, when. I'm patient, Meg, and relentless in my way. I'm starting to get my edge back. It's been blunted a long time, but it's coming back. You'll just have to deal with that."

"Interesting. A little scarier than I expected, but interesting."

"And it's because I love you, and I trust you, that I'm going to show you this."

He opened the file on his desk. Taking the copied pages of Patrick Galloway's journal, he handed them to her.

He saw the instant she recognized the handwriting, the way her body went stiff and still, the quick, almost inaudible drawing in of breath. Her gaze flicked up to his once, briefly, then riveted on the pages in her hand.

She said nothing as she read them. She didn't weep or rage or tremble as another woman might have done. Instead, she picked up her wine again, sipped slowly and read the pages straight through.

"Where did these come from?"

"They're copies from the pages out of a notebook he had inside his parka. Coben gave them to me."

"How long ago?"

"Few days."

There was a little burn in the center of her belly. "And you didn't tell me. You didn't show me."

"No."

"Because?"

"I needed to evaluate, and you needed to settle."

"Is that part of your edge, Chief? Making unilateral decisions?"

"It's part of my professional responsibilities, and my personal feelings. You can't discuss this with anyone, until I determine otherwise."

"You've shown them to me now because in your professional opinion you've evaluated and I've settled."

"Something like that."

She closed her eyes. "You take care, don't you? Professionally, personally. It's pretty much the same to you, the caring."

He said nothing, and she opened her eyes. "No point in tossing a bunch of bullshit out at you when you did what you thought was right. Probably was right."

Knowing it wouldn't go down easy now, she set the wine aside. "What does Coben think?"

"It's more what his superiors think at this point. The theory is Max killed Galloway, then killed the third man. When your father's body was discovered, fear of discovery and remorse drove him to suicide."

"That's how they'll write it up, close it down, whatever the cop-speak for it is."

"I think so, yes."

"Poor Carrie." She leaned forward, laid the pages back on his desk. "Poor Max. He never killed Patrick Galloway."

"No," Nate said and closed the file again. "He didn't."

TWENTY-ONE

THEY PACKED INTO Town Hall for Max Hawbaker's memorial. It was the only place big enough to hold the crowd. It was interesting to Nate how many showed up—in work clothes or Sunday clothes, in Alaskan tuxedos or bunny boots. They came because he'd been one of them, and his wife and kids still were. They came, Nate thought, whether they thought he was a small-town hero or a murderer.

And many did believe the latter. Nate saw it in their eyes or heard it in snatches of conversation. He let it go.

Max was eulogized with warmth and with humor— and the name Patrick Galloway was carefully omitted from any public statement.

Then it was done. Some went back to work, and some went to Carrie's for what he always thought of as the post-funeral replay.

Nate went back to work.

CHARLENE AMBUSHED MEG as she off-loaded supplies from her plane. She grabbed her arm, tugged her away from Jacob. "I need to see him."

"Who?"

"You know who. I want you to fly me into Anchorage, to the funeral home that's holding his body till spring. I have a right."

Meg studied Charlene's face. "Well, I can't. It's too late to fly to Anchorage today, and I've got jobs booked. Iditarod's under way. People want to fly over the route, get pictures."

"I've got a right—"

"What brought this on?"

"Just because we didn't get married doesn't mean I wasn't his wife. His true wife, just the same as Carrie was to Max."

"Oh shit." Meg paced out two tight circles. "You know, I thought you showed a lot of class going to the memorial, looking Carrie right in the eye and giving her your condolences. And here you are working up a mad because she got all that attention."

"That's not it." Or only part of it, Charlene admitted. "I want to see him, and I will. If you won't take me, I'll call Jerk in Talkeetna, pay him to fly me down."

"You've been stewing about this since Max's memorial, haven't you? Just stewing and churning it around since then. What's the point, Charlene?"

"You've seen him."

"Score one for me."

"How do I know he's gone? How do I know it's him unless I see for myself? The way Carrie got to see Max."

"I can't take you."

"You'd make me go with a stranger?"

Meg looked back at the river. There'd been some

overflow. Cracks and gaps in the shifting ice that had the water below welling up, freezing thin. Dangerous business, because the new ice looked just like the rest and would break under you and take you down.

What you thought was safe would kill you.

There were handwritten warning signs. Nate's doing, she knew. He was a man who understood all about thin ice and the dangers of what looked safe and normal.

"Would you settle for a picture? A photograph?"

"What do you mean?"

She turned back. "If I brought you a picture of him, would that do it?"

"If you can go down and take his picture, why—"

"I don't have to. Nate has pictures. I can get one, bring it to you."

"Now?"

"No, not now." She yanked off her cap, drove her fingers through her hair. "He wouldn't like it. Evidence or something. But I'll get it tonight. You can look at it, satisfy yourself, and I'll take it back."

OUTSIDE THE STATION, Meg flipped through her keys and found the one marked PD. She'd left Nate sleeping and hoped he stayed that way until she got back. She didn't want to explain this little bit of insanity to him.

She let herself in, pulled out her penlight. Part of her wanted to poke around and enjoy the sensation of being somewhere she shouldn't. But more, she wanted to get this little chore over with and get back to bed.

She went straight into Nate's office. Here she risked the overhead lights, flipping them on before crossing to the covered corkboard.

She removed the blanket carefully. And it fell to the floor from her numb hands as she took one wavering step in retreat.

She'd seen death before and had never known it to be pretty. But those stark and graphic photos of Max Hawbaker had her breath whistling out.

Best not to think about it, not quite yet. Better to take the photo of her father—how much *cleaner* his death seemed—and take it to Charlene.

She slid the photo inside her jacket, turned the lights off and went back out the way she came.

Charlene was in her room, answered the door wearing a floral robe. There was a scent of whiskey, smoke, perfume.

"You'd better be alone," Meg said.

"I am. I sent him on. Where is it? Did you get it?"

"You're going to look, then I'm taking it back and I don't want to hear any more about this."

"Let me see. Let me see him."

Meg drew it out. "No, you can't touch it. You wrinkle it up or anything, Nate will know." She turned the photo face front.

"Oh. Oh." Charlene stumbled back, much as Meg had at the corkboard. "God. No!" She shot a hand out to stop Meg from putting the picture away again. "I need to . . ."

She stepped forward again and, at Meg's warning look, clasped her hands behind her back. "He . . . he looks the same. How can that be? He looks the same. All these years, and he looks the same."

"He never had a chance to look different."

"It would've been quick, do you think? Would it have been quick?"

"Yes."

"He was wearing that parka when he left. He was wearing it the last time I saw him." She turned, cupped her elbows with her hands. "Go away now." She shuddered, then pressed both hands to her mouth. "Meg," she began and spun around.

But Meg was already gone.

Alone, Charlene walked into the bath, turned on the lights and studied herself in the hard glare.

He'd looked the same, she thought again. So young. And she didn't. She never would again.

IT WAS MARCH IN ALASKA, but the longer days didn't make him think of approaching spring, however close the calendar crept toward the official day.

Nate awoke to daylight now and most often on the left side of Meg's bed. When he walked through town, he saw more of people's faces and less of sheltering hoods.

The plastic eggs hanging from the branches of snow-draped trees, the plastic bunnies crouched on white carpets of lawn didn't make him think spring, either.

But his first breakup did.

He watched, with a kind of buzzy wonder, the little

cracks creeping along the icy ribbon of river, like crazed zippers. Unlike the overflow, these didn't fill in and freeze up. It astonished him so much that it took him twenty minutes to stop staring and head back to the office.

"There are cracks in the river," he told Otto.

"Yeah? Little early for breakup, but we've had a warm spell."

Maybe, Nate thought, if he lived in Lunacy for, oh, a hundred years, he'd think of a few days of forties and damp, chilly lower fifties as a warm spell. "I want signs posted. I don't want a bunch of kids playing hockey falling through the ice."

"Kids got more sense than to—"

"I want signs posted, like we did for overflow, but more so. Check at The Corner Store, see if they've got any more sign board. Either Peach or Peter needs to write them. Ah, 'No skating, thin ice.'"

"It's not so much thin as—"

"Otto, just go get me a half dozen signs."

He grumbled, but he went. And Nate noticed Peach's lips were folded tight on a smile she was trying to suppress.

"What?"

"Nothing. Not a thing. I think it's a fine idea. Shows we've got concern for our citizenship, and order. But I think you could just write, 'Breakup, and steer clear.'"

"Write whatever you think best. Just write it." He started through the station to head out the back and find what he could use for stakes. "And don't let Otto write it."

When he was satisfied the signs were under way, he wrote and printed fliers off his computer and set out to distribute them.

He pinned them up in the post office, the bank, the school, worked his way to The Lodge.

There, Bing came over and read behind his shoulder—and snorted.

Saying nothing, Nate read his own words.

BREAKUP IN PROGRESS.
NO SKATING, WALKING OR OTHER
ACTIVITIES WILL BE PERMITTED ON
THE RIVER, BY ORDER OF THE LUNACY
POLICE DEPARTMENT.

"I spell something wrong, Bing?"

"Nope. Just wonder who you think's stupid enough to go skating around on the river during breakup."

"Same sort of person who jumps off a roof to see if he can fly after he's read a couple Superman comics. How long does breakup take?"

"Depends, doesn't it? Winter started early, now spring's doing the same thing. So we'll just see. River breaks up every frigging year, so does the lake. Nothing new."

"A kid goes out there fooling around, falls through the ice, we could be going to another memorial."

Bing pursed his lips thoughtfully as Nate walked out again.

He still had fliers in his hand when he saw movement behind the display window of *The Lunatic*.

He crossed over, found the door was locked. Knocked.

Carrie studied him through the glass a minute, then opened up.

"Carrie. I'd like to post one of these in your window here."

She took it, read it, then walked to her desk to get tape. "I'll put it up for you."

"Appreciate it." He glanced around. "You here alone?"

"Yes."

He'd interviewed her twice since the memorial, and each time her thoughts and answers had been scattered and vague. He'd tried to give her time, but time was passing. "Have you been able to remember any more details from that February?"

"I tried to think about it, write things down like you said, at home." She taped the flier, face-out on the glass. "I couldn't do it there. I couldn't seem to do it at my parents' when I took the kids down for a couple weeks. I don't know why. I just couldn't get the thoughts out or the words down. So I came here. I thought maybe . . ."

"That's fine."

"I wasn't sure I could come here. I know Hopp and some of the other women came in and . . . cleaned up after—when they were allowed to, but I wasn't sure I could come back here."

"It's hard." He'd gone back to the alley, forced himself to go back. And all he'd felt was numb despair.

"I had to come back. There hasn't been a paper since . . . it's been too long. Max worked so hard, and this meant so much to him."

She turned around, drawing careful breaths as she looked around the room. "Doesn't look like anything really. Doesn't even look like a real paper. Max and I went to Anchorage, Fairbanks, even Juneau, to tour a real paper, real newsrooms. His eyes would just light up. Doesn't look like much here, but he was proud of it."

"I don't agree with you. I think it looks like a lot."

She struggled to smile, nodded briskly. "I'm going to keep it going. That's something I decided today. Just to-day before you came in. I thought I'd let it go, that I just couldn't do this without him. But when I came back here today, I knew I had to keep it going. I'm going to put an edition together, see if The Professor's got time to help me, maybe knows a couple of kids who want to work, get some journalist experience."

"That's good, Carrie. I'm glad to hear it."

"I'll write something down for you, Nate, I promise. I'll think back and I'll try to remember. I know you wanted to go through his papers and such. I haven't been back there yet."

She didn't have to look at the back office for Nate to know she meant the room where Max had been found.

"You can, if you want."

The State cops had been through that room, Nate thought. He still wanted his pass at it, but not now. Not when anyone walking by would see he was inside and wonder why.

"I'll come back for that. He kept an office at home?"

"A little one. I haven't been through his things. I keep putting it off."

"Anybody at your place now?"

"No. Kids are in school."

"Is it all right with you if I go in now, look around? If I need to take anything, I'll write you up a receipt."

"You go ahead." She went to her purse, fished out keys and took one off a ring. "This is to the back door. You keep it as long as you need it."

HE DIDN'T WANT TO PARK in front of the Hawbaker house. Too many people talked about something just that small.

Instead, he parked by a bend in the river. He didn't notice any cracks in the ice and wondered if he'd jumped the gun on the ones in town. He hiked the back way, through a patch of woods. Colder here, he thought, colder under the trees where the sun couldn't fight through. There were tracks—snowmobile, skis. Cross-country team, he decided, from the high school. He spotted other tracks that weren't human and hoped he wasn't going to come face-to-face with the moose he'd run off.

He didn't know enough about them to be sure they didn't hold grudges.

The snow was deeper than he'd anticipated and made him curse himself for not slapping on his snowshoes. So he did what he could to use the tracks.

He saw a streak he thought might be a fox and, when he stopped to catch his breath, spotted a herd of shaggy-coated deer. They trudged along, no more than fifteen feet to his north. He could only assume he was down-wind as they didn't so much as give him a glance. So he stood watching them until they wound their way out of sight.

He worked his way to Carrie's back door, past what he assumed was a garden or toolshed, around the building on stilts that would be their cache. Someone had cleared the back stoop, and there was a stack of firewood, covered with a tarp, by the door.

He used the key and stepped inside a combination mudroom and laundry area. Since his boots were wet and caked with snow, he took them off, leaving them and his coat.

The kitchen was clean, almost to a gleam. Maybe that's what women did, or some women, when they were coping with grief. They got out the cleanser and the mop. And the polishing cloth, he thought as he continued through the house, the vacuum cleaner. There wasn't a speck of dust to be found. Nor any of the usual clutter of living.

Maybe that was the point. She wasn't ready to live again yet.

He went up, identified the kids' room by the posters on the walls, the disorder on the floor. For now, at least, he bypassed the master bedroom where the bed was carefully made and a patchwork throw was draped over the back of a chair.

Did she sleep there now, unwilling, unable to lie down on the bed she'd shared with her husband?

Beside the bedroom was Max's office. And here was the clutter, the dust and debris of normal living. The desk chair had a strip of duct tape along one of the seams—the everyman's repair job. The desk itself was scarred and battered, an obvious second- or thirdhand purchase. But the computer on it looked new or very well tended.

There was a desk calendar, one of those cubes that followed a theme and gave you a picture and a saying each day. Max's was a fishing theme, and it had a cartoon man holding up a minnow-sized fish and claiming it was bigger when he'd hooked it.

The date was January nineteenth. Max hadn't made it back home to rip it off to reveal the next day's joke.

There was no message written on it, no handy clue such as: Meet [insert name of killer] at midnight.

Nate bent to go through the trash can under the desk. He found several other pages of the cube, some with notes.

IDITAROD ART—POV DOG?

BATHROOM TAP DRIPPING. CARRIE PISSED. FIX!

And the one from the day before his death, the one covered with scribbles of one word: PAT.

Nate took it out, placed it on the desk.

He found several envelopes indicating Max had sat there, paying bills on one of the days shortly before he died, a couple of candy wrappers.

He went through the desk drawers, found a checkbook—$250.06 on the balance after the bill-paying stint—two days before he died. Three passbooks for savings accounts. One for each of his children, one joint for him and his wife. He and Carrie had a $6,010 nest egg.

There were envelopes, return address labels. Rubber bands, paper clips, a box of staples. Nothing out of the ordinary.

In the bottom drawer he found four chapters of a manuscript. The top page indentified it as:

COLD SNAP

A Novel

by Maxwell T. Hawbaker

Nate put it on the desk and got up to search the shelf unit running along one wall. To his pile, Nate added a box of floppy disks and a scrapbook holding newspaper articles.

Then he sat down to test his computer skills.

It wasn't password-protected, which told him Max hadn't thought he had anything to hide. A run through the documents netted him a spreadsheet on which Max had carefully listed mortgage and time payments. Family man, Nate thought, responsible with his money.

Nothing he could find on finances showed any large sums, anything out of the ordinary. If Max had been blackmailing his killer, he hadn't recorded the income alongside his monthly debits.

He found more of the novel and the start of two more. A check through the floppies showed that Max had conscientiously backed them up. There were a few bookmarked sites—fishing for the most part.

He found some saved e-mail: fishing buddies, responses from a couple of people regarding sled dogs. Follow-ups, Nate assumed, on the planned Iditarod article.

He spent an hour threading through, but nothing jumped out and yelled *clue!*

Gathering up what he had, he carted it down to the

mudroom where he confiscated an empty box to dump it all into.

He wandered back into the kitchen. The kitchen calendar had a bird theme. No one had thought or bothered to turn it over to February much less March.

More than half the little squares had notes. PTA meeting, hockey practice, book report due, dentist appointment. Normal family routine. The dentist appointment had been Max's, Nate noted, and he'd been due for it two days after his death.

He flipped it up, glanced over February, at March. A lot of notes there, too, with GONE FISHING in large capital letters over the second weekend in March.

Nate let the page fall again. Routine, normal, ordinary.

But there was that single calendar page from the trash can upstairs, covered with the name Pat.

Four pairs of snowshoes hung in the mudroom.

Studying them, he put on his boots, his coat, hefted the box and started out again.

He was back in the woods again, up to mid-shin in snow, when the gunshot blasted through the quiet. Instinctively, he dropped the box, dug under the coat for his own weapon. Even as he gripped it, there was a thunder in the woods. A single deer, a thick-bodied, heavily antlered buck, leaped into view and continued its leaping gallop.

With his heart thudding, Nate started moving in the direction it had come from. He'd made it about twenty yards when he saw the figure melt out of the trees—and the long gun it carried.

They stood for a moment in the echoing stillness,

each with a weapon in his hand. Then the figure lifted his left hand, shoved back his hood.

"He scented you," Jacob said. "Spooked and ran even as I fired. So I missed."

"Missed," Nate repeated.

"I'd hoped to take some venison to Rose. David hasn't been able to hunt lately." He lowered his gaze, slow and deliberate, to Nate's sidearm. "Do you hunt, Chief Burke?"

"No. But when I hear a gunshot, I don't go looking for who fired it unarmed."

Jacob made an obvious business of clicking on the safety. "You found him, and I go home without meat."

"Sorry."

"It was the deer's day, not mine. Do you know your way out?"

"I can find it."

"Well, then." Jacob nodded, turned and, moving with grace and ease in his snowshoes, melted back into the trees.

Nate kept his weapon out as he walked back, as he picked up the box he'd dropped. He didn't holster it again until he was back in his car.

He drove to Meg's to push the box into the back of a closet. It was something he had to pursue on his own time. Since his pants were wet to the knees, he changed, then went down to the lake with the dogs to check for any sign of breakup before he drove back into town.

"SIGNS ARE UP," Otto told him.

"So I see."

"We've gotten two complaints already, about minding our own business."

"Anybody I need to talk to?"

"Nope."

"You got two calls, Chief, from reporters." Peach tapped the pink While You Were Out notes on her counter. "About Pat Galloway and Max. Follow-up, they said."

"They have to catch me first. Peter still on patrol?"

"We sent him out for lunch. It was his turn." Otto scratched his chin. "Ordered you an Italian sub."

"That's fine, thanks. Would a man go hunting two, three miles from his own place, when he's got acres of hunting ground where he lives?"

"Depends, wouldn't it?"

"On what?"

"What he was hunting, for one."

"Yeah. I guess it would depend on that."

THE CRACKS IN THE RIVER lengthened and widened as the temperatures held above freezing. From the banks, Nate saw his first sight of the cold, deep blue shimmer between the gleam of white. Fascinated, he watched it spread and heard what sounded like artillery fire. Or the crashing fist of God.

Plates of ice heaved up, swamped and surrounded by that blue, then floated placidly, like a newborn island.

"Something almost religious about your first breakup," Hopp commented as she walked up beside him.

"My first breakup was with Pixie Newburry, and it was more traumatic than religious."

Hopp stood in silence as ice crackled and boomed. "Pixie?"

"Yeah. She had these big almond-shaped eyes, so everybody called her Pixie. She dumped me for this kid whose father had a boat. It was the first wave in a sea of broken hearts for me."

"Sounds shallow to me. You were better off without her."

"Didn't seem like it at twelve. I didn't think this would happen so fast."

"Once nature decides to move, there's no stopping her. And you can bet she'll slap us back with a few more licks of winter before she's done. But breakup's a time for celebration around here. We're having an informal breakup party at The Lodge tonight. You'll want to put in an appearance."

"Okay."

"You've been spending more time at Meg's than The Lodge, sleeping arrangement–wise." She smiled when he merely looked at her. "It's been mentioned, here and there."

"Is my choice of sleeping arrangements a problem—official-wise?"

"No, indeed." She cupped her hand around a cigarette, used a thick silver Zippo to light it. "And on a personal front, I'd estimate that Meg Galloway's no Pixie

Newburry. It's been mentioned, too, here and there, that there are lights on at Meg's pretty late at night."

"Maybe we have insomnia." She was the mayor, Nate reminded himself. And Galloway's journal hadn't referred to a woman on the mountain. "I'm spending some of my off time on the Galloway matter."

"I see." She stared out at the river as the blue and the white battled. "Most people go fishing, read a juicy book or watch TV on their off time."

"Cops aren't most people."

"You do what pleases you, Ignatious. I know Charlene's planning to bring Pat back here, soon as she's able, and bury him. Wants a full-fledged funeral. The ground ought to be thawed enough soon to manage it by June, unless we get another long freeze."

She drew in smoke, sighed it out again. "Part of me wishes that would be that. The dead are buried, and the living have to live. It's hard on Carrie, I know, but you keeping this going won't bring her husband back."

"I don't believe he killed Galloway. And I don't believe he killed himself."

Her face stayed perfectly still, her eyes stayed on the busy river. "That's not what I want to hear. God's pity on Carrie, but that's not what I want to hear."

"Nobody wants to hear they may be living next door to someone who's killed twice."

She shuddered now, once and violently, and drew on the cigarette. She puffed at it hard, expelling smoke in bursts. "I know the people who live next door to me and a mile away and three miles from that. I know them by face and name and habits. I don't know a murderer, Ignatious."

"You knew Max."

"Oh God."

"You climbed with Galloway."

Her eyes sharpened now and focused on his face. "Is this an interrogation?"

"No. Just a comment."

She breathed in and out while the ice cracked. "Yes, I did. My man and I did. I enjoyed it, too, the challenge of it, the thrill of it, in my younger days. Bo and I settled for hiking, a night of camping in good weather the last few years he was alive. That Bo was alive," she said.

"Who'd he trust most when he was on the mountain? Who did Galloway trust up there?"

"Himself. That'd be the first rule of climbing. You'd better trust yourself first and last."

"Your husband was mayor back then."

"It was more honorary than official in those days."

"Even so, he knew the people around here. Paid attention. I bet you did, too."

"And?"

"If you put your mind to it, thought back to February of '88, you might remember who, besides Galloway, wasn't in Lunacy. Who was away for a week or more."

She tossed the cigarette down where it sizzled against the snow. Then she kicked snow over it to bury it from view. "You're giving a lot of credit to my memory, Ignatious. I'll think about it."

"Good. If you remember anything, come to me. Just me, Hopp."

"Spring's coming," Hopp said. "And spring can be a bitch."

She walked away, leaving him by the river. He stood in the chilly wind, watching that river come back to life.

TWENTY-TWO

IT WASN'T JUST river ice that cracked and heaved during breakup. Streets, frozen through the long winter, burst with fissures the size of canyons and potholes wide enough to swallow a truck.

It didn't surprise Nate that Bing had the contract for road repair and maintenance. What did surprise him was that no one seemed to give much of a damn that the repair and maintenance moved at the pace of a lame snail.

He had other things to worry about.

People, he discovered, cracked, too. Some who had held on to their sanity through the dark, relentless winter appeared to think the tease of spring was a good time to let it go.

His cells were revolving doors for the drunk, the disorderly, the domestic disturbances and the just plain dopey.

The sound of horns tooting and catcalls brought him to the bedroom window just after dawn. A light snow had fallen during the night, hardly more than a dusting that lay thin and sparkling on the streets and sidewalks under the rising sun.

The lights on the barricades around the two-foot pothole he'd named Lunatic Crater blinked red and yellow. Around those blinking lights he saw a man dancing what appeared to be a jig. That might have been surprising enough for sunrise entertainment, but the fact that the man was buck-assed naked added a certain panache.

A crowd was gathering already. Some were clapping—maybe keeping time, Nate speculated. Others were shouting—encouragement or derision in equal measures.

With a sigh, Nate toweled off his half-shaven face, grabbed a shirt and shoes and headed down.

The dining room was deserted, with a few plates of half-eaten breakfast as testament to the draw of a naked guy dancing on Lunatic Street.

Nate grabbed a jacket off a hook and walked out in his shirtsleeves.

There were whistles and stomping feet—and a dawn temperature Nate judged hadn't quite come up to the freezing mark as yet. He nudged his way through the gathered crowd. He recognized the dancer now. Tobias Simpsky, part-time clerk at The Corner Store, part-time dishwasher at The Lodge, part-time disc jockey at Lunacy Radio.

He'd changed the jig to some kind of western-movie Indian war dance.

"Chief." Rose, with Jesse's hand in hers and the baby snuggled in a pack at her breast, smiled serenely. "Nice morning."

"Right. Is today some particular event? A pagan ritual I might've missed hearing about?"

"No. Just Wednesday."

"Okay." He passed through the onlookers. "Hey, Toby? Forget your hat this morning?"

Still dancing, Toby tossed back his long, brown hair

and threw out his arms. "Clothes are only a symbol of man's denial of nature, of his acceptance of restrictions and loss of innocence. Today, I merge with nature! Today I embrace my innocence. I am *man!*"

"Just barely," someone called out, giving the crowd a good laugh.

"Why don't we go talk about that?" Nate took his arm and managed to flap the jacket over his hips.

"Man is a child, and a child comes naked into the world."

"I've heard that. Show's over," Nate called out. He tried to arrange the jacket while guiding Toby across the street. The man had grapefruit-sized goose bumps on every inch of exposed skin. "Nothing much to see here anyway," he muttered under his breath.

"I drink only water," Toby told him. "I eat only what I gather with my own hands."

"Got it. No coffee and doughnuts for you."

"If we don't dance, the dark will come back, and the cold winter. The snow." He looked around, wildly now. "It's everywhere. It's everywhere."

"I know." He got him inside, into a cell. Figuring Ken was the closest he had to a shrink, he contacted him to request a house call.

In the next cell Drunk Mike snored away, sleeping off a toot that had had him wandering into a neighbor's house instead of his own the night before.

Including Drunk Mike, he'd had six calls between eleven and two. Slashed tires on Hawley's truck, a portable radio turned up to full blast and left on Sarrie Parker's doorstep, broken windows at the school, more yellow graffiti on Tim Bower's new Ski-doo and on Charlene's Ford Bronco.

Apparently even the thought of spring stirred up the natives.

He was thinking about coffee, about his missed breakfast, about what drove a man to dancing naked on a snowy street when Bing came slamming in. He was big as a tank and looked ready to commit murder.

"Found these in my gear." He slapped two fishing rods onto the counter, then jabbed the auger, which looked like a curly sword, before slamming it down as well. "I ain't no thief, and you better find out who stowed them there so I'd look like one."

"Would these belong to Ed Woolcott?"

"Got his name engraved on the damn rods, doesn't he? Just like that prissy gnat-ass to have his name plated on overpriced fishing rods. I'm telling you right now, I'm not having him say I took them. Clean his clock good and proper if he does."

"Where did you find them?"

He worked his hands into fists. "You try to say I took 'em, I'll clean your clock, too."

"I didn't say you took them, I asked where you found them."

"In my shack. Went out last night. Gonna tow my shack in for the season. Found them then. Mulled over what to do about it, and this is what I'm doing." He jabbed a finger at Nate. "Now you do what you're supposed to do."

"When's the last time you were in your shack before last night?"

"Been busy, haven't I? Couple of weeks, maybe. If they'd been there, I'd have spotted them right off, just like I did. I don't use that prissy-assed gear."

"Why don't you come back to my office, Bing, and sit down."

He readied meat-slab fists again, bared his teeth. "What for?"

"You're going to make an official statement. Details like if you noticed if anything else was disturbed, added or subtracted, if your shack was locked, who might want to get your non-prissy ass in hot water."

Bing scowled. "You're gonna have to take my word on it?"

"That's right."

Bing jutted his bearded chin. "All right, then. But it's gonna have to be quick. I got work to do, don't I?"

"We'll make it quick. You get that crater fixed on Lunatic before it swallows a family of five."

Since Bing was a man of few words, the statement took under ten minutes.

"Do you and Ed have a history I should know about?"

"I put my money in his bank, take it out as I need it."

"You two socialize?"

Bing's answer was a snort. "I don't get invites to dinner at his place and wouldn't go if I did."

"Why's that? His wife a lousy cook?"

"Likes to put on airs—both of them—like they were better than the rest of us. He's an asshole, but so's better than half the world's population." He shrugged his massive shoulders. It was like watching a mountain stretch. "I got nothing against him, particularly."

"Can you think of anyone who'd have something against you? Enough to want to cause you trouble?"

"I mind my own and expect people to do the same. Anybody's got a problem with that, I'll—"

"Clean their clock," Nate finished. "I'll see Ed gets his property back. Appreciate you bringing it in."

Bing sat another moment, drumming his thick fingers against his wide thighs. "I don't hold with stealing."

"Me, either."

"Don't see why you're so fired up to lock up a man who's had a few drinks or punches somebody who gets in his face, but a thief's different."

Nate believed he spoke his own truth. There'd been violence on Bing's record, but no theft. "And?"

"Somebody took my buck knife and my spare gloves out of my rig."

Nate pulled up another form. "Give me a description."

"It's a goddamn buck knife." He hissed through his teeth when Nate simply waited. "Got a five-inch blade, closed-lock back, wood handle. Hunting knife."

"And the gloves?" Nate prompted as he keyed in the description.

"Work gloves, for Christ's sake. Cowhide, fleece lining. Black."

"When did you notice them missing?"

"Last week."

"And you're reporting it now because?"

Bing didn't speak for a minute, then moved those mountainous shoulders again. "Maybe you're not a complete asshole."

"I'm touched. Let me blink these sentimental tears out of my eyes. You lock your rig?"

"No. Nobody's been stupid enough to mess with my stuff."

"Always a first time," Nate said.

When he was alone, and waiting for the town doctor to come give Toby some sort of psych eval, Nate studied the reports on his desk. A decent stack of reports, he thought. Maybe not the sort of load he'd been accustomed to in Baltimore, but a definite stack. With petty theft and petty vandalism leading the pack.

Enough so, he mused, that he'd been kept busy the last couple of weeks. So busy he'd had little time to spare for his unofficial investigation.

Maybe it wasn't coincidence. Maybe it wasn't some cosmic reminder that he wasn't Homicide any longer.

Maybe somebody was nervous.

HE CALLED ED IN, and watched the man's face light up when he saw the rods and auger.

"I take it those are yours."

"They sure are. I'd given up on them, certain they'd made their way to some pawnshop in Anchorage. Good work, Chief Burke! You've made an arrest?"

"There's no arrest. Bing found them mixed in with his gear in his ice shack last night. He brought them in to me first thing this morning."

"But—"

"Is there any reason you can think of why Bing would have broken into your shack, defaced it, taken those, then brought them in to me today?"

"No." Ed stroked a hand over each rod in turn. "No, I guess not, but the fact remains he had them."

"The only facts are he found them and returned them. Do you want to pursue this?"

Ed blew out a breath, stood for a moment with his face reflecting a man struggling with some inner war. "Well . . . I honestly can't see why Bing would've taken them, much less turned them in if he had. I have them back, and that's the important thing. But it doesn't address the vandalism or the theft of nearly a full quart of scotch."

"I'll keep the case open."

"Good. Good, then." He nodded toward the window, to beyond where ice floes floated on the deep, dark blue. "You survived your first winter."

"Looks like."

"There are some who don't expect you to put yourself through the experience a second time. I've wondered myself if you plan to go back to the Lower 48 after your contract."

"I suppose that depends on whether or not the town council offers to renew my contract."

"I haven't heard any complaints. Well, nothing major in any case." He picked up the rods, the auger. "I should get these stowed."

"I need you to sign for them." Nate nudged a form across his desk. "Let's keep it official."

"Oh. Absolutely." He looped his signature on the proper lines. "Thank you, Chief. I'm glad to have my property back."

Nate noticed him glance at the draped blanket, as he had twice before. But there were no questions or comments about it.

Nate rose to shut the door himself, then he walked to the board, uncovered it. On a list of names, he penciled a line, connecting Bing to Ed. And added a question mark.

THE CLOUDS ROLLED BACK in by afternoon and, through them, Nate spotted the red slash of Meg's plane. He was on his way back from investigating a call reporting a dead body by the stream in Rancor Woods. It turned out to be an old pair of boots stuck in the snow, which the holidaying bird-watchers renting the cabin had spotted through their field glasses.

Tourists, Nate thought, as he tossed the boots—likely abandoned by other tourists—in the back of his car.

Then he heard the familiar thunder of the bush plane and watched Meg slide out of the clouds.

By the time he got to the skinny dock on the river, she'd already landed. The floats on her plane were another sign of spring, he thought. He walked over, feeling the dock sway under him, while she and Jacob unloaded the supplies.

"Hey, cutie." She dropped a box on the dock and made it shudder. "Saw you out by Rancor Woods. My heart went pitty-pat, didn't it, Jacob?"

He chuckled under his breath and carried a large box down the dock to his truck.

"Bought you a present."

"Yeah? Give it up."

She reached into another box, pushed the contents around and pulled out a box of condoms. "Thought you might be shy about buying your supply at The Corner Store."

"Whereas I wouldn't be shy about having you wave them around on a public dock." He grabbed them out of her hand, stuffed them in his jacket pocket.

"I got you three boxes, but I'll keep the other two in a safe place." She winked, then bent to pick up a carton. He lifted it first. "I'll carry it."

"Careful with it. It's an antique tea set. Joanna's grandmother wanted her to have it for her thirtieth birthday." She hauled out another box, walked with him. "What are you doing hanging around the docks, Chief? Looking for loose women?"

"Found one, didn't I?"

She laughed, gave him a little elbow jab. "We'll see if you can make me looser later."

"It's movie night."

"Movie night's Saturday."

"No, they moved it, remember? Conflict with the high school Spring Fling."

"Right, right. I've got a couple of dresses in this load for that. What's the movie?"

"Double feature. *Vertigo* and *Rear Window*."

"I'll bring the popcorn."

She loaded the box in the truck, studied him as he loaded his. "You look tired, Chief."

"A lot of people seem to have spring fever. It's keeping me busy. Busy enough I haven't been able to give certain areas as much time or attention as I'd like."

"You're not just talking about my naked body." She looked back to her plane where Jacob was getting the last of the cargo. "My father's been dead for sixteen years. Time's relative."

"I want to close this down for you. For him. For myself, too."

She twined a lock of his hair around her finger. He'd let her trim it for him. A sign, she thought, of a courageous man. Or one loopily in love.

"Tell you what. Let's take the night off from all of it. Just go to the movies, eat popcorn and fool around."

"I've got more questions than I have answers. I'm going to have to ask you some of them. You may not like them."

"Then let's definitely take the night off. We've got to deliver this stuff. I'll see you later."

She hopped in the cab of the truck and sent Nate a quick wave as Jacob pulled out. But she watched him in the sideview mirror until they'd turned.

"He looks worried," Jacob commented.

"His kind always worries. Why do I find that so attractive?"

"He'd like to shield you. No one else ever did." He smiled a little when she turned to stare at him. "I taught you, listened to you, cared for you. But I never shielded you."

"I don't need to be shielded. Or want to be."

"No, but knowing he would attracts you."

"Maybe. Maybe." She'd have to think about that one. "But his wants and mine are bound to ram headlong into each other before long. Then what?"

"That depends on which one's still standing after the collision."

With a half laugh she stretched out her legs. "He doesn't stand a chance."

SHE'D HOPED TO HAVE TIME to get home, clean herself up, polish herself up, and set the stage for a night of marathon sex. It was a way to keep things interesting and basic and, she admitted, thoughtless. But she believed it wouldn't hurt him to be thoughtless for a little while.

He thought entirely too much, and it was contagious.

But she didn't have time, not after delivering all the cargo, collecting her fees. She had to settle for popping the corn in The Lodge's kitchen while Big Mike serenaded her with show tunes.

It wasn't a hardship to listen to Big Mike sing as he worked. She caught up on the news as Rose passed in and out of the kitchen, and she cooed over pictures of Willow and new shots of Big Mike's toddler.

It was, she thought, almost like being home in the warmth of the active kitchen, listening to chatter and music. And there was the added benefit of being able to pilfer a slice of Big Mike's applesauce cake.

"Got yourself a movie date," Big Mike said between tunes. "*Ro*-mantic."

Meg ate the cake with her hands, standing beside the stove. "Could be, unless he hogs the popcorn."

"Got little stars in your eyes, little stars and hearts."

"Uh-uh," she managed with her mouth full.

"Sure do. Him, too." He made kissy noises—an odd sound, Meg thought with a laugh, coming out of a buff, bald black man. "I got them in my eyes the first time I saw my Julia. Still do."

"So here you are, baking great applesauce cake for a bunch of sourdoughs."

"I like baking cake." He plated fried fish, red potatoes and French-cut green beans. "But for Julia and my little Princess Annie, I'd do just about anything. This is a good place to live, a good place to work, but if you got love, anyplace is."

He segued from show tunes to the Beatles' "All You Need Is Love," while Meg polished off the cake and Rose came in for orders.

It was a good place to live, Meg mused as she filled a paper bag with the popcorn, shook it to distribute butter and salt. She was just going to have to figure out what to do about the love.

She walked over to Town Hall in a chilly damp that promised rain.

Nate was late, which surprised her. He hustled in just as the lights dimmed.

"Sorry. Had a call. Porcupine. Tell you later."

He tried to settle into the movie, to the mood, to the moment. But his thoughts kept circling around. He'd connected Ed and Bing on his board that morning.

Drawn together by stolen fishing gear. Something that had all the earmarks of a prank or a kid's adventure. There were dozens of other connections, linking person to person.

They were all around him, sitting in the dark, watching Jimmy Stewart play a cop after a breakdown.

Been there, done that, Nate mused. Stewart would spiral down, too. He'd suffer and he'd sweat his way into an obsession.

And he'd get the girl, lose the girl, get the girl, lose the girl. A merry-go-round of pain and pleasure.

The girl was the key.

Was Meg? As Patrick Galloway's only child, wasn't she the living symbol of him? If not the key, another link?

"How long are you going to circle before you land?"

"What?"

"Looks like a holding pattern to me." Meg angled her head, and he realized the lights were back on for intermission between the features.

"Sorry. Zoned out."

"I'll say. You didn't get close to your share of the popcorn." She rolled up the bag, left it on the seat. "Let's get some air before the second feature."

They had to take it in the open doorway, like most of the movie crowd. The clouds that had rolled in had burst open sometime during Kim Novak's transformation. The rain Meg had scented gushed out of the sky, pummelled the ground.

"We'll have some flooding," Meg said, frowned through the clouds of smoke from those brave and drenched souls who stood just outside with cigarettes cupped in umbrellaed palms. "And black ice on the roads when the temperature drops a little more."

"If you want to get home now, I'll take you. I'll need to come back, keep an eye on this."

"No, I'll stay for the second feature, see how it goes. Just as easy turn to snow again."

"Let me check on a couple of things. I'll meet you back inside."

"There's a cop for you, ever vigilant." She saw his face change, rolled her eyes. "Not a complaint, Burke. Jesus. I'm not going to whine and go pouty if I end up watching a movie by myself. And I can get myself home if I need to. I can even handle the rest of tonight's planned entertainment on my own if you're not around to service me. I have fresh batteries. You look at me and see her, it's going to piss me off."

He started to say he hadn't, but she was already walking away. And it would've been a lie anyway. Conditioned response, he thought, and tried to roll the weight of it off his shoulders.

Still carrying it, he picked Peter, Hopp, Bing, The Professor, out of the crowd.

He spent intermission, and a little beyond it, coordinating and confirming procedure for flooding.

By the time he rejoined Meg, Grace Kelly was trying to convince Jimmy Stewart to pay more attention to her than the people in the apartment he could see from his rear window.

He took Meg's hand, linked fingers. "Knee jerk," he murmured in her ear. "Sorry."

"Leave off the knee and you've got it right." But she turned her head, brushed her lips over his. "Watch the movie this time."

He did or tried to. But just as Raymond Burr caught Grace Kelly snooping around his apartment, the door banged open behind them.

Light ran in behind Otto, causing most of the audience to boo and shout at him to close the damn door. He came in fast and wet, ignoring the curses as he zeroed in on Nate.

Nate was already up and moving toward him.

"You need to come outside, Chief."

For the second time that day, Nate went out in his shirtsleeves, this time to the sizzle of sleet on pavement and the icy sting of it on his skin.

He saw the body immediately and, dragging the hair out of his face, moved through the wet to the curb.

He thought at first it was Rock or Bull, and his heart went thick in his throat. But the dog that lay in blood and freezing rain was older than Meg's, with more white in his coloring.

The knife that had been used to slash his throat lay buried in his chest.

He heard someone scream from behind him. "Get them back inside," he ordered Otto. "Control the situation."

"I know this dog, Nate. It's Joe and Lara's old dog, Yukon. Harmless. Barely got a tooth left in his head."

"Get these people back inside. Either you or Peter bring me out something to cover him up with."

Peter came on the run moments after Otto went in.

"Jacob gave me his slicker. God, Chief, it's Yukon. It's Steven's dog, Yukon. This isn't right. This just isn't right."

"Do you recognize the knife? Look at the handle, Peter."

"I don't know. There's a lot of blood, and . . . I don't know."

But Nate knew. His gut told him it was going to be a buck knife. It was going to be Bing's missing buck knife. "We're going to take this dog down to the clinic. You're going to help me load him in the back of my car. But you're going to go over and get the camera first so we can record this scene."

"He's dead."

"That's right, he's dead. We're going to examine him at the clinic, after we record the scene here. Once we have him loaded, I need you to go back inside, tell Joe and Lara their dog's with me, and where. Go get the camera now."

He looked up, caught a movement out of the corner of his eye. When he straightened, he saw Meg on the sidewalk, holding his jacket.

"You forgot this."

"I don't want you out here."

"I've already seen what somebody did to that poor dog. Poor old Yukon. It's going to break Lara's heart."

"Go back inside."

"I'm going home. I'm going home to my own dogs."

He grabbed her arm. "You're going back inside, and when I've cleared it, you're going to The Lodge."

"This isn't a police state, Burke. I can go where I want to go."

"You're going to do what the hell I tell you. I'm going to know exactly where you are, and it's not going to be alone, five miles out of town. There's ice on the roads, hazardous conditions, flash flooding, and somebody who'd be cold enough to cut this dog's throat from ear to ear. So you get your ass back inside until I tell you otherwise."

"I'm not leaving my dogs out—"

"I'll get your dogs. Get inside, Meg. Get inside, or I'll haul you in and lock you in a cell."

He waited five thrumming seconds with nothing but the crackling hiss of sleet striking the ground. She spun around, stormed back in.

He waited where he was, outside in the rain, beside a dead dog until Peter came roaring back.

He took the camera, took several Polaroids, tucking them into the pocket of his jacket.

"Help me load this dog, Peter. Then you go in, follow the orders I gave you. I want you to tell Otto to escort Meg to The Lodge and see that she stays there until I say different. Is that clear?"

Peter nodded. His Adam's apple bobbed, but he nodded. "Ah, Ken's inside, Chief. I was sitting just behind him during the movie. Do you want him out here now?"

"Yeah. Yeah, send him out. He can ride with me."

He shoved his dripping hair out of his eyes while thin fog twined around his ankles. "I'm going to count on you to keep order, Peter. I want you to disperse the crowd inside, send everyone on their way. Advise them to go home, let them know we're taking care of things."

"They're going to want to know what—what happened."

"We don't know what happened yet, do we?" He looked back at the dog. "Keep everyone calm. You're good at talking to people. You go in there and talk to your people. And, Peter, pay attention to who's in there. I want you and Otto to make a list of everyone who's inside."

And, Nate thought, I'll know everyone who isn't.

They loaded the dog into the vehicle. As Peter hurried back into Town Hall, Nate crouched down by his right rear tire. Beside it, just under the axle, was a pair of bloody gloves.

He opened the door, dug out an evidence bag. Lifting the gloves by the cuffs, he sealed them.

They would be Bing's, he thought. As the knife would be.

A knife and gloves Bing had reported stolen only hours before.

TWENTY-THREE

"IT WOULD'VE BEEN QUICK." Ken stood over the dog. And scrubbed his hands over his face.

"The neck wound did it," Nate prompted.

"Yeah. Yeah. Jesus, what kind of sick son of a bitch does this to a dog? You said, ah, you said the chest wound didn't show much blood. He was gone when whoever did this rammed the knife into the chest. You slice the neck like that, sever the jugular, that's game point."

"Bloody. Blood would've gushed."

"Yeah. God."

"Rain washed away some of it—most of it—but not all. And he was still a little warm when we found him. He'd been dead, what, maybe an hour, if that?"

"Nate." Shaking his head, Ken took off his glasses, polished them on the tail of his shirt. "This is way out of my league. Your guess on that would be as good, if not better, than mine. But yeah, an hour's about right."

"Intermission'd been over around an hour. He wasn't there when we went out between movies. And there was too much blood left for him to have been killed somewhere else and dumped. You knew this dog?"

"Sure. Old Yukon." His eyes went shiny, and he rubbed them dry. "Sure."

"He give anybody any trouble? Snap at somebody that you know of? Bite anyone?"

"Yukon? Barely got enough teeth left to gum up his own food. Friendly dog. Harmless. Maybe that's why I'm having a hard time keeping it together." He turned away for a moment, struggling for control. "Max . . . well, Max was horrible. A human being, for God's sake. But this dog . . . This dog was *old* and sweet. And defenseless."

"Sit down for a minute if you need to." But Nate stood where he was, looking down at the dog. At the fur matted with blood and still dripping with rain.

"Sorry, Nate. You'd think a doctor could handle himself better than this." He sucked in air, pushed it back out of his lungs. "What do you want me to do?"

"Joe and Lara are going to be coming along in a minute. I need you to keep them out of here until I finish."

"What are you going to do?"

"My job. Just keep them out until I'm done."

He lifted his camera, took more pictures. He wasn't a coroner, but he'd stood over enough dead bodies, witnessed enough autopsies to guess that the knife strike had been executed from over the dog's head, a little behind. A left-to-right stroke. Straddled him, lifted his head up, sliced.

Blood jets out, coats the gloves, maybe the sleeves, maybe even splashes back some. Dog goes down, bury the knife in him. Ditch the gloves, walk away.

A couple of minutes, with the rain giving cover, with a couple hundred people—maybe a little more—inside the building, focused on Jimmy Stewart.

Risky, he thought as he dusted the handle of the knife for prints, but calculated. Cold.

There was nothing on the knife but blood. He bagged it, then dug up a plastic sack. He put the knife and the photographs inside. And went out to speak to the Wises.

The rain had turned to a thin, wet snow by the time Nate tracked down Bing. He found him in his enormous garage by his log house. His weather radio was on as he tinkered under the hood of his truck.

There were a couple of other vehicles inside and what looked like a small engine or a motor up on blocks. One of the drawers on a huge, rusted, red toolbox was open. Above a long counter was a peg-board holding more tools, with a calendar beside it featuring a mostly naked blonde with enormous breasts.

A muscular-looking sewing machine—sewing machine?—sat on a wood table in the far corner. And over that was a moose head.

The place smelled like beer stirred with smoke and grease.

Bing squinted over at Nate, one eye closed against the smoke that drifted up from the cigarette clamped in his lips. "We get more rain tomorrow, the river's going to come up and kiss Lunatic Street. Gonna need the sandbags I got back of the truck."

Sandbags, Nate thought with a glance at the sewing machine. He couldn't quite picture Bing sewing up sandbags, but he supposed there were bigger wonders in the world.

"You left the movie early."

"Seen enough. Gonna be busy by morning. What's it to you?"

Nate stepped forward, held out the bagged knife. "Yours?"

Bing drew the cigarette out of his mouth as he turned. He'd have to have been blinded by more than a little smoke to miss the blood on the handle and blade.

"Looks like it." He tossed the cigarette down, heeled it to pulp on the oil-stained concrete. "Yeah, it's my knife. Looks like it's been used some, too. Where'd you find it?"

"In Joe and Lara's dog, Yukon."

Bing took one step back. Nate saw it, the quick, jerking step of a man who'd been sucker punched. "What the hell you talking about?"

"Somebody used this to slit that dog's throat, then jammed it in his chest so I wouldn't have any trouble finding it. What time did you leave the movie, Bing?"

"Somebody killed that dog? Somebody killed that dog?" Awareness slid over the shock in his eyes. "You're saying I killed that dog?" His fist tightened over the wrench still in his hand. "Is that what you're saying?"

"You take a swing at me with that, I'll take you out. You want to spare yourself that humiliation, because believe me, I can do it. Put it down. Now."

Rage trembled over his face, quaked visibly through his body. "You've got yourself a big, bad temper, don't you, Bing?" Nate said softly. "The kind that's earned you some assaults on your record, had you spending a few nights here and there behind bars. The kind that's pushing you right now to crack my skull like an egg with that wrench. Go ahead, try it."

Bing heaved the wrench across the room where it smashed a chip out of the cinder-block wall. He was breathing like a steam engine, and his face was red as brick.

"Fuck you. Sure I punched a few faces, cracked a few heads, but I'm no goddamn dog killer. And if you say I am, I don't need a wrench to bust your head open."

"I asked you what time you left the movie."

"I went out to catch a smoke at intermission. You saw me. You started in on how we had to prep for possible flooding. I came back here. Loaded those damn sandbags." He jerked a thumb toward the bed of his truck where at least a hundred sandbags were stacked. "Figured I'd tune up the engine while I was at it. I've been here ever since. Somebody went to Joe's place and killed that dog, it wasn't me. I liked that dog."

Nate took out the bagged gloves. "Are these yours?"

Staring at them, Bing rubbed the back of his hand over his mouth. The red was dying out of his cheeks, with clammy white rising. "What the hell's going on here?"

"Is that a yes?"

"Yeah, they're mine, I'm not denying it. I told you somebody took 'em, took my spare gloves and my buck knife. I reported it."

"Just this morning, too. A cynical person might wonder if you were covering yourself."

"Why the hell would I kill a dog? Damn, stupid old dog?" Bing scrubbed at his face, then shook another cigarette out of the pack in his breast pocket. His hands shook visibly.

"You don't have a dog, do you, Bing?"

"So that makes me a dog hater? Christ. I had a dog.

He died two years ago this June. Got cancer." Bing cleared his throat, drew hard on his cigarette. "Cancer took him."

"Somebody kills a dog, you have to wonder if he had problems with the dog or the people who owned it."

"I didn't have any problem with that dog. I got no problem with Joe or Lara or that college boy of theirs. You ask them. You ask them if we had any problems. But somebody's got problems with me, that's for damn sure."

"Any idea why that might be?"

He shrugged, jerkily. "Only thing I know is I didn't kill that dog."

"Keep available, Bing. If you plan on leaving town for any reason, I want to know about it."

"I ain't going to stand by while people point the finger at me."

"Stay available," Nate repeated, and went out the way he'd come in.

MEG NURSED A BEER and her temper as she waited. She didn't like waiting, and Nate was going to hear about it when he got back. He'd snapped orders at her like she was some sort of half-wit, green recruit and he was the general.

She didn't like orders, and he was going to hear about that, too.

He was going to get both ears full when he got back. Where the hell was he?

She was worried sick about her dogs—no matter how the sensible part of her insisted they were fine, that Nate would keep his word and get them for her. She should have been allowed to get them herself instead of being under some sort of half-assed house arrest.

She didn't want to be here, worrying, helpless, sipping beer and playing poker with Otto, Skinny Jim and The Professor to pass the time.

She was up twenty-two dollars and change, and she didn't give a damn.

Where the hell was he?

And who the hell did he think he was, telling her what to do, threatening to lock her in jail? He'd have done it, too, she thought as she drew the eight of clubs to fill out a very pretty full house.

He hadn't been sweet, sad-eyed Nate when he'd stood out in the rain beside that dog. Beside poor, dead Yukon. He'd been something else, someone else. Someone she imagined he'd been back in Baltimore before circumstances had cut him off at the knees. Cut him off at the heart.

She didn't give a damn about that, either. She wouldn't give a damn.

"See your two dollars," she said to Jim. "Raise it two." And tossed her money into the pot.

Her mother had given Jim an hour break and was working the bar. Not that there was a lot of business, Meg thought as The Professor folded and Otto bumped her raise another two. Other than their table, there was a booth of four—Outsiders. Climbers waiting out the weather. The two old farts, Hans and Dex, had another booth, whiling away a rainy evening with beer and checkers.

And waiting, she knew, for whatever gossip might come in the door.

There'd be more in and out if the river rose. People coming in for a few minutes of dry and warm, ordering up coffee before they went out to sandbag again. When it was done, there'd be more. Piling in, wet and tired and hungry, but not ready to go home alone, not ready to break the camaraderie of bucking nature.

They'd want coffee and alcohol and whatever hot meal was put in front of them. Charlene would see they got it; she'd work until the last of them were gone. Meg had seen it before.

She tossed in two dollars to call when Jim folded.

"Two pair," Otto announced. "Kings over fives."

"Your kings are going to have to bow to my ladies." She set down two queens. "Seeing as they're cozied up with three eights."

"Son of a bitch!" Otto watched the nice little pile of bills and coins as Meg swept them away. Then he lifted his chin, pushed back his chair as Nate stepped in from the lobby. "Chief?"

Meg jerked around. She'd sat facing the outside door, waiting to pounce the minute he opened it. Instead, she thought sourly, he'd snuck in behind her.

"Could use some coffee, Charlene."

"It's good and hot." She filled a large mug. "I can fix you a meal. That'd be good and hot, too."

"No, thanks."

"Where are my dogs?" Meg demanded.

"In the lobby. Otto, I ran into Hopp and some others outside. Consensus is the river looks like it's going to hold, but we'll need to keep an eye on it. No more than a light snow coming down now. Forecasters say this system's going to head west, so we're probably in the clear."

He drank down half the coffee, held the mug out to Charlene for a refill. "It's flooded over on Lake Shore. Peter and I put hazard markers up there and across from the east edge of Rancor Woods."

"Those two spots are a problem if too many people piss on the side of the road," Otto told him. "The system goes west, we won't have a problem in town."

"We'll keep an eye," Nate repeated and turned toward the stairs.

"Just one damn minute. *Chief*." Meg stood in the doorway, a dog on either side. "I've got some things to say to you."

"I need a shower. You can say them while I'm cleaning up, or you can wait."

Her lips peeled back into a snarl as he carried his coffee up the steps. "Wait, my ass."

She stomped up behind him, the dogs in her wake.

"Who do you think you are?"

"I think I'm chief of police."

"I don't care if you're chief of the known universe, you don't get off snapping at me, ordering me, threatening me."

"I did get off. But I wouldn't have had to do any of those things if you'd just done what I told you."

"What you *told* me?" She shoved into the room behind him. You don't *tell* me. You're not my boss or my father. Just because I've slept with you doesn't give you the right to tell me what to do."

He yanked off his soaked jacket, then tapped the badge on his shirt. "No, but this does." He peeled off the shirt on the way to the bathroom.

He was still someone else, she thought. The someone else who'd lived behind those sad eyes, just waiting to muscle his way out. That someone was hard and cold. Dangerous.

She heard the shower start up. Both dogs continued to stand, their heads cocked as they looked up at her.

"Lie down," she murmured.

She marched into the bathroom. Nate was sitting on the toilet lid, fighting off wet boots.

"You sic Otto on me like some sort of guard dog and leave me waiting damn near three hours. Three hours where I don't know what's going on."

He looked at her, dead in the face, with eyes like flint. "I had work and more important things to do than keep you updated. You want the news?" He set the boots aside, rose to strip off his pants. "Turn on the radio."

"Don't you talk to me like I'm some sort of whiny, irritating female."

He stepped into the shower, ripped the curtain shut after him. "Then stop acting like one."

God, he needed the heat. Nate pressed his hands to the tile, dipped his head and let the hot water pour over him. An hour or two of it, he estimated, it might just reach his tired, frozen bones. A bottle or two of aspirin, parts of him might stop aching. Three or four days of sleep might just counteract the fatigue that trudging through icy flood water, hauling barricades, watching a grown man and woman weep over their murdered dog had drenched him with.

Part of him wanted the quiet, the quiet dark that he could sink into where none of it really mattered. And part of him was afraid he'd find his way back there, all too easily.

When he heard the curtain draw back again, he stayed as he was, arms braced, head down, eyes shut. "You don't want to fight with me now, Meg. You'll lose."

"I'll tell you something, Burke, I don't like being shuffled off like a petty annoyance. I don't like being ignored. Ordered around. I'm not sure I like the way you looked outside Town Hall tonight. So I couldn't see anything I recognized on your face, in your eyes. It pisses me off. And . . ."

She slid her arms around him, pressed her naked body to his so that he jerked straight. "It stirs me up."

"Don't." He clasped his hands over hers, prying hers apart before he turned to hold her at arm's length. "Just don't."

Deliberately she looked down. Deliberately she smiled as she looked up again. "Seems to be a contradiction here."

"I don't want to hurt you, and I would, the way I'm feeling right now."

"You don't scare me. You got me all churned up, spoiling for a fight. All of a sudden, I'm spoiling for something else. Give me something else." She reached up, ran her hand down his chest. "We'll finish fighting after."

"I'm not feeling friendly."

"Me, either. Nate, sometimes you just need something else. Just need to go somewhere else and forget for a little while. Burn up some of the mad or the hurt or the scared. Burn me up," she murmured. She gripped his hips now, squeezed.

She'd have been better off if he'd pushed her away. He was sure of it. But he yanked her toward him, so that warm, wet body collided with his, so he could find her mouth, ravage it.

She clamped around him, hooking her arms up his back so her fingers could dig into his shoulders. Nails biting flesh. The heat pumped out of her, and it reached his bones, seared through them, scoring away the tired and the cold line of anger.

Her hands streaked down him again, wet against wet, and her head dropped back to invite him to feast on her throat, her shoulders, anywhere he could find that soft, warm flesh.

The sound she made, the sound that simmered against his lips was one of erotic triumph.

"Here." She slid the soap out of the slot. "Let's clean you up. I like the feel of a man's back under my hands. Especially when it's all wet and slippery."

She had a voice like a siren. He let her use it on him, use her hands on him, let her think she was guiding him. When he pushed her back to the shower wall, the sleepy look in her eyes sharpened with surprise.

When she started to smile, he crushed his mouth to hers.

She'd been right, she thought dimly. He was someone

else, someone who took control, ruthlessly. Who took away choice, who could make her surrender it.

Even as his mouth took possession of hers, he twisted the soap from her hand. He ran it over her breasts, long, teasing strokes that had her nipples aching. Her breath trembled out in a sigh.

The tickle low in her belly told her she was ready. That she wanted. She needed. Rubbing her lips down the side of his neck, she murmured to him. "It's good with you. It's good. Be inside me now. Come inside me."

"You'll scream first."

She laughed, nipped—not so gently. "No, I won't."

"Yes." He hauled her arms over her head, cuffed her wrists with one hand. Pinned them there. "You will."

He slid the soap between her legs, rubbing it, sliding it, watching her as her body shuddered to orgasm.

"Nate."

"I warned you."

Something like panic lit inside her, panic quickly tangled with razor-edged pleasure as his fingers dipped inside her. She twisted, looking for freedom, for more. For him. But he drove her, past the point she could hold it, past the point she thought she could bear it. Her breath sobbed out, half-mad pleas as the water poured hot over her shaking body, as the steam blurred her vision.

When it burst in her, ripping a line between sanity and madness, he muffled her scream with his mouth.

"Say my name." He had to hear it, had to know she knew who had her. "Say my name," he ordered as he hoisted her by the hips and buried himself inside her.

"Nate."

"Again. Say it again." His breath was raw in his throat. "Look at me, and say my name."

"Nate." She fisted a hand in his hair, dug her fingers into his shoulder. She looked at his face, looked into his eyes. And saw him, saw herself. "Nate."

He took her, took her, took her until he was empty, until she was limp as water, her head dropped on his shoulder.

He had to brace a hand on the wet wall to catch his breath, to catch himself. He fumbled for the tap to shut off the shower.

"I need to sit down," she managed. "I really need to sit down."

"Hold on a minute." Because he wasn't sure she would, he boosted her up, half slinging her over his shoulder as he levered them out of the shower.

He grabbed a couple of towels, though he imagined with the heat they'd generated, the water would steam off them in a matter of minutes.

The dogs got to their feet when he walked into the bedroom with her. "Better tell your pals you're okay."

"What?"

"The dogs, Meg. Reassure your dogs before they decide I've knocked you unconscious."

"Rock, Bull, relax." She all but dripped out of his arms when he laid her on the bed. "My head's buzzing."

"Better try to dry off." He dropped one of the towels on her belly. "I'll get you a shirt or something."

She didn't bother to dry off, but only lay there enjoying the used, lax sensation weighting her body. "You

looked tired when you came in. Tired and mean, with a
thin coat of ice over it all. Same look you had outside
Town Hall. I've seen it a couple of other times—a quick
glimpse of it. Cop face."

He said nothing, only pulled on an old pair of sweats,
tossed her a flannel shirt.

"It's one of the things that stirred me up. Weird."

"The road's dicey out to your place. You're going to
need to stay here."

She waited a moment, letting her thoughts coalesce
again. "You shrugged me off. Before. Before when we
were outside." She could still see Yukon, the slash in his
throat, the knife buried to the hilt in his chest. "You
shrugged me off, and you gave me orders, a kind of ver-
bal strong-arming. I didn't like it."

Again, he said nothing, but picked up the towel to dry
his hair.

"You're not going to apologize."

"No."

She sat up to draw on the borrowed shirt. "I knew
that dog since he was a puppy." Because her voice wanted
to break, she pressed her lips together. Controlled it. "I
had a right to be upset."

"I'm not saying you didn't." He walked to the window. The snow was barely a mist now. Maybe the fore-
caster was right.

"And I had a right to be worried about my own dogs,
Nate. A right to go see to them myself."

"Partways there." He stepped away from the window
but left the curtains open. "Natural enough to worry,
but there was nothing to worry about."

"They weren't hurt, but they might've been."

"No. Whoever did this went for a solo dog, an old dog. Yours are young and strong and have two sets of healthy teeth. They're practically joined at the hip."

"I don't see—"

"Think for two seconds instead of just reacting." Impatience snapped in his voice as he tossed the towel aside. "Say somebody wanted to hurt them. Say somebody— even somebody they knew and let get close—tried to hurt one of them. Even managed to do it. The other'd be on him like God's own fury and tear him to pieces. And anybody who knows them enough to get close, knows that."

She drew her knees up to her chest, pressed her face against them and began to cry. Without looking up, she waved a hand to hold him off when she heard him move toward her.

"Don't. Don't. Give me a minute. I can't get the picture out of my head. It was easier when I was mad at you or turning that mad into sex. I *hated* sitting there waiting, not knowing. And I was scared for you, under it. I was scared something was going to happen to you. And *that* pissed me off."

She lifted her head. Through the blur of tears she could see his face, and that he'd shut down again. "I've got something else to say."

"Go ahead."

"I . . . I have to figure out how to say this so it doesn't sound lame." She dragged the heels of her hands up over her cheeks to dry them. "Even being mad and being scared and wanting to plant my boot up your ass for making me both, I . . . admire what you do. How you do it. Who you are when you do. I admire the strength it takes to do it."

He sat. Not beside her, not on the bed, but on the chair so there was distance between them. "Nobody I ever cared about—nobody outside of on the job—ever said anything like that to me."

"Then I'd say you cared about the wrong people." She got up, walked to the bathroom to blow her nose. When she came out, she stood leaning on the doorjamb, watching him from across the room.

"You went out and got my dogs for me. With all that was going on, you went out and brought them back for me. You could've sent someone else or just blown it off. Road's flooded, they'll have to wait. But you didn't. I have friends who'd have done the same for me, and me for them. But I can't think of any man I've been with, any man I've slept with, who would have done it."

A ghost of a smile touched his mouth. "Then I'd say you've slept with the wrong men."

"I guess I have." She went over and picked up the shirt he'd discarded when they'd come in. With some care, she unpinned the badge, then brought it to him. "This looks good on you, by the way. Sexy."

He gripped her hand before she could step back. Still holding it, he got to his feet. "I've got an awful need for you. It's more than I've had for anyone else, and may be more than you want."

"I guess we'll find out."

"You wouldn't have admired me a year ago. Six months ago. And you need to know that there are still days it seems like too much trouble to even get out of bed."

"Why do you?"

He opened his other hand, looked down at the badge. "I guess I've got an awful need for this, too. That's not heroic."

"Oh, you're so wrong." Her heart was lost. In that one moment it simply slid out and dropped at his feet. "Heroism's just doing more than you want to do or think you can. Sometimes it's just doing the crappy things, the unhappy things other people won't do."

She stepped closer, cupped his face in her hands. "It's not just jumping out of a plane onto a glacier ten thousand feet up because there's nobody else there to do it. It's getting out of bed in the morning when it seems like too much trouble."

Emotion swirled into his eyes, and he lowered his cheek to the top of her head. "I'm so in love with you, Meg."

Then he kissed her hair, straightened. "I need to go out. I want to check the river, patrol before I turn in."

"Can a civilian and her dogs do a ride-along on that?"

"Yeah." He ruffled a hand over her damp hair. "Dry your hair first."

"Will you tell me what you know, about Yukon?"

"I'll tell you what I can."

TWENTY-FOUR

HE WENT BACK to the scene of the crime in the early morning drizzle. Ten steps from the door, Nate thought. Left in plain view of anyone who might have come in or gone out of Town Hall. Plain view of anyone driving by, walking by.

More than left, he amended. Executed in plain view.

He walked inside, through to the meeting center. He'd ordered everything left as it was. The folding chairs, the big projection screen remained in place. He brought it back, into his head, the way it had been the night before.

He'd come in a little late, just before the lights had gone down. He'd scanned the crowd as much out of habit as looking for Meg.

Rose and David had been in the last row. Her first night out since the baby. They'd been holding hands. He remembered seeing them both at intermission—with Rose on the phone, probably checking with her mother, who was home watching the kids.

Bing had been near the back. Nate had ignored the flask he'd held between his knees. Deb and Harry, The Professor. A small clump of high schoolers, the entire Riggs family, who lived in a log cabin out past Rancor Woods.

He'd estimate that half the population had been there—which meant half hadn't. Some had left at intermission. Any of those who'd stayed might have slipped out and in again.

In the dark, while attention was focused on the screen.

He walked back to the lobby when he heard the outer door open and watched Hopp shove back her hood.

"Saw your car parked outside. I don't know what to think about this, Ignatious. I can't put two thoughts together about it."

She lifted her hands, let them drop again. "I'm going to go over and see Lara. Don't know what I'll say. This is such a crazy thing. Mean and crazy."

"I'll go with mean."

"But not crazy? Somebody carves up a harmless dog outside Town Hall, and that's not crazy?"

"Depends on why."

Her mouth flattened at that. "I can't see any why to it. Couple of people are saying we've got a cult, high school kids experimenting or some such thing. I don't believe that for one minute."

"It wasn't ritualistic."

"Others think it's some loony, camped out near town. Maybe it's a comfort believing none of us could have done such an awful thing, but I don't know that it makes me feel any better to think we've got a crazy lurking around who'd kill a dog that way."

She studied his face. "You don't think that."

"No, I don't think that."

"Are you going to tell me what you do think?"

"I think when somebody kills a local dog, in the middle of town, in front of a building where a good half of that town's sitting, he's got his reasons."

"Which are?"

"I'm working on it."

HE DROVE ALONG THE RIVER before heading to the station. It was a sulky gray today, with those plates and chunks of floating ice dull on its surface.

Meg's plane was gone, a clear symbol that he couldn't box her up somewhere safe and close. Bing and a two-man crew were patching a section of road. Bing's only acknowledgment as Nate slowed to pass was a long, steady stare.

He drove to the station to find Peach urging coffee on Joe and Lara. Peter stood by looking very much like a grown man struggling not to cry.

Lara, her eyes swollen and beet red, sprang up the instant Nate stepped into the room.

"I want to know what you're doing about Yukon. What are you doing to find the bastard who killed my dog?"

"Now, Lara."

"Don't 'Now, Lara' me," she said, whirling on her husband. "I want to *know*."

"Why don't you come back to my office. Peach, hold off anything that comes in, except an emergency, for the next few minutes."

"All right, Chief. Lara." She gripped Lara's hand in hers. "I couldn't be more sorry."

Lara managed a short bob of her head before she shot

her chin into the air and sailed into Nate's office. "I want some answers."

"Lara, I want you to sit down."

"I don't want—"

"I want you to sit down." His tone was quiet, but the authority in it had her dropping into a chair.

"The town voted for this police department. Voted to bring you in and to pay the tax that pays your salary. I want you to tell me what you're doing. Why you're not out there right now looking for that son of a bitch."

"I'm doing everything I can do. Lara," he said in that same quiet tone before she could speak again. "Don't think for a minute that I'm taking this lightly. That any of us are. I'm pursuing it, and I'll keep pursuing it until I can give you those answers."

"You've got the knife. The knife that—" Her voice broke, and her chin bobbled, but she sucked in air, pushed back her shoulders. "You ought to be able to find out who owned that knife."

"I can tell you that the knife was reported stolen yesterday morning, along with other items. I've talked to the owner, and I'm going to get statements from people who were in Town Hall last night. I can start with you."

"You think one of us killed Yukon?"

"That's not what I think. Sit down, Lara," he said when she leaped to her feet. "You were both at movie night. So let's go over what you saw, heard."

She lowered, slowly this time. "We left him outside." Tears swam into her eyes. "He was getting so he couldn't hold his bladder, so we left him outside. It was only for

a few hours, and he had his doghouse. If we'd left
him in—"

"You don't know if it would've made a difference.
Whoever did this could've broken in, taken him out.
From what I've heard, you gave that dog nearly fourteen
good years. You've got nothing to blame yourself for.
What time did you leave the house?"

Lara bowed her head, stared at her hands as her tears
plopped onto them.

"Right after six," Joe said, and began to rub his wife's
shoulder.

"You go straight to Town Hall?"

"Yeah. We got there about six-thirty, I guess. Early,
but we like to sit close to the front. We dumped our jack-
ets on the chairs. Three, four rows back, on . . . on the
left side. And we socialized awhile."

Nate took them through it. Who they had talked
with, who had sat near them.

"Anyone ever complain to you about the dog?"

"No." Joe sighed. "Well, maybe a few times when he
was a puppy. He used to bark if a leaf stirred. And he got
out once and chewed up Tim Tripp's boots from off his
back stoop. But that was years ago, and Tim got kind of
a kick out of it because the damn boots were almost bigger than Yukon. He settled down, after he got out of the
puppy stage, he settled down."

"How about the two of you? Have you had a problem
with anyone lately? An argument?"

"I got into it some with Skinny Jim over the Iditarod. It
got pretty heated. But that sort of thing happens. People

get worked up over the Iditarod, and they've got their favorites."

"I had to call Ginny Mann into the school because her boy hooked twice." Lara fumbled out a tissue. "She wasn't happy about it or with me."

"How old's her boy?"

"Eight." She blinked rapidly. "Oh God, Joshua couldn't have done that to Yukon, Nate. He's a good kid—just doesn't much like school, but he wouldn't have killed my dog because he was mad at me. And Ginny and Don, they're good people. They couldn't . . ."

"Okay. If you think of anything else, you let me know."

"I want—I want to apologize for the way I jumped on you before."

"Don't worry about that, Lara."

"No, it wasn't right. It wasn't right and it wasn't . . . You saved my son's life."

"I wouldn't go that far."

"You helped save it, and that's the same thing to me. I shouldn't've come in here the way I did. Joe tried to calm me down, but I wouldn't be calmed. I loved that damn dog."

AFTER THEY'D LEFT, Nate uncovered his case board. As he pinned up the pictures he'd taken the night before, Peter came in. "Okay, Chief?"

"Yeah."

"I feel like I should've been able to handle Mrs. Wise. I got twisted up. I, well, Steven and I hung out together a lot, and . . . I grew up with that dog. My dad, he has the sled dogs, and they're great. But not the same as a pet. Even when Steven went to college, I'd go over and see Yukon sometimes. I guess that's why I had some trouble with everything last night, too."

"You could've told me."

"I just . . . I was just twisted up. Um, Chief? Is that going to be just an open case board now? I mean, should we put copies of notes and other case-related items on the board?"

"No."

"But . . . you've got Yukon up there now."

"That's right."

"You think what happened to Yukon's related to the others? I feel stupid, but I don't understand."

"Thinking they're related might be stupid."

Peter stepped closer. "Why do you?"

"At this point I've got no clear motive for anyone killing that dog." Nate walked around to his desk, unlocked a drawer and took out the sealed knife and gloves. "These belong to Bing. He reported them stolen yesterday morning."

"Bing?" Peter's eyes widened. *"Bing?"*

"He's got a temper on him. He's got a sheet, and most of it deals with assaults. Violent behavior."

"Yeah, but . . . God."

"We've got a few ways to look at this. Bing gets in an argument with Joe somewhere along the line. Or Joe and Lara do something that aggravates him. He stews about it, decides to teach them a lesson. So he decides to kill the dog, reports the knife and gloves as stolen, then goes off after intermission last night, knowing the Wises are inside. He gets the dog, brings him back. Kills him, leaves the knife and gloves figuring he's covered because he'd reported them stolen. Then he goes home and works in his garage."

"If he was mad at Mr. or Mrs. Wise, why didn't he just punch Mr. Wise in the face?"

"Good question. Another way we can look at it is, somebody wanted to cause Bing some trouble. He pisses a lot of people off, so that's no stretch."

He eased a hip onto his desk, his eyes on the board. "They steal his knife and gloves. They use them to kill the dog, leave them where they'll be found. Or . . ."

He moved to the counter, started a pot of coffee. "We ask ourselves how Galloway's murder, Max's death and the killing of a dog might be connected."

"That's just it. I don't see."

"The killer left us one big clue. Cryptic or obvious, depending on which angle you look from. The dog's throat was slit. That's what killed him. But the killer doesn't toss the knife aside. He takes another minute. Had to roll the dog over to do it. To bury the knife in its chest. Why?"

"Because he's sick and he's mean and—"

"Put that aside and look at the board, Peter. Look at Galloway. Look at the dog."

He struggled with it, Nate could see. With looking close at the grisly pictures. Then he let out a little breath, as if he'd been holding it. "Chest wound. They both have a blade of some kind in the chest."

"Could be coincidence, or maybe somebody's trying to tell us something. Now, take another step. Where's the connection between Galloway, Max and the Wises?"

"Well, I don't know. Steven and his parents moved here when I was about twelve, I guess. That was after Galloway was gone. But they knew Mr. Hawbaker. Mr. Wise ran an ad in *The Lunatic* most weeks for his computer servicing. And Mrs. Wise and Mrs. Hawbaker took some classes together. The exercise class at the school and the quilting class Peach has going."

"Something else connects them. To our knowledge they didn't know Patrick Galloway, but for sixteen years everyone believes Galloway just took off. Now they don't. Why?"

"Well, because they found him when . . . Steven. Steven's the one who found him."

"Get away with murder for sixteen years, then some dumbass college boy and his idiot friends screw it up for you." Nate listened to the coffee plop into the glass pot. "A pisser, all right. If they hadn't been up there—that time, that place—odds are things would be fine. Another avalanche—nature's or one the State set off to clear the mountain—that cave could've been buried again. For years. Maybe forever, if your luck held."

He eased a hip down on his desk while the coffee brewed. "Now you've got to go and kill again. Kill Max, or induce him to kill himself. You'll get away with that, too. You believe that. You have to believe that, but there are cops in Lunacy now. Not just state, but town cops, right underfoot. What do you do about that?"

"I . . . I can't keep up."

"You distract them. Vandalism, petty thievery. Little things that keep them occupied, just in case they're thinking about more important things. You pay that dumbass college boy back, and you give the cops something else to worry about at the same time. Two birds. But you can't resist being a little fancy, giving them an elbow in the ribs. So you mimic your first murder by shoving the knife in the dog's chest."

He got up, poured coffee for both of them. "Now, it could be you're so fucking arrogant and full of yourself that you use your own knife, your own gloves. Strong possibility when you profile Bing Karlovski. Or you're so clever, so full of yourself, you plant them so the finger points elsewhere. If that's the case, why Bing? Where's he connect?"

"I swear I don't know. I'm trying to get all this into my head. Maybe it doesn't have to connect. Bing's ornery. He irritates people. Or there was just an easy chance to steal the knife."

"None of it's chance. Not this time. We need to find out where Bing was—exactly where he was in February of 1988."

"How?"

Nate sipped his coffee. "For a start, I'm going to ask him. Meanwhile I want statements from everyone who was at movie night, and everyone who wasn't. That's going to take time. You tell Peach to make a list that divides the township and outlying into three parts. We'll each take one."

"I'll tell her right now."

"Peter?" Nate stopped him at the door. "Weren't you scheduled to work last night? To cover the desk?"

"Yeah, but Otto said he didn't feel like going to the movies so we switched. That's okay, isn't it?"

"Sure." Nate sipped his coffee again. "That's fine. Go ahead and get Peach started on that list."

Nate crossed to the board and drew lines connecting Joe and Lara Wise with Max and with Bing.

"Nate?" Peach peeked in. "You still want me to hold things out here?"

"No, whatcha got?"

"Had a report of gunfire and a bear sighting. Same people who reported the dead body that was a pair of boots. I gave both of them to Otto, since he was already out on patrol. Gunfire was Dex Trilby's truck, which is older than I am, backfiring."

"And the bear was what, a squirrel standing on a log?"

"No, the bear was a bear. Those idiot Outsiders put up a bunch of bird feeders around the cabin, draw the birds in. Well, a bear can't resist fresh bird feed. Otto ran it off, and made them take down the feeders. He's a little irritable after having to go out there twice already today. So if something else comes in, I thought I'd hand it off to you or Peter."

"You do that."

"Well, then, Carrie Hawbaker just came in and wants to see you. She wants me to give her the items for the police log."

"Good, go ahead. I guess we'll have *The Lunatic* up and running again."

"Looks that way. She says she wants the official statement on what happened last night for the paper. Do you want me to take care of it?"

"No." He flipped the blanket over his board. "Send her on back."

She looked better than the last time he'd seen her. Steadier and not quite so sunken around the eyes. "Thanks for seeing me."

"How are you doing?" he asked and closed the door.

"Getting through, getting by. It helps to have the kids—they need me—and the paper." She took the chair he offered and set the canvas briefcase she carried on her lap. "I'm not just here about the items for the police log. Though, God, it's an awful thing about Yukon."

"It is."

"Well. I know you wanted me to think about back when Pat disappeared. To write down details. I did some." She opened the bag to take sheets of paper. "I thought I'd remember it all. I thought everything would just coming flooding back. But it didn't."

Nate saw the papers were neatly typed and written in a formal outline style. "It looks like you remembered plenty."

"I put down everything. A lot of things that couldn't matter. It was long ago, and I have to admit now that I didn't pay much attention to Pat's leaving. I was teaching, and wondering how I was going to get through another winter—my second—here. I was thirty-one, and I'd missed my goal of being married by my thirtieth birthday."

She smiled a little. "That was one of the reasons I'd

come to Alaska in the first place. The ratio was in my favor. I remember feeling a little desperate, a little sorry for myself. And annoyed with Max because he hadn't asked me. That's why I remember—you'll see it written there—that he was gone a couple of weeks that winter. I think it was that February, I'm not absolutely sure. Days tend to freeze together in the winter, especially if you're alone."

"Where did he tell you he was going?"

"That I do remember, because I got snippy about it. He said he was going to Anchorage, down to Homer—a few weeks in the southeast, interviewing bush pilots and getting some of them to fly him around. For the paper, and research for the novel he was writing."

"Did he do a lot of traveling back then?"

"He did. I put that down, too. He said he'd be gone maybe four or five weeks, and that didn't sit well with me, especially with things still up in the air between us. I remember because he was back sooner than he said, but he didn't even come to see me. People told me he'd holed up at the paper. Was practically living there. I was too mad to go see him, either."

"How long before you did see him?"

"It was a while. I was pretty mad. But finally I got mad enough *to* see him. I know it was the end of March or the very start of April. We had the classroom decorated for Easter. Easter hit the first Sunday in April that year. I looked it up. I remember sitting there with all those colored eggs and bunny drawings while I was stewing about Max."

She ran her hand over her stack of papers. "This part I remember perfectly. He was at the paper, locked in. I had to bang on the door. He looked terrible. Thin and unshaven, his hair all which way. He smelled. There were papers all over his desk."

She sighed a little. "I can't remember what the weather was like, Nate. What it looked like in town, but I can remember exactly how he looked. I can remember exactly how it looked in his office. Coffee cups, dishes all over the place, trash cans overflowing, trash on the floor. Ashtrays full of butts. He used to smoke.

"I wrote it down," she said, and smoothed the papers again. "He was working on his novel—that's what I as-sumed—and looked like a madman. Damn if I know why I found that so appealing. But I gave him what-for. Told him I was done. If he thought he could treat me that way, he could just think again, and so on. I just raved and ranted, and he didn't say a thing. When I'd run out of steam, he got down on one knee."

She stopped a moment, pressed her lips together. "Right there, in all that mess. He said he wanted a sec-ond chance. He needed one. And asked me to marry him. We were married that June. I wanted to be a June bride, and since I'd already missed the thirtieth-birthday deadline, a couple more months didn't matter."

"Did he ever talk about the time he was away?"

"No. And I didn't ask. It didn't seem important. All he said was that he'd learned what it was like to be alone, really alone, and he didn't want to be alone again."

Nate thought about the lines connecting the names on his list. "Did he ever have a particular run-in or a par-ticular friendship with Bing?"

"Bing? No, not a buddy sort of thing. Max tried to stay on his good side, especially since he knew Bing had asked me out."

"Bing?"

"'Asked me out' is probably a euphemism. He wasn't interested in dining and dancing, if you follow me."

"And did you ever . . ."

"No." She laughed, cutting herself off in midstream and looking shocked at herself. "I haven't laughed, not really, since . . . It's terrible to laugh at this."

"The thought of you and Bing strikes me funny. How'd he take being turned down?"

"Oh, I don't think it was a big deal." She brushed it off with the back of her hand. "I was handy, that's all. New female in the very small pack. Men like Bing would try to cut the new one out of the herd, see if he could get some sex and maybe a couple of home-cooked meals out of it. Nothing against him, it's natural enough in a place like this. He wasn't the only one who made moves. I went out with a few that first winter. Even The Professor and I had dinner a couple times, though it was plain as plain he had a major crush on Charlene."

"That would be before Galloway left?"

"Before, during, after. He's always had a thing for her. But we had dinner a couple of times, and he was a perfect gentleman. Maybe a little more gentlemanly than I was looking for, to tell the truth. But I wasn't looking for someone like Bing."

"Because?"

"He's so big and crude and rough. I went out with

John because I liked his looks and his intellect. And with Ed once because, well, why not? Even Otto, after his divorce. A woman—even one who's not very pretty and past thirty—has a lot of choices in a place like this, if she's not too picky. I chose Max."

She smiled into middle distance. "I still would." Then brought herself back. "I wish I could tell you more. Looking back, I guess I can see that Max was troubled. But he always seemed troubled when he worked on one of his books. He'd put them away for months and months at a time, and everything was normal. But as soon as he'd pull one out and start, he'd close in. I was happier when he'd forget the books."

"Anyone ever make a move on you after you were married?"

"No. I recall Bing telling me, right in front of Max, that I was selling myself short or cheap or something like that."

"And?"

"Nothing. Max made a joke out of it, bought Bing a drink. He wasn't one for confrontations, Nate. Went miles out of the way to avoid one, which is one of the reasons, I guess, he didn't make it on a big-city paper. You saw what he did when you brushed him off after you first got here. He went to Hopp. That was his way. He wouldn't have come in here for a showdown with you on his own because he just didn't have the tools for any sort of battle. He never did."

"Was Max a movie fan?"

"Just about everyone in Lunacy is. One dependable

form of community entertainment. He really loved doing reviews on what we had coming up. Speaking of
movie night, I really do want a statement about what
happened last night."

"Peach can give you the report for the log."

"I'll see her about that, but I think, something like
this, we'll want to run more than an item. Otto found
him," she began as she started to dig out a notebook.

"Yes. Give us a couple days on this, Carrie. By then I
should have something more cohesive to give you."

"Do you mean you expect to make an arrest shortly?"

Nate smiled. "You've got your reporter hat right back
on. What I mean is I'll have my notes, statements, the incident report coordinated."

She rose. "I'm glad my kids weren't there last night. I
almost insisted they go, just so they'd get out and do
something normal. But they had a couple of friends over
for pizza instead. I'll check back with you tomorrow."

"I was just wondering," he said as he walked her to
the door, "was Max a fan of *Star Wars*?"

She stared at him. "Where did that come from?"

"Just a dot I'm trying to connect."

"He wasn't. Not just that he wasn't a particular fan,
which was baffling to me because he loved that sort of
thing. Big epic stories with lots of special effects. But he
wouldn't watch those. We had a *Star Wars* marathon on
movie night about six, seven years ago. Well, whenever the
twentieth anniversary of the original was. He wouldn't go,
and the kids were mad to go. I had to take them myself.
And write the reviews for the paper, now that I think

about it. When the new ones came out, I ended up taking the kids all the way to Anchorage to see them for the first run. He stayed home.

"What hat did you pull that one out of?"

"Cop hat." He gave her a little nudge to urge her out. "It's not important. You see Peach about the log item."

NATE TIMED IT so that he walked over to The Lodge when Bing and his crew broke for lunch. He stepped inside as Rose served Bing a beer. His eyes met Bing's over it. He strolled over, nodded casually to the two men on the opposite side of the booth.

"You boys mind finding another table so Bing and I can have a private conversation?"

They didn't like it, but they picked up their coffee mugs and moved to the next empty booth.

"I got lunch coming," Bing began. "And I got a right to eat it without you sitting here spoiling my appetite."

"See you got that pothole filled in. Thanks, Rose," he said when she brought him his usual coffee.

"You ready for lunch, Chief?"

"No. Nothing right now. River's holding," he continued to Bing. "Maybe we won't need those sandbags."

"Maybe we do, maybe we don't."

"February 1988. Where were you?"

"How the living fuck do I know?"

"In 1988, the Los Angeles Dodgers won the Series, the Redskins took the Super Bowl. Cher won an Oscar."

"Lower 48 crap."

"And in February, Susan Butcher won her third Iditarod. Hell of a feat for a girl from Boston. Finished in eleven days and just under twelve hours. Maybe that refreshes your memory."

"It refreshes that I lost two hundred bucks on that race. Damn woman."

"So, what were you doing a few weeks before you lost the two bills?"

"A man remembers losing two hundred because of a woman. He don't necessarily remember every time he scratches his ass or takes a piss."

"You take any trips?"

"I was coming and going as I damn well pleased then, same as now."

"Maybe you went down to Anchorage, saw Galloway there."

"I've been down to Anchorage more times than you can spit. Couple hundred miles doesn't mean anything up here. I might've seen him there a time or two. Seen plenty of people I know there. I do my business and they do theirs."

"You play hard-ass on this, you'll be the one who pays for it."

The heat burned into his eyes. "You don't want to go threatening me."

"You don't want to go stonewalling me." Nate leaned back with his coffee. "You figured you should be the one wearing this badge."

"Better than some cheechako, one that got his own partner killed. One that woulda washed out if that thin blue line hadn't held him up."

It seared straight into his gut, but he drank the coffee,

held Bing's eyes. "Been doing your homework, I see. But the fact is, I'm wearing the badge. I've got enough right now to take you in, charge you and lock you up for what was done to that dog."

"I never touched that dog."

"If I were you, I'd put a little more effort into remembering where I was when Patrick Galloway left town."

"Why do you want to beat this dead horse, Burke? Make you feel important? Max killed Galloway, and everybody knows it."

"Then it shouldn't bother you to verify your own whereabouts."

Rose came over with a slab of meat loaf, a mountain of mashed potatoes and a small sea of gravy. "Anything else I can get for you, Bing?" She set a bowl of snow peas and tiny onions beside the plate.

Nate saw him struggle, watched him draw himself back. His voice was even, a shade on the gentle side when he answered. "No thanks, Rose."

"You enjoy that. Chief, just let me know if you want anything."

"I'm through talking to you," Bing said, and forked up a huge bite of meat loaf.

"How about some lunchtime small talk, then? What do you think of *Star Wars?*"

"Huh?"

"You know, the movies. Luke Skywalker, Darth Vader."

"Fucking idiot," Bing mumbled under his breath and scooped up gravy drenched potatoes. "*Star Wars,* for Christ's sake. Let me eat in peace."

"Great story, memorable characters. Under all the jazz, it's about destiny—and betrayal."

"It's about making a killing at the box office and merchandising." Bing waved his fork before he dug in again. "Buncha guys flying around in spaceships, whapping each other with light swords."

"Sabers. Light sabers. The thing is, it took some time, some sacrifice, some loss, but . . ." He slid out of the booth. "The good guys won. See you around."

TWENTY-FIVE

THERE WERE ELEVEN SENIORS in the last-period English lit class. Nine of them were awake. John let the two snoozers catch their late-afternoon catnap while one of the more alert mangled the Bard's words in her reading of Lady Macbeth's "Out, damned spot," scene.

He had enough on his mind, and supervising the discussion on *Macbeth* was only a small part of it.

He'd been leading discussions like this for twenty-five years, since the first time he stepped nervously in front of a classroom of students.

He'd been only a few years older than those he'd taught back then. And perhaps more innocent and eager than the majority of his students.

He'd wanted to write great and awesome novels, filled with allegories on the human condition.

He hadn't wanted to starve in a garret, so he'd taught.

He'd written, and though the novels were never as great or awesome as he'd hoped, he'd published a few. Without teaching he might not have starved in that garret, but he wouldn't have eaten well.

He'd felt the demands—and, God help him, the joys—of teaching overwhelming for the intellectual young man who wanted to write great novels. So he'd taken the leap, the brave and foolish leap, and had run to Alaska. There he would experience, he'd live simply, he'd study the human condition in that primitive place, that wide-open isolation it represented to him. He'd write novels about man's courage and tenacity, his follies and his triumphs.

Then he'd come to Lunacy.

How could he have known, a young man not yet thirty, the true meaning of obsession? How could he have understood—that bright, idealistic and pathetic young man—that one place, one woman could chain him? Could keep him willingly shackled no matter how they defied and denied his needs?

He had fallen in love—become obsessed, he was no longer sure there was a difference—the moment he'd seen Charlene. Her beauty was like a golden willow, her voice a siren's song. Her reckless and joyful sexuality. Everything about her enchanted and engulfed him.

She was another man's woman, the mother of another man's child. But it made no difference. His love, if that's what it was, hadn't been the pure and romantic love of a valorous knight for a lady, but the lustful, sweaty need of a man for a woman.

Hadn't he convinced himself she would cast Galloway off? He was careless with her. Selfish. Even if he hadn't been blinded by love, John would have seen that. Resented that.

So he'd stayed and waited. Changed the course of his life and waited.

After everything he'd done, all his plans, his hopes, he was still waiting.

His students got younger and younger, and the years died behind him. He could never get back what he'd cast away, what he'd wasted.

And still, the single thing he wanted would not be his.

He glanced at the clock, saw another day had gone to dust. Then, catching a movement out of the corner of his eye, saw Nate leaning against the jamb of the open door of his classroom.

"Your papers on *Macbeth* are due next Friday," he announced to a chorus of groans. "Kevin, I'll know if Marianne writes it for you. Those of you who're on the yearbook committee, remember there's a meeting tomorrow at three-thirty. Make sure you've arranged transportation home, if necessary. Dismissed."

There was the general clatter, shuffle, chatter he was so used to he no longer noticed.

"What is it about high schools," Nate began, "that can make a grown man's palms sweat?"

"Just because we survived the hell of it once, doesn't mean we can't be thrown back into the pit."

"Guess that's it."

"You'd have done well enough, I'd wager," John said, as he packed some papers into his battered briefcase. "You've got the looks, the attitude. Decent enough student, I'd say, did well with the girls. Athletic. What did you letter in?"

"Track." Nate's lips curved. "Always could run. You?"

"Your classic nerd. The one that screwed the curve for the rest of the class."

"That was you? I hated you." With his thumbs hooked in his pockets, Nate strolled in, looked at the notes on the blackboard. "*Macbeth,* huh? I got Shakespeare okay if somebody else read it. Out loud, I mean, so I could hear the words. This guy killed for a woman, right?"

"No, for ambition at the *urging* of a woman. With the seeds for it all planted by three more."

"He didn't get away with it."

"He paid, with his honor, with the loss of the woman he loved to madness, with his life."

"What goes around."

John nodded, lifted an eyebrow. "Did you drop by to discuss Shakespeare, Nate?"

"Nope. We're investigating the incident last night. I need to ask you some questions."

"About Yukon? I was in Town Hall when it happened."

"What time did you get there?"

"A few minutes before seven." He glanced over absently as some of the liberated students raced laughing down the hall. "Actually, I'm doing an extracurricular group on Hitchcockian storytelling for the tenth- through twelfth-graders. Gets some of the kids involved, earns them extra credit. A dozen of my students signed up for it."

"Did you go out between seven and ten?"

"I went out at intermission, had a smoke, got some of the punch the elementary school committee was selling. Which was more palatable when I doctored it."

"Where were you sitting?"

"Toward the back, opposite side from my students. I didn't want to inhibit them or be barraged with questions. I was taking notes on the movies."

"In the dark?"

"Yes, that's right. Just a few key points I wanted to make sure to bring forward in discussion. I'd like to help you on this, but I don't see how I can."

He walked over to lower the blinds on the room's single window. "After Otto came in, after we knew what had happened, I went back to The Lodge. I was upset. We all were. Charlene, Skinny Jim and Big Mike were running the place."

"Who was there?"

"Ah, Mitch Dauber and Cliff Treat, Drunk Mike. A couple of hikers." As he spoke, he policed the room, gathering up dropped pencils, crumpled balls of paper, a hair clip.

"I got a drink. Meg and Otto came in shortly, and after things settled down a little, we played some poker. We were still playing when you got there."

Nate nodded and put away the notebook he'd pulled out.

John tossed the paper in the trash, put the other items in a shoe box on his desk. "I don't know anybody who'd do that to a dog. Especially Yukon."

"Nobody else seems to, either." Nate glanced around the classroom. It smelled like chalk, he thought. And that teenage perfume of gum, lip gloss and hair gel. "Do you ever take time off during the school year? Give yourself a break and just head out?"

"I've been known to. Mental-health breaks, I'd call them. Why?"

"I'm wondering if you took a mental-health break back in February of 1988."

Behind his lenses, John's eyes went cool. "It would be hard to say."

"Try."

"Should I be talking to a lawyer, Chief Burke?"

"That would be up to you. I'm just trying to get a picture of where everyone was, what everyone was up to when Patrick Galloway was killed."

"Shouldn't the State Police be the ones trying to get that picture? And if I'm not mistaken, haven't they drawn their conclusions?"

"I like my own drawings. You wouldn't say it was a secret that you've been, let's say, partial to Charlene for a long time."

"No." After taking off his glasses, John began to polish them, slowly, thoroughly, with a handkerchief from his jacket pocket. "I wouldn't say it's a secret."

"And were partial to her when she was with Galloway."

"I had feelings, strong feelings for her, yes. They hardly did me any good as she married someone else less than a year after Galloway left."

"Was murdered," Nate corrected.

"Yes." He replaced his glasses. "Was murdered."

"Did you ask her?"

"She said no. She's said no every time I've asked her."

"But she slept with you."

"You're treading on very personal ground now."

"She slept with you," Nate continued, "but she married someone else. Slept with you while she was married to someone else. And not just you."

"That's private. As much as anything can be in a place like this. I'm not going to discuss it with you."

"Love's a kind of ambition, isn't it." Nate tapped a finger on the copy of *Macbeth* still sitting on John's desk. "Men kill for it."

"Men kill. Half the time they don't need any excuse."

"Can't argue with that. Sometimes they get away with it. More often they don't. I'd appreciate it if you'd think back, and when you remember where you were that February, you let me know."

He started for the door, turned back. "Oh, I wondered, did you ever read any of the books Max Hawbaker started?"

"No." Though his voice was calm, a dull anger still rode in his eyes. "He was secretive about them. A lot of aspiring writers are. I had the impression he talked about writing a book more than he actually wrote."

"Turns out he started a few. I've got the copies. They all sort of circle around to the same thing. A theme, I guess you'd call it."

"That's not atypical for a fledgling writer either. Even an experienced one will explore a theme from several angles."

"His seems to be about men surviving nature—and each other. Or not surviving. Always ends up being three men, no matter how many it starts out with, it comes down to three. The one he did the most on is about three men climbing a mountain, in the winter."

Nate jingled loose change in his pocket when John remained silent.

"He only had a few chapters complete, but he had notes on the rest, like an outline or scattered scenes he was going to plug in. Three men go up the mountain. Only two come back." Nate paused a moment. "A lot of novels are autobiographical, aren't they?"

"Some," John said evenly. "It's often a device used for a first novel."

"Interesting, isn't it? It'd be even more interesting to find out who that third man was. Well, I'll be around. You let me know if you recall where you were that February."

John stood where he was until Nate's footsteps stopped echoing down the hall. Then he sat, slowly, at his desk. And saw his hands were shaking.

NATE WALKED IN on an informal meeting at Town Hall. He did so deliberately and wasn't surprised when conversation snapped off when he came in the door.

"Sorry to interrupt." He scanned the faces of the town council, faces he'd come to know. More than one of them registered embarrassment. "I can wait until you're finished if you want."

"I think we're about wrapped up here," Hopp said.

"I disagree." Ed planted his Vasque Sundowners on the floor, folded his arms over his chest. "I don't think we've resolved anything—and I think this meeting should continue—and, I'm sorry, Chief, remain closed until things are resolved."

"Ed." Deb leaned forward. "We've hashed this around six dozen ways. Let's give it a rest."

"I move we continue."

"Oh, move it up your ass, Ed." Joe Wise got to his feet.

"Joe." Hopp jabbed a finger at him. "We're informal here, but that doesn't mean we're going to start a rumble. Since Ignatious is here, and his name's come up in this meeting, let's get his input."

"I agree." Ken rose, dragged another chair into the circle they'd formed. "Have a seat, Nate. Listen," he said before anyone could object, "this is our chief of police. He should be a part of this."

"The fact is, Ignatious, we're discussing recent events. And your handling of them."

"Okay. I take it some aren't satisfied with my handling of them."

"Well, the fact is . . ." Harry scratched his head. "There've been some rumblings around town that we've had more trouble here since we hired you than before. Seems like we have—not that I see how that's your fault—but it seems we have."

"It might have been a mistake." Ed firmed his jaw. "I'll say that right to your face. It might have been a mistake to hire you, anyone for that matter, from Outside."

"The reasons for going Outside were valid," Walter Notti reminded him. "Chief Burke has done, is doing, the job he was hired to do."

"That may be, Walter, that may be. But—" Ed held up his hands. "It could be some of the less lawful elements of this town look at that as a kind of dare. So they're more active, you could say. People around here don't like being told what to do."

"We voted to have a police force," Hopp reminded him.

"I know that, Hopp, and I was one who voted aye, right here in this room. I'm not saying Nate's to blame for the way it's worked out. I'm saying it was a mistake. Our mistake."

"I'm stitching up the Mackies less often since Nate got here," Ken put in. "I had less patients coming in than usual for treatment after fights, less domestic violence. Last year Drunk Mike was brought in twice with frostbite after somebody found him passed out on the side of the road. This year he's still going on benders, but he's sleeping them off safe in a cell."

"I don't think we can blame having a police force for you getting your equipment stolen, Ed, or your shack graffitied." Deb spread her hands. "We can't blame having law for Hawley getting his tires slashed, or for windows being broke at the school or any of that stuff. I say we blame it on parents not sitting hard enough on their kids."

"A kid didn't kill my dog." Joe looked apologetically at Nate. "I agree with what Deb said, and with what Walter and Ken said before that, but a kid didn't do that to Yukon."

"No," Nate said. "It wasn't a kid."

"I don't think hiring you was a mistake, Nate," Deb continued, "but I think we've all got a responsibility to this town, and we ought to know how you're handling it.

What you're doing to find out who's doing these things and who did that to Yukon."

"That's fair. Some of the incidents mentioned may very well have been kids. The broken windows at the school certainly were, and since one of them was careless enough to drop his penknife, they've been identified. I talked to them and their parents yesterday. Restitution will be made, and both of them will get a three-day suspension—during which time, I doubt they're going to have a real good time."

"You didn't charge them?" Ed demanded.

"They were nine and ten, Ed. I didn't think locking them in a cell was the answer. A lot of us," he said remembering the sealed juvenile file on Ed's record, "do stupid things, get in trouble with the law when we're kids."

"If they did that, maybe they did the other things," Deb suggested.

"They didn't. They got set down in school by their teacher, broke a couple of windows. They sure as hell didn't hike all the way out to Ed's ice shack or sneak out of the house at night and walk the two miles to Hawley's to slash his tires and spray paint all over his truck. You want my input? Your trouble didn't start since you hired me. Your trouble started sixteen years ago when somebody killed Patrick Galloway."

"That's something that's shaken everybody up," Harry said, nodding to the others around the room. "Even those of us who didn't know him. But I don't see what it has to do with what we're discussing here."

"I think it does. So that's how I'm handling it."

"I don't follow you," Deb said.

"Whoever killed Galloway is still here. Whoever killed Galloway," Nate continued as everyone began talking at once, "killed Max Hawbaker."

"Max killed himself," Ed interrupted. "He killed himself because *he* killed Pat."

"Someone wants you to believe that. I don't."

"That's just crazy talk, Nate." Harry pushed back air with both hands. "Just crazy talk."

"Crazier than Max killing Pat?" Deb rubbed her fingers over her throat. "Crazier than Max killing himself? I don't know."

"Quiet!" Hopp held up both hands and shouted over the noise. "Just quiet down a damn minute. Ignatious." She drew a breath. "You're saying that someone we know has killed twice."

"Three times." His gaze was flinty as it scanned the room. "Two men and an old dog. My department is investigating, and will continue to investigate, until this individual is identified and arrested."

"The State Police—" Joe began.

"Whatever the findings and the opinion of the State authorities, my department will investigate. I swore to protect and serve this town, and I will. Part of that investigation will require each one of you to account for your whereabouts and activities last night between nine and ten P.M."

"Us?" Ed bellowed it. "You're going to question us?"

"That's right. In addition, I'm going to be looking for the whereabouts and activities of everyone during the month of February 1988."

"You—you—" Ed blustered to a halt, then, gripping the edge of his chair, pushed himself forward. "You intend to question us, as *suspects*? This is over the top. This is beyond belief. I'm not going to be subjected to this or have my family and my neighbors subjected to this. You're exceeding your authority."

"I don't think so. But you guys can vote to cancel my contract, pay me off. I'll still investigate. I'll still find the person responsible. That's what I do." He rose. "I find the people responsible. So you can have your meetings, your votes, your discussions. You can take my badge. I'll still find the one responsible. That's the only person who has to worry about me."

He strode out, leaving the raised voices and insulted faces behind.

Hopp caught up with him on the sidewalk. "Ignatious, wait a minute. Wait just a minute," she snapped when he kept walking. "Damn it!"

He stopped, jiggling the keys in his pocket.

She scowled up at him as she finished pulling on her coat. "You sure know how to liven up a town council meeting."

"Am I fired?"

"Not yet, but I sure don't think you won any popularity votes in there." She tugged the hip-length coat, the color of a Concord grape, closed. "You might've been a little more tactful about it."

"Murder's one of those things that short circuits all my tact switches. Then there's the matter of walking in on a meeting where my professional status is being questioned."

"All right, all right, maybe that was poorly done."

"If you or anyone else has a problem with how I'm doing the job, you should've come to me with it."

"You're right." She pinched the bridge of her nose. "We're all upset, we're all on edge. And now you've dumped this in our laps. Nobody liked thinking Max had done what it seemed clear he'd done, but it was a hell of a lot easier to think that than what you're suggesting."

"I'm not suggesting it. I'm saying it, flat out. I'm going to find out what I need to know, however long it takes, and whoever I have to step on along the way."

She pulled her cigarettes and lighter out of her coat pocket. "I can see that plain enough."

"Where were you sixteen years ago, Hopp?"

"Me?" Her eyes popped wide. "For Christ's sake, Ignatious, you don't honestly think I climbed up No Name with Pat and stuck an ice ax in him. He was twice my size."

"But not your husband's. You're a tough-minded woman, Hopp. You've done a lot around here to preserve your husband's vision. You might do a lot to protect his name."

"That's a filthy thing to say to me. A filthy thing to say about a man you didn't even know."

"I didn't know Galloway, either. You did."

Fury covered her face as she took a step back. She turned away, marched back into Town Hall. The door slammed like a cannon shot behind her.

HE KNEW MURMURS AND MUTTERS would be going around, so Nate decided to stay visible. He had his dinner at The Lodge. From the glances tossed his way, he imagined the statements he'd made at the meeting were making their way around Lunacy's frosty grapevine.

And that was fine. It was time to shake things up.

Charlene brought his salmon special to the booth herself, then slid in across from him. "You've sure got people wondering and worried."

"Do I?"

"I'm one of them." She picked up his coffee, sipped, then wrinkled her nose. "I don't know how anybody can drink this without sweetening it up some."

He pushed the dispenser of sugar packets over. "Help yourself if you want it."

"I will." She tore open two packets of Sweet'N Low, poured it in and stirred it up.

She was wearing a shimmery gray shirt, the sort that clung to a woman's curves, and had scooped back her hair to show off dangling silver earrings. After tapping the spoon on the side of the mug, she sampled.

"That's better." Then she kept both hands around the mug, as she leaned intimately toward Nate. "When I first found out about Pat, I went a little crazy inside. I'd have been ready to believe you if you'd told me Skinny Jim had put that ax in him—and he didn't come along until five or six years after Pat had been gone. But I've calmed down some."

"That's good," Nate said, and continued to eat.

"Maybe knowing I can bring him back here and bury him when the ground's ready helped. I like you, Nate, even though you wouldn't give me a tumble. I like you well enough to tell you you're not doing anybody any good with all this."

Nate slathered butter on a roll. "And what would 'all this' consist of, Charlene?"

"You know what I'm saying—this talk about us having a murderer running around. Something like that gets whispered about enough, people might start to believe it. It's bad for business. The tourists aren't going to come here if they think they could get murdered in their beds."

"Cissy?" he called with his eyes still on Charlene's. "Can I get another cup of coffee here? Is that what it comes down to, Charlene? It comes down to money. To your profit-and-loss statement."

"We've got to make a living here. We've got—"

She broke off as Cissy set another mug on the table, filled it with coffee. "You need anything else, Nate?"

"No, thanks."

"We do a lot of business here over the summer. We've got to if we don't want to live on the PFD all winter, and winter's long. I've got to be practical, Nate. Pat's gone. Max killed him. I'm not letting myself hold that against Carrie. I wanted to, but I'm not letting myself. She's lost her man, too. But Max killed Pat. God knows why, but he did."

She picked up her coffee again, sipped it while she gazed out the dark window. "Pat took him up there, some wild hair, I expect. Max looking for a story or article or some shit, and Pat figuring he could have an adventure and make a few dollars. The mountain can make you crazy. That's what happened."

When he said nothing, she touched a hand to his. "I've thought about it, like you asked me to. And I remember that Max didn't come in here for damn near a month that winter. Maybe more. Back then, this was the only place for miles in any direction you could get a hot meal, and he was a regular. I used to wait on him almost every night. But he didn't come in."

Absently, she reached over, broke a small chunk off Nate's dinner roll. "He called in orders a few times," she said as she nibbled on bread. "We didn't do deliveries, still don't, but Karl, he was soft-hearted. He ran the food over to the paper himself. He told me Max looked sick and a little crazy. I didn't pay any attention. I was brooding over Pat and busy trying to make ends meet. But you told me to think back, and I did, and I remember that."

"All right."

"You aren't paying attention to me."

"I heard everything you said." He met her eyes. "Who else didn't come in much that February?"

She let out an impatient breath. "I don't know, Nate. I only thought about Max because he's dead. And because I was remembering, all of a sudden, that Carrie and I both got married that summer. The summer after Pat was gone. That's what made me think of it."

"Okay. Now think about people who are still alive."

"I think about you." She laughed, waved a hand. "Oh, don't get all tight-assed. A woman's got a right to think about a good-looking man."

"Not when he's in love with her daughter."

"Love?" She began to drum her fingers on the table.

"Well, you are just out for all sorts of trouble, aren't you? Taking on the town council so everybody's looking at you sideways, getting Ed and Hopp all pissed off, now talking about loving Meg. She hasn't kept a man more than a month since she figured out what to do with one."

"I guess that means I hold the current record."

"She'll chomp a piece out of your heart then spit it right in your face."

"My heart, my face. Why does it bother you, Charlene?"

"I've got bigger needs than she does. Bigger, stronger needs." Her earrings spun and glinted when she tossed her head. "Meg doesn't need anything or anyone. She never did. She made it clear a long time ago she didn't need me. She'll make it clear soon enough that she doesn't need you."

"That may be. Or it may end up I make her happy. Maybe that's what bothers you. The idea she might end up happy, and you can't quite get there."

His hand snaked out, gripped her wrist before she could hurl the coffee in his face. "Think again," he said quietly. "A scene's going to embarrass you a lot more than me."

She jumped violently out of the booth and stalked across the room, up the stairs.

For the second time that day, Nate heard the bullet shot of a slammed door.

And in its echo, he finished his dinner.

· · · · ·

HE DROVE OUT TO MEG'S, hoping his blood would cool and his brain clear by the time he got there. The gloom of the past few days had lifted, leaving brilliant stars in a black-glass sky. A slice of moon rode over the trees, and a shimmery fog slithered low to the ground. Bare branches on the trees, Nate noticed. The snow was still thick on the ground, but the branches had shaken off the snow.

A part of the road was still flooded so he had to ease his way around the barricade and through the foot of standing water.

He heard a wolf call, lonely and insistent. It might be hunting, he thought, for food. For a mate. When it killed, it killed for purpose. Not for greed, not for sport.

When it mated, he'd read, it mated for life.

The sound died off as he drove through the night.

He could see the smoke rise from Meg's chimney, hear the soar of her music. Lenny Kravitz this time, he thought. Rocking on mists of doom and fields of pain.

He parked behind her, then just sat. He wanted this, he realized, wanted it maybe more than he should. To come home. To deal with the day, then shake it off and come home to music and light, to a woman.

The woman.

Hearth and home, Meg had said. Well, she'd nailed him. So if he ended up with that chunk of his heart spat in his face, he had no one to blame but himself.

She opened the door as he walked up, and the dogs rushed out to dance around him. "Hi. Wondered if you'd find your way to my door tonight." She cocked her head. "You look a little rough around the edges, Chief. What've you been up to?"

"Winning friends, influencing people."

"Well, come on inside, cutie, have a drink, and tell me about it."

"Don't mind if I do."

LIGHT

Is it so small a thing
To have enjoy'd the sun,
To have lived light in the spring,
To have loved, to have thought, to have done;
To have advanced true friends, and beat
   down baffling foes . . . ?

MATTHEW ARNOLD

We burn daylight.

WILLIAM SHAKESPEARE

TWENTY-SIX

"CHIEF." PEACH OFFERED HIM a sticky bun and a cup of coffee almost before he got in the door.

"You know, you keep baking these things, I'm not going to be able to sit in my desk chair."

"It'd take more than a few sticky buns to pork up that cute little behind. Besides, it's a bribe. I need to ask if I can take an extra hour for lunch tomorrow. I'm on the May Day planning committee. We're going to meet tomorrow and try to finish coordinating the parade."

"Parade?"

"May Day parade, Nate. It's on your calendar and not that far off."

May, he thought. He'd played with the dogs a bit that morning in Meg's yard. In snow up to the tops of his boots. "That'd be May first?"

"Come hell or high water, and we've had the parade in both. School band marches. The Natives wear their traditional dress and play traditional instruments. All the sports teams are in it, and Dolly Manners's dance classes. More people who live here participate in it than watch it, but we get tourists and Outside folk come in from all over."

She fussed with the vase of plastic daffodils on her counter. "It's a good time, and the past couple years we've done some advertising. We did even more this year, drumming up media interest and whatnot. Charlene puts it on The Lodge's web page and does package deals. And Hopp pushed and got us included in the events page of a couple of magazines."

"No kidding. Pretty hot stuff."

"Well, it *is*. It's a full-day event. We have a bonfire and more music that night. Weather's too bad, we move that to The Lodge."

"You have a bonfire in The Lodge."

She punched his arm playfully. "Just the music."

"Take whatever time you need."

Big parade, Nate thought. Bookings at The Lodge, meals served, customers in The Corner Store, browsing the local artists and craftsmen's work. More money, more business at the bank, the gas station. More business period.

That could be cut considerably by too much talk of murder.

He glanced over when Otto came in. "Isn't it your day off?"

"Yeah."

Nate could see something in his eyes, but played it light. "You come by for the sticky buns?"

"No." Otto held out a manila envelope. "I wrote up where I was, what I was doing and so forth in February of '88. On the night Max died, and when Yukon got killed. Thought it'd be better all around if I put it down before you had to ask me."

"Why don't you come back to my office?"

"Don't need to. I got no problem with this." He

puffed out his cheeks. "A little problem, maybe, but less doing it like this than having you ask. I don't have much of an alibi for any of the three situations, but I wrote it down."

Nate set down the bun to take the envelope. "I appreciate it, Otto."

"Well. I'm going fishing."

He left, passing Peter on the way out.

"Hell," Nate muttered.

"You're in a tight spot." Peach gave him a little rub on the arm. "You've got to do what you've got to do, even if it means hurting feelings and getting danders up."

"You're not wrong."

"Um." Peter looked back and forth between them. "Something wrong with Otto?"

"I hope not."

Peter started to follow up, but Peach gave a quick shake of her head. "Well, the reason I'm late is my uncle came by this morning. He wanted to tell me there's a guy squatting north of town by Hopeless Creek. There's an old cabin there. It looks like he's moved in. Nobody'd care much except my uncle thinks he may have broken into his work shed, and my aunt says there's food missing from the cache."

He grabbed a sticky bun, bit in. "He—my uncle— went by to check it out this morning before he came to see me, and he says the guy came out with a shotgun and ordered him off his property. Since he had my cousin Mary with him—taking her into school—he didn't hang around to reason with the guy."

"All right. We'll go reason with him." Nate set his

untouched coffee and Otto's envelope on the counter. Then went to the weapon cabinet and got two shotguns and ammo. "Just in case reason doesn't work," he told Peter.

The sun was bright and hard. It seemed impossible that only a few weeks before, he'd have made this trip in the dark. The river wound beside the road, cold blue, forming a keen edge of color against the snow that still lined its banks. The mountains stood, clear as monuments carved in glass, against the sky.

He saw an eagle perched on a mile marker post, like a golden guard to the forest behind him.

"How long's this cabin been empty?"

"Nobody's lived in it, officially, as long as I can remember. It's run-down and built too close to the creek so it floods out every spring. Hikers might use it for a night now and then, and ah, kids might use it for . . . you know. Chimney's still standing, so it'll hold a fire. Smokes something awful though."

"Meaning you've used it for . . . you know."

Even as he smiled, color edged Peter's cheekbones. "Maybe once or twice. What I heard was a couple of cheechakos built it way back. Going to live off the land, pan the creek for gold. Figured they'd get by on subsistence, and after a year start collecting their PFD. Didn't know squat. One of them froze to death, the other went crazy with cabin fever. Maybe ate some of the dead guy."

"Lovely."

"Probably just bullshit. But it adds to it when you're taking a girl there."

"Yeah, pretty romantic stuff."

"You want to turn off up there." Peter pointed. "It's a little rough going."

After about three yards bumping and grinding his way along the narrow, snow-packed rut, Nate decided Peter was the master of understatement.

The trees were thick and smote out the sun, so it was like driving through a tunnel paved by sadistic ice demons.

He rolled his tongue back, so it wouldn't get in the way of his teeth when they snapped together, and muscled the wheel.

He wouldn't have called it a clearing. The dilapidated square of logs hunched in a hacked-out square of trash willows and spindly evergreen on the icy bank of the spit of creek. It huddled there in the shadows, one window boarded, the other crisscrossed with duct tape. A sagging length of porch sat over a few stacked cinder blocks.

A filthy Lexus four-wheel-drive with California tags stood in front. "Call Peach, have her run those tags, Peter."

While Peter used the radio, Nate debated. There was smoke puffing sluggishly out of the tilted chimney. And a dead mammal of some sort hung nastily over a post by the door.

Nate unsnapped his weapon but left it holstered as he eased out of the car.

"That's far enough!" The cabin door swung open.

In the dimness Nate could see the man and the shotgun.

"I'm Chief Burke, Lunacy Police. I'm going to ask you to lower that weapon."

"I don't care who you say you are or what you say you want. I'm on to your tricks, you alien bastards. I'm not going back up there."

Aliens, Nate thought. Perfect. "The alien forces in this sector have been defeated. You're safe here now, but I need you to lower your weapon."

"So you say." But he eased out another foot. "How do I know you're not one of them?"

Early thirties, Nate estimated. Five-ten, a hundred and fifty. Brown hair. Wild eyes, color undetermined. "I have my ID, stamped and certified after testing. You lower that weapon so I can approach, I'll show it to you."

"ID?" He looked confused now, and the shotgun lowered an inch.

"Underground Earth Forces certified." Nate tried a sober nod. "Can't be too careful these days."

"They bleed blue, you know. I got two of them the last time they took me."

"Two?" Nate lifted his eyebrows as if duly impressed, and watched the gun lower another inch. "You're going to need to be debriefed. We'll get you back to control, get your statement on record."

"We can't let them win."

"We won't."

The gun barrel angled toward the ground, and Nate stepped forward.

It happened too fast. It always happened too fast. He heard Peter open the car door, say his name. He was watching the man's face, his eyes—and he saw it come into them. Panic, rage, terror all at once.

He was already cursing, already ordering Peter to get down. Get down! as he cleared his weapon from the holster.

The shotgun blast shook the air, sent some bird screaming in the trees. A second pumped out as Nate dived for cover under the car.

He was set to roll out the other side when he saw the blood on the snow.

"Oh, God. Oh, Jesus Christ. Peter."

His body went to lead, and for an endless moment he shook under the weight of it. He could smell the alley—the rain, overripe garbage. Blood.

His breath came too fast, the high edge of panic making his head light, the bitter wash of despair turning his throat to dust. He carried it all with him as he crawled through the snow.

Peter was sprawled behind the open door of the car, his eyes wide and glassy. "I think . . . I think I'm shot."

"Hold on." Nate clamped a hand over Peter's arm where his jacket was torn and bloody. He could feel the warm flow—and the anvil slam of his own heart in his chest. With one eye cocked toward the cabin, he dug out a bandanna.

If there were prayers running inside his head, he didn't recognize them.

"It's not too bad, is it?" Peter moistened his lips, angled his head down to look. And went white as bone. "Man."

"Listen to me. Listen." Nate tied the bandanna tight over the wound, tapped Peter's cheek to keep him from passing out. "You stay down. You're going to be all right."

Not going to bleed out on me. Not going to die in my arms. Not again. Please God.

He pulled Peter's weapon out of the holster. Closed Peter's hand around it. "You got this?"

"I . . . I'm right-handed. He shot me."

"You can use your left. He gets by me, you don't hesitate. Listen to me, Peter. He comes out here, you shoot. Aim for body mass. And you shoot until he's down."

"Chief—"

"Just do it."

Nate bellied back to the rear of the car, opened the door and slid in. He slid out again with both shotguns. He could hear the man inside the house, raving. The occasional blast of fire.

He could hear the sounds of the alley merging with it. The rain, the shouts, the running footsteps.

He bellied back to Peter, laid one of the shotguns over his lap. "You don't pass out. Hear me? You stay awake."

"Yes, sir."

There was no one to call for backup. This wasn't Baltimore, and he was on his own.

Crouched, the shotgun in one hand, his service revolver in the other, he dashed across the icy stream and into the trees. Bark exploded. He felt a knife-splice of a flying splinter hit his face just under his left eye.

That meant the shooter's attention was on him now, and away from Peter.

In the cover of trees, he plowed through the snow.

His partner was shot. His partner was down.

His breath whistled out as he tried to run through knee-deep snow, circling the cabin.

Braced behind a tree, he studied the layout. No back door, he noted, but another window on the side. He could see the shadow of the shooter on the glass, knew he was waiting there, watching for movement.

Nate pumped the shotgun one-handed and fired.

Glass exploded, and with that sound, the screams, the return fire filling his ears, he used his own tracks to run back toward the front of the cabin.

Shouts and shots sounded behind him as he cracked through the ice of the stream, scrambled through the frigid water and leaped toward the front of the house.

He barreled onto the sagging porch and kicked open the door.

He had both weapons pointed at his man—and part of him, most of him, wanted to cut loose with them. Drop him, drop him cold, as he had the murdering bastard in Baltimore. The murdering bastard who'd killed his partner and ripped his own life to pieces.

"Red." In the shambles of the cabin, the man looked at him. His lips trembled into a smile. "Your blood's red." And dropping the gun, he fell to the filthy cabin floor and wept.

HIS NAME WAS Robert Joseph Spinnaker—a financial consultant from L.A., and a recent psychiatric patient.

He had claimed multiple alien abductions over the past eighteen months, stated that his wife was a reproduction, and attacked two of his clients during a meeting.

He'd been listed as missing for nearly three months.

Now he slept peacefully in a cell, reassured by the color of the blood on Nate's face and Peter's arm.

Nate had done little more than lock him up before he'd rushed back to the clinic so he could pace the waiting room.

He went over the entire event a hundred times, and each time he saw himself doing something different, just a little different that kept Peter from being hurt.

When Ken came out, Nate was sitting, his head in his hands.

He jerked up immediately. "How bad?"

"Getting shot's never good, but it could've been a hell of a lot worse. He'll be wearing a sling for a while. He's lucky it was bird shot. He's a little weak, a little groggy. I'm going to keep him a couple more hours. But he's good."

"Okay." Nate let his knees give way and lowered to the chair again. "Okay."

"Why don't you come back, let me clean those cuts on your face."

"Just some scratches."

"The one under your eye's more of a gash. Come on, don't argue with the doctor."

"Can I see him?"

"Nita's with him now. You can see him after I treat you." Ken led the way, gestured for Nate to get on an exam table. "You know," he said as he cleaned the cuts, "it'd be stupid for you to blame yourself."

"He's green. He's grass, and I took him into an unstable situation."

"That's not showing much respect for him or the job he signed on to do."

Nate hissed in a breath at the sting under his eye. "He's a baby."

"He's not. He's a man. A good man. And you taking on the weight lessens what happened to him today—and what he did."

"He got up, broke cover and got to the door after me. He could barely keep his feet, but he came to back me up."

Nate met Ken's eyes as Ken fixed on a butterfly bandage. "His blood was on my hands but he came through the door to back me up. So maybe I'm the one who can't handle himself."

"You did handle yourself. I got most of it from Peter. He thinks you're a hero. If you want to pay him back for what happened, don't disillusion him. There." Ken stepped back. "You'll live."

HOPP WAS IN THE WAITING ROOM when Nate came out, along with Peter's parents and Rose. They all stood, began talking at once.

"He's resting. He's fine," Ken assured them. And Nate kept walking.

"Ignatious." Hopp hurried out after him. "I'd like to know what happened."

"I'm walking back."

"Then I'll walk with you, and you can tell me. I'd like to get it straight from you rather than the various accounts blowing around town at this point."

He told her, briefly.

"Would you slow down? Your legs are longer than my whole body. How'd your face get hurt?"

"Tree shrapnel. Flying bark, that's all."

"Flying because he was shooting at you. For God's sake."

"The fact that my face got cut up is probably why both Spinnaker and I are still standing. Fortunately I bleed red."

So does Peter, he thought. He'd bled plenty of red today.

"The State Police coming to get him?"

"Peach is contacting them."

"Well." She drew a breath. "He's been out and about being crazy for three months. Squatting out there God knows how long. He could be the one who killed poor Yukon. He could be the one who did that."

Nate found his sunglasses in his pocket and put them on. "He could be, but he's not."

"Man's crazy, and it was a crazy thing. He could've thought Yukon was some alien in a dog suit. It makes sense, Ignatious."

"Only if you believe this guy happened to sneak into town, hunt up an old dog, brought the dog outside Town Hall and sliced his throat—having previously stolen the buck knife. That's a little too broad for me, Hopp."

She took his arm so he'd stop. "Maybe because you'd

rather believe otherwise. Maybe because believing otherwise is giving you something to get your teeth into.
More than breaking up a few fights or keeping Drunk
Mike from freezing his sorry ass. Did it ever occur to you
that you're tying all this together, looking for a killer
among us because you want it to be so?"

"I don't want it to be so. It is so."

"Damn stubborn . . ." She set her teeth, turned to the
side until she controlled her temper. "Things won't settle down around here if you keep stirring them up."

"Things shouldn't settle down around here until they're
resolved. I've got to go write up my report on this."

NATE SPENT THE NIGHT in the station, most of it listening to Spinnaker's earnest reports of his alien experiences. To keep him calm, if not quiet, Nate sat outside
the cell, making notes.

And was deeply thrilled to see the State Police arrive
the next morning to relieve him of his prisoner.

He was also surprised to see Coben on the detail.

"Maybe you should consider renting a room down
here, Sergeant."

"I figured this would be an opportunity to touch
base on other matters. If we could take a minute in your
office."

"Sure. I've got the paperwork on Spinnaker for you."

He walked into his office, picked up the paperwork.
"Assault with deadly on police officers, et cetera. The
shrinks will soften that up, but it won't make my deputy
any less shot."

"How's he doing?"

"He's okay. He's young, resilient. It caught him mostly in the meaty part of the arm."

"Any time you walk away, it's a good day."

"There's that."

Coben walked over to the board. "Still pursuing this?"

"Looks like."

"Making any headway?"

"Depends on where you're standing."

Lips pursed, Coben rocked back on his heels. "Dead dog? You're linking that?"

"Man's gotta have a hobby."

"Look, I'm not fully satisfied with the resolution of my case, but I've got restrictions on me. A lot of it does depend on where you're standing. We can agree there was an unidentified third man on that mountain when Galloway was killed. Doesn't mean he killed Galloway or had knowledge thereof. Doesn't mean he's still alive, for that matter, as it's more logical that the individual who killed Galloway also disposed of this third man."

"Not if the third man was Hawbaker."

"We don't believe it was. But *if* it was," Coben continued, "it sure as hell doesn't mean this unidentified third man had anything to do with Hawbaker's death—or the death of some dog. I've got a little wiggle room, unofficially, to confirm the identity of the third man, but it's not taking me anywhere."

"The pilot who took them up was killed in unexplained circumstances."

"There's no proof of that. I've looked into it. Kijinski

paid off some debts and made more during the period between Galloway's death and his own. So that's hinky, I'll give you that. But there's no one to confirm he took them up."

"Because all but one of them's dead."

"There are no records, no flight logs. No nothing. And nobody who knew Kijinski, or will admit to it, who remembers him booking that flight. He may very well have been the pilot, and if so, it's just as logical to assume Hawbaker disposed of him as well."

"Might be logical. Except Max Hawbaker didn't kill three men. And he didn't come back from the grave and slit that dog's throat."

"It doesn't matter what your gut tells you. I need something solid."

"Give me time," Nate said.

TWO DAYS LATER, Meg strolled into the station, flipped a wave at Peach and went straight back to Nate's office.

A glance at his board barely broke her stride. "Okay, cutie, I'm springing you."

"Sorry?"

"Even thoughtful, dedicated, hardworking cops get a day off. You're due."

"Peter's on inactive. We're a man short."

"And you're sitting here brooding about that and everything else. You need head-clearing time, Burke. If something comes up, we'll head back."

"From where?"

"It's a surprise. Peach," she called as she started back out. "Your boss is taking the rest of the day off. What do they call it on *NYPD Blue*? Personal time."

"He could use some."

"You can cover it, can't you, Otto?"

"Meg—" Nate began.

"Peach, when's the last time the chief took a day off?"

"Three weeks, a little more, by my recollection."

"Head-clearing time, Chief." Meg grabbed his jacket off the hook herself. "We've got a clear day for it."

He took one of the two-ways. "An hour."

She smiled. "We'll start with that."

When he spotted her plane at the dock, he stopped dead. "You didn't say this head-clearing time involved flying."

"It's the best method. Guaranteed."

"Couldn't we just take a drive, have sex in the back-seat of the car? I find that's a really good method."

"Trust me." She kept his hand firmly in hers and used her other to brush the cut under his eye. "How's that feeling?"

"Now that you mention it, I probably shouldn't fly with a wound like this."

She cupped his face, leaned in and kissed him, long, slow and deep. "Come with me, Nate. I have something I want to share with you."

"Well, when you put it that way."

He got in the plane, strapped in. "You know, I've never taken off from the water. Not when the water was . . . wet. There's still some ice. It wouldn't be good to run into the ice, right?"

"A man who faces down an armed mental patient shouldn't be so jittery about flying." She kissed her fingers, tapped them on Buddy Holly's lips and began to glide over the water.

"Sort of like waterskiing, but not," Nate managed, then held his breath as she gained speed, kept holding it as the plane lifted off the water.

"I thought you were working today," he said when he decided it was safe to breathe again.

"I passed it to Jerk. He'll be dropping off supplies later. We've got parade stuff coming in, including a whole case of bug dope."

"You and Jerk run drugs for insects."

She slid her eyes in his direction. "Insect repellant, cutie. You survived your first Alaska winter. Now we'll see how you fare in the summer. With mosquitoes as big as B-52s. You won't want to walk three feet out of the house without your bug dope."

"Roger on the bug dope, but I'm not eating Eskimo ice cream. Jesse says it's made from whipped seals."

"Oil," she said on a laugh. "Seal oil or moose tallow. And it's not bad if you mix in some berries and sugar."

"I'll take your word because I'm not eating moose tallow. I don't even know what the hell it is."

She smiled again because his shoulders had relaxed, and he was actually looking down. "Pretty from here, isn't it, with the river, the ice, and the town all lined up behind it?"

"It looks quiet and simple."

"But it's not. It's not really either of those. The bush looks quiet, too, from the air. Peaceful and serene. A harsh kind of beauty. But it's not serene. Nature will kill you without a minute's thought, and in nastier ways than a crazy guy with a gun. It doesn't make her any less beautiful. I couldn't live anywhere else. I couldn't be anywhere else."

She soared over river and lake, and he could see the progress of breakup, the steady march of spring. Patches of green spread as the sun worked on the snow. A waterfall rushed down a cliff side with the sparkle of ice gleaming out of deep shadows.

Below them, a small herd of moose lumbered across a field. Above, the sky curved like a wild, blue ribbon.

"Jacob was here that February." Meg glanced at him. "I wanted to get that out of the way—maybe off both our minds. He came to see me a lot when my father was gone. I don't know if my father asked him to, or if it was just Jacob's way. There might've been a couple days here and there I didn't see him. But not as much as a week at a stretch, not a long enough time for him to have climbed with my father. I wanted you to know that, for certain, in case you needed to ask him to help you."

"It was a long time ago."

"Yeah, and I was a kid. But I remember that. Once I thought back on it, I remembered. I saw more of him than I did of Charlene in those first few weeks after my father left. He took me ice fishing and hunting, and when we had a storm come in, I stayed at his place for a couple of days. I'm telling you that you can trust him, that's all."

"All right."

"Now, look to starboard."

He glanced right and watched them fly off the edge of the world, over a channel of blue water that seemed entirely too close for comfort. Before he could object, he saw an enormous chunk of that blue-white world crack off and tumble into the water.

"My God."

"This is an active tidewater glacier. And what you're watching is called calving," she said as other boulders of ice broke and fell. "I guess because in the cycle, it's more a kind of birth than death."

"It's beautiful." He was all but plastered against the windscreen now. "It's amazing. Jesus, some of them are the size of a house." He let out a laugh as another shot off into the air and barely registered the shimmy of the plane in a pocket of turbulence.

"People pay me good money to fly them over here to see this, then spend most of their time with their eyes glued to the lens of a video camera. Seems like a waste to me. If they want to see this on a movie, they should rent one."

It wasn't just the show, Nate thought, the spectacle of it. It was that cycle—violent, inevitable, somehow mythic. The sights—jagged boulders of blue ice heaving themselves into the air. The sounds of it, creaks, the thunder and the cannon shots. The gushing up of the water on impact, the rising of the white into a shimmering island that streamed along on the churning fjord.

"I have to stay here."

She guided the plane up, circling so he could watch from another angle. "Here, in the air?"

"No." He turned his head, grinned at her in a way she rarely saw. Easy and relaxed and happy. "Here. I can't be anyplace else, either. It's good to know that."

"Here's something else that might be good to know. I'm in love with you."

She laughed as the plane shuddered through rough air; then she punched it through, and bulleted up the channel while ice fell around them.

TWENTY-SEVEN

CHARLENE HAD ALWAYS LOVED what passed for spring in Alaska. She loved the way the days kept stretching out, longer and longer until there was nothing but light.

In her office she stood at the window, her work neglected on her desk, and stared out at the street. Busy. People walking, driving, going, coming. Townspeople and tourists, country dwellers in for supplies or company. Fourteen of her twenty rooms were booked, and she'd be at capacity for three days the following week. After that, the strong, almost endless light would draw people in like flies to honey.

She'd work like a dog through most of April, into May and straight through until freeze-up.

She *liked* to work, to have her place crowded with people, the noise and the mess they made. The money they spent.

She'd built something here, hadn't she? She'd found what she wanted—or most of what she wanted. She looked out to the river. Boats were on it now, slipping their way through the melting islands of ice.

She looked beyond the river, beyond to the mountains. White and blue, with green beginning to spread slowly, very slowly at their feet. White at their peaks, forever white in that frozen, foreign world.

She'd never climbed. She never would.

The mountains had never called to her. But other things had. Pat had. She'd felt that call blow through her, a thousand trumpets, when he'd roared into her life. Not yet seventeen, she remembered, and still a virgin. Stuck, hadn't she been stuck, in those flat Iowa fields just waiting for someone to pluck her out?

The original midwestern farm girl, she thought now, desperate for any escape. Then he'd come, churning up all that dull air on his motorcycle, looking so dangerous and exotic and . . . *different*.

Oh, he'd called to her, Charlene remembered, and she'd answered that call. Sneaking out of the house on those chilly spring nights to run to him, to roll naked with him on the soft green grass, free and careless as a puppy. And so desperately in love. That burning, blistering love maybe you could only feel at seventeen.

When he'd gone, she'd gone with him, walking out on home, family, friends, speeding away from the world she knew, and into another—on the back of a Harley.

To be seventeen, she thought, and that daring again.

They'd lived. How they'd *lived*. Going wherever they wanted, doing whatever they liked. Through farmland and desert, through city and tiny town.

And all the roads they'd wandered had led here.

Things had changed. When had they changed? she wondered. When she realized she was pregnant? They'd been so thrilled, so stupidly thrilled about the baby. But things had changed when they'd come here with that seed planted inside her. When she'd told him she'd wanted to stay.

Sure, Charley, no problem. We can stick around awhile.

A while had become a year, then two, then a decade, and God, *God,* she'd been the one to change. To push and prod at that wonderful, reckless boy, to nag and hound him to be a man, to be what he'd run from. Responsible, settled. Ordinary.

He'd stayed, more for Meg, she knew, more for the daughter who was the image of him than for the woman who'd given him that child. He'd stayed, but he'd never settled.

She'd resented him for that. Resented Meg. How could she do otherwise? She wasn't *built* to do otherwise. She'd been the one to work, hadn't she? To make sure there was food on the table and a roof over their heads.

And she knew, when he'd gone off, to pick up jobs, to take a break, to climb his damn mountains, that he'd gone to whores.

Men wanted her. She could make any man want her. And the only one she really wanted had gone to whores.

What were his mountains but other whores? Cold, white whores that had seduced him away from her? Until he'd stayed inside one and left her alone.

But she'd survived, hadn't she? She'd done better than survive. She'd found what she wanted here. Most of what she wanted.

She had money now. She had her place. She had men, young, hard bodies in the night.

So why was she so unhappy?

She didn't like to think long thoughts, to look inside

herself and worry about what she'd find there. She liked to *live*. To move, to keep in motion. You didn't have to think when you were dancing.

She turned, vaguely irritated by the knock on her door. "Come on in."

She smoothed her face out, and the sultry smile was automatic when she saw John. "Well, hi there, good-looking. School out? It's that late already?" She patted her hair as she looked at her desk. "And here I've been daydreaming, wasting the day away. I'm going to have to get out there and see what Big Mike's whipping up for tonight's special."

"I need to talk to you, Charlene."

"Sure, honey. I've always got time for you. I'll make us some tea, and we'll get all cozy."

"No, don't."

"Baby, you look all frowny and serious." She crossed to him and skimmed a finger down each of his cheeks. "Of course you know I love when you're serious. It's so sexy."

"Don't," he said again and took her hands.

"Is something wrong?" Her fingers tightened on his like wires. "Oh God, is someone—something else—dead around here? I don't think I can take it. I don't think I can *stand* it."

"No. It's nothing like that." He let go of her hands, eased back a step. "I wanted to tell you, I'll be leaving at the end of the semester."

"You're taking a vacation? You're going to be taking a trip just when Lunacy's at its best?"

"I'm not taking a vacation. I'm leaving."

"What're you talking about? Leave? For good? That's just nonsense, John." The flirty smile faded, and something hot and sharp stabbed in her belly. "Where would you go? What would you do?"

"There are a lot of places I haven't seen, a lot of things I haven't done. I'll see them. I'll do them."

She felt her heart sink as she looked up into his dependable face. The ones who matter, her mind whispered, leave you. "John, you live here. You work here."

"I'll live and I'll work somewhere else."

"You can't just . . . why? Why are you doing this?"

"I should've done it years ago, but you get into the drift. Float your life away. Nate came to see me at school last week. Some of the things he said made me think, made me look back over . . . too many years."

She wanted to find her anger, the sort that pushed her to shout, to break things. The sort that swept her clean. But there was only dull worry. "What does Nate have to do with this?"

"He's the change. Or the rock in the stream that caused the change. You drift, Charlene, like water in a stream, and maybe you don't notice as much as you should what's going by."

He touched her hair, then dropped his hand again. "Then a stone drops into the stream, and it disrupts. It changes things. Maybe a little, maybe a lot. But nothing's quite the same again."

"I never know what you're talking about when you go on like that." She pouted as she turned around and kicked at her desk, and the gesture made him smile. "Water and rocks and streams. What does that have to do with you coming in here like this and telling me you're leaving. You're going away. Don't you even care how I feel?"

"Entirely too much for my own good. I loved you the first minute I saw you. You knew it."

"But not anymore."

"Yes, then, now, all the years between. I loved you when you were with another man. And when he was gone, I thought, Now, she'll come to me. And you did. To my bed, at least. You let me have your body, but you married someone else. Even knowing I loved you, you married someone else."

"I had to do what was right for me. I had to be practical." She did throw something now—a little crystal swan. But its destruction gave her no satisfaction. "I had a right to look out for my future."

"I would've been good to you, and for you. I'd have been good to Meg. But you chose differently. You chose this." He spread his hands to indicate The Lodge. "You earned it. You worked hard. You built it up. And while Karl was alive, you still came to me. And I let you. To me and to others."

"Karl wasn't after sex, or hardly. He wanted a partner, someone to take care of him and this place. I kept my end," she said passionately. "We had an understanding."

"You took care of him and this place. And when he died, you kept taking care. I've lost track of the times I've asked you to marry me, Charlene, the number of times you've said no. The number of times I've watched you go off with someone else or slide into my bed when there wasn't someone else. I'm done with it."

"I don't want to get married, so you're just going to take off?"

"You slept with that man the other night. Part of the hunting group. The tall one with dark hair."

She jerked up her chin. "So what?"

"What was his name?"

She opened her mouth, realized her mind was blank. She couldn't remember a face, much less a name, and barely remembered the groping in the dark. "What do I care," she snapped out. "It was just sex."

"You're not going to find what you're looking for, not with nameless men nearly half your age. But if you have to keep looking, I can't stop you. That's been clear enough right from the start of this. But I can stop being your fallback position."

"Go on, then." She scooped up a pile of paperwork from her desk, threw it into the air. "I won't care."

"I know. If you did, really did, I wouldn't go."

He stepped out of the room and closed the door behind him.

HE WAS DAZZLED BY THE LIGHT. Nate couldn't get enough of it, no matter how long the day lasted, he wanted more. He could feel it penetrating flesh and bone, charging him.

He hadn't woken from a nightmare in days.

He woke to light, worked and walked through it in the day. He thought in it and ate in it; he soaked in it.

And each night he watched the sun slide down behind

the mountains, he knew it would rise again in a few hours.

There were still nights when he'd slip out of Meg's bed, walk out with the dogs for company to watch the lights play havoc with the night sky.

He could still feel the wound, throbbing under the scars on his body. But he thought the pain was a healing one now. He hoped to God it was. A kind of acceptance for what he'd lost and an opening to what he could have.

For the first time since he'd left Baltimore, he called Jack's wife, Beth.

"I just wanted to know how you were. You and the kids."

"We're okay. We're good. It's been a year since . . ."

He knew. A year today.

"Today's a little rough. We went out this morning, took him flowers. The firsts are the hardest. The first holiday, first birthday, first anniversary. But you get through it, and it's a little easier. I thought—hoped—you'd call today. I'm so glad you did."

"I wasn't sure you'd want to hear from me."

"We miss you, Nate. Me and the kids. I worry about you."

"I'm okay, too. Better."

"Tell me what it's like there. Is it awfully cold and quiet?"

"Actually, it's around sixty today. As for quiet . . ." He looked over at his board. "Yeah. Yeah, it's pretty quiet. We've had some flooding. Not as bad as in the southeast but enough to keep us busy. It's beautiful."

He turned to his window now. "Like nothing you can

imagine. You have to see it, and even then it's hard to imagine."

"You sound good. I'm glad you sound good."

"I didn't think I'd make it here." Anywhere. "I wanted to. I didn't care so much until I got here. Until I was here, and then I wanted to. But I didn't think I would."

"Now?"

"I think I will. Beth, I met someone."

"Oh?" There was a laugh in her voice, and he closed his eyes to hear it. "Is she wonderful?"

"Spectacular, in so many ways. I think you'd like her. She's not like anybody else. She's a bush pilot."

"A bush pilot? Isn't that one of those people who fly around in those tiny planes like maniacs?"

"Pretty much. She's beautiful. Well, she's not, but she is. She's funny and tough, and she's probably crazy, but it fits her. Her name's Meg. Megan Galloway, and I'm in love with her."

"Oh, Nate. I'm so happy for you."

"Don't cry," he said when he heard the tears.

"No, it's good. Jack would find a million ways to tease you, but under it, he'd have been happy for you, too."

"Well, anyway, I just wanted to tell you. I just wanted to talk to you and tell you and say that maybe sometime you and the kids could come up. It's a great place for a summer vacation. By June it won't be dark till midnight, and then they tell me it's more like twilight than dark. And it's warmer than you think, or so they tell me. I'd like you to see it, to meet Meg. I'd like to see you and the kids."

"I can promise we'll come for the wedding."

His laugh was a little jerky. "I haven't moved in that direction."

"I know you, Nate. You will."

When he hung up, he was smiling. The last thing he'd expected. He left the board uncovered—a kind of symbol that he was investigating in the open now—and walked out of his office.

It still gave him a jolt to see Peter with his arm in a sling. The young deputy sat at his desk, punching keys one-handed.

Desk duty. Paperwork detail. A cop—and that's what the kid was—could die of sheer boredom.

Nate walked over. "Want to get out of here?"

Peter looked up, one finger of his good hand poised over the keyboard. "Sir?"

"Want me to uncuff you from that desk for a while?"

Light came into his face. "Yes, sir!"

"Let's take a walk." He grabbed a two-way. "Peach, Deputy Notti and I are on foot patrol."

"Um. Otto's already out," Peter told him.

"Hey, crime could be rampant out there for all we know. Peach, you've got the helm."

"Aye, aye, captain," she said with a snicker. "You boys be careful."

Nate took a light jacket from a peg. "Want yours?" he asked Peter.

"Nah. Only Lower 48ers need a jacket on a day like this."

"That so? Well, then." Deliberately, Nate rehung the jacket.

Outside it was brisk enough and overcast. Rain was

probably on its way, and undoubtedly, Nate thought, he'd regret the gesture of leaving the jacket before they were finished.

But he headed down the sidewalk with the damp, frisky air blowing through his hair. "How's the arm?"

"Pretty good. I don't think I need the sling, but between Peach and my mother, it's not worth the grief."

"Women get all fussy when a guy gets himself shot."

"Tell me about it. And try to be, you know, stoic about it, and they're all over you."

"I haven't talked to you too much about the incident. Initially I told myself I'd made a mistake taking you out there."

"I spooked him when I got out of the car. Incited the situation."

"A squirrel dropping an acorn would've spooked him, Peter. I said initially I told myself I'd made a mistake. The fact is, I didn't. You're a good cop. You proved it. You were down. You were hurt and dazed, but you backed me up."

"You had the situation controlled. You didn't need backup."

"I might have. That's the point. When you stand with someone in a volatile situation, you have to be able to trust him—no reservations."

The way he and Jack had trusted each other, he thought. So you'd go through the door, into the alley, no matter what waited in the dark.

"I want you to know I trust you."

"I . . . I thought you had me on the desk because you were trying to ease me out."

"I've got you on the desk because you're injured. In the line, Peter. A commendation regarding your actions during the incident is going in your file."

Peter stopped, stared. "A commendation."

"You earned it. It'll be announced at the next Town Hall meeting."

"I don't know what to say."

"Stoic works."

They crossed the street at the corner to swing up the other side. "I have something else to tell you, and it's sensitive. Regarding the investigation our department is conducting. The homicides."

He caught Peter's quick glance. "Whatever the State Police have determined, this department is treating them as homicides. I have several statements from individuals giving their whereabouts during the times in question. Most of those statements, however, can't be corroborated, at least not to my satisfaction. That includes Otto's."

"Oh, but Chief, Otto's—"

"One of us. I know. But I can't cross him off the list because he's one of us. There are a lot of people in this town, or outlying it, who had the opportunity for these three crimes. Motive's a different thing. The motive for the two subsequent arrow back to Galloway. What was the motive for his murder? Crime of passion, gain, cover-up? Drug-induced? Maybe a combination of those motives. But whoever it was, he knew."

Nate scanned the streets, the sidewalks. Sometimes it was what you knew that waited in the dark. "He knew them well enough to do that winter climb with his killer and with Max. Just the three of them. He knew his killer well enough to indulge in, I guess we'd call it role-playing while they were up there, enduring harsh conditions."

"I don't understand what you mean."

"He had a journal. It was on him—and left on him. Coben gave me a copy."

"But if he had a journal, then—"

"He never used the names of his companions. They were on some sort of lark. The kind that tells me if he hadn't been killed up there then, he'd have died on some other climb unless he'd straightened up. They were smoking grass, popping speed. Playing *Star Wars*. Galloway as Luke, Max as Han Solo, and ironically enough Galloway's killer in the Darth Vader role. The mountain became that ice world they were on."

"Hoth. I like the movies," Peter added with a little hunch to his shoulders. "I collected the action figures and stuff when I was a kid."

"Me, too. But these weren't kids. They were grown men, and somewhere along the line, the game got out of hand. Galloway wrote how Han—I believe that was Max—injured his ankle. They left him behind in a tent with some provisions and kept going."

"That proves Max didn't kill him."

"Depends on how you angle it. You could speculate that Max decided to follow, caught up with them in the ice cave and went crazy. You could further speculate that Max held the Vader role and killed both his playmates. Those aren't my personal theories, but they're theories. And the State accepts the second one."

"That Mr. Hawbaker killed both guys? *Then* got himself down alone? I can't see it."

"Why?"

"Well, I know I was just a little kid when all this happened, but Mr. Hawbaker never had a rep for being, you know, bold and, um, self-sufficient. You'd have to be both to handle that descent."

"I agree. Later in the journal, Galloway wrote that the Darth character was showing signs of—let's call it lunacy—anger, risk-taking, accusations. A lot of drugs involved in this and, from what I've read, a by-product of the strain, altitude sickness, the high some climbers get from being up there."

Nate watched Deb come out of The Corner Store to take Cecil for a walk. The dog was wearing a bright green sweater.

"Galloway was worried, worried about this guy's state of mind," he continued as he casually exchanged waves with Deb. "About getting them all down safe. His last journal entry was written in the ice cave. He never got out of it, so he was right to be worried. But he still wasn't worried enough to take definite steps to protect himself. There were no defensive wounds on the body. His own ice ax was still in his belt. He knew his killer, just like Max knew his. Just like Yukon knew the man who slit his throat.

"We know him, too, Peter." He sent another wave to Judge Royce, who strode toward KLUN with a cigar clamped between his teeth. "We just haven't recognized him yet."

"What do we do?"

"We keep going through what we know. We keep working with the layers until we know more. I'm not telling Otto about the journal. Not yet."

"God."

"This is tougher on you. These are people you've known all your life, or a good part of it."

He nodded down the street where Harry stood on the sidewalk outside The Corner Store catching a smoke and talking to Jim Mackie. Across from them Ed walked briskly in the direction of the bank but stopped to exchange a word with the postmistress, who was out sweeping her stoop.

Big Mike came out of The Lodge and jogged, undoubtedly heading for The Italian Place and his daily bout of shoptalk with Johnny Trivani. His little girl let out belly laughs as she rode his shoulders.

"Just people. But one of them, out here on the street, inside one of these buildings or houses, in a cabin outside of town, is a killer. If he has to, he'll kill again."

HE WENT TO MEG'S every evening. She wasn't always there. Jobs were picking up as the weather warmed. But they had an unspoken agreement that he would come and stay. He'd tend the dogs, see to some of the chores.

He was leaving his things there, such as they were, little by little. Another unspoken agreement. He kept his room at The Lodge, but it was more a storage area for his heavy winter gear at this point.

He could've moved that to Meg's, too. But that would've been the line. The official we're-living-together line.

He saw the smoke from her chimney before he made the turn, and his mood cranked up another notch. But there was no plane on the lake, and it was Jacob's truck in her drive.

The dogs bolted out of the woods to greet him, with Rock carting one of the mastodon bones they liked to gnaw on. It looked fresh to Nate, and he left the dogs playing an energetic tug-of-war with it as he went inside.

Nate could smell blood before he was halfway to the kitchen. Instinctively his hand went to the butt of his weapon.

"I brought meat," Jacob said without turning around.

There were a couple of thick planks of something bloody on the counter. Nate relaxed his hand.

"She doesn't have much time to hunt these days. Bear are awake. It's good meat for stew, meat loaf."

Bear meat loaf, Nate thought. What a world. "I'm sure she'll appreciate it."

"We share what we have." Jacob continued calmly wrapping bear meat in thick white paper. "She told you I was with her most days during the time her father was taken."

"Was taken? That's an interesting way to put it."

"His life was taken from him, wasn't it?" Jacob finished wrapping the meat, then picked up a black marker and wrote a date on the packages. It was such a housewifely gesture that Nate blinked.

"She told you this, but you don't trust her memory, or her heart."

"I trust her."

"She was a child." Jacob washed his hands in the sink. "She could be mistaken, or could, because she loves me, be protecting me."

"She could."

Jacob dried his hands, picked up the packages of meat. When he turned, Nate saw he wore an amulet around his neck. A dark blue stone over a faded denim shirt.

"I've talked to people." He walked into the little mudroom where Meg kept a small chest freezer. "People who aren't so willing to talk to police. People who knew Pat and Two-Toes." He began to stack packages in the freezer. "I'm told, by these people who will talk to me and not the police, that when Pat was in Anchorage, he had money. More money than was usual for him."

He closed the freezer, walked back into the kitchen. "I'm having a whiskey now."

"Where'd he get the money?"

"He worked a few days at a cannery, took an advance on his pay, I'm told. He used it to play poker." Jacob poured three fingers of whiskey into a glass. Held a second glass up, with a question on his face.

"No, thanks."

"I believe this may be true, because he liked to play, and though he often lost, he would consider it . . . payment for the entertainment. It seems this time he didn't lose. He played two nights, and most of one day. Those who talk to me say his winnings were big. Some say ten thousand, others twenty, others more. It may be like a fish that grows bigger with the telling. But there's agreement that he played and won and had money."

"What did he do with the money?"

"That, no one knows, or admits to knowing. But some say they saw him last drinking with other men. This isn't unusual, so no one can say who the men were. And why should they remember such a thing over so long a time?"

"There was a whore."

Jacob's lips curved, just a little. "There always is."

"Kate. I haven't been able to locate her."

"Whoring Kate. She died, maybe five years ago. Heart attack," Jacob added. "She was a very large woman and smoked two, maybe three, packs of Camels a day. Her death wasn't much of a surprise."

Another dead end, Nate thought.

"Did these people who talk to you but not to cops tell you anything else?"

"Some say Two-Toes flew Pat and two others, or three others, no more than that, to climb. Some say to climb Denali, some say No Name, some say Deborah. The details aren't clear, but there's memory of the money, the pilot, the climb and two or three companions."

Jacob sipped his whiskey. "Or I could be lying and be the one who climbed with him."

"You could," Nate acknowledged. "It'd be ballsy. A man who hunts down a bear's got balls."

Jacob smiled. "A man who hunts down a bear eats well."

"I believe you. But I could be lying."

This time Jacob laughed and downed the rest of the whiskey. "You could. But since we're in Meg's kitchen, and she has love for us both, we can pretend to believe each other. She has more light now. She's always been bright, but now she's brighter, and she burns off the shadows in you. She can take care of herself. But . . ."

He took the glass to the sink, rinsed it, set it to drain, then turned back. "Take care with her, Chief Burke. Or I'll hunt you down."

"Noted," Nate replied when Jacob walked out.

TWENTY-EIGHT

NATE BIDED HIS TIME. It seemed he had plenty of it. Since he made it a point to stop by The Lodge restaurant and see Jesse daily, it wasn't a problem to find an opportunity for a private word with Charlene.

He found Rose taking advantage of a mid-morning lull by sitting down in a booth refilling condiment dispensers.

"Don't get up," he said when she started to slide out. "Where's my buddy today?"

"We have cousins down from Nome, so Jesse has playmates for a few days. He's been showing off his uncle, the deputy," she said with a smile. "But he wants to bring them all into town to meet his good friend, Chief Nate."

"Really?" He could feel his own grin spreading from ear to ear. "Tell him to bring them on, and we'll give them a tour of the station." And he'd radio Meg, see if she could find him a bunch of toy badges when she picked up supplies.

"You wouldn't mind?"

"I'd get a kick out of it."

He leaned over to take a peek at Willow in her carrier. "She's awfully pretty."

He could say it with truth now. Her cheeks had

grown plump and sort of pinchable. And her eyes, so dark, seemed to latch on to his as if she knew things he didn't.

He held out a finger. Willow wrapped hers around it, shook it.

"Is Charlene in her office?"

"No, in the storeroom off the kitchen. Doing inventory."

"Okay if I go back?"

"You'll want a flak jacket," Rose warned as she dumped ketchup into a bright red squeeze bottle. "She's been in a mood the last few days."

"I'll risk it."

"Nate. Peter told us about the commendation. He's so proud. We're so proud. Thank you."

"I didn't do anything. He did."

Since her eyes filled, he made his escape quickly.

Big Mike was at the counter making what looked like enough salad to feed an army of rabbits. He had the radio on to local, and Yo-Yo Ma's deep and passionate cello streamed out.

"Crab Florentine à la Mike's the lunch special," he called out. "Buffalo salad for the heartier appetites."

"Yum."

"You going in there?" Mike asked when Nate turned toward the storeroom. "Better take a sword and shield."

"So I hear." But Nate opened the door, and since you could never tell with Charlene, left it open for safety's sake.

It was a large, chilly room lined with metal shelves that were loaded with canned and dry goods. A couple of tall coolers held tubs of perishables, with a chest freezer squeezed in between them.

Charlene stood among them, briskly scribbling on a clipboard.

"Well, I know where to head in case of thermonuclear war."

She flipped him a glance, one that held none of her usual steamy come-on. "I'm busy."

"I can see that. I just want to ask you a question."

"Nothing but questions out of you," she muttered, then raised her voice to a shout. "I'd like to know why we're down to two cans of kidney beans."

Big Mike's answer was to turn the radio up.

"Charlene, give me a couple of minutes and I'll be out of your way."

"Fine, fine, *fine!*" She slapped the clipboard against a shelf, hard enough that Nate heard the wood crack. "I'm just trying to run a business here. Why should that matter to anybody?"

"I'm sorry about whatever's bothering you, and I'll make this as quick as I can. Do you know anything about Galloway having substantial poker winnings between the time he left here and when he went up the mountain?"

She made a sound of derision. "As if." Then her eyes narrowed. "What do you mean, *substantial*?"

"A few thousand anyway. I've got a source that says he might've played a couple of nights and hit."

"If there was a game, he probably played. He hardly ever won, though, and hardly ever won more than a couple hundred if he got lucky. There was that one time in Portland. He won about three thousand. And we blew it on a fancy hotel room, a big steak dinner, a couple bottles of champagne from room service. He bought me an outfit for it. A dress and shoes, and a pair of little sapphire earrings."

Her eyes went shiny. But she shook her head and shoulders briskly and dried the tears up on her own. "Stupid. I had to sell the earrings in Prince William to pay for motorcycle repairs and supplies. Lot of good they did me."

"If he had won money, what would he have done with it?"

"Pissed it away. No." She laid her forehead on one of the shelf posts, and looked so tired, so lost, so sad that he risked rubbing her shoulder.

"No, not right then. He knew I was on a tear about money. If he'd gotten his hands on some, he'd have played a little maybe, but he'd have held on to the bulk of it, so he could bring it home and shut me up."

"Would he have banked it? In Anchorage?"

"We didn't have a bank in Anchorage. He'd've stuffed it in his pack and hauled it home for me to deal with. He didn't have any respect for money. A lot of people that come from it don't."

She lifted her head. "Are you saying there was money?"

"I'm saying there's a possibility."

"He never sent any home that time. He never sent home a dime."

"If he had money and was going on a climb?"

"He'd have left it stuffed in a drawer, if he kept his room. Or if he didn't keep his room, he'd have taken it with him. The State Police didn't say anything about money."

"He didn't have any on him."

None, Nate thought as he went out again. No wallet, no ID, no cash. No pack. Just matches and the journal, zipped into the pocket of his parka.

On the sidewalk, he took out his notebook. He wrote down MONEY, circled it.

The saying was "Follow the woman," he thought, but a cop knew if money was around murder, you always, always followed the money.

He wondered how he could find out if anyone in Lunacy had come in to a tidy little windfall sixteen years before.

Of course, it was just as likely Galloway kept a room, left the money in it. And the maid, the owner or the next person to occupy it just got really lucky.

Or he'd taken it with him in his pack. His killer hadn't opened it up before he'd tossed it into a handy crevice.

But why should the killer take the pack at all if not for a reason? For supplies—and woo-hoo, look what else we've got here. Or just to dump it in a panic, thinking if the body was found it wouldn't be identifiable.

But if there had been money, Nate was willing to bet the killer had known it was there and had helped himself. Who—?

"People might wonder why they're paying taxes so the chief of police can daydream out on the street."

He shook himself back, looked down at Hopp. "Are you everywhere?"

"As often as possible. I'm on my way in to get a cup

of coffee and brood. And plot." She wore irritation on her face as visibly as she wore her green-checked shirt.

"What's up?"

"John Malmont just tendered his resignation. Says he's leaving at the end of the school year."

"Leaving teaching?"

"Leaving Lunacy. We can't afford to lose him."

She took out her Zippo, but only stood snapping the top open and shut. Talk around town was she was wearing the patch.

"He's a superior teacher, and added to that, he's helping Carrie with *The Lunatic,* he runs all the school plays, heads up the yearbook committee, puts us on the tourist map with articles he gets published in magazines. I've got to sit down and figure out how to keep him."

"Did he say why he decided to leave? All of a sudden?"

"Just that it was time for a change. One minute we're planning our summer book club, which he heads up, and the next he's packing. Son of a bitch!"

She rolled her shoulders. "I'm having coffee *and* pie. Pie à la mode." She snapped the lighter violently. "That'll get the brain cells working. He's not leaving without a fight."

Interesting, Nate thought. Interesting timing.

BURKE HAD TO GO. That was the bottom line now. Poking and prodding into matters that were *none of his business.*

Well, there was more than one way to run a pain-in-the-ass cheechako out of town. There were those who said Burke had risen above that status now that he'd survived his first winter.

But he knew some remained cheechakos no matter what they survived.

Galloway had been one. When push came to shove, he'd been gutless and mewling and sneaky. Most of all sneaky.

The man had been an asshole, pure and simple. Why should anyone give a *damn* that he was dead?

Done what had to be done, he told himself as he carried the heavy plastic bags through the woods. Just like he was doing what had to be done now.

Burke would be dealt with. Another gutless, mewling, sneaky asshole. Oh, my wife left me for another man. Woe is me. Oh, I got my partner killed. Boo hoo. I have to run away where nobody knows me so I can wallow in my own muck of self-pity.

But that wasn't good enough. Had to try to be a big shot. To take *over* what wasn't his. Could never be his.

Yeah, he'd be dealt with, and life would get back to normal.

He hung the plastic bags in the trees closest to the house while the dogs whined and batted their tails.

"Not this time, boys," he said aloud and hung another from the eave by the back door, just out of sight of the doorway. "Not this time, fellas."

He gave the dogs a brisk rub, but they were more interested in sniffing at and licking his hands.

He liked the dogs. He'd liked Yukon. But that old dog had been half blind, arthritic and damn near deaf on top of it. Putting him down had been a mercy, really. And had made a point.

He walked back toward the woods, stopping at the edge to look back. There were some patches of earth where the snow was busily melting in the sun, where the rains had washed it clear. A few sprigs of green were rising out of it.

Spring, he thought. And once the ground thoroughly warmed, they'd bring Pat Galloway home for the last time.

He planned to stand at the grave site, with his head respectfully bowed.

IT WAS JUST SOFTENING to twilight when Nate got home. He waited by the side of the road while Meg walked over from the lake, over boggy green with thinning patches of snow, he noted.

She carried a box of supplies and wore a bright red shirt that made him think of some flashy tropical bird.

"Wanna trade?"

She looked at the pizza box he held, sniffed at it. "No, I got it *and* your toy badges. But I like a man who brings dinner. How'd you know for sure I'd be back for dinner, or were you planning on eating all that yourself?"

"I heard your plane. Finished up what I was doing, walked up to The Italian Place and got this. Figured you'd have to off-load your cargo, and the timing would be pretty close."

"Close to perfect. I'm starved." She carted the supplies into the house and straight back to the kitchen.

"And it so happens one of the things I picked up today is what's billed as an exceptional cabernet."

She pulled out the bottle. "You game?"

"Sure. In a minute." He set the pizza aside, laid his hands on her shoulders and kissed her. "Hi."

"Hi, cutie." Grinning, she grabbed his hair, yanked him down for a harder, longer kiss. "Hello, boys." She crouched down for a quick rub and wrestle with her dogs. "Didja miss me, huh, didja?"

"We all did. Last night we consoled ourselves with a bear bone and mac and cheese. Jacob supplied the bone, and the bear meat that's in your freezer."

"Umm, good." She pulled out a plastic bag, shook it so the contents jingled, then tossed it to him.

Inside he found silver pin-on stars. "Cool."

"You said seven, but I got you a dozen. You can have some on hand if you want to deputize more kids."

"Thanks. What do I owe you?"

"You're running a tab. We'll catch up. Open that bottle, will you, Chief?" She slid her hand in the pizza box and tore off a slice. "Missed lunch," she said with her mouth full. "Had to set down—a little engine trouble—and it cost me a couple of hours."

"What kind of engine trouble?"

"Nothing dire. All fixed now, but I could use pizza and wine, a hot shower, and a man who knows how to rub me in all the right places."

"Looks like we can handle all of that."

"You keep getting this half-smile going on. What's that about?"

"Things. You want to sit down and eat, or are you just going to stand there and stuff it in your face?"

"Stand here." She took another huge bite. "Stuff."

"Okay. Should this breathe or something?"

"Not when I'm washing down pizza with it. Gimme."

He poured her a glass and another for himself. Then he pulled out a slice and leaned back on the counter to eat it. "You know the day Peter was shot."

"Hard to forget. He used to follow me and Rose around like a puppy. He's doing okay, right?"

"He's fine. But that day, when I saw the blood on the snow, when I got to him and had his blood on my hands, part of my mind wiped out. No, more rolled back. To Jack. I was back in that alley again. I could see it, hear it, smell it. And I wanted to sink away somehow. Just go away."

"That's not the way I heard it."

"That's what was going on, inside." He'd get this out first, Nate thought. Make sure she saw him as he'd been, as he was, and as he hoped to be. "It seemed like a long time. A long time crouched there in the snow, with him bleeding on me. But it wasn't. And I didn't sink away."

"No, you didn't. You drew his fire away from Peter."

"That's not the point."

"Cutie." She moved forward, gave him a light kiss, moved back again to lean on the counter. "You're such a cop."

"I controlled the situation. Did the job and got everybody out of it alive. I could've killed him. Spinnaker."

He saw her take that in, just a slight angling of her head.

"I could've done it, and for an instant I considered it. Nobody would've questioned it. He'd shot my deputy, shot at me. He was armed and dangerous. It wasn't like in the alley with Jack. Then my partner was down—my partner was dying," he corrected, "and I was down, and that son of a bitch kept coming."

He looked down at his wine while she listened, while she waited. He set it on the counter. "There was no choice, and here I had one. And I considered blowing him to hell. You should know that. You should know it was in me to do that."

"Do you expect me to care if you had? He tried to kill my friend, tried to kill you. I wouldn't have cared, Nate. I guess you should know that's in me."

"It would've been . . ."

"Wrong," she finished. "For you. For the man you are, for the kind of cop you are. So I'm glad you didn't. Your right and wrong are more defined than mine. That's just the way it is."

"It was a year ago that Jack died."

Sympathy swam into her eyes. "Oh boy, you just keep getting punched in the gut, don't you?"

"No. No, I called Beth on the day. Jack's wife. I called her, and it was good. She was good. And talking to her, I realized I wasn't going to sink again. I don't know when I got out of the pit, exactly, and sometimes the ground's still a little soft and unstable under my feet. But I'm not going back down."

"You never were." She poured more wine in her glass. "I know people who have or who probably will. The kind who fly into the side of a mountain on a clear day or go off into the bush to die. I know them. They're part of the outer world I run in away from here. Burned-out pilots or some Outsider who stumbles up here because he can't take the world anymore. Women beat down from being abused or neglected for so long they'll just lie down and let the next man kick them to death on the street.

"You were sad, Nate, and a little lost, but you were never one of them. You've got too much core to be one of them."

He said nothing for a moment, then he reached out, touched the ends of her hair. "You burned away my shadows."

"Huh?"

The half-smile came back to his lips. "Marry me, Meg."

For a moment she stared at him, those crystal-blue eyes full power on his. Then she tossed the half-eaten slice of pizza into the box.

"I *knew* it!" Throwing her hands up, she spun around on her heels and clomped around the kitchen with enough violence to have the dogs leaping up to sniff at her. "I just *knew* it. Give a guy some good sex, a couple of hot meals, soften up enough to say you love him and—*boom!*—next breath it's marriage talk. Didn't I tell you. Didn't I tell you?" She whirled around to jab a finger at him. "Hearth and home, tattooed on your butt."

"Looks like you nailed me."

"Don't you smirk at me."

"A minute ago it was a half-smile, and you thought it was kind of cute."

"I changed my mind. What do you want to get married for?"

"I love you. You love me."

"So? *So?*" Her arms were still flapping around, and now the dogs figured it was a game and made playful little lunges at her. "Why do you want to screw that up?"

"Just crazy, I guess. What are you, chicken?"

She sucked air in her nose, and her eyes went to cold fire. "Don't you play that crap on me."

"You got marriage fear?" He leaned back on the counter, picked up his glass again and sipped his wine. "The brave little bush pilot gets shaky in the knees when the M word comes up. Interesting."

"My knees are not shaking, you jerk."

"Marry me, Meg." His half-smile went full blown. "See, you went pale."

"I did not. I did not."

"I love you."

"You bastard."

"I want to spend my life with you."

"Goddamn it."

"I want to have babies with you."

"Oh." She gripped her hair and pulled as an indescribable sound ground out of her throat. "Cut it out."

"See?" He contemplated another slice of pizza. "Chicken."

Her right hand closed into a fist. "Don't think I can't take you down, Burke."

"You already did, first time I saw you."

"Oh, man." The fist dropped to her side. "You think you're cute, you think you're smart, but what you are is stupid and simple. You've already been through this marriage thing, got the shit kicked out of you, and here you are asking for more."

"She wasn't you. I wasn't me."

"What the holy hell does that mean?"

"First part's easy. There's nobody else like you. I'm not who I was when I was with her. Different people make, well, different people. I'm a better man with you, Meg. You make me want to be a better man."

"Oh God, don't say things like that." She could feel her eyes burn. The tears rising up from her heart were hot and strong. "You're the man you always were. Maybe you were shaky for a while, but anybody is when they've been beaten up and tossed aside. I'm not better, Nate. I'm selfish and contrary and . . . I was going to say inconsiderate, but I don't see why it's inconsiderate to live your life the way you want. I'm mean when I want to be, I don't care about rules unless they're mine, and I'm here, I'm still here in this place, because I'm half crazy."

"I know. Don't change."

"I knew there was going to be trouble with you, New Year's Eve, when I went with that stupid impulse and brought you out to see the northern lights."

"You wore a red dress."

"You think I'm such a girl I'll go all squishy because you remember what color dress I wore?"

"You love me."

"Yeah." She blew out a long breath, wiped her hands over her wet cheeks. "Yeah, I do. What a damn mess."

"Marry me, Meg."

"You're just going to keep saying that, aren't you?"

"Until I get an answer."

"What if the answer's no?"

"Then I'll wait, work on you a little at a time and ask you again. Giving up doesn't work for me, so I'm done with it."

"You didn't give up. You were just hibernating."

He smiled again. "Look at you, standing there. I could look at you forever."

"Jesus, Nate." Her heart ached, literally ached so she had to rub the heel of her hand over it. And that ache, she realized, sweet at the center, smothered out the panic. "You kill me."

"Marry me, Meg."

"Oh well." She sighed. Then she laughed because the sweetness spread through everything else. "What the hell. I'll give it a shot." She took a running leap that would've knocked him flat if he hadn't had his back to the counter. Her legs wrapped around his waist, her mouth crushed down on his. "This goes south, it's on your head."

"Goes without saying."

"I'll be a terrible wife." She rained kisses over his face, his throat. "I'll irritate you and make you crazy half the time. I'll fight dirty and I'll stay pissed off when you win, which will be rarely." She leaned back, framed his face with her hands. "But I won't lie to you. I won't cheat. And I'll never let you down when it matters."

"It'll work for us." He rested his cheek on hers and just breathed her in. "We'll make it work. I don't have a ring."

"You'll need to rectify that, ASAP. And spare no expense."

"Okay."

Laughing, she leaned back, way back so he had to shift his stance to keep a hold on her. "This is just crazy enough to be right." She reared back up, locked her arms around his neck. "I think it's time we went upstairs and had insane engagement sex."

"I was counting on that." He hitched her up a bit and carried her out of the room. When she nipped her teeth into his throat, he took a shaky breath. "Does it have to be upstairs? How about on the stairs. Or just on the floor right here. Then later, we could . . . Damn it."

The dogs ran barking to the door, and an instant later, he saw the glare of headlights cross the window.

"Lock all the doors," Meg murmured dreamily, still working on his throat. "Turn out all the lights. We'll hide. We'll get naked and hide."

"Too late. But we're going to remember where we were, and after we get rid of whoever that is—even if we have to kill them—we'll pick it up again."

"Deal." She hopped down. "Hold!" she ordered the dogs, who sat, quivering at the door. She opened it, recognized the man who got out of the car. "Friend," she told the dogs, then lifted a hand in greeting. "Hey, Steven."

"Hey, Meg." He bent to pet the dogs. "Hi, guys, hi. How's it going? Ah, I saw Peter, and he said Chief Burke was out here. I wanted to see him a minute, if that's okay."

"Sure. Come on in. Outside, boys, time for a run."

"Hi, Steven, how're you doing?"

"Chief." He shook hands with Nate. "A lot better than the last time you saw me. I wanted to thank you again, in person and when I was a little more with it, for what you did for me. For us. You, too, Meg."

"Heard you kept all your digits."

"Ten fingers, ten toes. Well, nine and a half toes. Really lucky. All of us were. I'm sorry to bother you at home . . . I mean when you're off duty."

"It's no problem."

"Go ahead and sit down," Meg invited. "You want some wine? A beer?"

"He's underage," Nate said even as Steven started to accept. "And he's driving."

"Cops," Meg grumbled. "Always pooping on the party."

"Maybe a Coke or something if you've got it handy."

"Sure."

Steven sat, drummed his fingers on his knees. "I'm home for a couple of days. Spring break. I wanted to come sooner, but I've got a lot of stuff to catch up on. Missed a lot of classes when I was out, you know."

"You making them up?"

"Yeah, putting in a lot of long nights, but I'm making up time. I wanted to come when I heard about Yukon." His voice trembled, and the fingers on his knees dug in.

"I'm sorry."

"I remember when we got him. I was just a kid, and he was this goofy ball of fluff. It's hard. Hardest on my mom. He was like her baby or something."

"I don't know what I'd do if anyone hurt my dogs,"

Meg said as she came back into the room. She handed Nate one of the glasses of wine she had in each hand, then took the can of Coke under her arm and gave it to Steven.

"I know you're doing all you can. Somebody told me you had some crazy guy around—Jesus, he shot Peter." He shook his head as he opened the can. "And some think maybe this guy did that to Yukon. But . . ."

"You don't think so," Nate prompted.

"Yukon was friendly, but he wouldn't have gone with a stranger. I just don't think he'd have gone with somebody he didn't know. Not without a fight. He was old, and mostly blind, but he wouldn't have left the yard with somebody he didn't know."

He drank deep. "Anyway, that's not why I came by. I just wanted to get that out. It's about this."

He hitched up his hips as he dug in the front pocket of his jeans. He pulled out a small silver earring in the shape of a Maltese cross. "It was in the cave," he said.

Nate took it. "You found this in the cave, with Galloway?"

"Scott did, actually. I forgot about it. I guess we all did. He saw this about a foot from . . ." He glanced at Meg. "From the body. Sorry."

"It's okay."

"He chipped it out. I don't know why, something to do. He put it in his pack. By the time we all got off the mountain, the shape we were in, the hospital and shit, he just forgot about it. He found it in his stuff and remembered and gave it to me because I was coming home. We thought it was probably your father's, Meg, so you should have it. Then I thought how it should probably go through the cops first, so I figured I should bring it to Chief Burke."

"Did you show this to Sergeant Coben?" Nate asked.

"No. Scott passed it to me right before I left to come home, and I wanted to get home. I thought it was all right to do it through you."

"That's fine. Thanks for bringing it by."

"I DON'T KNOW if it was his," Meg said when she was alone with Nate. "It could've been. He wore an earring. He had a few. I can't remember exactly. A couple of studs, a gold hoop. But it might've been his. It could've been something he bought in Anchorage while he was gone. It might have been . . ."

"His killer's," Nate finished, studying the earring in his palm.

"Are you going to give it to Coben?"

"I'm going to think about it awhile."

"Put it away, will you? Can we put it away for tonight? I don't want to be sad."

Nate slipped it into the breast pocket of his shirt, buttoned it closed. "Okay?"

"Okay." She laid her head on his shoulder, laid a hand over the pocket. "You can show it to Charlene tomorrow. Maybe she'd know. But for now—" She set her hands on his shoulders, boosted herself up again. "Where were we?"

"I think we were over there."

"And now we're here. And look! There's a nice comfy

couch behind you. How quick can you get me naked on it?"

"Let's find out."

He dropped backward, pulling her around at the last minute, so she fell, laughing, under him. Her legs were still hooked around him as she tugged his shirt out of his pants, scraped her nails up his back.

"I expect you to ring the big bell tonight, since I'm an engagement-sex virgin."

"I'm going to work my way up to the big bell." He unbuttoned her shirt, taking his lips on a trail down the opening to the button of her jeans. "Ring all the little ones on the way up."

"I admire a man with ambition."

She felt his tongue slide over her, his teeth scrape over exposed flesh as he peeled the jeans down her legs.

She was going to marry this man. Imagine that? Ignatious Burke, with his big, sad eyes and strong hands. A man just packed with patience and needs and courage. And honor.

She brushed a hand through his hair. She'd done nothing in her life to deserve him. And somehow that made it all that much more wonderful.

Then his teeth nibbled along her inner thigh, her system shuddered and she stopped thinking altogether.

He worked his way up her and down her, over her, around her, washed through with the knowledge that she belonged to him now. To cherish and protect, to hold up and to lean on. Love for her was like a sun inside him, shining strong and white.

He found her lips again, sank into them, into all that heat and power.

In some part of his brain, he heard the dogs barking, a frenzied cacophony that cut through the sexual buzz. Even as he lifted his head to tune in to the sound, Meg was shoving him away.

"Something's at my dogs."

She sprinted out of the room even as he rolled off the couch. "Meg! Wait a minute. Wait a damn minute."

He heard something, something that wasn't a dog, sound outside the house, and he ran after her.

TWENTY-NINE

SHE HAD A RIFLE and was yanking open the back door by the time he caught her. He made a leap, slapped the door closed.

"What the hell are you doing?"

"Protecting my dogs. They're going to get mauled out there. Back off, Burke, I know what I'm doing."

Too rushed for niceties, she rapped the butt of the rifle into his belly and was both furious and astonished when instead of buckling, he stood his ground and shoved her back.

"Give me the gun."

"You've got your own. They're my dogs." A pulsing, clacking roar cut through the frenzied barks. "It'll kill my dogs!"

"No, it won't." He didn't know what *it* was, but from the sound of it, it was bigger than any dog. He slapped on the outside lights, then picked up the gun he'd laid on her counter, pulled it out of the holster. "Stay here."

Later, he would wonder why he'd thought she'd listen to him, listen to reason. Be safe. But when he opened the door, his gun lifted, held in combat stance, she bolted out, ducking under his arm, whirling her body and the barrel of the rifle toward the sounds of vicious war.

There was an instant of wonder struck into him, tangled with fear and a terrible respect. The bear was massive, a great hulk of black against the patchy snow. Its teeth gleamed sharp and deadly in the light as its jaws opened, and it bellowed viciously at the dogs.

They went at it, short, testing lunges, snapping, snarling. He saw blood splattered over the ground, a pool of it soaking into the thawing ground. The raw smell of it, and the pungent odor of wild animal, stung the air.

"Rock, Bull! Here! Come here, now!"

Too far gone, was Nate's only thought as Meg called out. Too far gone to listen even to her. They'd already made their choice between fight or flight, and the blood lust was on them.

The bear dropped onto all fours, its back hunched, and the sound it made was nothing like the growls Hollywood assigned to its breed. It was more. More savage, more chilling. More real.

It swiped out, razor claws sweeping, and sent one of the dogs tumbling off into the snow on a high-pitched yelp. Then it rose up on its hind legs. Taller than a man, wide as the moon. Blood on its fangs and its eyes mad with battle.

He fired as it charged, fired again as it got down on all fours to rush them. He heard the explosion of Meg's rifle, once, twice, booming through his own fire. It screamed, it seemed like a scream to him, as blood flew, as it matted its fur.

It fell less than three feet from where they stood, and it shook the ground under Nate's feet.

Meg shoved the rifle at Nate and jumped down to run

to the dog who limped toward her. "You're all right, you're okay. Let me see. Just grazed you, didn't he? You stupid, *stupid* dog. Didn't I tell you to come?"

Nate stayed where he was a moment, making certain the bear was down for good while Rock sniffed around the body, nosed into the blood.

Then he walked down to where Meg knelt in nothing but a pair of panties and an open shirt. "Get inside, Meg."

"It's not too bad." She was crooning to Bull. "I can fix it. Baited. Baited the house, do you see? Bloody meat." Her eyes were hard stones as she gestured to the chunks of half-eaten meat near the back of the house. "Hung meat, fresh meat at the house, probably at the edge of the woods. Lure the bear in. Bastard. That's what the bastard did."

"Get inside, Meg. You're cold." He pulled her to her feet, felt her trembling. "Take these. I'll get the dog."

She took the guns, whistled for Rock. Inside, she laid the guns on the counter and dashed for a blanket and first-aid supplies. "Lay him on that," she called out when Nate carried the dog in. "Get down with him, keep him quiet. He's not going to like this."

He did as she asked, held the dog's head and said nothing while she cleaned the cuts.

"Not deep, not too deep. Probably scar. War wounds, that's okay. Rock, sit!" she snapped out when he tried to wiggle under her arm to sniff at his companion.

"I'm going to give him a couple of shots here." She took out a hypo, tapped it with a steady hand, squirted out a small stream. "Hold him still."

"We can take him in to Ken."

"It's not that bad. He wouldn't do any more than I can do here. Going to give him this, make him groggy so I can stitch up the deeper cuts. We'll give him an antibiotic after, wrap him up, let him sleep it off."

She pinched a hunk of fur, then slid the needle in. Bull whimpered and rolled his eyes pitifully up at Nate. "Just relax, big guy, you're going to feel better in a minute."

He stroked the dog while Meg started to suture. "You keep all that stuff around the house?"

"Out here, you never know. Maybe you slice your leg or whatever cutting wood, power's out, roads are blocked, what are you going to do?"

Her brows were knitted as she worked, her voice calm and matter-of-fact. "Can't depend on getting to a doctor for every damn thing. There now, baby doll, nearly done. We're going to keep you nice and warm. I've got this salve here. It'll help it heal and keep him from gnawing at it 'cause it tastes foul. Gonna bandage him up. Take him in tomorrow, have him looked at, but it's not too bad."

When the dog was sleeping under a blanket with Rock curled beside him, she picked up the wine bottle and drank from it. Now her hands shook violently. "Jesus Christ."

Nate took the bottle from her, set it carefully aside. Then he gripped her elbows and jerked her an inch off the floor. "Don't you ever, *ever* do anything like that again."

"Hey!"

"Look at me. Listen to me."

She hardly had a choice as his voice was booming, and his face, rigid with fury, engulfed her vision.

"Don't you ever take a risk like that again."

"I had to—"

"No, you didn't. I was here. You didn't have to go running out of the house, half naked, to take on a grizzly."

"It wasn't a grizzly," she shouted back at him. "It was a black bear."

He dropped her back on her feet. "Damn it, Meg."

"I can take care of myself and what's mine."

He spun back around, his face so full of rage, she backed up a step. This wasn't the patient lover; it wasn't the cold-eyed cop. This was a furious man with enough heat blasting out to boil her alive.

"You're mine now, so get used to it."

"I'm not going to stand around and act helpless because—"

"Helpless, my ass. Who wants you to act helpless? There's a big fucking difference between acting helpless and running out of the house in your underwear when you don't know the situation. There's a big damn difference, Meg, when you try to shove me aside by ramming the butt of a rifle in my gut."

"I didn't . . . did I?" Oddly enough it was his full-blown temper that cut hers down to manageable, that allowed her to think again. "I'm sorry, I'm sorry. That was wrong."

She pressed her hands to her face, took several deep breaths until the fear, the anger, the shaky aftermath of both eased.

"Some of the other stuff was probably wrong, but I just reacted. I . . ." She held out a hand, palm out for peace, then picked up her wine again. She sipped slowly to soothe her raw throat.

"My dogs are my partners. You understand you don't

hesitate when your partner's in trouble. And I did know the situation. There wasn't time to explain it. And I haven't taken time to tell you it felt . . . all kinds of good and different things to know you were beside me out there. Even if I didn't act like it, I knew you were there, and it mattered."

Her voice thickened so she pressed the fingers of her free hand to her eyes until she had it under control. "You want to be mad, I won't hold it against you. But maybe you could wait to finish yelling at me until I get some clothes on. I'm cold."

"I guess I'm finished." He stepped toward her, pulled her into his arms and held on like fury.

"Look at that. I'm shaking." She burrowed into him. "I wouldn't be if you weren't here to hang on to."

"Let's get you dressed." He kept an arm around her until they were in the living room, then he walked over to put another log on the fire.

"I've got a need to take care of you," he said quietly. "I'm not going to drown you in it."

"I know. I've got a need to take care of myself, but I'll try not to shove you away with it."

"Okay. Now, explain about the baiting."

"Bears like to eat. That's why you bury or seal your scraps when you're camping, why you carry any food supplies in sealed containers and hang them up, away from camp. That's why you build a cache for supplies and have it on stilts, and the ladder you use to get up to them comes down every time you do."

She pulled on her pants, scooped a hand through her hair. "Bears get a scent of something to eat, they mosey on over to snack, and they can climb a ladder. You'd be surprised what can climb a ladder. They'll even wander into town, a populated area, to get into garbage cans, bird feeders and so on. You might have one try to get in the house, just to see if there's something more interesting to eat inside. Mostly you can scare them off. Sometimes you can't."

She buttoned up her shirt, edged closer to the fire. "There's meat on the ground out there, and I bet we'll find some shreds of the plastic it was in. Somebody put it there, hoping to bring a bear in toward the house, and you can be pretty confident that kind of baiting will work this time of year. Bears are just waking up. They're hungry."

"Someone laid the bait, hoping you'd step into the trap."

"No, not me. You." And that had her stomach churning. "Think about it. Had to be baited sometime today, before I got back. If someone'd tried that while we were here, we'd have heard the dogs carrying on. Say you were out here alone tonight, like you were last night, what would you have done if you'd heard the dogs start up like we did?"

"I'd've gone out to see why, but I'd have gone out armed."

"With your handgun," she said with a nod. "Maybe you can take down a bear with a handgun, or scare it off with one—if you're lucky enough and get off enough shots before it takes it out of your hand and eats it. Mostly, you're just going to make it mad. And a bear who's busy chowing down or fighting a couple of angry huskies? He'd have gotten through my dogs, Nate. Odds are they'd have done some damage before it ripped them to pieces. And if you'd been out there alone with that nine-millimeter, you might have been ripped to pieces, too. Odds are. Wounded bear, enraged bear, he'd come right through the door after you, too. That's what someone was counting on."

"If so, I must be making someone very nervous."

"That's what cops do, don't they?" She rubbed a hand over his knee when he sat beside her. "Whoever it was wanted you dead or in a world of hurt. And didn't mind sacrificing my dogs to do it."

"Or you, if things had gone differently."

"Or me. Well, he's got me pissed off now." She patted his knee before she rose to pace. "Killing my father, that hurt me. But he'd been gone a long time, and I could deal. Tracking him down, tossing him in a cell, that'd be enough. But nobody comes after my dogs."

She turned and saw that half-smile was back. "Or after the guy I'm going to marry, especially before he's bought me a really expensive ring. You still mad at me?"

"Not so much. I will always have that image of you standing out there in your red panties with that red shirt open and blowing back in the wind while you held a rifle. But after a while, it's going to be erotic instead of terrifying."

"I really do love you. It's the damnedest thing. Okay." She scrubbed her hands hard over her face. "We can't leave that carcass out there. It'll bring all kinds of other interested visitors, and the dogs will be rolling over it in the morning. I'm going to call Jacob, have him help me deal with it, and he can see if he can find any signs from whoever left the bait."

She saw his face, stepped forward.

"I can see your brain working. Jacob was here today and with bear meat. He wouldn't have done this, Nate. I can give you several specific reasons why, over and above the fact that he's a good man who loves me. First, he'd never put my dogs in jeopardy. He loves them and respects them too much. Second, he knew I was coming home tonight. I touched base with him after I did the engine work. Third, if he wanted you dead, he'd just jam a knife in your heart and bury you somewhere you'd never be found. Simple, clean, straightforward. This? This was sneaky and cowardly and not a little desperate."

"I agree with you. Call him."

IN HIS OFFICE THE NEXT MORNING, Nate studied his most recently collected evidence. Some scraps of white plastic, which looked like the same material used at The Corner Store to bag produce, some scraps of meat he'd sealed in an evidence bag.

And a silver earring.

Had he seen it before? That earring? There was something on the fringes of his memory, a finger tap on the brain, trying to wake it up.

A single silver earring. Men wore them more now than they once had. Fashions changed and evolved, and even a suit wouldn't be smirked at for sporting an earring these days.

But sixteen years ago? Not as mainstream, not as

common for a man. More a hippy sort of thing or a musician, an artist, a biker, a rebel. And this wasn't a discreet little stud or a tiny sporty hoop, not with that cross dangling.

It made more of a statement.

It wasn't Galloway's. He'd checked the photographs, and Galloway had died with a hoop in his ear. Best he could tell, using a magnifying glass, Galloway's other ear had been unpierced.

He'd check with the ME to be sure.

But he knew what he was looking at belonged to the murderer.

The little back piece—what the hell did they call that—was missing. He could see, in his mind's eye, that faceless figure, rearing back with the ax, and the little earring falling off, unnoticed. Bringing the ax down, bringing it home.

Had he stood there, watching Galloway's shocked face as his friend had slid bonelessly down that icy wall? Had he stood there, staring, studying? Shocked himself or pleased? Thrilled or appalled? Hardly mattered, Nate thought. The job was done.

Take the pack, check it? No point in leaving supplies *or* the money, if the money was in there. Have to be practical. Have to survive.

How long before he'd noticed the loss of the earring? Too late to go back and check, too insignificant a detail to worry about.

But it was always the details that built the case—and the cage.

"Nate?"

Still holding the earring, he reached for his intercom. "Yeah?"

"Jacob's here to see you," Peach told him.

"Send him back."

He didn't get up, but instead leaned back in his chair as Jacob came in and closed the door behind him. "Expected you to come by this morning."

"There are things I want to say I didn't want to say last night in front of Meg."

Jacob wore a buckskin shirt over faded jeans, and the thin string of beads around his neck held a polished, brown stone. His silvered hair was drawn back in a long tail. His exposed lobes sported no jewelry.

"Have a seat," Nate invited, "and say them."

"I'll stand and say them. You'll use me to finish this, or I'll do what I have to do on my own. But this will end." He stepped forward, and for the first time in their acquaintance, Nate saw undisguised rage on Jacob's face.

"She is *my* child. She's been mine more years than she was Pat's. This is my daughter. Whatever you think about me, whatever you wonder, you will *know* that. I'll be a part of finding who put her in danger last night, one way or the other."

Nate rocked forward in his chair, rocked back again. "You want a badge?"

He saw Jacob's hands ball into fists, then open again, slowly, just as slowly as the rage went under some enigmatic mask. "No. I don't think I'd like a badge. Too heavy for me."

"Okay, we'll keep my . . . use of you unofficial. That suit you better?"

"It does."

"These people you were asking questions of, ones who told you about the money? Is it possible wind of that blew back here to Lunacy?"

"More than possible. People talk, especially white people."

"And if that wind blew, it wouldn't be a stretch to conclude, due to your connection to Galloway and to Meg, that you'd pass the information to me."

Jacob shrugged.

"Why not just shut you down before you got it to me?"

And now Jacob smiled. "I've lived a very long time and am very hard to kill. You haven't and aren't. This business last night was sloppy and stupid. Why not just shoot you in the head when you're alone by the lake? Weigh you down with stones and sink you. I would."

"I appreciate that. He doesn't use the direct approach. No, not even with Galloway," Nate said as Jacob looked at the board. "That was a moment of madness, of greed, of opportunity. Maybe all three. It wasn't planned."

"No." Considering now, Jacob nodded. "There are easier ways to kill a man than climbing a mountain."

"One stroke of the ax," Nate continued. "One. Afterward, he's too . . . delicate to yank it out again, to dispose of the body. That would be too direct, too involved. Same with Max. Stage a suicide. Max was as responsible as he is—he can look at it that way. The dog? Just a dog, a cover, a distraction—and an indirect slap at Steven Wise. He won't come at me face-to-face."

He pushed the earring across the desk. "Recognize that?"

Jacob frowned over it. "A bauble, a symbol. Not a Native one. We have our own."

"I think the killer lost it sixteen years ago. Long forgotten. But he'll remember it if he sees it again. I've seen it before. Somewhere." Nate picked it up, let the cross twirl. "Somewhere."

HE CARRIED IT WITH HIM. It wasn't strictly procedure, but Nate kept the earring in his pocket as he went about town business.

He said nothing to anyone about the incident at Meg's, and he asked her and Jacob to do the same. A little game with a killer, he thought.

In that burgeoning spring while the days lengthened and the green overtook the white, he went about his duties, talked with the people of his town, listened to their troubles and complaints.

And checked the earlobes of all the men he came in contact with.

"They can close up," Meg told him one night.

"What?"

"The holes in your ear—or wherever you decide to skewer yourself." She danced her fingers lightly over his penis.

"Please." He couldn't quite submerge the shudder and made her laugh. Wickedly.

"I've heard it can really add something to the . . . thrust."

"Don't even think. What do you mean, close up?"

"They can heal up. If you haven't had it for long, and

you quit wearing anything in it, they"—she made a slurp-
ing sound—"close up again."

"Son of a bitch. Are you sure?"

"I used to have four in this one." She tugged her left
ear. "Got an urge and jabbed a third and fourth hole in."

"Yourself? You did it yourself?"

"Sure. What am I, a weenie?" She rolled over on him,
and since she was naked, his mind wandered away from
the conversation before he dragged it back again.

"I wore four for a few weeks, but it started to be too
much trouble, so I ditched the extras. And they closed
up." She reached over to turn on the light, then angled
her head. "See?"

"You could've told me that before I looked at earlobes all over town and made notes on who had pierc-
ings."

She rubbed his earlobe. "You might look cute with
one."

"No."

"I could do it for you."

"Absolutely no. Not in the ear or anywhere else."

"Spoilsport."

"Yeah, that's me. I've got to rethink this now, since
my short list is no longer viable."

She rose up to straddle him, to take him in. "Think
later."

HE DROPPED INTO THE LODGE and spotted Hopp and
Ed having a meeting over buffalo salad. He stopped at
their booth. "Can I interrupt a minute?"

"Sure, slide in." Hopp made room for him. "We're going over what you'd call fiduciary matters. Gives me a headache and perks Ed here right up. We're trying to figure out how to stretch the budget to building a library. Section off part of the proposed post office for it, at least for now. What do you think?"

"Sounds like a nice idea to me."

"We're agreed on that." Ed dabbed at his lip with a napkin. "But we need a little more elastic in the budget to make the stretch." He winked at Hopp. "I know that's not what you want to hear."

"We get people involved, get donations for materials, for labor. We get books donated or go begging for them. People pull together if you get them excited about a project."

"You can count me in," Nate told them. "If and when. Meanwhile, I got a fiduciary type of question myself. I was going to drop by to see you, Ed. Bank question, goes back a few years, so it may tax your memory."

No hole in his ear, Nate thought as Ed nodded.

"When it comes to banking, my memory's long. Hit me."

"It deals with Galloway."

"Pat?" He lowered his voice, glancing around the restaurant. "Maybe we shouldn't discuss this here. Charlene."

"It won't take long. I've got a source saying Galloway got himself a good pile of cash playing poker when he was in Anchorage."

"Pat loved to play poker," Hopp commented.

"That he did. I played with him more than once.

Small stakes, though," Ed added. "I can't imagine him winning much."

"Source says otherwise. So I was wondering, did he send any money back, into his account here in town, before he went on that climb?"

"Not that I recall. Not even a paycheck. We were a smaller operation in those days, as I told you before." His eyes narrowed in thought. "Though by the time Pat left, we'd built an actual vault and had two part-time tellers. Still I was involved in nearly every transaction."

Rubbing his chin, he sat back. "Pat didn't bother with the finances. He wasn't one to come into the bank to deposit, or withdraw for that matter."

"How about when he left town for work? Did he usually send money back?"

"Now, he did, sometimes. I do remember Charlene coming down once, even twice, every week—more than two months—checking to see if he had anything direct deposited after he left that time. If there was any big money, which I tend to doubt, he might've banked it there, or just as likely stuffed it in a shoe box."

"I'll go with Ed on the second," Hopp said. "Pat never did think twice about money."

"People who come from it usually don't." Ed gave a shrug. "Then there's us," he said with a wink at Hopp, "who have to do some finagling if we want to have a town library."

"I'll let you get back to that." Nate scooted out. "Thanks for the time."

"He ought to spend his time on town business." Ed shook his head as he lifted his coffee.

"I guess he figures this is."

"We need May Day, Hopp, if we're going to get that library."

"Agreed. So far he's keeping it low-key. He's just going to have to see it through until he's satisfied it was Max who killed Pat. Tenacious Ignatious," she said. "That's how I'm thinking of him these days. Boy just won't let go. It's a good quality to have in your chief of police."

JACOB HAD BEEN RIGHT: Some people wouldn't talk to cops. Even with Jacob there, Nate hadn't been able to squeeze any more juice out of the trip he took to Anchorage.

Not that it was a wasted trip.

He hadn't gone to see Coben. He should have, he admitted as Jacob skimmed over the lake. He should have taken the earring in, but he hadn't.

He wanted a little more time there. A little more time to pull it together.

He let his shoulders relax when the plane was on the water. "Thanks for going with me. You want me to secure the plane? You coming in?"

"You know how?"

"It's a boat with wings at this point. I know how to secure a boat to dock."

Jacob nodded toward Meg, who walked down to meet them. "You have other business."

"Yeah, I do. See you later then."

He stepped out onto the flotation, praying he didn't lose his balance and mortify himself by pitching into the lake. But he stepped safely on one end of the dock just as Meg stepped on the other.

"Where's he going?" she called out, when Jacob glided away.

"Said there was other business." He reached for her hand. "You're back early."

"No, you're back late. It's nearly eight."

He looked up at the sky, still bright as noon. "I'm not used to it yet. Woman, where's my supper?"

"Ha ha ha. You can throw a couple of moose burgers on the grill."

"Moose burgers, a personal favorite."

"You get anything more in Anchorage?"

"No, at least not investigationally. And how was your day?"

"Actually, I was in Anchorage briefly myself. And since I was there, I happened to wander into this shop where they happened to have wedding dresses."

"Really?"

"Stop grinning. I'm still firm on not wanting a big, fancy deal. Just a wild party right here at the house. But I decided I do want a kick-ass dress. One that'll make your eyes pop out."

"Did you find it?"

"That's for me to know and you to find out." She stepped up on the porch ahead of him, then gave him a smacking kiss. "I like my moose burger well-done and the bun lightly toasted."

"Check. But before we dine, I did a little marriage shopping today myself."

"Oh yeah?"

"Oh yeah." He pulled the ring box out of his pocket. "Guess what this is."

"Mine. Gimme."

He flipped the top open and had the pleasure of seeing *her* eyes pop when she saw the full-cut solitaire flanked by sparkling channel cuts on a platinum band.

"Holy shit!" She grabbed it out of the box, held it aloft and jumped off the porch. She danced around the yard, crowing out sounds he took as approval.

"Does that mean you like it?"

"Sparkly!" She spun laughing circles all the way back to him. "This, Chief Burke, is a ring. How much did it set you back?"

"Jesus, Meg."

She kept laughing, like a loon. "I know, tacky. And I don't really want to know. It's a killer, Nate, an absolute killer. It's stupid and extravagant, so it's perfect. Absolutely perfect."

She held it out, then dropped it into his open palm. "Okay, put it on me, and hurry up."

"Excuse me, but can we have a little dignity for this part?"

"I think we've already crossed the point of no return on that." She wiggled her fingers. "Come on. Give it up."

"Good thing I didn't wrack my brain trying to come up with something poetic to say when I did this." He slipped it on her finger where it sparkled insanely. "Be careful you don't put your eye out with that thing."

"When do I go splat?"

"Sorry?"

"I just keep falling more and more in love with you.

When do I finally hit bottom and go splat?" She framed his face in the way that always made his heart roll over in his chest. "I don't know if I'm perfect for you, Nate, but you sure as hell are for me."

He took the hand that wore the ring and kissed it. "If and when we splat, we'll do it together. Let's go make moose burgers."

THIRTY

"WHAT ARE THESE?"

Meg looked at the ring of keys in Nate's hand, deliberately furrowed her brow. "Those would be keys."

"Why do you need so many keys?"

"Because there are so many locks? Is this a quiz?"

He jingled them in his palm while she continued to give him a sunny, innocent smile. "Meg, you don't even lock your doors half the time. What are all these keys about?"

"Well . . . There are times a person needs to get into a place, and hey, that place is locked. Then she would need a key."

"And this place that, hey, is locked, wouldn't be the property of that person. Would that be correct?"

"Technically. But no man is an island, and it takes a village, and so on. We're all one in the Zen universe."

"So these would be Zen keys?"

"Exactly. Give them back."

"I don't think so." He closed his fist around them. "You see, even in the Zen universe I'd hate to arrest my wife for unlawful entry."

"I'm not your wife yet, buddy. Did you have a search warrant for those?"

"They were in plain sight. No warrant necessary."

"Gestapo."

"Delinquent." He cupped her chin in his free hand and kissed her. Opening the rear hatch of his four-wheel, he called the dogs. "Come on, boys. Let's go for a ride."

She refused to leave the dogs alone at the house now. They went with her, to Jacob's, or on a day when jobs made that inconvenient, to the run at The Lodge.

He gave the still-healing Bull a little help on the jump.

"Fly safe," he said to Meg.

"Yeah, yeah."

With her hands jammed in her pockets, she headed down to the plane, then turned and walked backward. "I can get more keys, you know. I have my ways."

"You sure do," Nate murmured.

He waited, as was his habit, for her to take off. He liked to watch her glide from water to air and to stand while the stillness erupted with her engines. While he did, he let himself think of nothing but her, of them, of the life they were building.

She was already working in what he'd discovered— after the snow had melted—was a pair of flower beds flanking her porch. She talked of columbine and trollius and of the wolf urine she sprinkled around to protect them from moose.

Her delphiniums, she promised, would reach near ten feet in the long days of summer.

Imagine that, he thought. Imagine Meg Galloway, bush pilot, bear killer, illegal-entry addict, tending a garden. She claimed her dahlias were as big as hubcaps.

He wanted to see them. Wanted to sit on the porch with her on some endless summer night with the sun ruling the sky and her flowers spread out in front of the house.

Simple, he thought. Their life could be made up of thousands of simple moments. And still never be ordinary.

Her plane rose up, and up, a little red bird in a vast, blue sky. And he smiled, felt the quick lift in his heart when she dipped her wings, right then left, in salute.

When there was stillness again, he climbed in the car with the dogs. And thought of other things.

Maybe it was foolish to pin so much on an earring, a small piece of silver, and an unsubstantiated claim that Galloway had possessed an undisclosed amount of cash.

But he'd seen that earring before, and he'd remember. Sooner or later, he'd remember. And money was no stranger to murder.

He let it sift through his head as he drove into town. Galloway had possessed ready cash and a beautiful woman. Tried-and-true motives for murder. And in a place like this, women were rare commodities.

The parade committee had already started hanging the bunting for May Day. It wasn't the red, white and blue usual for small-town parades. Why would it be usual in Lunacy? Instead banners and bunting were a rainbow of blues, yellows, greens.

He saw an eagle perched on a swag of it, as if granting his approval.

Along the main street, people were sprucing up their homes and businesses for spring. Pots and hanging baskets of pansies and curly kale—both of which he'd learned didn't mind a chill—were already set out. Porches and shutters sported fresh coats of paint. Motorcycles and scooters replaced snowmobiles.

Kids started to ride bikes to school, and he saw more Doc Martens and Timberlands than bunny boots.

And still the mountains that ringed the shimmers of spring, that rose into a sky that held the light for fourteen hours a day, clung relentlessly to winter.

Nate parked, led the dogs to the run. They gave him pitiful looks, their tails sinking between their legs as they trudged inside.

"I know, I know, it sucks." He crouched, sticking his fingers through the chain link so they could be licked. "Let me catch the bad guy, then your mom won't worry so much, and you can stay home and play."

They whined when he walked away and gave him a bellyful of guilt.

He went in through the lobby and tracked down Charlene in her office.

"I hired three college students for the summer." She gave her computer a pat. "I'm going to need them with the bookings we've got."

"That's good."

"Local guides always take on a few, too. The place'll be hopping with pretty college boys by June." There was a glitter in her eyes as she said it, but to Nate, it looked more like defiance than anticipation.

"That'll keep us all busy. Charlene . . ." He closed the door. "I'm going to ask you something, and you're not going to like it."

"Since when has that stopped you?"

No way to be delicate, he decided. "Who's the first person you slept with after Galloway left?"

"I don't kiss and tell, Nate. If you'd ever taken me up on it, you'd know that."

"This isn't gossip, Charlene, and it isn't a game. Does it matter to you who killed Pat Galloway?"

"Of course it does. Do you know how hard it is to plan his funeral, knowing he's still in some morgue and *not* knowing exactly when I can bring him home? I ask Bing every other day when he thinks the ground'll be soft enough to dig. To dig my Pat's grave."

She snatched two tissues out of the box on her desk, sniffled into them.

"When my mother buried my father," Nate said, "she walked around the house like a ghost for a month. Longer, I guess. She did everything she had to do—like you are, but you couldn't reach her. You couldn't touch her. She went away somewhere. I was never able to reach her again."

Charlene blinked at tears, lowered the tissues. "That's so sad."

"You haven't done that. You haven't let it make a ghost out of you. Now I'm asking you to help me. Who moved on you, Charlene?"

"Who didn't? I was young and fine to look at. You should've seen me back then."

Something stirred, he reached out to grab the tail of it, when she exploded.

"And I was *alone!* I didn't know he was dead. If I'd known, I wouldn't have been so quick to . . . I was hurt and I was mad, and when the men came swarming around, why shouldn't I have taken my pick? Taken lots of picks?"

"There's no blame here."

"I slept with John first." Her shoulder jerked, and she tossed the tissue into her pink wastebasket. "I knew he had a crush on me, and he was so sweet about it. Attentive," she said, wistfully now. "So I went to him. But not only him. I filled up on it. I broke hearts and I broke up marriages. And I didn't care."

She steadied herself and, for once, looked quiet, almost thoughtful. "Nobody killed Pat because of me. Or if they did, they wasted their time. Because I never cared about any of them. I never gave them anything I didn't take back. He isn't dead because of me. If he is, I swear, I don't think I can live with it."

"He's not dead because of you." He walked around her, behind her, and laid his hands on her shoulders to rub gently. "He's not."

She lifted a hand, closed it over his. "I kept waiting for him to come back. For him to see I wasn't pining for him—and want me again. I swear to God, Nate, I think I waited for that until you and Meg went up there. Until you found him, I was waiting for him."

"He would've come back." He tightened his grip when she shook her head. "You get to know the victim when you do what I do. You get inside them and understand them better, a lot of the time better than people who knew them living. He'd have come back."

"That's the nicest thing anyone's ever said to me," she said after a moment. "Especially somebody who's not trying to get in my pants."

He gave her shoulders a pat, then took the earring out of his pocket. "Do you recognize this?"

"Hmm." She sniffled again, flicked her finger over her lashes to dry them. "It's sort of pretty, but I don't know, male. Not my kind of thing. I like splashier."

"Could it have been Pat's?"

"Pat's? No, he didn't have anything like that. No crosses. He didn't go for religious symbols."

"Have you ever seen it before?"

"I don't think so. Wouldn't remember if I had, I guess. It's not much of a thing."

HE DECIDED TO START showing it around, get reactions. Since Bing was having breakfast in The Lodge, Nate walked by his table, let the earring dangle from his fingers. "Lose this?"

Bing barely gave it a glance before staring back into Nate's eyes. "Last time I told you I lost something, I got nothing but grief."

"I like to get things back to their rightful owner."

"It ain't mine."

"Know whose it is?"

"Don't spend a lot of time looking at people's ears. And I don't want to spend any more time looking at your face."

"Nice to see you again, too, Bing." He put the earring away. Bing had trimmed his beard an inch or so, Nate noticed and figured it was his warm-weather look. "February 1988. I can't find anybody around who can tell me, absolutely, you were here through that month. Have found a couple who think maybe you weren't."

"People should mind their own, like I do."

"Max was gone, and I hear you had a hankering, let's say, for Carrie back then."

"No more than any other woman."

"Seems like a good time to have moved in on her some. You strike me as a man who doesn't let opportunities go to waste."

"She wasn't interested, so why waste my time? Shit. Easier to find one and pay the hourly rate. Maybe I went down to Anchorage that winter. There was a whore named Kate I had some transactions with. So'd Galloway. His business."

"Whoring Kate?"

"Yeah. Dead now. Damn shame." He shrugged it off as he ate. "Dropped dead of a heart attack between johns. They say, anyway." He leaned forward. "I didn't kill that dog."

"You say, anyway, and you seem more concerned with that than with two dead men."

"Men can take care of themselves better than an old blind dog. Maybe I was in the city some that winter. Maybe I ran into Galloway going through Kate's swinging door. Didn't mean a damn to me."

"You talk to him?"

"I had other things on my mind. So did he. Poker game."

Nate lifted his eyebrows as if mildly surprised, mildly interested. "Is that so? You're remembering a lot of details all of a sudden."

"You're in my face all the damn time, aren't you? Spoiling my appetite, so I've been thinking on it."

"You get in on the poker game?"

"I went for a whore, not to gamble."

"Did he mention plans to climb No Name?"

"He was yanking his pants up, Christ's sake, and I was about to yank mine down. We didn't chat. Said he was riding a streak, took a break to bang Kate and was heading back. Kate said something about the place being lousy with Lunatics, and that was fine with her. Business was good. Then we got down to it."

"Did you see Galloway again, after your business was concluded?"

"Don't remember seeing him." Bing stabbed at his food. "Maybe he came in the bar, maybe he didn't. I headed on up to see Ike Transky, trapper I knew used to have a place outside Skwenta, bunked with him a few days and did some hunting, little ice fishing. Came back here."

"Transky back you up on that?"

Bing's eyes went hard as agate beads. "Don't need anybody to back up what I say. Dead now, anyway. Died in '96."

Convenient, Nate thought as he walked out. The two people Bing named as potential alibis were dead or gone. Or you could turn the prism and look at it from a different facet.

Stolen gloves, a stolen knife, both left near a dead dog. Property of a man who'd seen and spoken to Galloway.

It wasn't too much of a stretch to imagine Galloway going back to that game or stopping for a drink with friends.

Guess who I just ran into on his way to bang Whoring Kate? Small world, Nate thought. Small, old world. If Bing was telling the truth, it might be the killer was worried Galloway had mentioned who else from Lunacy was playing poker and paying for whores.

Nate decided to make a few stops, dangling his single piece of evidence, on the way to the station.

Later in the day, he showed it to Otto.

The deputy shrugged. "Doesn't mean anything to me."

A coolness had come between them, a stiff formality Nate regretted. But it couldn't be helped.

"I always thought the Maltese cross was more military than religious."

Otto never blinked. "Marines I served with didn't wear earrings."

"Well." As he had at every stop through the day, Nate put the earring back in his pocket, buttoned it.

"It's going around that you're showing that thing to everybody. People are wondering why their chief of police is spending time on a lost earring."

"Full service," Nate said easily.

"Chief," Peach said from her counter, "we've got a report of a bear in Ginny Mann's garage, off Rancor. Her husband's out with a hunting party," Peach added. "She's home alone with her two-year-old."

"Tell her we're coming. Otto?"

WHEN THEY PULLED ONTO the pitted lane a mile and a half north of town, Otto flicked a glance at Nate. "I sure hope you don't plan to have me drive this thing around like a maniac while you lean out the damn window there and shoot warning shots over some bear's idiot head."

"We'll see what we see. What the hell is a bear doing in a garage?"

"He's not fixing a carburetor." At Nate's snicker, Otto grinned. Then sobered again as he remembered what was between them.

"Somebody forgot and left the door open, most likely. They might have a can full of dog food or bird food in there. Or the dumbass bear went in to see if there was anything interesting."

When they pulled up in front of the two-story cabin with attached garage, Nate saw the garage door was indeed open. He didn't know if the bear was responsible for the mess he could see inside or if the Manns just pitched things in there like it was the town dump.

Ginny opened the front door. Her red hair was piled up on her head, and her loose overshirt and hands were splattered with paint. "He went around back. He's been crashing around inside there for twenty minutes. I thought he'd just go on, but I was afraid he'd try to get through the door to the house."

"Stay inside, Ginny," Nate ordered.

"You get a look at him?" Otto called out.

"I got a look at him through the front when he lumbered up." Behind her there was the sound of insane barking and the wail of a toddler. "I had the dog inside and was upstairs working in the studio when Roger started carrying on. Woke the baby. I'm about to go crazy from the noise. Brown bear. Didn't look full-grown but big enough."

"Bears are curious," Otto commented as they checked their rifles and started around the side of the garage. "If he's a young one, he was likely just poking around and he'll run off quick enough when he sees us."

Around back, Nate could see the Manns had roped off a patch of ground for a garden. Apparently the bear had tromped through it coming or going and had spent some time beating up a plastic crate full of newspapers and mail-order catalogs.

Nate scanned and then gestured when he spotted a brown rump through the trees.

"There he goes."

"Better give him a little scare, get him running. Discourage him from coming back." Otto aimed the rifle skyward, fired two rounds. And Nate watched, with some amusement, as the bear hustled its fat rump and ran.

He stood watching its progress beside a man who was on his list of suspects.

"That was easy enough."

"More often than not, it is."

"Sometimes it's not. Meg and I had to take one down the other night at her place."

"Is that what got at her dog? I heard her dog got clawed up some."

"Yeah. It would've gotten at us, too, if we hadn't killed it first. Somebody baited the house."

Otto's eyes narrowed into slits. "What the hell are you talking about?"

"I'm talking about somebody hanging meat, fresh, bloody meat, in thin plastic bags, on Meg's house."

Otto's mouth went tight, then he turned sharply away, paced off several steps. Nate rested his hand on the butt of his weapon. "You're asking if it was me?" Otto strode back, stood toe-to-toe with Nate. "You want to know if I'd do something that cowardly, that vicious? If I'd do something that could get two people ripped to pieces? And one of them a woman?"

He jabbed his finger into Nate's chest. Twice. "I'll take you tossing my name into the hat when it comes to Galloway, even when it comes to Max. It galls me you'd toss it in there over Yukon, but I swallowed it, but I'll be goddamned if I'll take this. I was a Marine. I know how to kill a man if I need to. I know how to do it quick, and I know plenty of places I could get rid of a body where nobody on this earth would find it."

"That's what I figured. So I'm asking you, Otto, because you know the people around here, who'd stoop that low?"

He trembled. The rage was still on him, Nate could see. He had the rifle in his hand, but even in temper, it was pointed at the ground. "I don't know. But he doesn't deserve to live."

"The earring I showed you belongs to him."

Interest won over the anger in his eyes. "You found it out at Meg's?"

"No. In Galloway's cave. So here's what we're going to think about. Who did Galloway like and trust who could handle a winter climb? Who gained something by his death? Who wore this?" he added, patting his pocket.

"Who considered himself a badass back then, and could leave town for a couple of weeks without anyone commenting?"

"You're letting me back in?"

"Yeah. Let's go tell Ginny the coast is clear."

IT WAS A TOSS-UP who was more surprised when Meg swung by to pick up her dogs. She herself or Charlene, who was caught red-handed feeding the dogs table scraps.

"Didn't see why it should go to waste. These dogs hate being penned up."

"It's just until Bull's fully healed."

They stood there, awkwardly, while the dogs ate.

"Do you know what got at him?" Charlene asked after a moment.

"Bear."

"Well, God. He's lucky he only got a few scrapes." Charlene crouched and made kissing noises at Bull. "Poor baby."

"I always forget you like dogs. You never keep one."

"I've got enough to look after around here." She glanced over, and Meg's ring caught the sun and shot light. "I heard about that, too."

She gripped Meg's hand, pulling it up under her nose as she rose. "Joanna at the clinic got a load of it, told Rose and Rose told me. Seems I might have heard about it from you. He really stepped up to the plate, didn't he?"

"Lucky me."

"Yeah, lucky you." Charlene let Meg's hand go. She started to walk away, stopped. "Lucky him, too."

Meg said nothing for a moment. "I'm waiting for the shot."

"No shot. You look good together, better together than you look otherwise. If you're going to go and marry somebody, it might as well be somebody you look good with."

"How about somebody who makes me happy."

"That's what I mean."

"Okay. Okay," Meg repeated.

"Um. Maybe I could give you a party. Like an engagement party."

Meg dipped her hands into the pockets of her jean jacket. "We're not going to wait very long. Doesn't seem like we'd need a party when we'll only be engaged about a month."

"Well. Whatever."

"Charlene," Meg said before she could leave. "Maybe you could help with the wedding thing." She watched pleasure, and surprise, run over Charlene's face. "I don't want fancy, just something out at the house, but I want a party with it. A big one. You're good at putting those things together."

"I could do that. Even if you don't want fancy, you need good food, lots of liquor. And it should be pretty. Flowers and decorations. We could talk about it."

"All right."

"There's . . . there's something I have to do now. Maybe we could talk about it tomorrow."

"Tomorrow's good. Maybe since they've just eaten, I could leave the dogs here a little while, pick up some supplies and things."

"I'll see you tomorrow, then."

Charlene went in quickly before she could change her mind. She went straight up to John's room, knocked.

"It's open."

He sat at his cramped, little desk but stood when she came in. "Charlene. Sorry, I'm grading papers. I really need to get this done."

"Don't go." She leaned back against the door. "Please don't go."

"I can't stay, so I have to go. I've turned in my resignation. I'm helping Hopp find a replacement for me."

"There's no replacement for you, John, whatever you think about . . . about the other men. I've been bad to you. I knew you loved me, but I didn't let myself care. I liked knowing there was somebody who was there, whenever I needed him, but I didn't let myself care."

"I know. I know that all too well, Charlene. I've finally got the belly to deal with it."

"Please let me say this." Eyes pleading, she crossed her hands over her breasts. "I'm scared, and I've got to get it out before I run out of courage. I liked having men want me, seeing that look in their eyes. I liked taking them to bed, especially the young ones. So I could believe, in the dark, when their hands are on me in the dark, I haven't seen forty yet."

She touched her face now. "I hate getting older, John, seeing new lines in the mirror every day. As long as men want me, I can pretend the lines aren't there. I've been scared and angry a long time, and I'm tired."

She took a step forward. "Please don't go, John. Please don't leave me. You're the only one since Pat I could rest with, feel quiet with. I don't know if I love you, but I want to. If you stay, I'll try."

"I'm not Karl Hidel, Charlene. And I can't settle anymore. I can't sit in here with a book for comfort when you've taken someone else to bed."

"There won't be anyone else. There won't be other men, I swear. If you'll just stay and give me a chance. I don't know if I love you," she said again, "but I know thinking about being without you's breaking my heart."

"That's the first time in more than sixteen years you've ever come in this room and talked to me. Said anything real to me. It's a long time to wait."

"Too long? Tell me it's not too long."

He crossed to her, put his arms around her, his cheek to the top of her head. "I don't know. I don't think either one of us knows. So, I guess we'll have to wait and see."

NATE PINNED HIS BADGE on a khaki shirt that carried the Lunacy PD symbol on the sleeve. He'd been informed by her honor the mayor that May Day required a more official look.

When he strapped on his gun, Meg made a long *mmmmm.* "Cops are so sexy. Why don't you come back to bed?"

"I've got to go in early. Should already be there.

Including the participants, we're expecting close to two thousand in town today. Hopp and Charlene did some major PR."

"Who doesn't love a parade? All right, since you're being so official, give me ten and I'll fly you in."

"It'll take longer for you to do your systems checks and fly there than it will for me to drive it. Besides, you can't get ready in ten."

"Can too, especially if somebody goes down and makes the coffee."

Even as he looked at his watch and sighed, she dashed into the bathroom.

When he came back with two mugs, she was pulling her red shirt over a white scoop-necked tee. "Consider me amazed."

"I know how to budget time, cutie. This way we can have some wedding talk on the way in. I managed to pull the plug on Charlene's notion of renting a pergola and covering it with pink roses."

"What's a pergola?"

"Beats me, but we're not having it. She's majorly bummed because she claims it's not only romantic, but essential for the wedding photos."

"It's nice that the two of you are getting along."

"It won't last, but it makes life marginally easier for the time being." She gulped down coffee. "Two minutes for the face," she said and scooted back into the bathroom.

"She and Big Mike have their heads together on this behemoth wedding cake. I'm giving her her head there. I like cake. We're tangling about the flowers. I'm not being buried in pink roses, but we've agreed on a few things. Like getting a professional photographer. Snapshots are great, but this is a monumental deal, so we go with a pro. Oh, and she says you have to get a new suit."

"I already have a suit."

"She says you have to have a new one, and it has to be gray. Steel gray, not dove gray. Or maybe it was dove gray and not steel gray. I don't know, and I'm tossing you to the wolves on that one, Burke. You argue with her."

"I can buy a suit," he muttered. "I can buy a gray suit. Do I get to pick out my own underwear?"

"Ask Charlene. There, done. Let's go, aren't you ready yet? You're holding up the parade."

She laughed when he made a grab for her and let him chase her down the stairs.

They were at the door when he stopped, when it clicked into place for him, when that jolt of memory became knowledge. "Snapshot. God*damn*."

"What?" Meg pushed at her hair as he charged back upstairs. "You want a camera? Men. Jesus. And they're always harping about women not being on time."

She trudged back upstairs, then stared in astonishment while he dragged her albums and boxes of photos from the closet to dump them on the bed.

"What are you doing?"

"It's in here. I remember. I'm sure of it."

"What's in there? What are you doing with my pictures?"

"It's in here. Summer picnic? No, no . . . campfire shot. Or . . . damn it."

"Just a minute here. How do you know there's a

campfire shot in there or summer picnics or anything else?"

"I snooped. Scold me later."

"You can count on it."

"The earring, Meg. I saw it when I was looking through here. I know I saw it."

She shoved him aside so she could grab a stack. "Who was wearing it? Who did you see?" She scanned pictures, tossed them out like toy airplanes.

"Group shot," he murmured, straining to bring it into focus. "Party shot. Holiday . . . Christmas."

He grabbed the album she reached for and flipped through to the end. "There. Bull's-eye."

"New Year's Eve. They let me stay up. I took that picture myself. I took it."

Her hand trembled as she peeled back the plastic, pulled the photograph free. The edge of the tree was in the corner, the colored lights and balls blurry. She'd gone in close, so it was just the faces, nearly only the faces, though she remembered now that her father had his guitar on his lap.

He'd been laughing, with Charlene pulled tight against him so her cheek was pressed right up against his. Max had mugged his way in from behind the couch, but she'd cut off the top of his head.

But the one who sat on the other side of her father, his head turned slightly as he smiled at someone across the room, was clear.

As was the silver Maltese cross dangling from his ear.

THIRTY-ONE

"IT'S NOT PROOF, Meg, not a hundred percent."

"Don't give me that cop bullshit, Burke." As he drove, she sat with her arms folded tight at her waist, as if holding in pain.

"It's not bullshit. It's circumstantial. It's good, but it's circumstantial." His mind worked back, forward, covering the ground. "The earring was handled by at least two people before it came to me. No forensics. It's a common design, probably thousands of them out there during that time. He could have lost it, given it away, borrowed it himself. The fact that he wore it in a photograph taken more than sixteen years ago doesn't prove he was on that mountain. A brain-dead defense attorney could smash it in trial."

"He killed my father."

Ed holds a grudge. Hopp had told him that, after the run-in with Hawley.

All those connecting lines. Galloway to Max, Galloway to Bing, Galloway to Steven Wise.

You can add more. Woolcott to Max—the concerned old friend helping the widow with the memorial. Woolcott to Bing—implicating the man who might know, who might remember a casual conversation from sixteen years before.

Hawley's slashed tires and spray-painted truck—payback for the wreck, disguised as childish vandalism.

Money. Ed Woolcott was the money man. What better way to hide a sudden cash windfall than your own bank?

"That bastard Woolcott killed my father."

"That's right. I know it. You know it. He knows it. But building a case is a different thing."

"You've been building a case since January. Piece by step by layer, when the State basically closed it up. I've watched you."

"Let me finish it."

"What do you think I'm going to do?" She squinted against the sun. She'd walked out of the house without her sunglasses, without anything but her own bubbling need to act. "Walk up to him and put a gun in his ear?"

Because he heard it in her voice, the dark grief along with the bright rage, he laid a hand over hers. Squeezed. "Wouldn't put it past you."

"I won't." It took an effort to turn her hand over, to return that connection when it would have been easy to yank it back. Stay alone with the storming emotions. "But I'm going to see his face, Nate. I'm going to be there where I can see his face when you take him in."

The main street was already lined with people staking their claim on position. Folding chairs and coolers stood on curb and sidewalk, many already occupied or in use as people sat and slurped on drinks in plastic cups.

The air was already buzzing with noise, shouts and squeals and laughter spearing up through the blast of music from KLUN.

Trucks offering snow cones, ice cream, hot dogs and other parade food were parked on corners and down side streets. Rainbow bunting waved in the breeze.

Two thousand people, Nate estimated, and a good chunk of them kids. A normal day in Lunacy, he could've walked into the bank and taken Ed quietly in his office.

It wasn't a normal day, in any stretch.

He parked at the station, pulled Meg in with him. "Otto and Peter," he demanded of Peach.

"Out with the horde where *I* should be." Irritation marred her eyes as she smoothed a flowing skirt, the color of daffodils, over her ample hips. "We thought you'd be here before—"

"Call them both in."

"Nate, we've got over a hundred people already lining up on the school grounds. We need—"

"Call them both in!" he snapped. He kept walking, one hand on Meg's arm, into his office. "I want you to stay here."

"No. It's not only stupid and wrong for you to expect that, it's disrespectful."

"He's got a concealed license."

"So do I. Give me a gun."

"Meg, he's already killed three times. He'll do whatever he can to protect himself."

"I'm not something you can bundle away safe."

"I'm not—"

"Yes, you are. It's your first instinct, but get over it. I won't ask you not to bring your work home or complain when it interferes with my life. I won't ask you to be what you're not. Don't ask that of me. Give me a gun. I promise I won't use it unless I have to. I don't want him dead. I want him alive. Rotting. I want him healthy so he rots for a long, long time."

"I want to know what's going on." With her hands fisted on her hips, Peach filled the doorway. "I called those boys back, and now we've got no one out there keeping order. A bunch of high school boys have already run a tie-dyed bra up the flagpole, one of the draft horses kicked a tourist who's probably going to sue, and those lamebrain Mackie boys hauled in a keg of Budweiser and are already skunk drunk."

Frustration had the words shooting out like machine-gun fire. "They stole a bunch of balloons, too, and are, right this damn minute, marching up and down the street like fools. We've got reporters here, Nate, we've got media attention, and it just isn't the image we want to project."

"Where's Ed Woolcott?"

"With Hopp at the school by now. They're supposed to ride behind those damn horses. What is going *on?*"

"Call Sergeant Coben, in Anchorage. Tell him I'm taking a suspect in the Patrick Galloway homicide into custody."

"I DON'T WANT TO SPOOK HIM," Nate told his deputies. "I don't want violence or a panic in the kind of crowd we're dealing with. Civilian safety is first order."

"The three of us ought to be able to take him down pretty quick and simple."

"Maybe," Nate acknowledged. "But I'm not risking civilian lives on 'maybe,' Otto. He's not going anywhere. At this point, he has no reason to attempt flight. So we contain him. While we have this parade to deal with, at least one of us will have him in visual contact at all times."

He turned to the corkboard. "We've got Peach's parade route and schedule right here. He comes right after the high school band. That's position six on the program. They'll go from the school into the town proper, down Lunatic and out again. They'll stop here, at Buffalo Inlet, then turn off to come around the back way to the school to off-load. At that point, it won't be as crowded there, and we can take him quietly, with minimal civilian risk."

"One of us can go back up to the school grounds," Peter put in. "After they've gotten to the far end of town. Clear out the civilians."

"That's exactly what I want you to do. We take him quietly, at the end of the route. We bring him back here and let Coben know the suspect is in custody."

"You're just going to turn him over to the State cop?" Otto demanded. "Just here you go, pal, after you've done all the work?"

"It's Coben's case."

"Bullshit. State brushed this off. Didn't want the mess and bother and took the easy way."

"Not entirely true," Nate said. "But regardless, this is how it's done. How it's going to be done."

He didn't need collars and commendations. Not anymore. He just needed to finish the job. From dark to light, he thought. From death to justice.

"Our priorities are to maintain civilian safety and take the suspect into custody. After that, it's Coben's game."

"It's your call. Looks like I'll have to be satisfied to watch Ed shit bricks when you slap the cuffs on him. Bastard killed that poor old dog."

Otto glanced at Meg, colored a little. "And the others. Pat and Max. Just the dog was most recent, that's all."

"It's okay." Meg offered a grim smile. "As long as he pays for all of it, it's okay."

"Well." Otto cleared his throat, stared hard at the maps pinned to the corkboard. "When they go around the back roads, we'll lose visual," he pointed out.

"No, I'll have that covered. A couple of civilian volunteers." He glanced up as Jacob and Bing walked in.

"Said you had a job." Bing scratched his belly. "What's it pay?"

MEG WAITED until he'd dispensed two-ways and sent the men out to take up their initial positions. "And where am I in all this?"

"With me."

"Good enough." She'd pulled her shirt out to cover the holstered .38 at the small of her back.

"They might question why you're not doing the flyby, as scheduled."

"Engine trouble," she said as they started out. "Sorry about that."

The crowd was full of color and noise and cheers with the smell of grilling meat and sugar filling the air. Kids were running around a streamer-and-flower-decorated maypole erected for the event in front of Town Hall. He saw the doors of The Lodge were open, and Charlene was doing a brisk business with those who wanted a more substantial lunch than could be had on the street.

Side streets were barricaded against vehicular traffic. A young couple sat on one of the barricades making out with some enthusiasm while a group of their friends played Hacky Sack in the street behind them. A television crew out of Anchorage was doing a pan of the crowd from the opposite corner.

Tourists shot videos or browsed the folding tables and portable booths where local crafts and jewelry were sold. Beaded leather bags, dream catchers, elaborate Native masks hung on folding screens. Plain and fancy mukluks and handwoven grass baskets ranged over the folding tables or slabs of plywood set on sawhorses.

Though it was warm and sunny, caps and scarves made of qiviut, the underwool of the Arctic musk ox, sold briskly.

The Italian Place sold slices of pizza to go. The Corner Store had a special on disposable cameras and bug dope. A spin rack of postcards stood just outside the door. They ran three for two dollars.

"An enterprising little town," Meg commented as they drove through.

"It is that."

"And after today, a safer one. Thanks to you. Otto nailed that. It's thanks to you, Chief."

"Aw shucks, ma'am."

She rubbed a hand over his. "You say that like Gary Cooper, but you've got Clint Eastwood—Dirty Harry years—in your eyes."

"Just don't . . . I'm trusting you."

"You can." There was an icy calm over the rage now. If there was overflow, if that rage bubbled up and cracked the calm, she'd freeze it up again. "I need to be there, but . . . we can say this is your bear to take down."

"Okay."

"It's going to be a beautiful day for a parade," she said after a long breath. "The air's so still, though. Like it's waiting for something." They pulled up at the school. "I guess this is it."

The marching bands were decked out in bright blue uniforms with their brass buttons and instruments gleaming with polish. Horns clashed as different sections practiced, and adults in charge shouted out instructions.

Drums boomed.

The hockey team was already loading up, sticks clacking as they herded into position. They'd lead the parade, with their regional champions' banner hiding the rust on Bing's flatbed truck. A test of the recording and speakers had Queen's "We Are the Champions" pouring out.

"There you are." Hopp, snappy in a suit of hot candy pink, hurried up to him. "Ignatious, I thought we were going to have to run this show without you."

"Handling things in town. You've got a full house."

"And an NBC affiliate to document it." Her cheeks were nearly as pink as her suit with the excitement of it. "Meg, shouldn't you be getting up there?" She pointed skyward.

"Engine's down, Hopp. Sorry."

"Oh. Well, poop. Do you know if Doug Clooney's got his boat out on the river yet? I've been looking for Peach or Deb—they're supposed to be driving herd around here—but everyone's running around like chickens."

"I'm sure he's out there, and Deb's right over there, getting the hockey team settled."

"Oh. Good God, we're starting. Ed! Stop primping for five seconds. I don't know why I let them talk me into riding behind these horses. Don't see why we couldn't have gotten a convertible. It's more dignified."

"But not as much of a spectacle." Ed smiled broadly as he joined them. He wore a navy three-piece suit, bankerly with its chalk stripes and flashy with its paisley tie. "Guess we should've had our chief of police behind the horses."

"Maybe next time," Nate said easily.

"I haven't congratulated you on your engagement." His eyes were watchful on Nate's as he held out a hand.

He considered doing it now, right now. He could have him down and cuffed in under ten seconds.

And three elementary kids rushed between them, chased by another with a plastic gun. A pretty, young majorette in sparkles hurried over to retrieve the missed baton that landed near his feet.

"Sorry! Sorry, Chief Burke. It got away from me."

"No problem. Thanks, Ed." He extended his hand to complete the aborted shake and again thought—maybe now.

Jesse ran up, threw his arms around Nate's knees.

"I get to be in the parade!" the boy shouted. "I get to

wear a costume and march right down the street. Are you going to watch me, Chief Nate?"

"Absolutely."

"Don't you look handsome," Hopp commented, and crouched down to Jesse as the boy slipped his hand trustfully into Nate's.

Not here, Nate told himself. Not now. No one gets hurt today. "Hope you'll come to the wedding," he said to Ed.

"Wouldn't miss it. Couldn't settle for a local, eh, Meg?"

"He survived a winter. That makes him local enough."

"I suppose it does."

"Jesse, you better get back to your group." Hopp gave him a little pat on the butt, and he ran off, shouting, "Watch me!"

"Help me up into this thing, Ed. We're about to go."

"We're going to walk back down a ways," Nate said as they climbed into the buggy. "Things seem under control here. I want to make sure the Mackies are behaving themselves."

"Stealing balloons." Hopp cast her eyes to heaven. "I heard about that."

Nate took Meg's hand and strolled away. "Does he know?" she asked him.

"I'm worried. Too many people around, Meg. Too many kids."

"I know." She gave his hand a squeeze as the marching band's boots began to click on the pavement. "It'll be over soon. Doesn't take that long to get from one end of town to the other and back again."

It would be interminable, he knew. With the crowds,

the shouts and cheers, the blaring music. An hour, he told himself. An hour tops and he could take him without anyone getting hurt. No need to run into an alley this time, no need to risk the dark.

He kept his stride steady but unrushed as he passed the fringes of the crowd and made his way to the heart of town.

The trio of majorettes danced by, waving and tossing their batons to enthusiastic applause. The one who'd nearly beaned him shot Nate a big, toothy smile.

The drum major strutted in his high hat, and the band cut loose with "We Will Rock You."

He spotted Peter at the first intersection and turned his head to press his lips to Meg's ear. "Let's keep walking, down there to the balloon guy. I'll buy you a balloon. They'll pass us, and we'll keep them in sight a little longer."

"A red one."

"Naturally."

End of town circle around, he thought. The hockey team would already be done and moving back into town to see their friends, mix with the crowd. The band would head into the school to change out of their uniforms.

Out of the way. Most everyone out of the way. And Peter there to move any lingerers along.

He stopped by the clown with the orange mop of hair and a fistful of balloons. "Jeez, Harry, is that you in there?"

"Deb's idea."

"Well, you look real cute." Nate angled himself to see the buggy, the crowd. "My girl wants a red one."

Nate reached for his wallet, listening with half an ear

as Harry and Meg debated which shape would do. He watched Peter move down the opposite sidewalk, and as the band marched by, taking the sound with them, he heard the clip-clop of the horses.

Kids squealed and dashed out as Hopp and Ed tossed handfuls of candy. He passed bills to Harry and continued to turn as if watching the spectacle.

And spotted Coben, with his white-blond hair catching the sunlight, in the crowd. So, he saw instantly, did Ed.

"Damn it, damn it, why didn't he wait?"

Panic streaked across Ed's face. Seeing it, Nate began to fight his way through the crowd that was massed into a wall along curbside. He couldn't get there, not in time. He heard the cheers and shouts of the crowd like a tidal wave rushing around him. They applauded when Ed leaped out of the buggy, even when he pulled a gun from under his suit jacket.

As if anticipating a show, they started to part for him as he dashed for the opposite side of the street. Then there were screams and shouts as he knocked people aside, trampled over them when they fell.

Nate heard gunfire as he shoved his way to the street.

"Down! Everybody down!"

He sprinted across the street, leaped over shocked pedestrians. And saw Ed backing down the empty sidewalk behind the barricades, holding a gun to a woman's head.

"Back away!" he shouted. "You just toss your gun down and back away. I'll kill her. You know I will."

"I know you will." He could hear the shouts behind

him and the fading music as the band marched on without a clue. There were cars and trucks parked at the curb here, and buildings had side doors that would almost certainly be unlocked.

He needed to keep Ed's focus on him, before the man could use his panicked brain enough to think about dragging his hostage into a building.

"Where are you going to go, Ed?"

"Don't you worry about that. You worry about her." He jerked the woman so that the heels of her jogging shoes bumped the sidewalk. "I'll put a bullet in her brain."

"Like you did Max."

"Did what I had to do. That's how you survive here."

"Maybe." There was sweat on Ed's face. Nate could see it glinting in the sunlight. "But you won't walk away from this one. I'll drop you where you stand. You know *I* will."

"You don't throw that gun down, you'll have killed her." Ed dragged the weeping woman back another three feet. "Just like you killed your partner. You're a bleeding heart, Burke. You can't live with that."

"I can." Meg stepped up beside Nate, aimed her gun between Ed's eyes. "You know me, you bastard. I'll down you like I would a sick horse, and I wouldn't lose a wink of sleep over it."

"Meg," Nate warned. "Ease back."

"I can kill her and one of you first. If that's what it takes."

"Her probably," Meg agreed. "But she doesn't mean

anything to me. Go ahead, shoot her. You'll be dead before she hits the ground."

"Ease back, Meg." Nate lifted his voice now, and his eyes never left Ed's. "Do what I tell you, and do it now." Then he heard a chaos of voices, stumbling feet. The crowd was surging forward, Nate knew, with curiosity, fascination and horror outweighing simple fear.

"Drop the weapon and let her go," Nate ordered. "Do it now, and you've got a chance." Nate saw Coben come around the back and knew someone was going to die.

Hell broke loose.

Ed whirled, fired. In a flash, Nate saw Coben roll for cover and the splatter of blood from the bullet that caught him high on the shoulder. Coben's service revolver lay on the sidewalk where it had flown out of his hand.

Nate heard a second bullet thud into the building beside him and the sound of a thousand people screaming.

They barely penetrated. His blood was ice.

He shoved Meg back, sent her sprawling to the ground. She cursed him as he stepped forward, his gun steady. "Anyone dies today," he said coolly, "it'll be you, Ed."

"What are you doing?" Ed shouted as Nate continued to walk toward him. "What the hell are you doing?"

"My job. My town. Put down the gun, or I'll take you out like that sick horse."

"Go to hell!" With one violent move, he shoved the weeping woman at Nate and dived behind a car.

Nate let the woman slide bonelessly to the sidewalk. Then he rolled under another car, came up street-side.

Crouched, he glanced over to check on Meg and saw her soothing the woman whose life she'd claimed didn't mean anything to her. "Go," she snapped out. "Get the bastard."

Then she began to belly forward toward the injured Coben.

Ed fired, the bullet exploding a windshield.

"This ends here. It ends now!" Nate shouted. "Throw out your gun, or I'll come and take it from you."

"You're *nothing!*" There was more than panic, more than rage in Ed's voice. "You don't even belong here." There were tears. He broke cover, firing wildly. Glass shattered and flew like lethal stars; metal pinged and rang.

Nate stood, stepped into the street with his weapon lifted. He felt something sting his arm, like a fat, angry bee. "Drop it, you stupid son of a bitch."

On a scream, Ed swung around, aimed.

And Nate fired.

He saw Ed clutch his hip, saw him go down. And continued forward at the same steady pace until he'd reached the gun Ed had dropped as he'd fallen.

"You're under arrest, you asshole. You coward." His voice was calm as June as he shoved Ed onto his belly, yanked his arms behind him and cuffed his wrists. Then he crouched, spoke softly while Ed's pain-glazed eyes flickered. "You shot a police officer." He glanced without much interest at the thin line of blood just above his own elbow. "Two. You're done."

"We need to get Ken up here?" Hopp's query was conversational, but when Nate looked up to see her coming toward him, crunching broken glass under her dressy shoes, he saw the tremor in her hands, her shoulders.

"Couldn't hurt." He jerked a chin toward the people

who'd jumped over, crawled under or simply shoved barricades aside. "You're going to need to keep those people back."

"That's your job, Chief." She managed a smile, then it frosted as she stared down at Ed. "You know, that TV crew got damn near all of this on camera. Cameraman must be certifiable. One thing we're going to make clear in the upcoming interviews on this unholy mess. This one's the Outsider now. He's not one of us."

She shifted deliberately away from Ed, held out a hand to Nate as if to help him to his feet. "But you are. You sure as hell are, Ignatious, and thank God for it."

He took her hand and felt that light tremor in hers as she squeezed his hard. "Anybody back there hurt?"

"Bumps and bruises." Tears trembled in her eyes, were willed away. "You took care of us."

"Good." He nodded when he saw Otto and Peter working to move the crowd back.

Then he looked over, found Meg crouched in a doorway. She met his eyes. There was blood on her hands, but it appeared she'd fashioned an expert field dressing on Coben's wounded shoulder.

She brushed a hand absently over her cheek, smearing blood. Then she grinned and blew him a kiss.

THEY SAID IT WAS FORTUNATE no lives had been lost, and injuries to civilians, while plentiful, were mostly minor—broken bones, concussions, cuts and bruises all caused by falls and panic.

They said property damage wasn't extensive, broken

windows, windshields, a streetlight. Jim Mackie, with considerable pride, told the NBC affiliate reporter he was going to leave the bullet holes in his pickup.

They said, all in all, it was a hell of a climax to Lunacy, Alaska's May Day Parade.

They said a lot of things.

Media coverage turned out to be more extensive than the injuries. The violent and bizarre capture of Edward Woolcott, the alleged killer of Patrick Galloway, the Ice Man of No Name Mountain, was national fodder for weeks.

Nate didn't watch the coverage, and settled for reading reports in *The Lunatic*.

As May passed, so did the interest from Outside.

"Long day," Meg said as she came out on the porch to sit beside him.

"I like them long."

She handed him a beer and watched the sky with him. It was nearly ten and brilliantly light.

Her garden was planted. Her dahlias, as expected, were spectacular, and the delphiniums speared up, deeply blue, on five-foot stalks.

They'd reach taller yet, she thought. They had the whole summer, all those long days washed with light.

The day before, she'd buried her father, at last. The town had come out for it, to a man. So had the media, but it was the town that mattered to Meg.

Charlene had been calm, she thought. For Charlene, anyway. She hadn't even played to the cameras but had stood—as dignified as Meg had ever seen her—with her hand gripped in The Professor's.

Maybe they'd make it. Maybe they wouldn't. Life was full of maybes.

But she knew one sure thing. Saturday next, she would stand out here, in the light of the summer night, with the lake and the mountains in front of her, and marry the man she loved.

"Tell me," she said. "Tell me what you found out today when you went down to talk to Coben."

He knew she'd ask. He knew they'd talk it through. Not just because of her father. But because what he himself did, who he was, mattered to her.

"Ed switched lawyers. Got a hotshot from Outside. He's claiming your father was self-defense. That Galloway went crazy, and he feared for his life and panicked. He's a banker, and he kept banker's records. He's saying he won the twelve thousand that suddenly showed up in his account in March of that year, but they'll have witnesses that say different. So it won't fly. He says he had nothing to do with the rest of it. Absolutely nothing. That won't fly, either."

There was a cloud of mosquitoes near the edge of the woods. They buzzed like a chain saw and made him grateful for the bug dope he'd slathered on before coming outside.

He turned his head to kiss her cheek. "Sure you want to hear this?"

"Keep going."

"His wife's turned inside out, so she's spilled enough to rip his alibis for the time of Max's death and Yukon's. Put that in with the yellow spray paint in his toolshed, and Harry stating Ed bought some fresh meat from him the day we had our little encounter with the bear. Weave it all together, you've got a tight little net."

"Added to all that is the fact that he held a gun to a tourist's head, shot a state cop *and* our chief of police." She gave his biceps a quick kiss. All of which," she added, "was caught for the record by the NBC cameraman." She stretched, one, long, sinuous move. "Great TV. Our brave and handsome hero shooting the bastard's leg out from under him, while he himself was wounded—"

"Flesh wound."

"Standing that bastard down like Cooper in *High Noon*. I'm no Grace Kelly, but I get hot just thinking about it."

"Gosh, ma'am." He slapped at a sparrow-sized mosquito that got through the dope. "It wasn't nothing."

"And I looked pretty damn good myself, even when you sent me to the damn sidewalk."

"You look even better now. The lawyers will try to work it . . . diminished capacity, temporary insanity, but . . ."

"It won't fly," Meg finished.

"Coben'll wrap him up—or the DA will. Got their teeth in it now."

"If Coben had listened to you, you'd have wrapped him up without all that show."

"Maybe."

"You could've killed him."

Nate took a small sip of beer and listened to an eagle cry. "You wanted him alive. I aim to please."

"You do please."

"You wouldn't have done it, either."

Meg stretched out her legs, looked down at the worn toes of her ancient gardening boots. Probably needed new. "Don't be too sure, Nate."

"He's not the only one who can bait. You were razzing him, Meg. Pushing his buttons so he'd pull the gun off her and try for one of us."

"Did you see her eyes?"

"No, I was looking at his."

"I did. I've seen that kind of scared before. A rabbit, with its leg caught in a trap."

She paused to rub the dogs when they galloped up. "If you tell me, no matter how many fancy Lower 48 lawyers he hires, that he'll go to jail for a long, long time, I'll believe you."

"He'll go to jail for a long, long time."

"Okay, then. Case closed. Would you like to take a walk down by the lake?"

He drew her hand to his lips. "I believe I would."

"And would you then like to lie down on the bank of the lake and make love until we're too weak to move?"

"I believe I would."

"The mosquitoes will probably eat us alive."

"Some things are worth the risk."

He was, she thought. She rose, held out a hand for his. "You know, in a little while, when we have sex, it'll be all legal. That going to take any of the spark out of it for you?"

"Not a bit." He looked up at the sky again. "I like the long days. But I don't mind the long nights anymore. Because I've got the light." He wrapped his arm around her shoulder to draw her close to his side. "I've got the light right here."

He watched the sun, so reluctant to set, glimmer on the cool, deep water. And the mountains, so fierce and so white, mirrored their eternal winter on the summer blue.

Can't get enough of Nora Roberts?
Try the #1 *New York Times* bestselling
In Death series, by Nora Roberts
writing as J. D. Robb.

Turn the page to see where it all began . . .

NAKED IN DEATH

SHE WOKE IN THE DARK. Through the slats on the window shades, the first murky hint of dawn slipped, slanting shadowy bars over the bed. It was like waking in a cell.

For a moment she simply lay there, shuddering, imprisoned, while the dream faded. After ten years on the force, Eve still had dreams.

Six hours before, she'd killed a man, had watched death creep into his eyes. It wasn't the first time she'd exercised maximum force, or dreamed. She'd learned to accept the action and the consequences.

But it was the child that haunted her. The child she hadn't been in time to save. The child whose screams had echoed in the dreams with her own.

All the blood, Eve thought, scrubbing sweat from her face with her hands. Such a small little girl to have had so much blood in her. And she knew it was vital that she push it aside.

Standard departmental procedure meant that she would spend the morning in Testing. Any officer whose discharge of weapon resulted in termination of life was required to undergo emotional and psychiatric clearance before resuming duty. Eve considered the tests a mild pain in the ass.

She would beat them, as she'd beaten them before.

When she rose, the overheads went automatically to low setting, lighting her way into the bath. She winced once at her reflection. Her eyes were swollen from lack of sleep, her skin nearly as pale as the corpses she'd delegated to the ME.

Rather than dwell on it, she stepped into the shower, yawning.

"Give me one oh one degrees, full force," she said and shifted so that the shower spray hit her straight in the face.

She let it steam, lathered listlessly while she played through the events of the night before. She wasn't due in Testing until nine, and would use the next three hours to settle and let the dream fade away completely.

Small doubts and little regrets were often detected and could mean a second and more intense round with the machines and the owl-eyed technicians who ran them.

Eve didn't intend to be off the streets longer than twenty-four hours.

After pulling on a robe, she walked into the kitchen and programmed her AutoChef for coffee, black; toast, light. Through her window she could hear the heavy hum of air traffic carrying early commuters to offices, late ones home. She'd chosen the apartment years before because it was in a heavy ground and air pattern, and she liked the noise and crowds. On another yawn, she glanced out the window, followed the rattling journey of an aging airbus hauling laborers not fortunate enough to work in the city or by home 'links.

She brought the *New York Times* up on her monitor and scanned the headlines while the faux caffeine bol-

stered her system. The AutoChef had burned her toast
again, but she ate it anyway, with a vague thought of
springing for a replacement unit.

She was frowning over an article on a mass recall of
droid cocker spaniels when her telelink blipped. Eve
shifted to communications and watched her command-
ing officer flash onto the screen.

"Commander."

"Lieutenant." He gave her a brisk nod, noted the still-
wet hair and sleepy eyes. "Incident at Twenty-seven West
Broadway, eighteenth floor. You're primary."

Eve lifted a brow. "I'm on Testing. Subject termi-
nated at twenty-two thirty-five."

"We have override," he said, without inflection. "Pick
up your shield and weapon on the way to the incident.
Code Five, Lieutenant."

"Yes, sir." His face flashed off even as she pushed back
from the screen. Code Five meant she would report directly
to her commander, and there would be no unsealed inter-
departmental reports and no cooperation with the press.

In essence, it meant she was on her own.

BROADWAY WAS NOISY and crowded, a party that
rowdy guests never left. Street, pedestrian, and sky traffic
were miserable, choking the air with bodies and vehicles.
In her old days in uniform she remembered it as a hot
spot for wrecks and crushed tourists who were too busy
gaping at the show to get out of the way.

Even at this hour steam was rising from the stationary

and portable food stands that offered everything from rice noodles to soy dogs for the teeming crowds. She had to swerve to avoid an eager merchant on his smoking Gl-ida-Grill, and took his flipped middle finger as a matter of course.

Eve double-parked and, skirting a man who smelled worse than his bottle of brew, stepped onto the sidewalk. She scanned the building first, fifty floors of gleaming metal that knifed into the sky from a hilt of concrete. She was propositioned twice before she reached the door.

Since this five-block area of West Broadway was affec-tionately termed Prostitute's Walk, she wasn't surprised. She flashed her badge for the uniform guarding the en-trance.

"Lieutenant Dallas."

"Yes, sir." He skimmed his official CompuSeal over the door to keep out the curious, then led the way to the bank of elevators. "Eighteenth floor," he said when the doors swished shut behind them.

"Fill me in, Officer." Eve switched on her recorder and waited.

"I wasn't first on the scene, Lieutenant. Whatever happened upstairs is being kept upstairs. There's a badge inside waiting for you. We have a homicide, and a Code Five in number eighteen-oh-three."

"Who called it in?"

"I don't have that information."

He stayed where he was when the elevator opened. Eve stepped out and was alone in a narrow hallway. Se-curity cameras tilted down at her, and her feet were almost soundless on the worn nap of the carpet as she approached 1803. Ignoring the hand plate, she announced herself, holding her badge up to eye level for the peep cam until the door opened.

"Dallas."

"Feeney." She smiled, pleased to see a familiar face. Ryan Feeney was an old friend and former partner who'd traded the street for a desk and a top-level position in the Electronics Detection Division. "So, they're sending computer pluckers these days."

"They wanted brass, and the best." His lips curved in his wide, rumpled face, but his eyes remained sober. He was a small, stubby man with small, stubby hands and rust-colored hair. "You look beat."

"Rough night."

"So I heard." He offered her one of the sugared nuts from the bag he habitually carried, studying her, and measuring if she was up to what was waiting in the bedroom beyond.

She was young for her rank, barely thirty, with wide brown eyes that had never had a chance to be naive. Her doe-brown hair was cropped short, for convenience rather than style, but suited her triangular face with its razor-edge cheekbones and slight dent in the chin.

She was tall, rangy, with a tendency to look thin, but Feeney knew there were solid muscles beneath the leather jacket. But Eve had more—there was also a brain, and a heart.

"This one's going to be touchy, Dallas."

"I picked that up already. Who's the victim?"

"Sharon DeBlass, granddaughter of Senator DeBlass."

Neither meant anything to her. "Politics isn't my forte, Feeney."

"The gentleman from Virginia, extreme right, old money. The granddaughter took a sharp left a few years back, moved to New York and became a licensed companion."

"She was a hooker." Dallas glanced around the apartment. It was furnished in obsessive modern—glass and thin chrome, signed holograms on the walls, recessed bar in bold red. The wide mood screen behind the bar bled with mixing and merging shapes and colors in cool pastels.

Neat as a virgin, Eve mused, and cold as a whore. "No surprise, given her choice of real estate."

"Politics makes it delicate. Victim was twenty-four, Caucasian female. She bought it in bed."

Eve only lifted a brow. "Seems poetic, since she'd been bought there. How'd she die?"

"That's the next problem. I want you to see for yourself."

As they crossed the room, each took out a slim container, sprayed their hands front and back to seal in oils and fingerprints. At the doorway, Eve sprayed the bottom of her boots to slicken them so that she would pick up no fibers, stray hairs, or skin.

Eve was already wary. Under normal circumstances there would have been two other investigators on a homicide scene, with recorders for sound and pictures. Forensics would have been waiting with their usual snarly impatience to sweep the scene.

The fact that only Feeney had been assigned with her meant that there were a lot of eggshells to be walked over.

"Security cameras in the lobby, elevator, and hallways," Eve commented.

"I've already tagged the discs." Feeney opened the bedroom door and let her enter first.

It wasn't pretty. Death rarely was a peaceful, religious experience to Eve's mind. It was the nasty end, indifferent to saint and sinner. But this was shocking, like a stage deliberately set to offend.

The bed was huge, slicked with what appeared to be genuine satin sheets the color of ripe peaches. Small, soft-focused spotlights were trained on its center where the naked woman was cupped in the gentle dip of the floating mattress.

The mattress moved with obscenely graceful undulations to the rhythm of programmed music slipping through the headboard.

She was beautiful still, a cameo face with a tumbling waterfall of flaming red hair, emerald eyes that stared glassily at the mirrored ceiling, long, milk-white limbs that called to mind visions of *Swan Lake* as the motion of the bed gently rocked them.

They weren't artistically arranged now, but spread lewdly so that the dead woman formed a final X dead-center of the bed.

There was a hole in her forehead, one in her chest, another horribly gaping between the open thighs. Blood had splattered on the glossy sheets, pooled, dripped, and stained.

There were splashes of it on the lacquered walls, like lethal paintings scrawled by an evil child.

So much blood was a rare thing, and she had seen much too much of it the night before to take the scene as calmly as she would have preferred.

She had to swallow once, hard, and force herself to block out the image of a small child.

"You got the scene on record?"

"Yep."

"Then turn that damn thing off." She let out a breath after Feeney located the controls that silenced the music. The bed flowed to stillness. "The wounds," Eve murmured, stepping closer to examine them. "Too neat for a knife. Too messy for a laser." A flash came to her—old training films, old videos, old viciousness.

"Christ, Feeney, these look like bullet wounds."

Feeney reached into his pocket and drew out a sealed bag. "Whoever did it left a souvenir." He passed the bag to Eve. "An antique like this has to go for eight, ten thousand for a legal collection, twice that on the black market."

Fascinated, Eve turned the sealed revolver over in her hand. "It's heavy," she said half to herself. "Bulky."

"Thirty-eight caliber," he told her. "First one I've seen outside of a museum. This one's a Smith and Wesson, Model Ten, blue steel." He looked at it with some affection. "Real classic piece, used to be standard police issue up until the latter part of the twentieth. They stopped making them in about twenty-two, twenty-three, when the gun ban was passed."

"You're the history buff." Which explained why he was with her. "Looks new." She sniffed through the bag, caught the scent of oil and burning. "Somebody took good care of this. Steel fired into flesh," she mused as she passed the bag back to Feeney. "Ugly way to die, and the first I've seen it in my ten years with the department."

"Second for me. About fifteen years ago, Lower East Side, party got out of hand. Guy shot five people with a twenty-two before he realized it wasn't a toy. Hell of a mess."

"Fun and games," Eve murmured. "We'll scan the collectors, see how many we can locate who own one like this. Somebody might have reported a robbery."

"Might have."

"It's more likely it came through the black market." Eve glanced back at the body. "If she's been in the business for a few years, she'd have discs, records of her clients, her trick books." She frowned. "With Code Five, I'll have to do the door-to-door myself. Not a simple sex crime," she said with a sigh. "Whoever did it set it up. The antique weapon, the wounds themselves, almost ruler-straight down the body, the lights, the pose. Who called it in, Feeney?"

"The killer." He waited until her eyes came back to him. "From right here. Called the station. See how the bedside unit's aimed at her face? That's what came in. Video, no audio."

"He's into showmanship." Eve let out a breath. "Clever bastard, arrogant, cocky. He had sex with her first. I'd bet my badge on it. Then he gets up and does it." She lifted her arm, aiming, lowering it as she counted off, "One, two, three."

"That's cold," murmured Feeney.

"He's cold. He smooths down the sheets after. See how neat they are? He arranges her, spreads her open so nobody can have any doubts as to how she made her living. He does it carefully, practically measuring, so that she's perfectly aligned. Center of the bed, arms and legs equally apart. Doesn't turn off the bed 'cause it's part of the show. He leaves the gun because he wants us to know right away he's no ordinary man. He's got an ego. He doesn't want to waste time letting the body be discovered eventually. He wants it now. That instant gratification."

"She was licensed for men and women," Feeney pointed out, but Eve shook her head.

"It's not a woman. A woman wouldn't have left her looking both beautiful and obscene. No, I don't think it's a woman. Let's see what we can find. Have you gone into her computer yet?"

"No. It's your case, Dallas. I'm only authorized to assist."

"See if you can access her client files." Eve went to the dresser and began to carefully search drawers.

Expensive taste, Eve reflected. There were several items of real silk, the kind no simulation could match. The bottle of scent on the dresser was exclusive, and smelled, after a quick sniff, like expensive sex.

The contents of the drawers were meticulously ordered, lingerie folded precisely, sweaters arranged according to color and material. The closet was the same.

Obviously the victim had a love affair with clothes and a taste for the best and took scrupulous care of what she owned.

And she'd died naked.

"Kept good records," Feeney called out. "It's all here. Her client list, appointments—including her required monthly health exam and her weekly trip to the beauty salon. She used the Trident Clinic for the first and Paradise for the second."

"Both top-of-the-line. I've got a friend who saved for a year so she could have one day for the works at Paradise. Takes all kinds."

"My wife's sister went for it for her twenty-fifth anniversary. Cost damn near as much as my kid's wedding. Hello, we've got her personal address book."

"Good. Copy all of it, will you, Feeney?" At his low whistle, she looked over her shoulder, glimpsed the small gold-edged palm computer in his hand. "What?"

"We've got a lot of high-powered names in here. Politics, entertainment, money, money, money. Interesting, our girl has Roarke's private number."

"Roarke who?"

"Just Roarke, as far as I know. Big money there. Kind of guy that touches shit and turns it into gold bricks. You've got to start reading more than the sports page, Dallas."

"Hey, I read the headlines. Did you hear about the cocker spaniel recall?"

"Roarke's always big news," Feeney said patiently. "He's got one of the finest art collections in the world. Arts and antiques," he continued, noting when Eve

clicked in and turned to him. "He's a licensed gun col-
lector. Rumor is he knows how to use them."

"I'll pay him a visit."

"You'll be lucky to get within a mile of him."

"I'm feeling lucky." Eve crossed over to the body to
slip her hands under the sheets.

"The man's got powerful friends, Dallas. You can't afford to so much as whisper he's linked to this until
you've got something solid."

"Feeney, you know it's a mistake to tell me that." But
even as she started to smile, her fingers brushed against
something between cold flesh and bloody sheets.
"There's something under her." Carefully, Eve lifted the
shoulder, eased her fingers over.

"Paper," she murmured. "Sealed." With her protected thumb, she wiped at a smear of blood until she
could read the protected sheet.

ONE OF SIX

"It looks hand-printed," she said to Feeney and held
it out. "Our boy's more than clever, more than arrogant.
And he isn't finished."

EVE SPENT THE REST OF THE DAY doing what would
normally have been assigned to drones: She interviewed
the victim's neighbors personally, recording statements,
impressions.

She managed to grab a quick sandwich from the same
Glida-Grill she'd nearly smashed before, driving across

town. After the night and the morning she'd put in, she could hardly blame the receptionist at Paradise for looking at her as though she'd recently scraped herself off the sidewalk.

Waterfalls played musically among the flora in the reception area of the city's most exclusive salon. Tiny cups of real coffee and slim glasses of fizzling water or champagne were served to those lounging on the cushy chairs and settees. Headphones and discs of fashion magazines were complimentary.

The receptionist was magnificently breasted, a testament to the salon's figure sculpting techniques. She wore a snug, short outfit in the salon's trademark red, and an incredible coif of ebony hair coiled like snakes.

Eve couldn't have been more delighted.

"I'm sorry," the woman said in a carefully modulated voice as empty of expression as a computer. "We serve by appointment only."

"That's okay." Eve smiled and was almost sorry to puncture the disdain. Almost. "This ought to get me one." She offered her badge. "Who works on Sharon DeBlass?"

The receptionist's horrified eyes darted toward the waiting area. "Our clients' needs are strictly confidential."

"I bet." Enjoying herself, Eve leaned companionably on the U-shaped counter. "I can talk nice and quiet, like this, so we understand each other—Denise?" She flicked her gaze down to the discreet studded badge on the woman's breast. "Or I can talk louder, so everyone understands. If you like the first idea better, you can take me to a nice quiet room where we won't disturb any of

your clients, and you can send in Sharon DeBlass's operator. Or whatever term you use."

"Consultant," Denise said faintly. "If you'll follow me."

"My pleasure."

And it was.

Outside of movies or videos, Eve had never seen anything so lush. The carpet was a red cushion your feet
could sink blissfully into. Crystal drops hung from the
ceiling and spun light. The air smelled of flowers and
pampered flesh.

She might not have been able to imagine herself there,
spending hours having herself creamed, oiled, pummeled,
and sculpted, but if she were going to waste such time on
vanity, it would certainly have been interesting to do so
under such civilized conditions.

The receptionist showed her into a small room with a
hologram of a summer meadow dominating one wall.
The quiet sound of birdsong and breezes sweetened
the air.

"If you'd just wait here."

"No problem." Eve waited for the door to close then,
with an indulgent sigh, she lowered herself into a deeply
cushioned chair. The moment she was seated, the monitor beside her blipped on, and a friendly, indulgent face
that could only be droid's beamed smiles.

"Good afternoon. Welcome to Paradise. Your beauty
needs and your comfort are our only priorities. Would
you like some refreshment while you wait for your personal consultant?"

"Sure. Coffee, black, coffee."

"Of course. What sort would you prefer? Press *C* on your keyboard for the list of choices."

Smothering a chuckle, Eve followed instructions. She spent the next two minutes pondering over her options, then narrowed it down to French Riviera or Caribbean Cream.

The door opened again before she could decide. Resigned, she rose and faced an elaborately dressed scarecrow.

Over his fuchsia shirt and plum-colored slacks, he wore an open, trailing smock of Paradise red. His hair, flowing back from a painfully thin face, echoed the hue of his slacks. He offered Eve a hand, squeezed gently, and stared at her out of soft doe eyes.

"I'm terribly sorry, Officer. I'm baffled."

"I want information on Sharon DeBlass." Again, Eve took out her badge and offered it for inspection.

"Yes, ah, Lieutenant Dallas. That was my understanding. You must know, of course, our client data is strictly confidential. Paradise has a reputation for discretion as well as excellence."

"And you must know, of course, that I can get a warrant, Mr.—?"

"Oh, Sebastian. Simply Sebastian." He waved a thin hand, sparkling with rings. "I'm not questioning your authority, Lieutenant. But if you could assist me, your motives for the inquiry?"

"I'm inquiring into the motives for the murder of De-Blass." She waited a beat, judged the shock that shot into his eyes and drained his face of color. "Other than that, my data is strictly confidential."

"Murder. My dear God, our lovely Sharon is dead?

There must be a mistake." He all but slid into a chair, letting his head fall back and his eyes close. When the monitor offered him refreshment, he waved a hand again. Light shot from his jeweled fingers. "God, yes. I need a brandy, darling. A snifter of Trevalli."

Eve sat beside him, took out her recorder. "Tell me about Sharon."

"A marvelous creature. Physically stunning, of course, but it went deeper." His brandy came into the room on a silent automated cart. Sebastian plucked the snifter and took one deep swallow. "She had flawless taste, a generous heart, rapier wit."

He turned the doe eyes on Eve again. "I saw her only two days ago."

"Professionally?"

"She had a standing weekly appointment, half day. Every other week was a full day." He whipped out a butter yellow scarf and dabbed at his eyes. "Sharon took care of herself, believed strongly in the presentation of self."

"It would be an asset in her line of work."

"Naturally. She only worked to amuse herself. Money wasn't a particular need, with her family background. She enjoyed sex."

"With you?"

His artistic face winced, the rosy lips pursing in what could have been a pout or pain. "I was her consultant, her confidant, and her friend," Sebastian said stiffly and draped the scarf with casual flare over his left shoulder. "It would have been indiscreet and unprofessional for us to become sexual partners."

"So you weren't attracted to her, sexually?"

"It was impossible for anyone not to be attracted to her sexually. She . . ." He gestured grandly. "Exuded sex as others might exude an expensive perfume. My God." He took another shaky sip of brandy. "It's all past tense. I can't believe it. Dead. Murdered." His gaze shot back to Eve. "You said murdered."

"That's right."

"That neighborhood she lived in," he said grimly. "No one could talk to her about moving to a more acceptable location. She enjoyed living on the edge and flaunting it all under her family's aristocratic noses."

"She and her family were at odds?"

"Oh definitely. She enjoyed shocking them. She was such a free spirit, and they so . . . ordinary." He said it in a tone that indicated ordinary was more mortal a sin than murder itself. "Her grandfather continues to introduce bills that would make prostitution illegal. As if the past century hasn't proven that such matters need to regulated for health and crime security. He also stands against procreation regulation, gender adjustment, chemical balancing, and the gun ban."

Eve's ears pricked. "The senator opposes the gun ban?"

"It's one of his pets. Sharon told me he owns a number of nasty antiques and spouts off regularly about that outdated right to bear arms business. If he had his way, we'd all be back in the twentieth century, murdering each other right and left."

"Murder still happens," Eve murmured. "Did she ever mention friends or clients who might have been dissatisfied or overly aggressive?"

"Sharon had dozens of friends. She drew people to her, like . . ." He searched for a suitable metaphor, used the corner of the scarf again. "Like an exotic and fragrant flower. And her clients, as far as I know, were all delighted with her. She screened them carefully. All of her sexual partners had to meet certain standards. Appearance, intellect, breeding, and proficiency. As I said, she enjoyed sex, in all of its many forms. She was . . . adventurous."

That fit with the toys Eve had unearthed in the apartment. The velvet handcuffs and whips, the scented oils and hallucinogens. The offerings on the two sets of co-linked virtual reality headphones had been a shock even to Eve's jaded system.

"Was she involved with anyone on a personal level?"

"There were men occasionally, but she lost interest quickly. Recently she'd spoken about Roarke. She'd met him at a party and was attracted. In fact, she was seeing him for dinner the very night she came in for her consultation. She'd wanted something exotic because they were dining in Mexico."

"In Mexico. That would have been the night before last."

"Yes. She was just bubbling over about him. We did her hair in a gypsy look, gave her a bit more gold to the skin—full body work. Rascal Red on the nails, and a charming little temp tattoo of a red-winged butterfly on the left buttock. Twenty-four-hour facial cosmetics so that she wouldn't smudge. She looked spectacular," he said, tearing up. "And she kissed me and told me she just might be in love this time. 'Wish me luck, Sebastian.' She said that as she left. It was the last thing she ever said to me."

Presents

THE 2009 NORA ROBERTS COLLECTION

4 WORLD PREMIERE MOVIES
4 WEEKS IN A ROW

Beginning
Saturday, March 21
On Lifetime

NORTHERN LIGHTS
MIDNIGHT BAYOU
HIGH NOON
TRIBUTE

From
#1 *New York Times* Bestselling Author

NORA ROBERTS

Go to myLifetime.com for showtimes.

penguin.com

Now available from

NORA ROBERTS

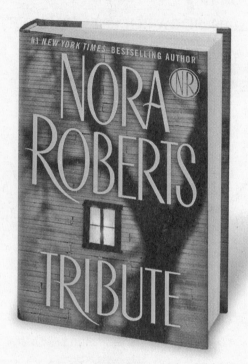

NoraRoberts.com